SAM MARIANO

CONTEMPT

CONTEMPT

COASTAL ELITE, #3

SAM MARIANO

Hello, dear reader.

This is the third book in the Coastal Elite series. If you've already read *Even if it Hurts* and *Undertow*, then you're in the right place!

If you haven't, you're gonna want to go back and start there. As the person who constructed this entire story, I can assure you this book does not stand on its own. Landon and Parker have history set up in *Undertow*, and there are side characters in this story that have developing plotlines that started in *Even if it Hurts*.

I also want to come out of the gates with this request: please, please do not compare Landon to Dare. They are *completely* different people. They are not meant to be alike, so if you go in with the expectation that they are, you're setting yourself up for failure. That would be like walking into a popcorn shop hoping to fill up on shrimp. You *could* leave mad about not getting any shrimp, but... why did you expect shrimp in a popcorn shop, you know?

Landon has issues, but he is *not* a psychopath. Quite the opposite, actually; he has plenty of emotional depth and baggage and wounds that have made him the bastard he is. The conditions that have crafted Landon wouldn't have impacted Dare at all. He wouldn't have cared. He also wouldn't have caught Parker's attention, because Parker is not attracted to Dare's calculated coldness. She's attracted to Landon's stupid hot head and damaged heart (despite her best efforts not to be).

Personally, it is not my goal to regurgitate the same characters and stories over and over again. There are certain character types and stories I am more drawn to than others, of course, so there will be similarities, but I'm not out here cloning the same story and characters over and over again. I'm also much more interested in characters than plots. I'm the same way as a reader. I need deep characters; I don't care if the story is about them going to the store and buying a bag of Doritos. With the right characters, anything can be interesting. But at the end of the day, every story has a different set of characters, and different people have different needs.

Parker does not need a hero like Dare. She doesn't want one, and if I gave her one, she would never be happy with him. If I paired up Parker with a hero like Dare, it would go about how it would go if I paired Dare up with Zoey (from *Untouchable*). At best, they would immediately break up because they legitimately would not like each other; at worst, he would end up murdering her. It is Parker's unprovoked empathy and compassion that made a lasting impression on Landon. Because Dare is a psychopath, this would not have made an impression on him at all. Honestly, the same core incident happening to him would have probably been shrugged off as an oddity and never thought of again, but it most assuredly would not have sparked a love story (however questionable that classification might seem at times when you're reading any of my books, lol).

Landon is an agent of chaos, but not like Dare was. He could never be like Dare was because wires that don't work in Dare's head *do* work in Landon's. He knows all the bad shit he does is wrong. He has a conscience, he just selectively chooses to ignore it.

This book is about Parker and Landon. The way *they* fit together. If either of them were different people, there would be no story, because they aren't interested in different people.

If you think misunderstood, wounded bad boy types who cause chaos and trouble are fun to read about, then I think you're gonna love Landon on his own merits.

TRIGGER WARNING: **If you DO NOT enjoy dubcon (and I do mean DUBIOUS) and/or noncon, this probably will not be the book for you.** The hero is very sexually aggressive with the heroine. He doesn't take no as a suggestion so much as... a sign that he's on the right track and should keep coming a little harder. He respects her, he isn't like that with other women (he can't be bothered to exert *any* effort on other women, he saves all his effort for her), but he considers the heroine his to play with, so... do not come here expecting enthusiastic consent. You will not get it. This is fiction, not real life.

There's also forced proximity mixed with a bit of... you know, him almost being her stepbrother (their parents got engaged in *Undertow*. Again, if you have not read *Undertow*, you really should read that one before this. Parker and Landon's story began in that book).

You're also going to have to trust me. This is not uncommon with my books, but if this series is your first Sam Mariano reading experience, just know that you're in the capable hands of someone who cares about your experience, and trust me even in moments you're not sure you should. ;) Reading my books can be a lot like dating my heroes. Trusting them even when it's scary is the only way it works.

I hope you enjoy the story, and thank you for reading. <3

"A true lover is continually and without interruption obsessed by the image of his beloved." -Andreas Capellanus

THE TOP BOX tilts as I make my way down the stairs as carefully as I'm able. I stop, looking up at it and hoping it settles because if it falls, every box on the stack will plummet down the stairs and I'll be lucky if I don't lose my balance and go with them.

I should have just carried fewer boxes and made a second trip, but this house has so many stairs, and we've been at this for so long. I just want to get it done so I can sit down.

Moving day.

Also known as my descent into the bowels of Hell.

I've been dreading today since the moment my mom told me we were moving in with the Atwaters. I couldn't even sleep last night, too busy tossing and turning and thinking way too much about all the possible horrors today—*and the rest of the days I have to spend here*—might hold.

Last time Landon and I were in a room alone together, he realized he can use my determination not to ruin things between his dad and my mom against me.

The time before that, he imprisoned me in my bedroom until I called the cops for help after he broke into my house.

And the first time...

Let's just say I'm really hoping we can make it through this year without there being a fourth.

I don't need the A I have in advanced statistics to know *that* is incredibly unlikely, but it is what I'm hoping for.

Moving in with the Atwaters seems a lot to my logical brain like standing on the deck of the Titanic with a bailer bucket, trying to throw water out faster than it can pour in so we don't sink.

I've seen the movie and read the books. My brain knows how that story ends, but my heart is another organ entirely. It *cannot* and *will not* be reasoned with. I am one thousand percent certain that by sheer force of my will, I will keep this goddamn ship afloat.

I will *not* let Landon Atwater sink it, no matter how hard he tries.

I only have to do this for a year.

Less, really.

More like eleven months. Just a slow blink in the overall span of my life.

I can do this.

I can carry the boxes, too. I smile, seeing the top box up there defying gravity as it settles into place. "Good box. I appreciate you."

When I was a kid, I always loved the movie *Matilda*. I didn't relate to the shitty family she had since my mom is legitimately the best, but I could relate to what her life must have been like after she got to live with Miss Honey. I liked to imagine my brain was so strong, it could move objects, too.

Looking at myself now, I think that's probably something I should have grown out of, but here I am, convinced I can move all the resistance in the world by the sheer force of my determination.

Oh well.

I'm gonna make it true.

I make my way down the stairs without dying and use my shoulder to push open the door of the Atwaters' in-home gym. I keep my ears peeled for the sound of weights being released and clanking into each other and feel relieved when I don't hear anything.

I haven't actually *seen* Landon in a while, and that makes me nervous. I need to put a tracker on him or something so I can be aware of his location in the house at all times.

Yeah, that's a good way to live.

I shove that unhelpful logic aside and turn the corner.

My heart slams to a stop when I catch sight of movement, then accelerates like it's on jet fuel when my mind grapples with the reality of what I'm seeing.

Landon Atwater, shirtless in just a pair of gray sweats and cross-trainers that probably cost more than my laptop. He's using a piece of gym equipment, a metal frame with a bar across the top. His feet aren't touching the ground and, without meaning to, I watch as he lifts himself until his chin goes above the bar. The muscles in his body flex with the effort, but he makes it look easy. He's glistening with sweat, so I guess he's been at it for a while.

That explains the heat in this room.

I'm so hot, I feel like I accidentally stepped into a sauna.

There *is* a sauna, but this room is just the workout area *and* it's air-conditioned. It shouldn't be so hard to breathe.

Must be the body heat he's generating.

When I pry my eyes from his distracting body and meet his gaze, I see it's locked on me, a smirk on his lips as he repeats the smooth movement of lifting himself—this time, aware that he has an audience.

Shit.

I tear my gaze away, pulse pounding, and try like hell to

steady the shaking of all *my* muscles. I'd like to believe they're suddenly wobbling on me because I've been carrying heavy things all day, but deep down, I know that's not it.

He makes me nervous.

I *hate* that he makes me nervous, but I guess it would be crazy if he didn't at this point.

My heart does another somersault when I hear him let go of the bar and drop to the ground.

Panic joins the fray of my muddled emotions and I spin around, trying to find somewhere to drop these boxes so I can get the hell out of here.

"Need help with that?"

I look back at him, my brown eyes wide with surprise. If he didn't have me so far off my game, I wouldn't squeak, "Okay," but... well, here we are.

Okay? That's not even the right response.

Yes, please.

No, thank you.

You're offering to help? Are you feeling feverish?

All acceptable responses to his question, and yet I came up with *okay*.

Ugh.

I'm obviously flustered, so his smirk grows even bigger. He grabs a white towel and slings it around his neck on his way over to me.

I turn and shift my hold on the stack of boxes to make it easier for him to grab, surprised and relieved at the offer of help.

Maybe he will *make an effort now that we're here and this is actually happening.*

Then he brushes right past me, and the heat in my face rises as my heart drops because *of course he did.*

Still holding the boxes and now fuming that I fell for such

an obvious taunt, I feel my wits starting to reorganize them-selves. The surge of emotion settles down and the fear goes with it so I can think straight.

Yeah, that was rude, but it's Landon Atwater—am I really surprised?

I just need to put the boxes down and leave. There's no reason for this to be a whole event.

Mom and Hayden can figure out where all this crap goes later. I find an empty corner to drop the boxes in, then I straighten, settling my hands on my hips and stretching my back.

God, moving sucks.

It would have sucked less if Mom would have let Hayden hire movers to handle everything like he offered to, but she said she doesn't trust them and she'd rather we move our things in ourselves.

I don't lift heavy things for fun, so this could not be less my thing.

Landon obviously does. If he weren't such an asshole, he would be *helping* us move in and getting his workout in that way, but here he is instead, working out in his gym like he would any other day.

Jerk.

On second thought, before I turn and leave, I pry open the tallest box and take out my pink yoga mat. When Hayden told me there was an in-home gym, I figured it made sense to keep it down here.

Now that I know the likelihood of running into Landon goes up in the gym—*I've seen his abs; I should have realized that before*—I think I'll just do my stretches in my bedroom.

I gasp when I turn and nearly crash into Landon. I fall back a step on instinct, and he takes two steps closer to give me even less space than I already had.

The claustrophobic feeling of being cornered prey fills my lungs and kicks my heart into overdrive.

I don't think, I just shove my yoga mat at him as hard as I can.

The open water bottle falls out of his hands and hits the floor, spilling all over the place. He's caught off-guard, so I'm able to shove him back just enough to clear space between us, then I toss the yoga mat at him before he has time to think about it.

He's a jock, so his impulse is to catch things when thrown at him.

His brow flickers with confusion when he catches the yoga mat. He's probably wondering why he did, but I know.

I'll commend myself for my quick thinking later, but right now, I need to get the hell out of here.

I make a mad dash to the staircase, my heart pounding with fear that he'll follow me.

His jock instincts might mean he catches thrown balls like a doofy dog, but his jock body means he's a hell of a lot faster than I am. I could barely get to my room ahead of him the night he broke into my house, and I had a lot more space between us than I do now.

But maybe amid the confusion with the yoga mat, he doesn't think to chase me quick enough, so he decides not to.

Maybe he just doesn't bother because he knows with me living here now, he'll have all the opportunities in the world if he wants to chase me.

Whatever the case, I'm far enough away from him that when he calls, "Parker," I turn to look back at him.

My yoga mat hangs at his side, so I can see that when I knocked his water bottle out of his hands, it spilled down his abdomen. The water darkens the front of his sweats and trails down his left leg. I realize, seeing the wet, clingy outline of the gray material against his crotch, that I gave him a bit of a cold shower.

I swallow.

Isn't cold water supposed to make those shrink?

His voice jolts me out of my thoughts, and my gaze meets his.

"Next time you spill something on me," he says slowly, "I'll make you lick it up."

My heart sinks like the Titanic.

Landon tosses the yoga mat at me. My arms are like limp noodles, but somehow, I catch it.

Then I haul ass upstairs, and even though I know he isn't following me, it *feels* like he is.

Through the living room.

Up the other staircase.

Down the hall toward my room.

I turn the lock as soon as I get the door shut, but even once I'm inside, I don't feel safe.

Living in this house, under the same roof as him, I have to wonder if I ever will.

I HEARD *Landon Atwater got arrested over the summer.*

Duh, everyone knows that. But did you know he got arrested for breaking into Parker Johansson's house?

I heard she invited him over and then lied about it so he'd get in trouble.

Please, "invited him"? I heard she begged.

It's like that montage in Mean Girls, but it's my actual first day of school, and people aren't speaking into a camera—they're talking *about* me *in front of me* as I navigate the halls on the way to my locker.

Is it true that his dad and her mom got engaged?

Were they even dating?

I heard she's pregnant.

What a golddigger.

I sigh, stopping outside the locker I've been assigned for the year and taking out my backpack so I can fill it up.

It has been the *longest* first day of school ever.

After a stressful morning—courtesy of Landon, of course—I walked through the doors of Baymont High determined that it would be a good first day of school.

At home, dealing with him is more stressful because I have

to try to shield Mom from the idea that living with him makes me uncomfortable. At school, I don't have to worry about that. Normally, I don't even have to worry about *him* because I avoid him as much as I possibly can.

I knew there was a slight chance people might be gossiping about me, but since the incident with Landon happened over the summer, I hoped no one would even know about it.

I should have known better. For all the wealth that lives here, Baymont is a small town, and word of all the crazy shit that goes on here tends to spread like wildfire—quickly, torching whole lives that happen to be in its path.

On top of that, my schedule is wrong. I had to spend half of lunch in the office trying to work out why Landon Atwater is in two of my classes when I *always* schedule my classes very carefully to ensure he isn't in any of them.

I guess it doesn't matter now. I live with the jerk; what difference will a couple of classes make?

As if that's not enough bad luck, the car I've had since my 16th birthday decided to die on me after the first load of boxes I drove over to the Atwater mansion. As frustrating as it was to have to deal with that on top of moving, I like to think the car was making a dramatic protest about its new home, and I can't really blame it.

Today, Landon is my ride home.

I'd rather walk, honestly, but Hayden reasoned that since Landon and I are coming home to the same place now, he could just give me a ride. It would be no trouble at all.

Mom brought me to school, as is tradition on the first day of a new school year. Before we left, she assured everybody that she would be home waiting for us after school—probably to ensure Landon didn't kidnap me or something once the lunatic has me in his car.

I'm dreading the ride home with him, but I'll try not to let him feel that. Even if the first day hasn't gone the way I hoped it would, I'm committed to this fresh start thing. This *will* be a fresh start, and it will go well, whether the rest of the world wants it to or not.

It *has* to.

This is one of those scenarios where failure truly isn't an option. Mom's happiness is on the line, and I refuse to stand in the way of it.

Once my bag is full of books, I exit the building and make my way toward the row of reserved student spaces. They're not for just *any* students, of course. Only those whose parents make generous donations to the school to reserve one for their little darling. I know Landon has one, so I walk down the sidewalk until I get to his sleek, deep green Jaguar.

He's not here yet, so I sit on the curb to wait for him. While I wait, I pull out my phone and see I have a text from Mom.

"Hey honey, how was your first day?"

I type back, "Good," even though it's a big, fat lie.

"No problems?" she returns promptly.

"Nope," I lie again. Then, I decide to amend it with some truth, "Well, some gossip, but nothing to worry about."

"How's Landon? Are you guys on your way home?"

"Not yet. I'm waiting by his car. I'm sure he won't be long."

"Okay. Text me when you're leaving."

"I will," I assure her.

Just then, I'm startled by a leg brushing so close to me, it nearly touches my shoulder. I look over and recognize Landon's shoes and the expensive jeans he was wearing this morning.

For a split second, I'm bowled over by the absolute strangeness of knowing what Landon is wearing today because I saw him snatch a bagel at breakfast before he left (because God forbid he sit down and enjoy the delicious food Mom made us for the first day of school).

Every other first day of school, keeping my eyes peeled for Landon has been one of the items on my to-do list. I avoid him, of course, but I need to know where he is (and if anything changed over the summer) in order *to* effectively avoid him.

My gaze skates up his muscular body until I'm meeting his cool green-eyed gaze.

He smirks, standing there looking down at me for a few seconds. "I like when you know your place."

Dull annoyance pours through my veins, but I don't let him get a rise out of me. That was a cheap shot for such a rich boy, and it doesn't deserve the reaction he wants.

Biting back the impulse to ask if that's the best he can do, I roll my eyes and grab my bag, standing so I can walk around to the passenger side.

I stop short when I see Brittany Benson already waiting on that side of the car.

My brow furrows as Landon puts down the roof to turn his car into a convertible, then slides in behind the wheel. Brittany hops in the passenger side with unmasked zeal, and my eyes widen with indignation.

"What are you doing?" I ask, glancing from her to him. "You're supposed to be my ride home."

He sucks in a breath through his teeth, feigning regret. "Got a better offer. Sorry."

Is he serious?

Brittany rifles through her purse to avoid looking at me, and I stare, dead-eyed, at Landon as the asshole fires up his noisy-ass car and backs out of his "reserved for spoiled rich boys" parking spot.

He's seriously going to leave me stranded here.

And he knows I'm not going to go home and tell our parents that it's day one of a new school year and he's already being an asshole. I can see it in the smirk on his stupid face, the glint of pleasure dancing in his dark green eyes.

"You're an asshole," I mouth, since his car is too loud for him to hear me, anyway.

His smirk grows as he thrusts the gearshift back into drive, then gives me a little mocking wave.

He is *the worst.*

My full backpack hangs heavily at my side. Landon hits the accelerator hard just to be an asshole so his car roars as he takes off toward the exit. "See you at home," he calls back.

Well, that's just fucking great.

Sighing, I swipe my phone screen and text Hannah. "Have you left school yet?"

She doesn't answer right away, so I look around the parking lot to see if I can spot her car. It's usually pretty easy to find. She has a pumpkin-orange Volkswagen Beetle, definitely the only one on the lot.

I see it a few rows back, so I walk over just in case she doesn't check her messages before she leaves.

She looks exhausted when I spot her on her way to the car. Hannah is usually up with the birds so she can start on her chores before school starts, so I imagine she is.

"Hey," she says softly.

"Hey. Landon blew me off," I explain, since she knew he was supposed to give me a ride home. "Can I ride home with you?"

"You want to come to my place?" she asks, mildly surprised.

"I know the wicked witch is home now, but I think Landon is taking some girl to his house to hook up with, and I'm not really interested in being there for that."

She grimaces sympathetically, popping her trunk so we can stow our backpacks. "Yeah, of course you can come over. We can squeeze in some homework before I have to stop to make dinner. I can't believe they gave us so much on the first day."

"It's Baymont High; I would've been stunned if they hadn't."

Hannah mumbles something about how many hours there are in a day, then she walks around to the driver's side.

The ride to Hannah's is peaceful.

I text Mom to let her know there was a change in plans and I'm going to Hannah's instead, but I'll be home for dinner.

Then I flick through social media and pull up Brittany Benson's account. She posted a picture of her and Landon driving down the road with the wind blowing through her hair. She's flashing a peace sign.

I close the dumb app and shove my phone into my purse.

I look up when we pull up to the gate outside Hannah's house. She has a grand, beautiful home even though Hannah doesn't have any money herself. She should. The house was hers, but her dad left it and everything else to Anae's terrible mother when he died and now Hannah's destitute. You can't tell by her digs, though.

That's kind of how I feel moving into the Atwaters' mansion, but I know I don't have it nearly as bad as Hannah.

We used to go to her room when I came over to study or do homework together, but last year Hannah was moved out of her childhood bedroom and stashed in the attic. There's not enough space or light up there, so we head to the kitchen to study.

Unfortunately, being in the kitchen means we are more accessible to her horrid roommates. I guess technically they would be considered her family, but they in no way treat her like family, so I won't dignify them with that title.

The evil stepsister comes in while we're working, and Hannah immediately tenses up. Anae notices and likes it, smirking as she walks to the refrigerator to get herself a bottle of water.

"I'm not interrupting your little study date, am I?" she says, her heels clicking across the floor as she approaches the table.

Hannah shakes her head wordlessly, focusing her attention on the page of notes she was just reading through.

Anae's gaze flickers to me. She looks me over briefly, her eyes cool and disinterested. "You're still around, huh?"

"Apparently," I murmur, turning the page in my textbook so she gets the message that we're busy and goes away.

"Parker something, right?"

"Johansson," I offer, even though I'm sure she doesn't care.

"So, are you two in love, or...?"

I do not like where she's going with this. My gaze flickers to Hannah, her face warming because she, too, knows where Anae is heading.

I don't fan the flames by answering her. Bullies are like fires; they should be deprived of oxygen and smothered out of existence.

I try to ignore her as I jot down a short answer to the next question on my homework assignment, but it proves impossible.

When she sees neither of us will swallow her cheap bait, Anae leans down, locks a slim arm around Hannah's neck in a mockery of closeness, and murmurs, "No, I guess not. You're still sad that your last girlfriend left, aren't you?"

Rage heats my blood to simmering. On impulse, I look up at Anae and say, "Are you still sad your boyfriend did?"

Hannah's jaw drops and her gaze darts to me, her eyes wide with horror.

Anae's eyes flash with cool anger and I get the tingly sensation at the nape of my neck animals must get when a hunter focuses them between the crosshairs of a deadly weapon.

"She didn't mean that," Hannah says quickly. "She was trying to be funny. Parker's not funny, that's all you need to know about her. Tragically unfunny. It's practically a condition. There should be fundraisers to raise awareness. She was just joking, though. She didn't mean—but it was a bad joke. Parker, tell her you're sorry."

I'm not sorry at all, but I know Anae is *legitimately* insane—she spent half of the last school year and the whole summer in a mental hospital for trying to kill a girl over a pair of shoes—so I probably shouldn't have said it.

I can't bring myself to back down, though. Years of being Hannah's friend have trained me to hate Anae Richards, not to be afraid of her.

"If Anae wants to apologize to you for her meanness, I'll be happy to apologize for mine."

"Are you popular?" Anae asks me.

I almost laugh. "No."

"But you don't live under a rock? You know fucking with me is a very bad idea?"

"I'm aware of your reputation," I confirm. "I'm not trying to fuck with you, I just don't like seeing people be assholes to my best friend."

She smirks at me. "You must have loved Dare, then."

"I am not a member of his fan club, no," I say, but I'm distracted as Anae leans in and runs the edge of her fingernail along Hannah's collarbone.

"Where's my necklace?"

My stomach drops. Hannah's face is already red, her gaze trained on the table.

"I don't have it," Hannah says.

Anae chuckles unpleasantly. "Yes, you do." She pulls her phone out of her back pocket and taps the screen a few times before holding it in front of Hannah's face.

Hannah loses several shades of color. "Where did you get that?"

I crane my neck and look over at the screen. It's a picture of Hannah on prom night junior year.

"Dare sent it to me. A parting gift from my king," she murmurs, tracing Hannah's collarbone again. "Cinderella wearing my dress. My necklace." She turns her face so Hannah can feel her breath on her ear as she speaks. "Where is it?"

Hannah swallows. "I had the dress cleaned. It's back in your closet."

"I don't *care* about the dress, Hannah," she snaps, grabbing Hannah's throat.

"Hey," I say, jumping up from the table.

"I sold it," Hannah cries. "Your mom halved my allowance while you were away. I had to sell the necklace. I needed the cash for school supplies and clothes. I could barely afford gas to get around town."

That's a lie. Her stepmom *did* cut back on her already minimal allowance, but before Anae came home, Hannah brought the necklace over to my house along with a taped-together photograph of her with her parents because she knew her valuables weren't safe in her own home.

"Aubrey gave it to me to sell," Hannah explains quickly. "I was never meant to keep it."

"Why did you?" Anae asks, still touching her neck.

I'm deeply uncomfortable with Anae's intimidation tactics. Sensing that, Hannah shoots me a pleading look to stay out of it.

I know Anae's bullshit is nothing new and Hannah can handle herself, but I don't *want* to stay out of it. The only reason I keep my mouth shut is I'm afraid I'll only make things worse for her once I'm gone if I intervene.

Anae speaks again. "Did you keep it because Aubrey gave it to you, or because Dare bought it?"

Hannah is too afraid to speak. I understand why. She's straddling two landmines. There is no right answer—only a wrong one and a more wrong one.

I've witnessed the shit Hannah has had to endure over the years, know how scared she was last year when Anae's boyfriend pulled her into their tangled web and threatened... actually, I'm not sure what he threatened her with because she wouldn't tell me, but I've surmised it was something evil to get Anae to target her.

"She hates Dare," I state, trying to help without getting between them. "Why would she keep something because it was from him?"

"I've hated Dare, too," Anae answers. "I still want the fucking necklace he bought me." Just to Hannah, she murmurs, "She doesn't get it, does she? She never brushed with him, doesn't know the way he crawls beneath your skin and lingers there even when he's not around. But *you've* brushed up against Dare, haven't you, Hannah?" she murmurs, causing Hannah to swallow audibly. "Dare told me he paid you a visit in your bedroom one night while I was asleep. Told me he didn't fuck you, but it turns out he lied to me quite a bit toward the end of our relationship." Her fingers slide around Hannah's throat with her long nails poised against her skin—not to hurt, just to threaten. "Did he?"

"No, of course not," Hannah says nervously.

"Why did he have a picture of you in his phone?"

"To send to you, apparently," Hannah mutters.

"Why does he want me to go after you?"

Hannah doesn't appear to have an answer for that question. "I don't know," she says softly.

"Because he's an asshole," I state, since they've both lost

their damned minds. "The guy was a complete psychopath. Why are we even still talking about him? He's gone, and good riddance. This is a new year, a Dare-free year for both of you."

They both look at me, Hannah uncertainly, Anae with a curious frown.

"We have a chance to start fresh this year. All of us. Why don't we *do it*? Anae, you don't just have a second chance at senior year, you have a second chance at *freedom*. If you do the same shit you did last year, you'll end up right back where you were before—or worse. We all know you should be rotting in a cell somewhere, but here you are instead. Why?"

"Because Dare didn't want me to rot away in prison," she answers promptly.

I blink. "No. That's the wrong answer."

She shakes her head firmly. "He made sure I didn't have to suffer for long. He convinced that awful girl to change her story to protect me."

That is not at all how that went down.

I see her stay in the psych hospital has done *wonders* for her.

Ignoring her obvious instability, I point at her encouragingly. "This is your chance to reinvent yourself. You said it yourself, the evil king is gone—you don't have to be the evil queen anymore."

"I like being the evil queen."

Trying to pull her along down this motivational road despite her apparent disinterest, I keep at it. "Fine, then be an independent queen, but you don't have to be evil. You're new to our class. Sure, people have heard stuff about you, but no one really knows you, right?"

She shrugs. "I guess not."

"So, you can make a new impression and new friends. Better friends. Rebrand."

"I like my brand."

"Okay." I sigh. "But... there's no reason for us to start this year out as enemies. We can *all* be nicer to each other. We can embrace the fresh start. We can pave a different path."

"Okay, I'm tired of this inspirational spiel, but it has given me an idea." Anae straightens. "I'm going to throw a party this weekend. I don't know who's who in your grade, but you do, so you can help me come up with a guest list. I don't have any friends yet and you two—" she eyes us both with distaste "—won't do at all, but you can help me with the party. And in return, I won't ruin your life for the mean things you've said to me today. We'll call it even."

She looks so proud of herself, like she's truly accomplished compromise. "Okay, well, I suppose that's a start," I say.

She claps. "Yay! I love this idea. Hannah, you can do all the prep. Parker will help me with the guest list." Dismissing Hannah and stepping around her on her way to me, Anae asks, "Who's the queen bee in your grade?"

It's her grade now, too, but I don't say that. "Um... probably Sierra McCall."

"What's she like?"

"Kinda snobby and obnoxious, but generous. She buys her friends a lot of stuff."

Anae nods as if evaluating what she's hearing. "That's a good way to get people to like you. Is she cunning?"

"I wouldn't say she's particularly cunning."

"I could dethrone her."

"Or you could just be her friend," I suggest.

"I only need your knowledge of the players, not your boring suggestions about embracing whatever stupid Kumbaya shit you have in your head."

"Noted."

"What about the boys? I know there's only one Dare, but anyone with Dare energy I could feed on for a while?"

"I don't believe we have any outright psychopaths—present company excluded, of course—but there are definitely some assholes."

She flashes me a smile. "I'm not a psychopath."

"You tried to kill a girl over a pair of shoes."

"It was a shirt, and I wasn't committed to killing her over the shirt, that was just an idea. I wanted to kill her because—" Cutting herself off, she visibly pushes it away. "No. We're not talking about Dare's vanilla cunt-cake anymore. She doesn't matter. Dare and I are end game. I'm not looking for a replacement king, just a pretty puppet to pass the time with until he gets bored and comes back for me."

"As long as you're staying realistic."

"You're as vanilla as she is. I wouldn't expect you to get it."

I don't care what flavor she thinks I am, so if I'm meant to be insulted... I'm not.

"Anyway, the boys."

"Let's see. There's Arden Prince. He's very wealthy and very attractive if you're into assholes, which you clearly are. Arden may be the hottest guy in our grade and definitely the most popular, but he's a player and he's kinda gross. I don't know if he has Dare energy. I didn't know Dare the way you guys did. Flowers don't wilt and die when he walks into a room, so my gut instinct is that he doesn't, but he is definitely *aware* of Dare and his whole legend-aura. Arden is accustomed to being at the top of the food chain, so being overshadowed by Dare after all the evil shit he pulled last year... I do think he feels a sense of competition with him. He'll definitely ruin some unsuspecting woman's life someday."

"Mm, sounds yummy."

"Then there's Malek Atwater. He's an established member

of the elite around here. His dad's some famous football player. He's as rich as God, but with the fidelity of Zeus, so... Malek's home life can be rocky. He's also an asshole. I would say Arden is sneakier, but Malek is an in-your-face asshole. Wholly unapologetic about how terrible he is and does not try to hide it."

Anae appears to consider. "Eh, I'll have to form my own impression when I meet him. Guys like that can be more trouble than they're worth. I'm happy to hear there are some contenders, though. Anyone else?"

Landon Atwater.

"Nope," I lie. "I mean, they have a friend group, there are other guys in it, of course, but those are probably the ones you would be most interested in."

"Have you fucked both of them?" she asks, glancing at me. "Which one's better in bed?"

"Um, no," I say a touch awkwardly. "I haven't had sex with anyone. Certainly not either of those jerks."

She makes a face like she finds me thoroughly disgusting, but the feeling is mutual, so I don't take offense. "This house is swimming in virgins. I hate it."

"This isn't advice I would ordinarily give someone, but maybe you should be less yourself when you're trying to make new friends this year."

She rolls her eyes. "I'm not an idiot, Parker. I know I have to wear a mask around the normies. I don't care what kind of impression I make on *you.* You're irrelevant."

She is endlessly delightful, isn't she?

"Anyway, I should probably be getting home. My mom will need help making dinner."

"Fine. Put together a guest list and we'll go over it tomorrow. No poor people, no pity invites. I want a top tier guest list, only the best of your grade. You only get one chance at a first impression, so do not fuck with me on this."

"I get it," I assure her as I gather my things.

Hannah shoots me an apologetic look, but I flash her a reassuring smile. It's not her fault Anae hijacked our study session, and it doesn't bother me when Anae is a bitch to me—I just can't stand by and watch her be horrible to Hannah.

DESPITE MY STALWART enthusiasm at the start of the day, I'm dragging a little by the time Hannah drops me off at home.

I haul my heavy backpack up the five million steps to the front door and droop as I carry it into the Atwater lair.

I don't stop until I get to the kitchen, but what I see when I get there gives me pause and cheers me up a little.

Mom is standing at the counter with a red spatula and a mixing bowl. Hayden is standing behind her, his arms wrapped around her waist, her body cradled against his while he watches her cook.

They are adorable.

I haven't been noticed yet, so when Mom smiles and tips her head back for a kiss, I know I'm witnessing a private moment between them. I should make my presence known, but I don't want to intrude.

"You're supposed to be helping," Mom teases.

"I *am* helping," Hayden insists.

"Helping distract me," Mom tosses back.

"I'm sorry. I'm working to accomplish *my* end goal, not yours. I should have been clearer."

Mom grins as he moves her hair aside and bends to kiss her neck. "And what is *your* objective here, counselor?"

I love seeing Mom happy, but I don't want to overhear much more of this conversation. That little reminder of their happiness was all I needed to cleanse my fatigue and bolster my commitment to peace as I enter the kitchen. "Hey, guys."

Mom automatically starts to move away from Hayden to put an appropriate amount of space between them, but Hayden pulls her right back.

"Hey, honey. How was studying at Hannah's?"

"Not great." I hoist my heavy backpack and drop it on a chair at the island. Unzipping it, I reach in for the papers Mom has to sign since it's the start of a new school year.

"No?" Mom asks worriedly.

I shake my head. "The Wicked Witch of the West is back, and she thinks I'm one of her flying monkeys this year. She's making me plan a guest list for a party I am almost certainly not even invited to."

Mom's frown deepens. "Do you want me to call her mom?"

"No. Jackie sucks, too. It doesn't matter, it's not a big deal." I flash her a smile. "Just a long day. I'm happy to be home."

"Who is the Wicked Witch of the West?" Hayden asks, trying to catch up when he has no clue what I'm talking about.

"Anae Richards."

His dark eyebrows rise. "Oh, that's right. I forgot she would be in your grade this year. You shouldn't hang out with that girl, Parker. She's very troubled."

"Tell me about it. Unfortunately, my best friend is her stepsister," I inform him. "Now, we're even in the same grade. Unless we adopt Hannah, avoiding Anae isn't really an option."

"Well, be very careful. She should be in prison, or at the very least, getting long-term psychiatric care."

"Mm-hmm," Mom murmurs pointedly. "And why isn't she?"

His eyebrows rise. "Hey, I wasn't *her* lawyer."

He wasn't, but *his* client was the reason Anae got off with such a light charge.

"It doesn't matter now. She's out, and we all have to deal with her." I hoist my backpack. "Since I can see you already have help making dinner..."

Hayden nods solemnly. "I'm very helpful."

A smile tugs at my lips. "... I'll go upstairs and do a little more homework."

"All right. You have about 45 minutes until dinner will be ready," Mom says.

"A little longer if I have my way," Hayden murmurs.

I crack a smile as I hear my mom say, "Stop it, you deviant," on my way up the stairs.

The real deviant is standing at the top of them.

My smile droops when I feel him looming like a bad dream on a sleepless night, falls off my face entirely when I look up and meet his hooded gaze.

I'm used to running in the opposite direction when that happens.

Now I can't.

Feigning indifference, I plod up the stairs without looking at him. I keep to one side so he can pass, but rather than come down, he stands at the top and waits for me.

Fantastic.

A wave of foreboding washes over me as I reach the top step. Rather than move out of the way because he obviously saw me coming up the stairs, he deliberately blocks my path.

"Can you move?" I ask, halting on the top step.

"What's the magic word?"

I'm too tired for his shit. "Don't be an asshole," I say flatly.

He smirks, stepping back so there's enough room for me to step onto the landing. "Not in the mood to play, huh? You must have had a long day. A lot of people talking shit about your golddigging mom?"

I grind my teeth together and turn the corner without bothering to answer him.

He was clearly about to head downstairs, but now that I'm upstairs, he turns and follows me instead.

Great.

"I heard a few rumors myself. Might have contributed to a couple. When's your mom due, by the way?"

"Look, I don't really have the energy to deal with you right now," I tell him, even knowing he won't care.

"Did you hear the one where you invited me over?"

He doesn't specify when, but I know when.

The night he broke into my goddamn house.

"Brittany didn't like that one," he says, as if letting me in on a secret. "Why's she the one with a throatful of cum if you're the one who can summon me with a text?"

I am simultaneously revolted and annoyed by what he just said. "Please stop talking."

"Am I offending your virginal sensibilities—again?"

We've made it to my bedroom, but I can't go inside because I don't want him to follow me, so I stop outside the door and turn to huff at him. "What do you want, Landon?"

"You didn't tell my dad I blew you off after school today, did you?"

"Nope."

He smirks like my answer amuses him. "Look at you, doing my bidding without even having to be told. What a good girl."

I give him a dead-eyed look. "Can I go now?"

He ignores the question and holds my gaze. "You didn't come straight home. Who gave you a ride?"

"None of your business."

His eyes narrow with dislike.

I smile. "Anything else?"

"It was Hannah, right?"

"Arden, actually," I lie, just to watch his handsome features turn to granite. "Yeah, he saw me sitting by your spot all by myself—a poor, discarded damsel-in-distress—and thought he'd ride in on his big white horse and save me."

"Bullshit," he says, but I can see he's not entirely certain I'm lying.

I smile suggestively. "It was quite a ride, too. He has a really big... horse."

I must have taken it too far because the granite cracks and a faint smile tugs at his full lips. "You're so fucking full of shit."

"Maybe. You should text him and ask if I'm a screamer. In the meantime, I have homework to do, and you're not allowed in my room, so..." I twist the doorknob behind me and slowly back into my bedroom.

He walks away, shaking his head.

I lock the door once it's closed and sigh with relief that he went away so easily.

This time.

It was probably due to the fact that our parents are right at the bottom of the steps more than his basic sense of decency, but I'll take what I can get.

IT'S late by the time I get my homework finished.

Mom and Hayden are already in bed.

I lost track of time. I meant to go downstairs and get myself a cold bottle of water while they were still awake so I didn't risk running into Landon—and if I did, there would be a buffer—but now I've missed my window, and my throat is dry.

I hate feeling so much dread at the notion of simply leaving the sanctuary of my bedroom to go downstairs and grab a drink from the fridge, but I'm like a little girl again, tiptoeing down the hall so as not to disturb the monsters that might live in the shadows.

I check each area before I enter, and when I make it to the kitchen, I feel like the winner of a board game Mom used to play with me when I was little.

Don't wake Daddy.

I smile faintly at the memory, but my safety still feels tentative when I open the massive refrigerator and search for the bottled water.

Since I'm downstairs alone, I look around at my new home as I uncap the bottle and take a refreshing sip. It's nothing like my old one.

Our old house was nice—nicer than we should have been able to afford—but it was a stripped-down model, lacking the high-end finishes and features the other houses in our neighborhood had. We were like paupers trying to blend in among the royals.

This house was built for a king.

I don't know why a house needs ceilings so high. They make the place feel cavernous. It's impeccably decorated, and I don't think Hayden is a hobbyist interior designer, so he probably hired someone to do the job.

Every piece fits except the ones we hauled in along with us.

Most of the boxes have been put away or at least taken to the places they're meant to be unpacked, but Mom doesn't know this house much better than I do, so there are a few stray boxes in the living room that don't seem to have a home yet.

I peek at the labels written on in black Sharpie. Mom

wanted everything to be neat and organized to make the moving process as smooth as possible.

I know she was anxious about it. Landon is a threat she lacks confidence they can contain, so she managed the nuisances she knew she *could* control.

She must have run out of steam because the box marked photo albums certainly seems like it should be in Hayden's study. I decide to take it there for her, but my muscles are already sore from all the boxes I carried the past few days, so they balk at my lifting a box full of heavy books.

I put the box down just inside the study since I'm not sure where something as personal as family photo albums would go.

I'm tempted to look around the glorious haven of books and sophistication, but I still feel like a guest here, and I don't want to get caught snooping.

When I return to the homeless boxes, I see the next one is labeled swim supplies. Our old house didn't have a pool, but this one does. More than that, it has a pool *house*, and that seems like the most logical place for this stuff.

I wedge my cold bottled water under my chin and, ignoring my groaning muscles, lift the box. Might as well move this one while I'm at it.

The pool looks so serene as I walk by. It's a nice night, too.

I've wanted to go in the pool since I found out we were moving here. I hadn't seen the Atwater mansion before, but Landon is on the swim team and their house is expensive, so it stood to reason they probably had one.

What a pool, too.

I take the box into the pool house and open it to see what's inside. The usual stuff—sunscreen, some beach towels, one of Mom's old bathing suit cover-ups. I stop when I grab *my* backup bathing suit. It's a bikini, and while Mom always sports a bikini at the beach, I usually opt for a one piece. My fair complexion means I burn if I even *think* about the sun for too long, so the more skin I have covered, the better. I'd swim in one of those scuba diving outfits if I had one.

But we were out shopping one day and decided to take a spontaneous trip to the beach to watch the sunset and play in the water for a bit. We could have just gone home, but the shop had a blue bikini and a green bikini on clearance. We grabbed those, put them on under our clothes in the dressing room, and hit the beach.

Since it's dark, I don't have to worry about sunburn tonight.

I look at the looming mansion, my gaze automatically finding the window of the room I know is Landon's.

I do have to worry about him, but his bedroom lights are off. The basement doesn't seem to be illuminated either, and it is late on a school night, so it's probably safe to assume he's sleeping.

A grin claims my lips as I snatch the bikini out of the box and run to the bathroom to change.

I feel far too naked as I practically tiptoe out of the pool house. I toss a beach towel on a lounge chair as I walk past, then I check the house for signs anyone else is awake, but thankfully, the place is still dark.

Pleasure washes over me as I submerge myself in the water. Even the sounds the water makes to accommodate me as I walk deeper into the pool bring me peace.

I've always loved the water.

As much as I loved our old house, the one thing that bugged me was that we didn't have a pool. Every single other house in the neighborhood did. Since I didn't have any friends in the neighborhood, I didn't have access to anyone else's, either.

I mean, my best friend has a pool, but unless her roommates are out, Hannah's house is a stressful place to be. I can't stand either of the people she lives with, and any time I *have* gone over there to swim with her, Jackie or Anae—or both—have found reasons to drag her out of the pool to do something for them, because God forbid she have a little fun.

I don't know how she stands them, but *I* can't. It's too hard to keep my mouth shut when I'm around them, and usually I do because I don't want to make Hannah's life any harder once I'm gone, but it is far from relaxing.

I spread my arms and lean back in the water, allowing my body to rise so I'm floating in the warm, rippling waves. I close my eyes and just breathe.

This is relaxing.

Living at the Atwaters' mansion is also much more stressful than when we lived alone at our pool-less house, but this almost makes up for it.

Sprinkle on how happy Hayden makes Mom, and the bar fills up.

Worth it.

Even if it doesn't feel that way sometimes.

I float around for a while, enjoying the water and recharging a bit. I know I'm losing sleep for every minute I'm out here and I may regret it tomorrow, but I don't know when I'll get to swim in this pool again.

Or, well, float.

Floating is quieter and I'm paranoid about waking anyone, so I haven't actually gone for a swim, but once I come to the sad conclusion that I need to get out of the pool and get my butt to bed, I allow myself to swim a few laps back and forth.

Paradise.

With great regret, I leave the water. My body feels heavier as I emerge from both the unpleasantness of gravity *and* my dread about leaving paradise and not knowing when I'll be able to return.

I grab the beach towel off the chair and wrap it around

myself. I check the house for lights one more time, then head inside the beach house to put my clothes back on.

Since it's late and I need to get some sleep, I don't unpack the rest of the box. I close it up and make a mental note to tell Mom where it is at breakfast tomorrow.

But just as I'm pulling my hair out of my tank top and preparing to head back inside, I notice something sheer and black lying on the floor in front of the couch. Frowning, I bend to pick it up.

At first, I think maybe it was something I knocked out of the box, but when I hold it up, I know immediately it's nothing of mine or Mom's.

I know because I recognize it as part of the shirt Brittany Benson was wearing when she hopped into Landon's Jaguar this afternoon.

All the peace I just found in the pool drains away in an instant.

My imagination can't help but conjure the interaction that would have led to her top coming off and winding up on the floor of this pool house.

Gross.

I'm tempted to throw the damn thing in the pool, but I'm sure the top was expensive—*maybe even dry-clean only*—so I swallow down my annoyance and turn off the lights, then head back to my room with Brittany Benson's fucking shirt balled up in my fist.

"AND THAT IS why I need you to return Brittany Benson's shirt."

Hannah shakes her head as the car slows down at the last stop sign before we reach Baymont High. The car on the other side stops at the same time, so Hannah waves for them to go ahead. "I don't really know her. I'm not even sure I know what she looks like. I think you should do it yourself."

"No, what I should do is give it to Landon. Since he likes her so much, *he* can return her stupid shirt." Without giving her long enough to respond, I go on. "How do you just... not realize you're missing half of your shirt? Honestly."

"I'm sure she did notice," Hannah says.

"And she didn't go back for it?"

She smiles faintly. "Of course not. 'Oh, hey, I think I left my shirt at your house the other day' is the perfect way to invite herself back if she wasn't sure he would invite her without the nudge. Sometimes I forget that for all your academic brilliance, you've lived in a boy-free bubble your whole life and you don't know how dating works."

I scowl. "Why would you want to see a guy you have to trick into inviting you back over?"

Hannah laughs and shakes her head. "*You* wouldn't, but some girls do. Any girl who likes Landon has to, because they all know by now *he's* never going to put in the effort to see *them.*"

I shake my head. "Mind boggling. Maybe I should slip a copy of *He's Just Not That into You* in the shirt before I give it back."

"Too late to stop at the bookstore now," Hannah jokes as we pull into the school parking lot.

Hannah finds an open spot near the back, and as we walk past the row of reserved spaces, I spot Landon hanging with Malek and Arden by their cars. Of course *they* don't have to search the lot for a parking spot.

My heart rate kicks up when Landon's brooding gaze locks on me. I realize with growing horror I'm holding Brittany's shirt and he can *see me.* Without thought, I shove it at Hannah.

"Will you give it to her for me?" I ask again.

Hannah sighs. "All right. I'll need to see a picture, though. I want to make sure I approach the right person."

I pull out my phone to pull up Brittany's profile so Hannah can see what she looks like. Since I was just on her socials yesterday, her name pops up immediately. I click the most recent picture—the one of her in Landon's car—but my heart stops at the sight of a new comment.

"*Troublemaker*" it says with a little winking emoji.

The comment is from Landon.

At around 3 AM.

When I was downstairs in the pool.

A cold sweat breaks out at the realization that he was awake and could have come out to the pool and gotten me alone —not just alone, but our parents were asleep, so he could have... he could have done anything.

Oh my god.

But shoving aside the horror of that realization makes room for a more important one.

This is the response Landon wants out of me.

It may be reaching to assume he knew I would be checking out her socials, that I would notice the time he posted it and from that realize he had been awake.

But honestly, it's not a huge reach for anyone who knows me. I'm very thorough.

Even if I missed the time thing, just his comment on her picture would be annoying, and it wouldn't be the first time he's used some girl to annoy me. It's an old play from the beginning of the book, one he's been using against me since middle school.

Like at the 8th grade fall ball when he sent Malek over to ask me if I wanted to slow dance with him, and I couldn't breathe or think straight. My brain screamed no, but my heart said yes, and when I cautiously made my way over to accept his invitation, I realized Landon was already out on the dance floor with Vanessa Jensen, watching me with a malicious smirk on his annoyingly handsome face.

I realized a long time ago that it was one of his ways of keeping tabs on me. We don't speak, but he needs to know he can still affect me if he wants to.

When he finds out I sent Hannah to return his latest bimbo's lost clothing item, he will be so fucking satisfied with himself.

"Give me the shirt."

Surprised, Hannah looks over at me. "What?"

"I'm being stupid. I'll give it to her myself."

"Are you sure?" she asks, watching my face as she hands back the shirt. "If it's going to upset you, it's not a big deal. I can take it to her."

"No. If I let him think it bothers me, he'll keep doing shit like this. If he sees I don't care, maybe he'll stop."

"You do care," she murmurs innocently.

I give her a dead look. "Your honesty is not helpful."

She snickers, hugging her books to her chest. "Sorry."

Once we're inside the school, Hannah heads off to class and I head off in search of my new best friend, Brittany Benson. I spot her talking to two other girls by the lockers, and I paste on a friendly smile as I approach.

One of the girls spots me and signals Brittany that trouble is coming.

I can tell because when Brittany turns, she already looks nervous.

"Hi," I say brightly.

"Hey," she returns awkwardly.

I can tell she feels like a mistress being confronted by her lover's wife, so I keep my smile friendly. Way friendlier than Parker-friendly. I'm shooting for Hannah-friendly. Nearby birds should be inspired to fly in the windows and perch upon my shoulder so they can chirp along gaily as I sing a lovely song.

Since this is unusual for me, it only serves to make the girl look more cautious.

I don't want her to start wondering if the forced cheerfulness is because I have a nail gun waiting for her in the car, so I thrust the sheer scrap in her direction. "I have your shirt," I say gracelessly.

Her eyes widen. "*You* found it?"

There's a subtle note of disappointment in her inflection, and that's all the evidence I need that Hannah was right. She left the shirt on purpose, and if anyone was going to find it, she wanted it to be Landon.

I picture her getting a little excited every time her phone vibrates, wondering if it will be him telling her she left an item of clothing at his place. Teasing her about what will happen when she comes back to get it.

I almost feel bad for her.

"Anae Richards is having a party this weekend. She wanted me to invite you."

The girl behind her was just giving me a judgy, unimpressed look, but she snaps to attention at the sound of that name. "Really? When? Where? At her place?"

"Isn't she like... unhinged? In a bad way?" the other girl whispers apologetically.

"She's a goddamn icon," the judgy one states, her gaze never leaving mine. "Is there an invitation?"

"Uh... no. It's very exclusive, and I'm only allowed to invite Brittany. Sorry."

I'm sure Anae would have appreciated having a fan around to stroke her ego, but I am not in the business of recruiting new minions for her, and this girl seems like she would be only too eager to sign up.

"Will Landon be there?" Brittany asks uncertainly.

My jaw tries to lock, but I force a nod and remind myself to be cool. "Yeah. Landon, Arden, Malek. Kind of a way for Anae to mingle with new people since it's a new year. It's a carefully curated crowd."

"And I made the cut?" she asks brightly.

The one salty about *not* getting an invite asks sharply, "Is Sierra going to be there?"

She's annoying me, so I glance from her to Brittany. "Everyone who made the list will get the details. She'll be in touch."

I don't crave popularity at all and I certainly don't like Anae Richards, but I can't deny feeling a bit powerful as I dismiss them and walk away knowing they covet the invitations only I can offer.

Unfortunately, I am going to have to get with Anae to figure out the invitation situation, but I was planning to go to

Hannah's after school again, anyway. I hate how tired she has been lately, so I'm going to roll up my sleeves and help her get some housework out of the way so the poor girl can get more sleep.

***

"I WANT it to have a very cool night club feel," Anae says, her arms spread as she gestures to the open space in the room we just killed ourselves moving furniture out of.

"I want to never move another heavy thing as long as I live," I state, wiping sweat from my forehead with the back of my hand.

Hannah puts her hands on her hips and stretches a bit. "Okay, you mean the lighting?"

"Of course the lighting, but we also need plenty of comfy places for people to sit or hook up or whatever."

"Sure. Gotta have the hookup spots," I say.

Anae nods. "For the menu, Hannah's going to make a spread. Carne asada fries, tacos, and then for a vegan option, we'll have jackfruit carnitas."

"I'm also going to make cucumber roll ups for an appetizer," Hannah says.

"She'll circulate and pass out the appetizers. For the actual meal, we'll set up a table over here and people can help themselves. It's not a dinner party, so we'll keep it informal." She gestures elsewhere. "We'll put a bar over here, and we need to set something up out by the pool, too. And let's do a feature table when people first walk in, something sexy and cool to set the mood." She clasps her hands together. "I've got it. You know those lipsticks that change colors when you kiss someone? We'll get those, and everybody will take one when they enter."

"We need to come up with something as far as invites, too," I tell her.

She nods, contemplative for a split second, then she smiles. "I've got an idea for that. Hannah, how soon can you get me the lip balms?"

"Um..." Hannah pulls out her phone. "I don't know, give me a sec."

"Ugh." Anae rolls her eyes as if utterly inconvenienced. Then, back to me, she says, "If Hannah ever gets her shit together and we can get the lipsticks fast enough, we'll shoot a teaser video. Maybe a little girl-on-girl kiss so guests see how the lipstick works, then a shot of my lips changing colors with sexy, provocative language like 'who will you kiss tonight?' Not that, I'll let you come up with the verbiage since you're the brainy one."

Hannah speaks up. "We may be able to get them tomorrow, depending on how many we order."

Anae looks at me expectantly. "How many are on the guest list?"

"We still need to go over that."

"A preliminary number," she says impatiently.

"I had 21."

"So 22 people counting me?"

I nod.

She looks to Hannah. "What quantity are they packaged in?"

"They come in packs of six."

"Perfect. Order 24, enough for everyone with a couple to spare." She glances at me. "Hey, maybe if none arrive damaged, you can hang around, after all."

"What an honor," I say dryly.

"Yes, it is," she says without a hint of irony. "I'm glad you understand."

I roll my eyes to myself as she bombards Hannah with a list of what needs to be done on top of all her usual chores.

At least once Anae has finished handing out her orders, she leaves us alone to do her bidding.

I watch her exit the room and still wait a good ten seconds before speaking to Hannah. "All right, enough about the party. What do you need me to help with?"

"You don't have to help me," she insists. "I have a pretty good handle on my cleaning schedule, honest. I appreciate the gesture, but—"

I silence her with an outstretched hand. "You're wasting your time and mine. I'm helping. Just tell me what needs to be done before I start guessing."

Hannah sighs, then her gaze drifts reluctantly to the stairs. "Well... I guess I could use help getting all the draperies down from the windows. I need to clean them, but taking them down requires using a stepladder. Sometimes Anae will catch me on it and give it a good rattle because she thinks it's funny, and I... do not think it's funny."

I stare at her. "And you wanted me to apologize for taunting her about Dare."

Hannah rolls her eyes as she turns and leads the way upstairs. "I wanted you to apologize because I don't want her to use you for target practice, not because she didn't deserve it."

"I can't believe I'm helping her plan a party."

"Hey, if she's busy picking out a party dress, then she doesn't have to torture me to bust her boredom."

"Still. It's bullshit. This is her house; she's the one who should be pitching in and helping out around here."

Hannah's quiet for a moment longer than I anticipated, so I glance over at her.

She doesn't say anything, but I can tell I've said something wrong.

I've known Hannah for enough years to know she won't tell me what since she wouldn't think I meant any harm, so I replay my words in my head and test them for insensitivity.

"I didn't mean to say it was her house," I say tentatively.

Hannah shrugs defensively, then tips her chin up. "It *is* her house, isn't it?" she murmurs, setting up the ladder and pushing down on it to make sure it's steady. "You didn't say anything that's not true. It was *supposed to be* my house, that's what *my* mom wanted, but... she died, and he married a selfish cow, and now here we are."

I grimace, grabbing the ladder to keep it steady as Hannah climbs up to retrieve the dusty drapes.

Hannah generally avoids talking about this. I think she knows her labor of love looking after this house is wasted effort, but since I brought it up by accident, I might as well ask. After all, the clock is ticking. Hannah's 18th birthday is fast approaching, and if she has given a single thought to what it might mean, she's never given me any indication.

"Um, I know you probably don't like thinking about this, but have you talked to Jackie about what's going to happen in October?"

Hannah's movements halt briefly. I watch her throat work, and then she gets back to gathering the dusty fabric without missing a beat. "No," she says tersely.

"Don't you think you should?" I ask, looking up at her. "I mean, legally, she only has to let you stay here until you're 18, right?"

"Let me?" Hannah laughs shortly, but there's no amusement. "I don't think I have to worry about being evicted, Parker. I'm essentially slave labor. If she got someone to work any harder for any less than I do, they'd have to be purchased from human traffickers. Why bother committing felonies when I'm so low risk?"

"Well, you're probably right. But just in case, I have an idea. The Atwaters have a pool house. It's not meant to be lived in so it's not huge, more of a guest house, but if Jackie did kick you out after your 18th birthday, I bet I could convince Hayden to let you live there while you finish out the school year. I haven't asked yet, but I've started planting seeds so that if the time comes, he'll be primed to say yes."

Hannah smiles faintly. "Shouldn't he keep the guest house free in case *Landon* needs to be evicted?"

I roll my eyes at the mere mention of Landon. "Even if he did act up, Landon isn't going anywhere unless I tell on him. It's entirely within my control."

Hannah shakes her head. "No, thank you. I already have one friend being held captive by a jerk. I want you free to sing like a bird if he ever gives you a reason."

HELPING HANNAH TAKES LONGER than expected—that house has a *lot* of windows—so by the time I get home, I expect I'll have missed dinner.

I feel bad about not texting Mom to let her know I was running later than expected, but I shot off a quick "on my way!" text before I left Hannah's so she'd know I'm coming.

The Atwater lair does not have the homey drop-zone we had at our old house, so once more, I lug my heavy-ass backpack all the way to the kitchen. I look around for a plate of food Mom might have set aside for me, but there's nothing in the microwave, and looking around, I don't even see any signs anything was cooked.

Grabbing my phone out of my back pocket, I shoot her a text, "Are we being proper Californians now and having a juice entrée for dinner tonight?"

"With some kale chips, of course. What kind of mother do you think I am?"

I crack a smile. "Where are you?"

As I'm pressing send, I hear the patio door slide open. Mom comes in looking adorable in a sun hat and a blue dress. Hayden trails behind her, still dressed from work.

Mom looks so light and happy, like someone who just got back from vacation—or maybe even someone still *on* vacation. "Hey honey."

Hayden stops beside the staircase while Mom enters the kitchen. My gaze follows his to the stairs, and a moment later, Landon comes down.

"What?" he demands, his voice heavy with annoyance.

His dad looks up at him. "We're going out for dinner. Do you want to come?"

"What do you think?" Landon shoots back bitingly.

Ignoring the sullen ass, I ask Mom, "Where are we going?"

"The club," she answers.

I don't mean to brighten so visibly, but I could use a pick-me-up, too, and hearing we're having a Landon-free dinner at the club is much more appealing now than it was even the first time we went.

If Landon had been there, the whole evening would have gone differently. I would have been distracted by him, and I never would have noticed the handsome dark-haired valet. I wouldn't have been having an enjoyable, relaxing time with my family, so maybe he wouldn't have noticed me, either.

I don't know if he'll even be working tonight, but on the off chance he is, I already feel happier. "Okay," I chirp. "Do I have time to shower?"

Mom laughs at first, but when she sees I'm serious, she looks at me oddly. "No. Why would you need to shower before we leave?"

My cheeks warm, and not just because I realize now that was a bit silly.

It's because I can feel Landon's gaze locked on me.

It's the sensation I always got at Baymont High when he would catch me off-guard by showing up somewhere I wasn't expecting to see him.

"Right, yeah, of course." I shake my head to dismiss the silly idea of needing to shower to go eat when I was perfectly presentable at school all day. "Just let me change clothes real quick, and then I'll be right down."

THERE'S a long list of things I know about Parker Johansson, but somewhere near the top is this: unless she's eating at the fucking White House, she is not the type of girl who needs to change clothes to go to dinner.

Parker isn't intensely focused on her looks. It's just not her thing. She's not into clothes and shoes. She doesn't spend a lot of time on her makeup, and the only time her nails are painted is when she does them herself—and probably at the behest of her mom or Hannah when they were painting theirs.

Parker is beautiful, but she knows what she has to offer the world has everything to do with what's *inside* her head, not what she puts on it.

The only time I have ever known her to change clothes to go to a second location is the night she came to a party *I* invited her to.

When she showed up, she wasn't wearing what she wore to school that day. She'd put on a pretty dress, and she'd even gone to the trouble of putting on lipstick or lip gloss or some fucking thing like that. All she ever put on her lips at school was Chapstick, and even that was infrequent.

She made a visible effort that night because she was coming to see me.

So, when Parker comes bouncing down the steps with shiny lips and a low-cut red dress on, all of a sudden, I'm feeling pretty hungry.

She doesn't even see me as she eagerly approaches her mom and my dad and tells them she's ready to go.

We can't fucking have that, now, can we?

"You know what?" I say, pushing up off the couch. "I think I'll go, too."

Parker's brown eyes widen ever so slightly, and I can see the flash of disappointment mixed with alarm that tells me all I need to know.

I smile and watch her guard inch up as she follows our parents out to the car.

I catch up to her easily and fall into step beside her. "That's some dress," I murmur.

Her long red hair bounces as she shoots me a dirty look, wordlessly commanding me to shut my stupid trap.

I grin and bump my shoulder into hers. "Hey, you should be happy. I'm letting you win a battle. You wanted me to come to family dinner, didn't you?"

"Yeah, I'm sure you're doing it for me," she mutters dryly, but she doesn't say anything else, and I don't bother pushing.

I know she won't rise to any of my bait with our parents in earshot, and I'm not looking to make trouble for her to contain right now, anyway. I just want to go to that club and see who Parker was so excited to see without me around.

At school, it's common knowledge that any asshole who even looks at Parker for too long is going to get a visit from me. Since middle school, the mere threat of it has sufficiently dissuaded most guys—and the more persistent ones got their asses kicked.

I *like* to fight, and none of them ever have.

The natural consequence is that Parker made it to senior year not only untouched, but probably with the notion that guys tend not to be that interested in her.

Parker's social circle has never extended far beyond school, so I never had to worry about her meeting guys in other places. She worked at her mom's dance school which is pretty much all girls, and she's in enough school clubs to keep her pretty busy at Baymont High.

Obviously, when I didn't live with her, there were certain places I couldn't monitor her. I would have never known if she went to a restaurant with her mom and some overzealous waiter flirted with her. I would have found out if it went beyond that and turned into something more, but it never did.

After last time I refused to go to dinner with them, she probably thought she had a safe haven at the club.

But if she thinks I'll fail to patrol my territory just because I'm pissed off at my dad, she's going to be very disappointed.

Parker watches out the window as we approach the club. I've seen the million-dollar view so many times I don't even notice it anymore, but since she's gazing at it, I do, too.

The sun drops lower and lower in the sky as we inch toward sunset. The country club is built on the side of a cliff with killer ocean views. Outside, tables are set up on the patio area where plenty of Baymont's more affluent citizens are enjoying their dinners.

Parker sighs softly, so I guess she enjoys the view.

I guess I do, too.

The car slows down under the portico. This place has valet parking, so my dad puts the car in park but leaves the engine running. Gemma grabs her purse and climbs out. Rather than get out on my own side, I scoot across and exit the same way Parker did so I can keep a close eye on her.

Dad gets out and approaches the valet stand.

Parker trails behind him, then lingers off to his side.

Typically, my father is a man who commands attention and respect.

Typically, a valet might offer a polite nod, but would hardly even notice whoever was with him.

So, when this valet's gaze lands on Parker first and he has to visibly remind himself to greet my dad, I fucking notice.

Most of the valets here are older, but he's a young guy, probably in his early twenties. He has dark hair that he keeps a little too long. I'm surprised management doesn't make him cut it or at least slick it back. He's wearing black slacks and a white dress shirt with a red vest over it like the other valets, but unlike the other valets, he's rolled the sleeves of his dress shirt up to just below his elbow, so the ink trailing down his tan left arm is clearly visible above his black watch.

He doesn't look like any fucking valet I've seen.

As soon as he has written down my dad's information, his dark gaze shifts back to Parker, a small smile tugging at his lips. "What book did you bring tonight?"

His tone is playful.

Familiar.

What the fuck.

"What?" Parker plays at innocence. "I've never brought a book anywhere with me in my whole life."

"Yeah, okay."

"I'm a social butterfly. Always talking to everyone. Definitely never spotted anywhere with my head in a book to avoid peopling."

"Of course," he teases. "I must have mistaken you for somebody else."

I'm boiling in my own skin at the way she jokes around with this chump like I'm not even fucking here.

Gemma must have noticed something was off—*do I look confused? I feel fucking homicidal*—because she steps closer and leans in to fill me in. "Last time we were here, we ran into some of your father's clients and got caught up, so Parker snuck off and—"

"I don't care," I snap without even meaning to.

Without fucking *thought*, and I regret it an instant later because I *do* care. I want to know what I missed at the dinner I didn't come to. I want to know every exchange that's ever taken place between Parker and this stupid asshole.

The sound of my voice shatters Parker's focus and she seems to remember I'm here this time.

Her smile dies, and for the merest sliver of a second, I feel like an asshole for killing it.

But all I have to do is look at Aladdin on my way by and that feeling dissipates because his appreciative gaze is glued to her ass.

My hands clench into fists at my sides. It takes every scrap of willpower I possess not to turn and swing on him right fucking now.

Blood burns its way through my veins like molten lava as I resist the urge, scorching the surface as it flows through me.

All I hear is the buzzing of rage in my ears as my dad goes through the motions of getting us a table and the girls follow him outside.

By the time we get to the nice corner table with a perfect sunset view, I've managed to rein in my temper enough that I don't make a fucking spectacle, but even that pisses me off.

What I *want* to do is haul Parker away from this table and get her somewhere alone.

Alone, I can demand to know every word and lingering look that has ever passed between them before I choke her with my cock. Show her little ass what happens when she flirts with other guys.

The only reason I don't is our fucking parents.

If I wait until we're alone, I can get away with a hell of a lot more than if I lose my temper and do some stupid shit in public.

Doesn't make me want to any less, though.

I think Parker can feel it as she takes her seat at the table. One side is a booth, two chairs on the other side. Parker must strongly prefer the booth side, because she slides in without offering it to anyone else.

Then she dares a glance in my direction for the first time since we walked away from her little boyfriend at the valet stand.

I smirk, but I can feel it's fucking malicious.

Just wait until I get you alone.

She's already uneasy, then I drop into the booth beside her instead of taking the chair my dad left open next to him.

Gemma hesitates, her gaze drifting uncertainly in my father's direction.

He wants to believe we can play at being one big, happy family, so he subtly nods and grabs her waist, pulling her around to his side of the table and pulling out the empty chair beside him.

Gemma sits reluctantly, smoothing down her skirt as she does. She's sitting across from me, and she knows I don't like her, so she's tense. I slide her an indolent smirk that makes her even more uncomfortable as I stretch out my arm and rest it on the top of the booth behind her daughter's back.

Parker's posture straightens until it's as rigid as her mother's, but it's a gut reaction. As soon as I notice, she tries to relax before anyone else does.

"Should we get an appetizer?" Parker asks with manufactured pep.

My father is as invested in this futile effort as she is, so he picks up his menu and glances at the starters section. "There are enough of us this time. We might as well. You were interested in the charcuterie board last time, weren't you?"

Parker smiles, looking down at the menu. "Yes. My favorite part is the 'pickled stuff.' You don't expect to see 'pickled stuff' in the description on such a fancy menu."

"What about the charred octopus?" he asks.

Parker's face screws up. "Ew, no. That's so mean."

He cocks an eyebrow. "Mean?"

"You want to kill an octopus?" she demands, as if discussing a puppy massacre.

"Well, I wasn't planning on getting out my spear and doing it myself."

Gemma cracks a faint smile, but Parker remains disgusted. "It's barbaric. I'm not eating it, and—full disclosure—I'll be annoyed at you if you do."

My dad nods, eyebrows lifted. "All right, then. Pickled stuff it is."

"When Parker was a little girl, she befriended an octopus at the Baymont Aquarium," Gemma explains.

"His name was Frank, and he was adorable," Parker says primly.

"They played hide-and-seek," Gemma continues.

"He was an excellent hider."

"Frank was a very smart octopus who enjoyed sneaking out of his tank sometimes and scaring the bejeezus out of his caretakers."

Parker sighs. "Too adventurous for his own good, that Frank."

"The last time he got out, Frank made it to the kitchen of the little aquarium bistro."

"Uh-oh," Dad murmurs.

Gemma nods solemnly. "When the cook found him, he just thought somehow an octopus meant for the dinner menu had slipped through without being thoroughly... prepared."

"Murdered," Parker amends dramatically. "How sadistic is it that the bistro serves seafood in a place where marine life *literally lives*, anyway?"

"We do not eat octopus," Gemma concludes. "Ever."

Parker huffs, crossing her arms and sinking back against the booth in annoyance. Her annoyance quickly turns to alarm when she remembers where I put my arm.

She immediately sits forward again to avoid touching me, subtly scooting forward on the seat as a brunette in a server's uniform approaches the table.

"How are you this evening, Mr. Atwater?"

"We're well, Jenna. Thank you," my dad replies politely.

"I'll bring around water for the table in just a minute, but what else can I get you to drink? Can I start you off with a selection from the bar?"

"Yes," I say.

"No," Dad answers dryly, shooting me a look.

"I want the sunset lemonade," Parker volunteers.

"I'll have white wine," Gemma says.

"Iced tea," I say.

"Make that two," Dad adds. "And we're going to get an appetizer."

"The grilled octopus," I say before he can continue.

The waitress nods and starts to write it down, but just as the nub touches her notepad, Parker swats me in the stomach and says, "No, don't write that down." Glaring at me, she says, "Are you serious?"

"What?" I ask innocently. "Maybe I like octopus. Maybe it's my favorite thing in the world."

"It isn't," my father says firmly, shooting me a look across the table. "You don't even like octopus. We aren't ordering it."

Jenna is confused, so I tell her, "Some of us have very strong feelings about octopuses." I glance at Parker. "Octopi?"

"Both are acceptable, but the correct way to pluralize it is octopuses. Octopus isn't truly Latin, it was a word borrowed from the Greeks, so there's no need to change it to octopi when using the plural form."

I nod, looking back at the waitress. "She's the octopus expert. My expertise is with a different kind of pus."

Her teeth sink into her bottom lip as she bites back a little smile, her eyes glinting with amusement. I give her a little wink, and her cheeks bloom with color.

Growling with annoyance, Parker pushes me and starts to slide in my direction with the force of a steamroller.

I don't realize until she's practically on my lap and saying, "Move," that she wants out.

It's hell passing up an opportunity to grab her ass and make her regret pushing herself on me, but I can't make a move like *that* at the table unless I want to raise alarms so high, I won't be able to get away with shit.

Gemma's doe-eyes are wide and set on her daughter.

Parker murmurs, "I have to pee," but I know she just hates seeing me flirt.

I'm feeling pretty fucking smug about it, so I move out of her way, but I stay *in the way* enough that she has to brush her ass against me to move out from behind the table.

I laugh to myself a little as she huffs and strides away without looking back.

Dad shoots me an unamused look as I take my seat again.

"What?" I ask innocently.

"Do you have to taunt her?"

"I do. I have a quota to meet."

The waitress clears her throat. "So, no octopus then?"

"No octopus," my father confirms. "We'll take the charcuterie board and a basket of bread."

I roll my eyes, then tell whoever cares, "I need to take a piss."

Gemma, transparently afraid I'm going after her daughter, says, "I should go with Parker and wash my hands, too."

I smirk as I stand, but don't bother looking back to see if she's following me.

I don't go to the bathroom, either.

I can get Parker alone at home anytime I want, so I don't need to do it in a place like this where the chances of getting caught are so much higher.

Instead, I take a lap by the bar, and when the bartender is facing away from me, I reach back and help myself to a bottle. Then I head outside to put a nice dent in it while I watch the sun disappear into the ocean.

"ARE we ready to order yet, or do you need some more time?"

This is the third time the waitress has approached the table for our order since Landon disappeared.

"We need just another minute or two," Mom says apologetically. "I'm sorry."

"No worries," the waitress says brightly. "I'll circle back in a few more minutes."

The waitress walks away for the third time, and Hayden looks at his watch. "This is ridiculous," he says, pushing his chair back. "I'm going to see if he's in the bathroom. We're not making her come back again."

"Okay," Mom says with a little nod.

Once Hayden is gone, she looks across the table at me, her smile frail and doubtful. "Great first family dinner, huh?"

"I'm mentally collecting things for the scrapbook page as we speak."

"It seems Landon is in an unpleasant mood."

"That is his permanent state," I inform her. "It's fine. If he doesn't order this time, maybe we should have Hayden order something he knows he likes and just take it home for him."

Looking around, she says, "I don't see how we can leave

until we find him. We can't just leave him here without a way home. We all came together."

"Honestly, knowing Landon, he's already gone. He only wanted to come to dinner to annoy me. Once his mission was accomplished, he probably texted Malek and had him come pick him up."

"Without telling us?"

Mom is shocked that anyone would behave in such a way.

Clearly, I've spoiled her.

I crack a smile, reaching for an almond and a sliver of cheese. "This is so good. At least the pickled stuff doesn't disappoint." To further my point, I grab a slice of pickled peach and pop it into my mouth. Who knew *that* would be good? "Aside from their monstrous disregard for octopuses, the chef is a genius."

Hayden comes back to the table, but I can tell from the look on his face he didn't find him. "Landon's not in the bathroom."

Of course he isn't. We've been waiting for close to a half hour now. Our perfect sunset view was wasted, and now the ocean is a mysterious dark abyss that's slightly uncomfortable to look at given who we're eating with.

Mom tries to be helpful. "Parker said he might have texted Malek to come get him and just left without telling us. Do you think he might have done that?"

Hayden sighs as he pulls out his chair and takes his seat. "There's probably a pretty good chance that's exactly what happened." Hayden motions for the waitress, and since she has been waiting on us for so long, she rushes right over. "We're ready to order now."

AFTER A DELICIOUS MEAL and enjoyable company, Hayden tells the waitress we're ready for our bill. I consumed three glasses of the sunset lemonade since we wasted so much time waiting for Landon, so I tell them I need to pee again before we leave.

The bathrooms are past the front lobby, but as I'm on my way through, my gaze catches on something that demands a double take.

Landon?

I was sure he'd left, but I know what the back of his head looks like. As my brain catches up with the familiar sight of his clothing, I veer left without a clear plan.

"Hey," I call out.

His steps slow, and he glances back at me over his shoulder.

I look past him at the valet stand. It seems like that's where he was heading, so a wave of trepidation washes over me.

"I thought you left."

Landon spins around to face me, but while his steps slow to a crawl, he doesn't entirely stop.

What is he doing?

I don't know, but I don't believe any good can come out of it, so I speed up to close the distance between us more efficiently. "What are you doing out here?"

He gestures toward the valet station, in the same direction he's still moving. "Got some business to take care of."

"No."

He smirks. "What? Afraid I'll hurt your boyfriend's feelings, or is it his pretty face you're worried about?"

I roll my eyes, but the verification of what I didn't want to admit I thought—that he was going to talk to Javi—injects sheer alarm into my bloodstream. Without proper care or thought, I reach out and grab the fabric of his T-shirt, using it to pull him back in my direction.

"You're not going to harass the valet."

"Sure I am." He says it almost congenially, and that's when my brain registers the sheen in his eyes, the odd aura of playfulness despite him being in the process of doing an asshole thing.

"You've been drinking," I say flatly.

He holds up his thumb and forefinger with a small space between them. "Little bit." He sways forward, but not because the alcohol has made him unsteady on his feet; he loops an arm around my waist and tugs me against his hard, muscled body.

My heart drops clear out of my body. "Landon," I say, instinctively pushing at him to create some distance between us. It doesn't work, though. His arm is a steel band capable of holding more resistance than I'm physically capable of.

He angles his head and leans close to my neck, then his voice sends shivers everywhere when he murmurs lowly, "You smell good."

My stomach does several somersaults. "Your dad is going to kick your ass. We need to get you out of here."

"Aw, you don't want me to get in trouble? Thought you hated me."

Sighing, I keep a hand pushing against his chest to keep him on track. "Give me your phone."

He can't grab his phone and my ass at the same time, so I do not get the phone.

"Is everything okay over there?"

My blood freezes in my veins before promptly turning into steam and evaporating when my skin heats to what must be one thousand degrees.

I peek past Landon's broad shoulders and see Javi coming toward us, his dark brow furrowed with concern.

"Fine! Everything's fine," I call out. Then, to Landon, "Get your damn phone out."

"It's in my pocket. If you want it, help yourself."

Sighing heavily, I shove at him again with renewed annoyance. It's just as useless as all the other shoves, and more frustrating because if he won't let me go and Javi sees what an ass he's being, there's a risk of more people being brought into this. If other people get involved, I lose control.

I know Javi is just doing his job, but I really need him not to right now.

Since he's no help at all, I fish Landon's phone out of his pocket. Of course, it's locked, so I hold the screen up to his face. "Put in your passcode."

Instead, he places his thumb on the screen, his moody green stare locked on me. "You gonna go through it? Bet you've been wanting to, huh? Make sure you steer clear of the messages from Brittany." Leaning close, he stage whispers, "She likes to send nudes."

"You're disgusting," I bite out, but I'm not really focused on him being a moron right now. I'm swiping through his contacts, trying to find Malek before the valet reaches us.

I don't want to risk taking Landon inside. We're seated out back with a view of the water, but the whole back wall of the restaurant is floor to ceiling windows to provide that view for the most patrons. If I take him inside, the odds of one of our parents spotting him go way up.

The moment I dread approaches when Javi stops beside us, glancing from Landon to me, and then asking, "You're sure everything's all right?"

Sighing, I tell him, "If our parents find him this way, he's going to get in so much trouble."

Javi's eyes widen. "This is your brother?"

"No! God, no. Ew."

"Sorry," he says, holding his hands up. "You said..."

"He's my..." I find I can't quite get the word out of my mouth. "My mom and his dad are getting married," I say instead.

Landon finally lets go of me, but only so he can turn toward Javi.

Before he can summon any horrible words to say, I intervene. "Please go," I tell Javi. "I've got this under control."

He doesn't appear convinced, but when I literally shoo him away while putting the phone to my ear, he reluctantly starts walking back to the valet stand.

"What a fucknut," Landon mutters.

"What? For leaving me alone with *you?*" I ask dryly as the phone rings. "Maybe *he's* not the fucknut."

He shakes his head. "I don't know what you see in that guy."

"Oh my god, I don't see anything in him. I don't *know* him. This is the second time in my life I have been near him." The call goes to voicemail, and I mutter a curse under my breath.

Ending the call, I think who I should call next.

Arden, but despite being Landon's friend, I'm not sure he's the one to call in a crisis. If I had to put money on it, I'd guess *he* was the one who made the call to abandon Landon the night he broke into my house. Arden may have been enjoying the ride, but he wasn't about to go down for it.

I do have a moment of lucidity when that thought clashes with my present reality of trying to cover Landon's ass so he doesn't get in trouble—*again*—but it's shut down just as quickly.

The stakes are too high. I know Hayden is fed up with Landon's antics, and I don't know him well enough to know if this would be enough for him to boot Landon out of the house.

As tense as things are between them, he could be looking for a reason for all I know.

This can't be it.

Right now, I don't feel unsafe. I am in control of the situation, and Landon is being obnoxious but not dangerous.

I'll buy him a little more time to adjust if I can.

"If any of your goddamn friends would pick up the phone," I mutter to myself as I press Arden's number and put the phone to my ear.

"You could take me home," he suggests. "The fucknut knows who you came with. I bet he'd give you the keys. Not like we live far."

I shake my head before I even have time to process my refusal.

After all the shit he said to me the night he broke into my house, he's out of his mind if he thinks I'm going anywhere alone with him when he's been drinking.

Right now, we are in public. That's why I feel safe.

The dynamic would shift very quickly if that changed.

There's also the outside chance he's trying to get Javi in trouble. I could see Hayden deciding to have the car pulled around while I'm in the bathroom and realizing Javi gave it to someone who didn't have the ticket.

The realization that his dad could come out here any minute injects a little urgency into the situation. I've been gone long enough that I probably should be finished and out of the bathroom by now. If I don't return soon, Mom might come looking for me. We guessed that Landon probably blew us off and left, but she's paranoid about him, so if I'm gone for more than an appropriate length of time, her mom senses might start tingling.

I don't know who else to call.

Wait, yes I do.

Oh, I hate the thought of making that call, but I bet if I called Brittany to come get him, she'd be here before we got off the phone.

Before I can make a decision, a voice from behind causes my heart to stop. "Landon?"

"Shit," I whisper. Widening my eyes at Landon, I say, "Just be quiet and keep it together."

Then I turn around and manufacture a smile that—upon reflection—is a bit too much. "Look who I found!"

Hayden is scowling as he approaches.

I don't know what to do with Landon's phone, but it occurs to me I should probably hide it. It wouldn't be an ordinary thing to see me holding Landon's phone.

This stupid dress is sheath-like so there are no folds to hide it in, but I try to cover the phone with my hand, then press it against my thigh for good measure.

Of course, not seeming to know what to do with my hands only draws Hayden's attention *to* them.

"Is that Landon's phone?"

"Yep. He lost it."

It's the first thing I can think of.

"But he found it," I add just as quickly, holding up the phone like evidence. "Obviously."

Hayden regards me suspiciously.

"Do you want us to wait for the car?" I ask before he can ask any questions. "You can just go get Mom. And my purse," I add, realizing I left it at the table along with my leftovers. "I'll take the ticket and get the car?"

"Sure," Hayden drawls, his gaze drifting to his son.

All I can think is thank *God* he didn't come out here two minutes ago when Landon had his hands all over me.

The memory triggers a shiver, but I shake it off and flash

what I hope is a normal-looking smile to invite Hayden to accept my plan.

He hands over the ticket, and I grab Landon's wrist so I can haul him with me like an untrustworthy toddler.

My heart races as I run through the car ride home. Outside, I didn't smell the liquor on his breath until I got close, but in the enclosed space in the car...

"We need gum. Maybe gum will help."

I have gum in my purse, but it's back at the table. I can't give him a piece to start chewing now.

"Why are you trying so hard to help me?"

The question catches me off guard. I look up at Landon, and our eyes lock by accident.

My tummy turns over, so I quickly shift my gaze away. "You've done a lot of stupid things that you deserve to get in trouble for, but getting drunk alone at the country club to avoid having dinner with us is very low on that list."

"What do you care? I've spent six years being an asshole to you. Shouldn't you want to see me go down any way I can?"

Maybe.

And maybe all the layers of empathy I have for him are results of my own imagination and not even rooted in reality.

Maybe it's *not* that it's legitimately tough on him to have a new woman moving into the house and taking his mom's place.

Maybe it's *not* kicking up old wounds to see Hayden moving on after six years.

Maybe it *doesn't* feel like a betrayal to his mother's memory, like he has been abandoned all over again because it's plain to see that Hayden truly is *happy* with my mom, and maybe they didn't have much of a relationship at this point, but they had that. For the past six years, they've both buried themselves in the sand so they didn't have to face the prospect of moving on without her.

Now, his dad is moving on.

Landon hates my mother with a passion that simply isn't rooted in logic. My mom is a sweetheart, and if he gave her a chance, there's no reason he shouldn't like her.

All the snide remarks. Does he think I haven't noticed? He's angry that his dad moved her in. He's angry that he loves her.

Why else would he be so angry about that?

Maybe it's just because I saw how he coped with his big feelings when he was twelve, and I haven't seen any evidence that he's gotten better at it since then, but when Landon is hurt, I know he lashes out. My mom hasn't done anything to hurt him, unless it was that.

I can't relate to that, but I can understand how he feels.

I didn't lose a parent I adored. Hayden is replacing no one for me.

Mom did tell me Hayden hasn't been serious with anyone since his wife died, so I have a pretty good idea that I'm right about all this being new to him. And given even at school, his focus was on spreading rumors about her over me...

He's hurting.

He'll probably never admit that, but it doesn't matter.

I don't need verification. It's what I believe, and it makes sense, so unless new information comes in and proves me wrong, that's what I'm going with.

We approach the valet stand, so I don't have to answer him. My face feels warm when I meet Javi's gaze. He probably thinks I'm an idiot babysitting my same-age...

Ugh, no, I can't say the word—even in my head.

"Can we get the car, please?" I ask sheepishly.

He eyes the ticket I'm holding out for him to take, then glances at Landon before looking back at me. "Sure. Just a minute."

I don't know what we're waiting for, but a moment later, a BMW pulls up and an older man in the same uniform—though without the rolled-up sleeves—climbs out of the car.

"I'll take that," Javi says, walking around to take the keys and hand him ours. "Can you grab the Maserati in spot 14?"

The man looks briefly confused, but he nods and trades keys with Javi before heading back toward the parking lot.

"Couldn't go get it yourself, huh?" Landon asks.

Javi shakes his head. "I'm busy."

Since he's just standing there, Landon says, "Doing what?"

Javi holds his gaze, then he picks up the stack of blank parking tickets and taps each end to make sure they're nice and neat.

"Oh, my mistake. That seems pretty fucking important."

"Whole place might collapse if I don't get it done."

This is not a friendly exchange, so before Landon can do anything idiotic and escalate it, I grab his T-shirt and drag him away toward the black metal bench off to the left. "We'll wait over here. Thank you."

"Don't wander too far," Javi calls after me.

Landon starts to turn back, but I tighten my grip and yank him toward the bench. "Come on."

"I don't fucking like that guy."

"Really? I couldn't tell," I murmur, releasing his shirt so I can smooth my skirt under my legs and sit on the bench.

Landon drops into the empty space beside me and crosses his arms as he spreads out. "You never answered me, either."

I try to keep my gaze from drifting to his muscular thighs.

What lovely columns this portico has. So... thick and... pretty.

Probably not worth all the trouble they cause, but nice to look at, regardless.

"Not going to now either, huh?" Landon says.

Reluctantly, I meet his gaze. "Hm? What was the question?"

"Why you're being so fucking nice."

"Oh. Right. Because I'm madly in love with you," I say flatly.

The corner of his mouth tips up and he nods. "Knew it."

"Yeah," I say, nodding along. "I can't eat. Can't sleep. I go through so many notebooks because I can't stop doodling your name."

"And here people think you're just studious."

"I'm not sure Parker Atwater works, so if we get married, I'll probably keep my last name."

His lips curve up more and he shakes his head. "All right, smartass."

Landon's phone buzzing in my hand steals my attention. I look at the screen on impulse, then I hold the phone out to him.

He glances at the screen, then snatches the phone and answers it. "Hey."

It's Malek, probably returning the call since I didn't leave a message.

"Yeah," Landon says. "Any chance you can swing by the country club and pick me up? Got roped into a family dinner thing and..." He trails off, smirking as his gaze shifts to me. "Yeah. All right, cool. I'll meet you around front."

He stands and ends the call without another word. As he slips the phone into his pocket, he says, "Look at that. Problem solved."

"You didn't have to..." I start, but I don't even know how to finish.

In the enclosed space of Hayden's car, it's unlikely that nobody else would notice the alcohol on his breath. It's probably better that he gets a ride home with Malek, even if our parents will think he's just being a jerk.

"It's better this way." Then, his eyes sparkling a bit as he backs away, he says, "This way, I live to torture you another day."

I crack an absurd smile and roll my eyes. "Oh, yay."

He smirks, and with one last lingering look, turns and saunters off down the walking path away from the portico.

SINCE LANDON WENT to Malek's after dinner, I take advantage of his absence to go for a swim in the pool.

Afterward, I eye up the pool house and consider how Hannah would like it if she had to live there. I decide it needs a desk for her to do her schoolwork at, so I'll do a little browsing online once I finish my homework and see what I can find.

I'm still using the towel to squeeze pool water out of my hair when I come inside. Hayden is standing in the living room. I want to ask if he's amenable to pool house modifications, but one look at Mom standing worriedly at Hayden's side as if waiting for more information redirects every thought in my head.

My gaze shoots to Hayden's face. I just figured he was on a work call, but a work call wouldn't worry Mom. And now that I'm looking at him, I note Hayden's locked jaw, the glint of anger in his eyes.

The last time he looked like that was when he had to come to the police station to pick up Landon after he broke into my house.

What did he do now?

Since he's with Malek, there's a good chance they did something idiotic.

"Yes," Hayden says. "Of course. I assure you it won't happen again. And please extend our apologies to Javier."

Javier?

My heart sinks. I drop the towel to my side, damp hair forgotten, and approach Hayden as he ends the call.

"What did they say?" Mom asks.

"What happened?" I ask, since I need them to start at what I missed while I was swimming.

He answers Mom first. "They won't be pressing charges."

Pressing charges?!

"What happened?" I demand again, eyes wide.

Hayden sighs tiredly and uses one hand to massage his temples. Mom moves behind him and gently massages his shoulders to help ease the tension. "It appears that when Landon 'lost his phone' he also stole an entire bottle of Johnnie Walker from behind the bar. After draining half of it, he decided to pull a prank on the valet. He found his way to the employee area in the back and broke into Javier's locker so he could plant the stolen bottle there. Then, he called to report that when we used the valet service for dinner tonight, he thought he smelled liquor on the guy's breath. When management looked into the report, they found the liquor in Javier's locker and fired him."

I gasp.

Hayden holds up a hand. "Since he was innocent, Javier fought it, and when he pressed the issue and told them he'd be happy to take a breathalyzer test to prove he was sober, management decided to review the tapes. Of course, the security footage did not show Javier stealing the liquor and stashing it in his locker. It showed *Landon* doing it."

"So Javi isn't fired?"

Hayden shakes his head. "It's all straightened out now. We'll have to give him a hell of a tip next time we have dinner there," he adds dryly.

"Is Landon even allowed back?" Mom asks.

"Of course." He says it so casually, as if it was the only expected outcome. "You throw a little money at these things and they're settled pretty easily, but that's not the point." He shifts his attention back to his phone. "I need to call my brother. Parker, can you do me a favor?"

I nod.

"Can you run upstairs and pack Landon a bag?"

My heart drops. "A bag?"

"He has a brown leather weekend bag in his closet. Just fill it with his toiletries and enough clothes for a couple of days."

I bite anxiously on my bottom lip. "Where's he going?"

"He's grounded. He'll be staying with his cousin."

"Okay... Should I pack electronics? Does he have a laptop or an iPad I should...?"

"No. Pack his charger for his phone, and if you see his school bag up there, bring that. He doesn't need anything else."

I don't know how Landon will feel about me going into his room when he's not home, but I don't say that. I know *I'm* not super comfortable with it, but that's mostly because I feel like I'm going where I shouldn't be, and I'll be paranoid about him showing up while I'm in there and trapping me.

I know he won't, though.

Hayden is downstairs, and if Landon does show up at the house, I'm sure Hayden will deal with it.

Landon's door is closed, of course. When I push it open, all the scents I associate with him waft my way.

It's dark outside now, so the only light in this space is from the moon. Landon doesn't have an ocean view like I do. That strikes me as surprising.

I don't turn the light on right away.

I probably should. I have no idea if Landon is tidy or more of a slob, but I imagine there are piles of things I could trip over on my way to the window.

Since I'm here, I can't resist looking out and seeing what he sees.

My stomach drops when I get to the window and immediately realize he has a perfect view of the pool. The lights were off when I looked so I assumed he was asleep, but the lights are off now, and I couldn't ask for a clearer view of me slicing through the water.

Well.

That's not great.

I guess I'll never be able to take another late-night swim again in my life.

Realizing I wore a bikini because I thought no one was watching makes me feel even more embarrassed about it.

Ugh.

Sighing, I cross the room more quickly than I made my way to the window and flick on the light.

I'm a little surprised by what I see. I guess I expected Landon's space to be chaotic like he is, but his bedroom is sleek and modern with high ceilings (like the rest of the house) and an entire wall of windows behind the bed.

His bed is huge, too. Maybe it's only king-sized to fill the enormous space, but it looks cozy with six pillows lined up against the headboard, a perfectly made bed with the comforter turned down, and a fuzzy blanket laid across the bottom in case he wanted something a bit cozier.

Hayden mentioned a housekeeper comes twice a week, so I guess she must have been here this morning.

There's a nightstand by his bed, and a couple of chairs in

the room. On impulse, I sit on the long black chaise lounge in the corner by the windows so I can see the view from there.

Yep, a prime pool-stalking location.

If Hannah does move into the pool house, I'll have to warn her about Landon's view. Not that he's ever been remotely interested in Hannah or I think he would deliberately creep on her, but I know firsthand it can feel like you have privacy out there, and it turns out you really don't.

I don't think he'd have a very good view from the bed at any natural angle given the height of the headboard, so I figure he must have been on the chaise lounge when he was watching me.

Curiosity satisfied, I head for his closet and grab the weekend duffle Hayden mentioned. I put it down on the black chair close to his bed, then I try to orient myself a bit.

Where are his clothes?

I don't see a dresser. There's a bookshelf against the wall that he does not use for books, and a desk and chair where his laptop is plugged in.

I open the door at the far end of the room and flick on a light.

This is his bathroom.

It's massive, with a walk-in shower on the left side that spans most of the room. At the end, behind the shower, there's a linen closet. On the right side of the room, a long black marble countertop with a sink. Behind that, the toilet has its own separate room.

My bathroom is nice, but this bathroom is insane.

It feels like an invasion of his privacy to be in here, but I remind myself Hayden sent me up and get to collecting the items I expect him to need if he's going away for a couple of days.

Back in the bedroom, I open the second door expecting to

find a small walk-in closet much like mine, but as with the bath-room, this one is much larger. And as with his bedroom, it gives an air of sophistication I don't associate with Landon.

Why do none of his spaces seem to fit him?

Resisting the urge to delve deeper into the world of Landon Atwater, I refocus on what I'm meant to be doing in here and grab him some clothes. I try not to pay too much attention to his underwear—*my god, Hayden, why? Why send me to do this?*—and manage to emerge from the closet without dying from the mortification of being in Landon's room without his knowledge or permission and handling his *underwear.*

Once his bag is packed, I hoist it over my shoulder and hit the light on my way out of the room. I close the door so it's just as he left it aside from the items I removed.

Hayden is off the phone and waiting for me on the couch with Mom. He stands when he sees me coming down the stairs.

"Thank you, Parker."

"I couldn't find a school bag," I tell him.

"It may be in his car. I'll grab it." He reaches for the bag, but before he can take it, the sound of the front door opening steals everyone's attention.

I feel the temperature in my body shoot way up when Landon comes striding down the hall.

"What are you doing here?" Hayden asks.

"Oh, I live here," Landon shoots back like a smartass. Then he adds more bitingly, "At least for now, right?"

"Yeah, thanks to me," Hayden replies, the annoyance thick in his tone. "Because *I* consistently clean up your messes. If your own behavior dictated where you're sleeping, you'd be in a jail cell. Maybe I should have let them put you in one, because you don't seem to be learning anything by me bailing you out. This is the last time, Landon. Next time you pull something like this, you can find your own way out of it."

Landon nods with attitude. "All right, I see how it is. You'll pick the scheming bellydancer over me, you'll pick Aladdin over me—is there anyone I come before? Just curious." Then he waves a dismissive hand in Hayden's direction before starting up the stairs. "Nah, don't bother answering. You're a professional liar, doesn't fucking matter what you say."

"That's a convenient way to frame it, Landon. You tried to get a man *fired* for no fucking reason, and *I'm* the villain. You can't mess with people's lives for your own amusement."

"Like you haven't," Landon shoots back, shaking his head in apparent disgust.

"I don't do things without reason," Hayden states.

"Neither do I," Landon answers. "And tried to get him fired?" he asks, the ridicule thick in his tone. "Please. I didn't try very fucking hard, now did I? I was just messing with him tonight. If I want the asshole fired," now his gaze shifts to me, "I'll make sure to put in a little more effort and get the job done."

My stomach sinks because that definitely felt like a threat, and I'm not sure it was subtle enough for our parents to miss it.

Mom surprises me by inserting herself into the conversation. "Why do you have a problem with Javier? He was perfectly nice to all of us."

I start to sweat at Mom zeroing in on that. Of course Javier was polite to all of us—he was doing his job—but we all know he was a little *more* friendly toward me.

"Aladdin? Aw, what's not to like about him? Aside from the fact that he clearly wants to fuck your daughter, anyway."

"Landon," Hayden snaps.

Well, this is all the evidence I need that humans *can't* actually die from mortification.

Mom flinches at the crass way he speaks about me, but

while that would ordinarily deter her, she keeps pushing. "Why do you call him that?"

Landon's eyes widen. "Because the guy *looks* like fucking Aladdin, Gemma. Jesus Christ. He looks like he just popped out of the Disney cartoon and started parking cars. He's even got the vest. All he needs is a fucking monkey."

Mom considers that, then nods. "Now that you say that, I suppose I can see it." Then her gaze meets Landon's and she asks the million dollar question. "But even if he does like Parker, why do you care?"

Hayden doesn't seem to want Landon to answer this question. Before Landon can open his mouth, he snatches Landon's bag from my hands and walks it over to the stairs. "There's no sense in arguing about this anymore. What's done is done. I handled it this time, but if you do it again, you're on your own." Holding out the bag I packed for him, Hayden adds, "You're already packed, so there's no reason for you to go upstairs."

Landon stares at his father. A smirk tugs at his mouth, but there's no amusement dancing in his deep green eyes. It's pure malevolence. "You just couldn't wait to get me out of here, huh?"

"You know that's not true, Landon. All I want is for all of us to get along, and there's no reason we shouldn't be able to."

But we all know that's not true.

Landon is the reason.

He is the only wrench in the wheels of this new family functioning like a well-oiled machine.

Landon nods, holding his father's gaze. Then he turns around and comes back down the stairs. "All right. I'm out of here," he says, snatching the bag without stopping.

"You're not driving," Hayden states before he can make it far. "You're grounded. That means no car. And you've been drinking. I'll drive you."

"I'd rather walk," Landon states.

My stomach is in knots. I have a really stupid urge to go after him, but I'm afraid of him making things worse.

Hayden sighs, watching his son leave.

It's probably a little bit on purpose, but as soon as Landon is out the door, I remember his school bag.

"Wait, his school stuff is in his car," I say, already inching toward the dish where Landon drops his keys. "I'll just run out real quick and tell him in case he forgets."

"Parker," Mom calls after me, clearly objecting.

"I'll only be a minute."

I rush out before either of them can stop me.

My heart pounds as I head down the steps to the driveway. "Landon, wait."

He looks back over his shoulder. His steps slow, but he doesn't stop.

I have to jog to catch up to him. "I... I'm the one that packed your bag, and I couldn't find your school stuff. Your dad thought it might be in your car, but you got here before we could check, so..." I hold out his keys. "You may want to grab it."

He doesn't take the keys. Doesn't even look at them. Instead, he stares at me. "*You* packed my bag."

It feels like an accusation of betrayal, and it makes my stomach bottom out. "Your dad asked me to."

"You always do everything he tells you to?" he asks snidely.

I don't know what to say. I can understand Hayden's frustration with his son, but I can also understand how Landon is feeling. The things he said to his dad just now further cement my theory about why he has such a problem with my mom.

It's not her, personally.

It's his dad he really has the problem with, and the issues between them have built up for so many years... we just came into a mess. They probably need therapy or something to truly untangle it all.

And when I was younger I didn't get it, I just thought Landon was cruel, but now that I'm older, he reminds me of something I read once. I don't remember the exact phrasing, but it was something like, "sometimes the people who need love most ask for it in the most unloving ways."

Landon probably does need discipline, but it needs to be tempered with love and compassion. I think he still needs what I tried to offer him years ago. He pushed it away then, and I expect he will again because the old wounds never healed.

Lucky for him, I'm not fragile anymore. I can weather his rejection and cruelty without being as wounded by it as I was back then because I understand where it comes from now. I didn't before.

"I think it sucks that he's making you leave. Even if it is just for a couple of days. I think it sucks."

Landon's eyes narrow skeptically.

"I know you don't like having us here. I'm sure it's weird to have to share your space and your dad with other people after not having to for so long, but I really wish you'd give us a chance. You're coming at it with this me vs. them mindset, and it doesn't have to be that way. We want you to be a *part* of our family. We want to be part of yours. Things between you and your dad seem rough, but I don't think it has to be that way. If you both gave each other a little more grace, maybe—"

Before I can finish, Landon grabs my hips and walks me back until I'm pressed against his car. "I don't need your help mending my relationship with my daddy," he says a touch mockingly.

My heart does a somersault. It's not his words, but the way he's looking at me that triggers it. I've never been more aware of anything than his hand on my hip. A strange tension starts in my lower abdomen as his fingers flex, his grip tightening in preparation of me trying to get away.

I swallow. "I was just trying to—"

"I know what you were trying to do."

My heart beats faster as he holds my gaze. He's so close, and my brain is malfunctioning. I know I should do something. I should push him away, or try to turn away from him, but instead I stand paralyzed against the side of his car. My lungs seem to have halved in size, making breathing more difficult. There's a butterfly riot taking place in my lower tummy.

It's quiet enough that we both hear the front door open.

Landon takes a step back.

My legs feel like jelly, but I inch away from the car and hold out the keys.

Landon snatches them, then opens the passenger side door and grabs his bag. He does it without glancing back or doing anything that would give the impression he's even aware of the front door opening.

I'm not entirely steady on my feet, so I just stand here, but my gaze shifts to Mom standing in the doorway. I give a little smile and wave to let her know I'm okay. She returns both gestures, but doesn't go back inside the house. She's waiting for me.

Now that I've acknowledged her, Landon turns back with a smirk and a sarcastic little wave of his own.

He doesn't wait to see if she returns it.

He turns back to face me, then he drops his keys into the palm of my hand. "Enjoy your peace, Johansson." He starts walking down the driveway toward the road, but turns around long enough to say, "It won't last for long."

WHEN I COME DOWNSTAIRS the following morning, I don't have to wonder if Landon has grabbed his breakfast and left, or if I'll have a brush with him, or worry about how much damage he may do if I *do* have a brush with him and my mom witnesses it.

He isn't here.

It's the first time I've felt truly at peace since moving in with the Atwaters—aside from my brief stress vacation when I went night-swimming, but that peace was tarnished when I realized afterward I was being watched.

Probably.

I guess I never got verification, but in my mind, it's canon. It totally happened.

There's a middle-aged woman in a pale blue uniform with her salt and pepper hair pulled back in a bun standing at the stove when I come down.

She looks back at me, her dark eyes wide with surprise.

"I'm Parker," I tell her.

"Hello, Miss Parker. My name's Antonia. I'm Mr. Atwater's housekeeper."

I've never had a servant before. I'm not sure what to do. I

glance at the island where I would probably sit and wait for breakfast most mornings, but it feels tremendously awkward to just sit there while a stranger makes me breakfast.

"Hayden mentioned you came twice a week, but I didn't think it would be two days in a row."

Antonia frowns. "This is my first time here this week."

"Oh. Really? I didn't see anyone yesterday, but Landon's bed was made with such careful precision, I thought it must have been you."

"Oh, no. I don't make Landon's bed. He strips the bedding for me to wash when I come, but he makes it up himself every morning. Always has."

"Oh."

Misunderstanding my confusion, she adds, "That's his choice, though. I'd be happy to make yours if you'd like me to."

"Oh, you don't have to. I've never habitually made my bed, but maybe I could strip it once a week so you can wash the bedding?"

"If you want. Before your mother moved in, I worked a lot more, so I usually wash the bedding a few times a week. I figured since I'm only coming twice now, two would be good."

"Once a week is sufficient for me."

She nods pleasantly. "I'll make a note. Is there anything else I should know? Any food allergies? Favorite meals? Meals you hate?"

I open my mouth to answer, but before I can speak, Hayden comes around the corner. "She's highly opposed to octopus."

I crack a smile. "Good morning."

"Good morning, Parker."

Mom is right behind him. She flashes me a pleasant smile, then her gaze drifts to the housekeeper. I can tell by the slight furrow of her brow that she is also unsure what to do with a housekeeper. Her gaze drifts again, then she turns back to me brightly. "Do you want me to pack your lunch?"

"Already done," the housekeeper announces. "I made one for Landon, too."

"Oh, he isn't here this morning," Hayden tells her. "He's staying with my brother for a couple of days, so you don't have to make him anything Friday, either."

I'm hesitant to say anything, but since the thought popped into my head... "I could take it to him."

No one responds.

"I mean, we'll be in the same lunchroom. It's already packed..."

"You don't think he would taunt you for bringing him lunch?" Mom asks.

"I'm sure he will, but since I don't care..." I shrug.

"It's up to you, but you don't have to," she assures me. "I'm sure he was already planning to buy lunch today."

Before long, Antonia plates our food and we move to the dining room to enjoy our breakfast together. It still feels awkward afterward when I take my empty dishes to the kitchen where she's already cleaning, and she tells me just to leave everything on the counter and she'll clean it up.

Hayden is clearly accustomed to this, so he drops his dishes on the counter without hesitation and fetches his briefcase to make sure he has everything for work.

I grab both lunches Antonia packed from the refrigerator. When I turn around, Hayden is standing there with Landon's keys.

I frown at them, confused.

"Do you want to drive to school today?"

My eyes widen. "In Landon's Jag?"

He shrugs. "He won't be driving it."

"Um... I think that would make him pretty angry."

"Probably," he agrees. "But if he can't control his temper, he won't be getting it back anytime soon. Might as well give him some practice."

"I don't know," I say warily, eyeing the keys. "It's a very attractive car, but it's also a loud pain in the ass. I don't even really like it."

A lot like someone else I know...

"Well, you're free to take it if you'd like to."

"I think I'll pass, but thank you for the offer."

He nods and falls back to drop the keys in the key dish on the counter. "I can give you a ride on my way to the office. Maybe your mom can pick you up and take you to look at cars after school. I'd be happy to lease you something for the rest of the year, or even buy you one if you'll need a car beyond this year. I'm not sure what your college plans are."

My eyes narrow skeptically. "You don't have to buy me, Hayden."

His mouth tugs up ever so slightly. "I'm not trying to buy you, Parker. You're my daughter now. I'm taking care of you like one."

I FEEL a bit self-conscious when Hayden drops me off at school in his Maserati.

I've never been one to feel awkward or embarrassed about my mom dropping me off at school—*that never made any sense to me*—but after waking up in a seaside mansion and giving the housekeeper cooking me breakfast instructions on how best to serve me before being offered a Jaguar to drive to school in, I have never felt more like I've accidentally fallen into someone else's life.

It's only once I'm walking the halls at Baymont High with

my eyes peeled for a Landon sighting that anything feels remotely normal.

This is how it's meant to be.

I don't know what he's wearing today, or what he had for breakfast. I don't know if he's even here.

Not knowing makes me more aware, more watchful. It's as if he's around every corner, even though when I turn that corner, I never see him.

History class is next, though. If he's at school today, I'll see him there.

My stomach flutters at the thought. Gone is the delicious breakfast, apparently. Now it's a butterfly cavern.

My mind is at once frantic and incapable of concentrating as I enter the classroom. As if I'm the Secret Service, I check the perimeter, sweep the room.

There he is.

He's at his desk in the middle of the last row, but he's not sitting forward getting his books ready like I will be in a moment's time. Instead, he's turned around in his chair, talking to the guy seated behind him.

Trent Walker. He's a football player and one of the guys in their friend group. Not one I told Anae about because I knew instinctively he would be too vanilla for her, but he made the invite list.

Landon hasn't noticed me yet, but I'm hyper aware of any slight movement of his head that might change that.

I make it past his current line of sight and make a beeline to my desk without looking back. I wait for the telltale burn of his gaze when it hits me, but it never comes.

I should feel better that he hasn't noticed me. That should be a relief.

But it's not.

Instead of getting it over with, I find myself completely

preoccupied as I open my history textbook and organize my notes. My mind can't concentrate on any of the papers because try as I might to focus it, all I can think about is him.

This is why I have gone out of my way to avoid having classes with him.

I was lulled into a false sense of having my shit together this year because being in this class with him hasn't really bothered me for the last couple of days.

But it's because it wasn't my first sighting. There was no dread and anticipation of wondering what he might do that day.

It didn't feel the way it used to because it wasn't like it was before.

Today it is. Today I don't feel like "let's all make a fresh start" Parker with her "kumbaya shit," as Anae so eloquently put it.

Today I'm the Parker who doesn't have to be around Landon as long as she can avoid him at school, and I'm realizing now that Mom was right: I should *not* have brought him his lunch.

The mere thought of it reminds me so much of that day years ago when I approached his desk trying to be helpful...

Nope.

I'm not going to do it.

Maybe I'll split the extra lunch with Hannah or something, but I'm not delivering it to him like his dutiful little errand girl. The Parker I was a few hours ago didn't care, but flashback Parker kinda does, and I'm not inviting that kind of emotional chaos into my day.

Clearing as many thoughts of Landon as I can from my head, I give it a shake and roll out my shoulders, then I try harder to get ready to learn.

It's as impossible to trick my body into being completely

unaware of him as it would be for a gazelle to knowingly prance around in front of a hungry lion, but once the class gets going, I'm able to focus enough on the material to make it through.

As soon as class ends, I gather my things as quickly as possible and fly out the door.

I almost think I'm in the clear.

Then Landon sidles up beside me.

My whole body tenses at his proximity. Instinctively, I fall to the right a few inches to put more space between us.

He notices. I can tell by the way his lips tug up when he looks over at me. "Hey, Sis."

"Never say that again."

His eyes sparkle with amusement. "How's life without me?"

"Peaceful."

He moves to the right, eliminating my buffer space. I can't even create more because if I move over any farther, I'll ram into students stashing books in their lockers before they head off to lunch.

Rather than let him see his nearness bothers me, I stick my nose in the air and hug my books tighter against my chest. "How's exile?" I shoot back.

His smirk grows. "It's not so bad. Malek's house is bigger than mine, and *his* dad doesn't have a new lay he needs to impress with his parenting prowess, so he's not on my ass all the time. Not to mention their maid..." He pulls an obnoxious expression that seems to indicate she's hot.

My insides frost over. I shoot him a cool look. "How lovely for you."

"Mm-hmm," he agrees, amused that he's getting to me.

I should rise above it, but his obvious taunt accomplished exactly what he wanted it to. I'm so annoyed at him, I can't stop myself from blurting, "I doubt Brittany would be happy to hear that, but…"

He shrugs indolently. "I don't answer to her."

"That's not the flex you think it is," I say, rolling my eyes.

He cocks an eyebrow. "What, you *want* me to answer to her?"

"No, I just think if you don't give a damn about the girl, you should stop stringing her along and maybe let her find a guy who does."

Out of the corner of my eye, I see him shake his head at me. "Parker Johansson, defender of school slu—"

I throw out my hand, covering his mouth before he can finish. "If the next word out of your mouth isn't 'women,' I swear to God."

He grins, pushing my hand away. "You're so fucking easy to rattle."

"You wish." I drop my hand, making a show of swiping my palm down the side of my leg as if clearing it of Landon cooties.

"Why do you care how I treat her, anyway?"

I look over at him, unable to keep my wide-eyed disbelief off my face. "Because she's a human being whose only sin seems to be liking you, and it's fucking mean to treat her like…"

I trail off, unable to come up with the right word.

Landon takes advantage of my distraction, grabbing my arm in a steely grip and running me off the path I've been walking. Before I can do more than gasp an objection, he has me pushed into the empty space between a row of lockers and an open door.

He anchors a hand on the wall to cage me in before I can calculate the likelihood of success if I shove the door and make a run for it. He's to my front, the edge of a locker is to my left, and his muscular arm blocks the only possible escape on my right.

I tell myself to shove his arm or chop it or duck under it and get away from him, but in my head, all those actions will only cause him to drag me closer.

I'm not strong enough to hurt him, only to annoy him. It's not like he would be unable to grab me again and restrain me better that time. He might even want to, given I fought back. He'd want to prove a point, show me how much stronger he is —*physically, at least*—as if I don't already know. I picture that strong arm locked around my neck, my body forced back against his, his hot breath against my ear...

My lungs seem to shrink just imagining it.

I can't touch him. I'm afraid where that might lead.

I don't want to look at him either, but I don't have a choice. Avoiding his gaze would signify submission, so despite the sudden muscle weakness afflicting my entire body, I raise my gaze to meet his, my eyes narrowed with hateful displeasure.

Landon's mouth tugs up with a hint of malice. He leans in even closer. "Like the dirty little slut she is? Why do you care? Maybe she likes it." Then, his voice dropping suggestively, he adds, "Why don't you tell me why it *really* bothers you? You jealous, Johansson?"

I grind my teeth together. Comebacks fly from my brain to my mouth, but I swallow them all before any can escape.

I *refuse* to swallow his bait.

Instead, voice low and a touch shakier than I want it to be, I say, "Get away from me."

I'm not really worried about him pouncing on me here in the hall with so many people around, but the position we're in, the closeness of our bodies... My brain can't seem to convince my body it isn't in immense peril.

He doesn't budge. Instead, he asks softly, "Or what?" He brings his hand up, grazing my jawline with his knuckles before grabbing my jaw and forcing me to look up at him with my entire head instead of just my eyes. "You've got nothing to threaten me with, Parker. I'm the one holding every single card you care about. And you know I'll light every fucking one of them on fire."

I lick my lips, my heart pounding in my chest. I try to jerk my face from his grip, but it only tightens until it's almost painful. He pushes me back against the wall and brings his body closer, crowding me.

My heart tumbles and falls. My hollow tummy twists. The edges of my vision begin to darken, and I can feel fear taking over and shutting me down.

"Hey."

The sharp voice comes from behind Landon, and it pierces this bubble of aloneness he sucked me into.

Landon's grip eases, but he stares me down for a moment longer before he releases my jaw and takes a step back. He looks over at the intruder, irritation rolling off him at the interruption.

Malek's dark gaze hits me almost accusingly, as if it's *my* fault Landon cornered me.

But rather than verbalize the fucked-up sentiment, he just nods for Landon to follow him and starts walking. "Come on. I'm fucking hungry."

I stay there against the wall until Landon disappears from sight. My left arm is still curled protectively around my books. I'd completely forgotten I was carrying them.

I wait for the strength to return to my legs, and once I'm sure they'll carry me, I push off the wall.

But I don't feel any safer in his absence.

I don't feel hungry anymore, either.

And the prospect of going to the same lunchroom he'll be in, having to see him and feel his gaze on me from across the room?

Well, now it really does feel like the before times.

I fish my phone out of my purse and shoot off a quick text to Hannah. "You want to eat in your car today? I have two lunches."

She answers promptly. "Sure. Everything okay?"

No.

"Yeah," I text back. "I'll meet you by your car."

I DON'T KNOW what to wear to this stupid party.

I suppose it doesn't matter, but I want to dress like everyone else so I can blend in and avoid notice. Will all the other girls change into another outfit for the party? Anae and Hannah both mentioned dresses, so will most girls probably opt for dresses or skirts?

I'm uncomfortable when there are gaps in my knowledge about *anything*, but the truth is, I'm probably more anxious than I want to admit about going and just fixating on the clothing issue. I've never cared before if I'm meeting the societal norms of anything, let alone partygoing.

I haven't been to a high school party since sophomore year, and I don't know what to expect.

The last time I went to a party was the same reason I left it and haven't gone to another one since.

Landon Atwater.

We were twelve when his mom died.

I remember it happening because it was the oddest thing. It was weekend, a Saturday. I didn't *know* Landon other than being in his class. We weren't friends or anything, but I remember feeling all day like something horrible was about to happen. I didn't know what it was or why I felt that way. There was no discernible reason for my dread, but it followed me all day long.

We found out on Sunday about the accident. Mom and I were at the grocery store picking up ingredients for dinner and we ran into another parent. She asked Mom if she heard about what had happened to Sally Atwater, and before she said another word, I felt chills all over my body.

Mom and I were a bit numb walking away from the conversation. We didn't know the Atwaters, but we didn't need to be close to them to feel the horror of what had happened.

A member of our community went out on a boat with her son, and he had to come back without her.

I felt sick all night thinking about it. I couldn't sleep. I cried for him. I could not fathom how I would live without my mom, and I imagined he must feel the same about his.

When I gave up on sleep, I went into Mom's bedroom and asked her if she would get up and help me make something for Landon. Mom was always a smidge overprotective and didn't want me using the oven without supervision. She said it was common for people to cook for a family when they had suffered a loss like this, so we whipped up a batch of my best friend's famous banana nut muffins.

I knew that no quantity of muffins would make him feel any better, but I wanted to do *something* for him. Mom warned me that he probably wouldn't even be at school that day, but I wanted to have them ready just in case.

I felt like I was doing a good thing when I marched into middle school that morning with a container full of delicious breakfast muffins.

My heart ached when I walked into homeroom and saw Landon sitting alone at his desk.

Landon was never alone. He was one of the popular kids, so

he and his friends were usually gathered around someone's desk goofing off until the teacher told them all to take their seats.

Maybe his friends had already talked to him, or maybe they had no clue what to say, but he looked so alone and so sad, tears stung my eyes. I could feel his pain, and I wanted to ease it.

I unloaded my stuff at my desk and cleared away my own sadness figuring he didn't need any more. I wanted to be strong and supportive, to let him know that even if we weren't friends, I was there if he ever needed to talk.

So, I gathered up my courage and grabbed the muffins off my desk. I shook off the impression that Landon was too cool to approach and ignored people glancing at me, wondering what I was thinking as I pierced his bubble of beautiful popularity with my awkwardness and my braces.

He looked up, and the moment his wounded green eyes met mine, my heart melted into a puddle of goo that slowly dripped down into my stomach.

My voice shook awkwardly, and my heart pounded so loudly I was sure he could hear it. I had the perfect thing to say —I had rehearsed it all morning while I got ready for school— but I couldn't summon a single word with him looking at me.

"Can I help you?" he asked.

Understandable that he was confused. I was just standing there like a totem of awkwardness.

I cleared my throat and tried to retrieve any scrap of the speech I had prepared. "Um... I heard about your mom," I said softly. "I just wanted to tell you I'm so, so sorry. I can't even imagine..."

His jaw tightened. Anger flashed in his stormy green gaze. My stomach hollowed out, warning me that I should turn back before the waters got choppier, but I stayed my course.

"I thought you might—I mean, my mom said—I mean..." I

thrust the container of muffins toward him. "I made you some muffins."

Scowling, he looked at the container, then back up at me. "You made me muffins," he reiterated flatly.

I nodded. "Banana muffins. They're really good."

His eyebrows rose. "Yeah? Good enough to make me forget my mom's dead and it's my fucking fault?"

My heart dropped. My face fell. The muffins would have, too, but the top of his desk caught them.

"That's not true," I said on impulse.

His gaze filled with hate. It wasn't really me he was mad at, but in that moment he needed to punish someone, and I was standing in front of him looking like the perfect target.

He took the lid off the muffins and stood up. My heart started racing because he was standing so close to me. I shifted awkwardly, unsure what he was going to do. I tried to remember the other stuff I wanted to say, the stuff about how I was there if he wanted to talk.

But as I was trying to remember how I wanted to offer him comfort and support, he was grabbing one of the muffins I made him and moving to stand in front of me.

I didn't even try to move. I never dreamed he would be mean to me just for trying to be nice, so when he grabbed the front of my shirt and pulled it out, I just stood there not knowing what to do. He smashed the muffin against my chest, then crumbled what was left in his hand and dropped it down my shirt, coating my training bra and my tummy with sugar, nuts, and muffin crumbs. My shirt was tucked into my skirt, so the muffin was trapped inside.

Everyone saw what he did. People started laughing—just a stunned guffaw at first, but then laughter erupted from every kid in the room.

I stood there with the crushed muffin trapped in my shirt

and tears welling up in my eyes.

Landon smirked, malice in his eyes. "You know what? You were right," he said. "That did help."

I went back to my desk with tears sliding down my cheeks, my face and ears burning with humiliation. I gathered my stuff as quickly as I could and fled the school. I had a phone for emergencies, and I had to call and ask Mom to come get me.

Even though Landon was a massive jerk that day, I told myself I wouldn't hold it against him if, when I went back to school, he had reflected on how unnecessarily mean he had been and apologized. I knew he was hurting, and Mom explained in the car on the way home that when some people are in pain, they lash out. It doesn't make it right or fair and I certainly hadn't deserved that treatment, but maybe it was just the way his grief was coming out and I shouldn't take it personally.

Unfortunately, that apology never came.

I wasn't even on Landon's radar before, but he certainly knew I existed after that. He terrorized me every chance he got —just with pranks and making fun of me back then, stuff that made him look cool and made his dumb friends laugh, but when we got to high school, his harassment took a weird turn.

I went to a school football game with a couple of friends sophomore year. Landon isn't on the team anymore; he got in trouble too many times for fighting, but he was back then. I didn't look as awkward anymore. No more braces, just straight white teeth. No more training bra; mercifully, my B-cups had finally come in. I was by no means the kind of girl who attracted male attention as soon as she walked into a room, but I didn't look so much like the before version of Mia from *The Princess Diaries* anymore.

It was a different setting than the one he was used to seeing me in. I guess I thought that was why, when he caught my eye and walked over after the game, he invited me to come to the afterparty at his cousin's house. He told me they had a sweet pool so I should go home and get a bathing suit.

I was excited.

Looking back, I feel a little stupid because it was obviously a trick, but despite all the crap he had pulled over the years, I didn't look at Landon through a suspicious lens. Maybe I even had those stupid high school love stories in my head where the popular asshat notices the nerdy girl and stops being an asshat because, clearly, he now sees her for the beautiful person she has always been and he's madly in love with her.

I'd never admitted to being attracted to Landon because how could I possibly be attracted to someone who treated me like absolute garbage? But I wasn't blind, and his atrocious behavior was somehow not enough to make him unattractive to me.

Typically, it would be. His cousin Malek is widely regarded as a whole sex symbol at our school, and I could not be less attracted to that vile asshole if I tried.

Maybe the difference was the sympathy I had felt for Landon. It cushioned him from bearing the full brunt of his awfulness because, to me, even when he was being a bully, he was still the sad boy sitting alone at his desk and blaming himself for his mother being gone.

I couldn't hate Landon no matter how much he deserved it.

So, I went home and changed clothes. I put on a bathing suit underneath a party dress, even put on a bit of makeup.

In my mind, I imagined walking in and seeing his eyes glint with fondness when he caught sight of me. I imagined us talking all night long, sorting out every hurt caused by him being a jerk. I even went down imaginary roads that might lead to my first kiss before I left—something soft and romantic that would leave me floating on clouds as I made my way home.

It is heartbreaking how foolish I was.

I don't like to replay that night, but what actually happened was much closer to blatant assault. He ignored me for a good two hours and got drunk with his friends. He had only invited me, not Hannah or the other two girls we were at the game with, so there was no one else at the party for me to talk to, and I had a terrible time. But then, finally, he came over and got me. He grabbed my wrist and hauled me wordlessly through the crowd. My heart pounded and I thought, "This is it. It's finally happening."

But there was nothing sweet or romantic about it. He dragged me into a room and locked the door. I felt a first wave of fear wash over me, but that was silly. I'd gone to school with Landon forever; he wouldn't *hurt* me.

It didn't *feel* like he wouldn't hurt me, though.

The bedroom was dark because he hadn't bothered to turn the lights on. As he stalked toward me, I found myself backing away.

It was the first moment I realized maybe I shouldn't have come into that room with him.

He didn't say a single word to me, just backed me up against a wall. I looked up at him, confused. He slid his hands up under my dress to grab my hips and cage me in against the wall.

Fear wrapped its fingers around my throat. He smelled like liquor as he leaned in and roughly kissed my jaw, and I felt a sudden claustrophobic need to get away from him before he reached my mouth.

I had wanted him to be my first kiss, but not like that.

I pushed him away when I realized I needed to. I was still stunned, and he didn't take the hint. He grabbed my wrist again and pulled me back as I tried to move away from him. He pushed me over to the bed, then threw me down on the mattress and yanked down my bikini bottoms.

He got them off despite my confused attempts to stop him, and as his rough hand grabbed my naked hip to position me underneath him, the panic set in.

It couldn't be happening, but it was.

My heart raced as his weight crushed me. If I didn't get him off me and get out of that room, he was going to...

I fought him, and when I scratched his face, he was surprised enough that I managed to kick him off me and roll off the bed. I lunged for the door, ripped it open, and ran. My legs felt about as sturdy as two sticks of jelly as I fumbled with my purse, trying to get my phone out to call my mom just in case he came after me.

He didn't.

Not that night, anyway.

I didn't tell Mom or anyone else about what had happened. I felt so stupid, and I didn't even know how to process it myself, honestly. He'd invited me to that party just to attack me?

I kept my distance from him after that.

He never stopped being aware of me, and he never quit picking on me in front of his friends, but after that brush with him alone, I made sure he never got me alone again. I even went to the trouble of going to the office and transferring out of the only class we had together that year. Then, junior year, I was very hands-on in ensuring the school faculty knew I didn't want to be in any classes with him.

He never got me alone again until the end of summer when he broke into my house while my mom was out with his dad.

He chased me to my bedroom and trapped me inside. I sank to the floor with my back against the door, shaking with intensifying fear every time he slammed his hand against the wood and I felt the reverberations on the other side. I was terrified the door wouldn't hold, terrified of what he would do to me if it gave way.

From the moment he walked through the door, I feared he was there to finish what he had started that night at the party, but this time he wasn't silent, so I didn't have to wonder about his intentions.

This time, he told me exactly what he wanted to do to me when he got into my bedroom, so I knew I was right to be afraid.

I called the cops. It was the only thing to do.

I hadn't wanted things to escalate to that point, but he left me with little choice.

I was so angry and afraid by the time it was all over. I'd reached my limit making excuses for him and going out of my way to avoid him when I hadn't done a damn thing wrong. If jail was the only way I could assure I was safe from him, then jail was where he needed to be.

But his father is Hayden Atwater, the best criminal defense attorney in Baymont, probably in the whole state of California.

He knows all the right people, and he assured me that even if I pressed charges, he would make sure his son got out of it with no more than a slap on the wrist.

Kids in this town have gotten away with far more, so I knew he wasn't lying.

Hayden convinced me that it would be the most beneficial if Landon believed I chose not to press charges against him. He thought it might buy me a little good will. Certainly more than if I insisted on pressing charges and lost.

He also offered to pay off my mom's house as a "thank you" gift, but that was before he decided to hell with it and just proposed to her.

He's a bit impulsive, but I really like Hayden despite everything. I understand wanting to protect Landon even when he doesn't deserve it. I've battled the same impulse, and I'm not even related to him.

I could have never foreseen my mom falling for his dad. It would be amazing if Hayden were literally anyone else in the world.

But, unfortunately, he is Landon's father.

Landon is the landmine built beneath their relationship, and I have to spend the rest of the year standing on it so it doesn't explode and destroy everything.

I'm not feeling great that we're not even a week in and Landon has already had to go stay with his cousin for a couple of days. Earlier at dinner, Mom was quiet, and I could tell she wasn't, either.

A whisper of a memory replays in my head as I look at the three dresses laid out across my new bed. I remember helping Mom get ready for her first date with Hayden in her bedroom at our old house. I didn't know it was with him, but I could feel her excitement, and I hadn't felt it in so long. Mom is amazing, but she set her love life completely aside to focus on raising me, so I couldn't remember another time I'd seen her sparkle the way Hayden made her sparkle.

He loves her so fucking well, and she deserves that. They both do.

I grab the middle dress off the bed and march to the bathroom with renewed will.

It's just a party. Who cares?

It'll be at Hannah's house, and I'm the one who made the guest list, so I'll know people there.

Most importantly, I'm not that awestruck young girl anymore. Landon can no longer surprise me, and I won't follow him into any dark corners.

So honestly, what's the worst that can happen?

Maybe I'll even have a good time.

CHAPTER 10
PARKER

"NEED HELP WITH THAT?"

Hannah looks up and offers a smile as I approach the drink table where she's setting up for the party. "I've got it. We do still need one for the pool area, though. There's a smaller tub in the kitchen. If you want to, fill it about ¾ of the way full with ice. There's an open bag in the freezer."

"On it," I say, turning and heading for the kitchen.

Once I have a tub full of ice, I come back out to the main party room. Hannah has finished filling her tub, so I use the leftovers to fill mine. There are mini bottles of vodka and gin, and a couple of small bottles of water for anyone who wants one of those instead. Canned non-alcoholic beverages are plunged into a separate tub of ice, and Hannah made party punch distributed in two separate glass dispensers, one marked "designated driver friendly" that has colorful, melted sherbet mounds floating around on top.

My mouth waters just looking at it. I should probably be a proper unpaid worker and abstain, but... to hell with it. I'm unpaid. I'm getting some of that punch.

Hannah comes back and catches me dipping into the

goods. I flash her a guilty smile, then take a greedy sip of her amazing punch. "I couldn't resist."

Hannah chuckles. "You don't need to. I have enough to make a second batch in case this one runs out. Drink to your heart's content."

"In that case, can the second batch be just for me?" I ask, flashing her my best puppy dog eyes.

"Nice try." She glances at my tub. "I'll grab you a few mini waters to put in there, too."

"Don't we have an entire tub of full-sized waters?"

"Yes, but there may be some people who don't particularly want to drink, but they get dragged to the alcohol bins by friends or boys that do. I'm including a water option in the same container so she can easily grab this without drawing attention to it if she's feeling a bit pressured and doesn't want to go to a different bin."

I blink at her.

"It's not for you. But I've seen the guest list, and I know who will be here, so..."

Brittany.

It clicks. If she thought Landon would make fun of her for avoiding the drink bin in favor of a non-alcoholic option, she would absolutely grab a drink she didn't want and finish the whole thing.

I sigh. "She makes me so sad."

Hannah nods. "She needs a friend. I can't take her in, conflict of interest," she says, gesturing to me, "but for tonight, this will work."

I pull out my phone to check the time and see the party technically started three minutes ago. Anae assured me anyone cool would die before showing up exactly on time. She said we should expect people to start showing up 15 to 20 minutes after.

Hannah comes back with an armful of mini water bottles, but unfortunately, she's not alone.

Anae walks over in her insanely high heels and party dress, her blonde hair so perfect, I bet she had it done at a salon after school. As if she's the true lady of the house, she looks over the work we did while she was upstairs primping. "You're putting out bourbon, right? Chloe said Arden likes bourbon."

"Yes, we're putting out bourbon," Hannah assures her.

"He likes it neat. Don't put it in that ice."

She sighs faintly. "I know how to serve alcohol, Anae."

Hannah doesn't even drink, but she is the consummate hostess; of course she knows how to serve alcohol.

"Did you polish the glasses? I don't want him to think we can't afford proper help."

"Yes, I polished the glasses," Hannah says, to her immense credit, without a single hint of the annoyance she must feel bleeding through in her tone.

I wait until Anae leaves to inspect the setup by the pool, then I look over at Hannah as I plunge a mini bottle of water into the ice. "So, has she gone all-in on Arden?"

"I don't think so. She's just anxious about making a good impression on him. She's used to being the established one, and it has been confirmed several times this week that he's the top of the food chain now, so she wants to make sure he likes her. I'm sure starting over, especially after a setback like Dare, is difficult for her."

I couldn't care less about Anae's struggles, but before I can say as much, she comes back from the pool.

She must be satisfied by what she saw out there because rather than comment on it or bark at us to make changes, she does a little spin for us, her pink lampshade dress flying out to show off her long, slim legs. "What do you guys think?" she asks, striking a pose in front of an accent mirror hung up in the hallway.

"You look very pretty," Hannah says politely.

Anae turns and shifts her shoulders to look at herself from behind. "Right? Ten out of ten, would bang."

I roll my eyes, not bothering to offer my opinion of her outfit. She doesn't care about it, anyway.

"It's not too princessy, is it?" she asks, smoothing her hands down the puffy bottom. "It doesn't look like I'm trying to hide that I had a big dinner or anything?"

"Of course not," I say.

"Good." She misses a beat, then says, "Oh! Speaking of princesses. Hannah, come here."

"How is that a 'speaking of princesses'?" Hannah asks, but follows Anae over to a little red velvet loveseat we set up for the party and sits beside her, anyway.

Anae pulls her phone out of her clutch. "I want to show you something I found."

"Is this for the party?" I ask, approaching even though I wasn't invited. "It's probably too late to do much else. People will start showing up—"

"No, it's not about that," Anae says, waving me off. She taps and swipes at the screen, then tilts the phone so Hannah can see. "Look at these tattoos."

Tattoos?

Hannah frowns at whatever she is seeing on Anae's phone screen. I'm curious, so I walk over and sit on Anae's other side so I can look, too.

I am somehow shocked to see a picture of Dare—specifically, a picture of Dare and Aubrey on a beach in Italy. His arms are locked around her and she's laughing. There's a smirk on his handsome face and his dark hair's a little wet. His eyes aren't always expressive, but in this shot, you can tell he's having a good time. His caption reads, "I caught a mermaid."

"Are we really going to cyber stalk your ex right now?" I ask. "I thought we were focused. New start! Party! Whoo!" I say, pumping my fist into the air.

Anae ignores me and focuses on Hannah, since she's been successfully drawn in.

"What am I looking at?" Hannah asks, uncomprehending.

"He added to his tattoo."

"Okay. Why do I care?"

"Because you're on his arm."

Hannah's eyes widen. "What?" she asks sharply, scowling and looking closer at the screen.

"He has a Cinderella tattoo," Anae states, pointing to an exploded clock tower on his upper arm. "Look, the crow is him, he got that at the start of senior year to symbolize his house—he's onyx, wisdom, a black crow. Anyway. He changed the crow, it has a crown now. The crown is for me. He stole *my* crown. He was *my* evil king. I'm sure he told his dumb twat scoop of vanilla some other bullshit, but we all know *I'm* the evil queen. So, the crown is his tattoo to remind him of me. The mermaid is her, of course," she says, rolling her eyes. "But this clock tower with the hands set to midnight? This is clearly you, and the shard of glass in his mouth? Makes me feel like he's responsible for breaking Cinderella, and I do sense a darkness in you that was not there before."

Hannah eases back warily. "You're reading too much into this, Anae."

"I'm not. He got this ink for a reason. He's not one of those guys that just likes the way they look. I need to figure out what they mean. What's the significance of those of us who get tattoos? Initially, I thought it might be his trophy. He was never into physical trophies like I was, but what if *this* is his trophy?

He's turning his skin into a tapestry of all the lives he fucks with, you know?"

Anae's eyes are *bright* with excitement. This girl is entirely unhinged.

"But not everyone's on there. That dumb girl who wrote the haiku about Aubrey? Not on there, and a nail would have been incredibly easy to incorporate into the artwork. That dorky kid, Frank something, he's not on there, and that dumbass is in jail for a crime Dare committed. There are other people that didn't make the cut, too. He didn't ink them all into his skin. Only us. You, me, and Aubrey. Aubrey and I have both fucked him." She looks Hannah in the eyes. "So, I'm going to ask one more time—have you?"

"I told you I didn't, Anae."

Tapping Anae on the arm, I point out, "He could have tattoos for the other people. Maybe he just put them in a different place."

"Oh, that's true," Anae says, as if she hadn't considered that. A crease mars her perfect brow and she backs out of that picture, checking other posts to see if she can find ink anywhere else on his body. Since she's looking through a few beach posts, there's a lot of skin to look at.

While Anae is distracted, I glance over at Hannah. She's chewing on her bottom lip.

I'm concerned about her getting sucked back into this twisted web now that Anae is back. It was really hard on her last year. I thought she was finally clear of it once they moved and Anae wasn't around, but if Anae keeps bringing her focus back to the past, and especially if she finds new wrinkles Hannah hadn't considered...

I never met Aubrey and I have nothing against the girl, but being with Dare was *her* choice. I'm all for helping people when you can, but sometimes you have to let people live with their choices.

Hannah insists Aubrey didn't really know what she was getting into with him, that he deliberately misled her and only revealed the truth about himself once she'd fallen for him, but at the risk of sounding like an uncaring asshole, that's Aubrey's problem. If she's truly in trouble with him, then I hope she finds a way out of it, but not at Hannah's expense. I don't want my too-caring-for-her-own-good friend getting sucked back into Aubrey's vortex of dysfunction trying to save her. I don't know if she can make it out again.

When Hannah first told me about all this, I warned her that it was much easier for someone to pull you down when you offered a hand to help than for you to pull them up, so she had better make sure she had excellent footing. A stumble could prove fatal.

In Aubrey's case, if the devil really has a death grip on her ankle, it's even more likely.

But Hannah could not be convinced she lacked the Herculean strength to fight him, apparently, because every time she put distance between them, she let Aubrey suck her right back in.

"What if you're misinterpreting it?" Hannah suggests. "Maybe it's not symbolizing breaking Cinderella, but something with time. Like 'time's up' or 'it's only a matter of time,' or..."

Fear cuts through me when she utters that last guess. I cut in before Hannah inadvertently leads Anae somewhere crazy. "Maybe we should all stop trying to read into these tattoos he never even meant for us to see."

Anae's head snaps up. "Oh, he meant for me to see them. He didn't block me on any of his social media. He knew the first thing I would do when I got my phone back was check in on him, especially after he sent me that picture after prom.”

“Did it say anything else?” Hannah asks. “Did he just send the picture with no context, or was there a message attached?”

“I kept it,” she says, swiping away from his social media page and bringing up her old text messages with Dare.

The last message is from him to her. The time stamp says he sent it the morning after prom. There’s a picture of Hannah in a red dress wearing the rose necklace, and above it is a bubble of text that reads, “Thought you’d want to know Cinderella is playing with your toys while you’re away.”

I look to Hannah, who sits back and loses a shade of color.

I get it. It’s hard to look at that message as *not* siccing Anae on her.

I try to insert some reason. “Look, Dare’s cruel. We all know that. I get that you guys knew him so you’re trying to understand why he would do something like this, but the honest answer is probably just for his own sadistic amusement. He’s not even here and he’s messing with both of you. Can you imagine the pleasure he must feel knowing he can do that?”

Anae sighs—but it’s not the kind of sigh I would expect, it’s like she’s downright smitten. “He’s so wonderful. How could anyone not love this man? He’s so interesting.”

“He’s not. He’s just a shameless psychopath who leaves a path of destruction and broken lives in his wake.”

Anae shakes her head. “You’re so boring. You’re just like his stupid vanilla scoop. You don’t see his genius.”

“Well, she must see something in him since she rode off into the sunset with him,” I point out.

Anae narrows her eyes at me. “Ew. Whose side are you on?”

“Hannah’s. I don’t have a dog in this fight. I couldn’t care less about Chase Darington. I think he’s the worst, and I’m glad he's gone." Standing, I say, "Now, can you guys stop playing detectives over the *ink* he has chosen for his skin and come back to the present? We need to pick our stupid lipsticks."

Anae shakes her head, looking back at the screen. "I'm going to figure it out. I feel like he's still playing with me. He's leaving me messages, I just have to decode them and figure out what he wants me to do."

"Or you could not care what he wants you to do because he's literally living happily ever after with someone else, so honestly, fuck him."

She rolls her eyes. "Please. Aubrey is *not* his end game. Dare is a beast and she wants him to live in a cage. He'll get restless. Bored. Maybe he already is. Dare will never stay where he doesn't want to be, so once he tires of her, it's over. He'll ditch her just like he did me, and after spending this time with someone who doesn't understand him, who doesn't let him be who he is, he will remember me fondly. He will miss having me around, someone who understood and appreciated him for everything he truly is. We were the perfect couple. He just got distracted by her, that's all. He was used to me and he had a taste for something softer, something pure and sweet that he could sink his fangs into and pollute. But now he's used to the taste, or he's already polluted her and it's not fun for him anymore. He's probably bored to tears with his downgrade and realizing he made a massive mistake. That's why he left me all these clues. He wants me back."

"No," I say firmly, because her delusions are getting danger-ous. "Anae, he doesn't love you. He doesn't want to be with you. Look at the pictures. They're *happy*."

"You can project any image you want on social media," she insists.

"Why would he want you to think he's happy with her if he wants you to be with him? That literally doesn't make sense."

There's a knock at the door. Anae switches lanes like the psycho she is, smiling brightly. "Our first guest. Super lame to be the first guest."

I watch as Anae walks to the front door. When she's far enough away, I look back at Hannah. She's still sitting on the couch, her gaze unfocused. She's clearly somewhere else.

I sit down beside her and touch her thigh. "Hey, are you okay?"

Her gaze shifts to me. She nods, but doesn't say anything.

"She's crazy," I remind her. "Like, legit crazy. She's reading too much into things. There's nothing there."

"What if there is?"

I shake my head. "No way. He doesn't want her. If he did, he'd be with her. She's grasping at straws."

"Not about that," Hannah says. "He doesn't want Anae. He's not as interested in her as she is him, he never was. But some of the other stuff..."

I want to ask her to hurry up and spill before Anae comes back, but Hannah's struggling a bit, so I give her time to find her words.

Her gaze drops and she swallows. "There are things I didn't tell you about Dare. About prom night. He didn't send her that message until the morning *after* prom. I ran into him and Aubrey at prom, obviously, that's when he took my picture..."

I want to know what she held back, but before she can finish whatever she wants to tell me, Anae comes walking in with Brittany Benson.

Of course she's the first one here.

I glance behind them to see if that means Landon is here, too, but she seems to be alone.

"Look who I found," Anae says cheerfully, as if she's actually happy to see the girl.

"I guess I'm a little early," Brittany says, glancing at me. "Landon's coming with Malek, so…"

I know two things can be true at the same time.

I know I can feel bad for this girl for the blatant insecurity and load of issues she exhibits by clinging to a guy who could not give fewer fucks about her, and still also dislike her a little bit more every time she mentions him.

It doesn't sit right with me, though, so I try to shake it off.

I have already started down the path of being nice to her by inviting her to this party, so even if I only half mean it, I'm gonna keep going.

"Want to go pick out a lipstick?" I ask her.

She seems confused by my offer. Her gaze flits to Anae as if *she's* a safe person to use as a gauge for whether she should follow me.

God, her instincts are trash.

Anae wants to be rid of her, so she nods enthusiastically and shoos her toward me. "For sure. I think you look like a yellow, personally."

When we pulled the lipsticks out of the packs, Anae took one look at the yellows and pondered why they made such an ugly fucking shade. She said no one was going to pick that one, so of course she's trying to pawn it off on Brittany.

And, of course, Brittany grabs a yellow without hesitation since Anae told her to.

I sigh and snatch a yellow as well, so at least she's not the only one wearing the heinous shade.

THE PARTY IS in full swing which, of course, means the bathroom is *always* occupied. After what feels like the 14th time of trying the door and finding it locked, I head to the kitchen to complain.

Hannah is assembling a plate of cucumber roll-ups when I burst through the doors like Maleficent crashing a party she wasn't invited to.

She glances back over her shoulder. Seeing it's only me, she dismisses the show of drama and continues assembling snacks for Anae's guests.

"Two things," I say, holding up two fingers.

"What's up?"

"One, I don't know if you want to do anything about this, but Arden is getting a blow job in the library. He's sitting in front of the fireplace in one of the wing chairs. He didn't even bother to close the door."

She rolls a thin slice of cucumber and secures it with a toothpick. "Well, tell him the girl better swallow because I'm not cleaning that up."

"The second thing is that the bathroom down here is *still* occupied and my bladder is going to explode."

"You can use one of the upstairs bathrooms, just take the back staircase so no one sees you go up. I'll have enough clean-up to do when this party is over. I don't need people making messes upstairs, too."

That's what I was leaning toward, I just wanted to clear it with her first because I intended to take the main staircase and knew people might see me go up.

I'll take the back one since she asked me to, but making my way through dark, isolated corridors at a party Landon is also attending isn't something I'm excited about. I find him in the crowd and make sure he isn't looking my way before I disappear down the hall.

I have noticed him keeping an eye on me tonight.

And he has been drinking.

When Landon drinks, his inhibitions go right out the window.

Malek is supposed to drop him off after the party. I haven't figured out an ideal way to time my exit. Do I leave first and risk Landon following me? Or do I wait for him to leave and give him enough time to get home before I do?

Imagining him lying in wait for me is no more reassuring than the thought of him following me.

I really, really wish he would have just followed the rules for once and abstained from drinking at this stupid party.

Since thoughts of the present trigger immediate dread and anxiety, I shift my focus to the future.

We'll both be off at college this time next year. I don't know where Landon is going, but I'm certain it's not where I'm headed.

I only have to keep the peace long enough for Mom and Hayden to tie the knot. It's not like I'll have to deal with his shenanigans *forever*.

As I make my way down the corridor away from the party,

my mind teases me with a "what if?" scenario of if I *did*. If Mom and Hayden get married, but Landon never stops being a terror.

It's Christmas a decade from now. I'm visiting Mom with my loving, supportive husband who never terrorizes me. Landon is there with some Playboy bunny-looking date. Not the one he brought last year, of course. Landon isn't married in my daydream, he just flits from knockout to knockout, always leaving before anything can get real.

Every year, we come home for the holidays and I pretend everything is fine for Mom and Hayden—*who are still so happily married it makes unhappy couples sick*—and each year I have to be careful not to bump into Landon alone because he pulls the same shameless shit regardless of our parents, my husband, and whichever cute little bunny he has brought with him that year.

Daydream. More like a nightmare.

I shake it off as I approach the massive wooden doors that lead to Hannah's library. It used to be her dad's study, but the room is mostly unused now that he's gone. It's a travesty, too, because it's an amazing study.

Before I head upstairs, I swing into the library to relay Hannah's message. I'm no voyeur, but Arden isn't remotely seeking privacy.

No one else is in the library (which is why I wanted to come in here and wander around away from the party when I first stumbled across him), but the door is wide open. I knock on it to alert them that someone's coming in just in case they care.

Arden's attention doesn't even flicker in my direction. Some girl in an olive green crop top kneels on the ground between his legs with her long dark hair fisted in one of Arden's hands. He uses the makeshift ponytail to guide her head up and down, and I try to ignore the wet, sloppy sounds as I walk closer to them.

"Hannah said you better not leave a mess for her to clean up in here."

Arden's head falls back, and he shoots me a roguish smile. "You tell Hannah not to worry her pretty little head. Any girl lucky enough to have my cock in her mouth always swallows. Maybe I'll show her firsthand someday."

Ew.

I roll my eyes. "I don't think so. Hannah doesn't date players."

"Who said anything about dating?" he asks benignly.

The girl laboring over his lap pops off his dick to look up at him. "Are you seriously having a conversation about fucking someone else while I am blowing you?"

He looks down at her coolly. "I guess that indicates you're not doing a very good job, doesn't it?"

If I were her, I'd punch him right in the dick and storm out of the room, but she's obviously suited to his brand of evil because she flushes with embarrassment, steals a glance at me, then grips the base of his dick and takes it into her mouth again, apparently willing to try harder to please him.

That thing must be made of literal magic for anyone to put up with him. Shaking my head in vague disbelief, I turn to leave since I've delivered my message.

Before I reach the door, he calls, "Parker."

I pause and look back. "Yeah?"

His blue eyes twinkle with amusement. "I hear you're a screamer. Shame I don't remember our encounter."

"Oh, yeah. You really rocked my world."

He smirks. "You shouldn't joke like that with Landon. You know he's obsessed with you, and a bit of a hothead. I'm too handsome to get punched in the face."

"He is not," I mutter. "And you're gross, just in case no one has ever told you."

"This is why we're going to get married someday," he calls after me as I exit the library and start off down the hall.

I don't waste an eyeroll since he wouldn't see it, but ugh, he is the fucking worst.

At least my bladder finally gets some relief. I enjoy the moment of quiet before I head back downstairs, checking my phone and fixing my ugly yellow lipstick in the mirror before I leave the bathroom.

I didn't turn on the upstairs lights since I didn't want to draw attention to anyone being up here. A shiver of awareness travels down my spine as I glance down the long, dark hall toward the bedrooms.

During the day, this place is grand. But at night, it's spooky as hell.

I turn the other way back toward the staircase and gasp as I run into the solid wall of Landon's chest. My heart stops and my blood freezes in my veins. Cold fear starts at the nape of my neck and slithers down.

"What are you doing? No one's supposed to be up here."

"You're up here," he points out lazily.

I lick my lips, unconsciously moving a few steps back as he takes a slow step toward me. "Did you follow me?"

He tips his chin up. "What was that song you were singing?"

"What?"

"You were humming something in the bathroom."

Was I?

I can't remember. I also can't think straight with him backing me down the dark hall, so I stop moving. "We have to go back downstairs."

Not too bothered about what we're supposed to do, apparently, he holds out a tiny bottle of liquor. "I got you a drink."

I glance at it. It's Macallan 12. "I don't like whisky," I tell him.

"No?" He shrugs, uncaps it, and throws it back. "More for me, then."

I swallow as he caps the empty bottle and tosses it down the hall. I start as it hits the wood floor and rolls, emphasizing how quiet it is up here. "I think you've had enough," I say gently.

"Have I?" He closes the distance between us, grabbing my shoulders and forcing me back against the wall.

I reach for the first lifeline I can think of. "Brittany has been following you around all night. She's going to come looking for you."

He smirks. "I could tell her to hold your fucking ankles for me and she would. I don't give a fuck if she comes looking for me."

I hate that my gaze drifts to his lips, but I find it lingering there, looking for any hint of change to the color. I didn't try out the lipstick myself and I haven't been paying attention to other people. I don't know how dramatically the color changes when you kiss someone—*I suppose it depends on the kiss*—but I know Brittany is wearing yellow, just like me. Landon grabbed a blue, so if he kissed her tonight, there should be at least a hint of green, right?

It's too dark in the hall to tell for sure, but I think his lips are blue.

Unconsciously, I lick mine and look up at him.

There's heat in his eyes and alcohol in his veins, and that is a lethal combination.

I know I have to get him back downstairs before this can go bad, but my mind isn't clear enough to think of a way out.

This feels too much like sophomore year when he got me alone in a dark room, but it feels different, too.

We're older now.

And he has leverage he didn't have back then.

I didn't even know he *wanted* leverage over me back then. I didn't know anything, and now I know more than I want to.

"We have to go downstairs," I say. It's not clever or compelling. It's just what needs to happen.

Of course, Landon doesn't have any fucks to give about what needs to happen.

Rather than see reason and follow me back downstairs, he looks me over slowly, like he has all the time in the world. He grabs the hem of my dress and I gasp as he drags it up, the cool air hitting my exposed thighs.

"Landon, stop." I push the dress back down. He lets me, but only so he can grab my wrists and force them together above my head.

"Landon! I swear to god."

He holds my wrists with one hand, then uses the other to lift my dress again.

"Don't *do* this. I don't want to have to..."

"What? Tell on me?" He smirks, leaning forward and using his muscular body to pin me against the wall. His hand roams over my hip, then teases the waistband of my panties before he lets a threatening finger push past the band to touch my bare flesh. "I don't think you will, Parker. I think you like my dad. Not in a sick way, hopefully, but you definitely like the guy more than I fucking do. I can see it every time you talk to him. You get this excited glint in your eyes, like you've found a kindred spirit. You're weird, so our world is probably a little lonely for you, huh? My dad's an academic, too. Driven. Focused. You probably relate to him." He lets go of my hip so he can drag his fingers along the curve of my jawline. "That's all it is, right? You don't have some kind of crush?"

"That's sick," I whisper, turning my face away from his touch.

He shrugs, forcing my gaze back to him and leaning in to kiss my jaw. "So, if you want *my* dad to be your new daddy, you can't do the thing that would break the family up. You can't tell on me because then your mom will make you guys move out." His lips move toward my neck. "I can do any-fucking-thing I want to you, Parker, and you're not going to say a word. You're my favorite toy, and no one's going to stop me from playing with you."

"I am not your *toy*." I jerk my face away again, but this time when he grabs my jaw, it hurts enough to startle me.

"You're whatever the fuck I tell you to be."

I shake my head, my heart pounding as I look up at him. "This is not how this is going to work. You're right, I do want to keep the family together, but..."

You don't have to be part of it.

He doesn't know that Hayden said he would kick *Landon* out if Landon couldn't respect boundaries and tried to hurt me again.

I can't bring myself to tell him, either.

I've known since we agreed to move in it was a card I could keep in my back pocket for emergencies, but this feels like an emergency, and I can't bring myself to play it.

Even though I know Hayden would never turn his back on his son, that he would get him a place of his own to live in while he finished senior year, I can't fathom it not hurting Landon to know his dad would even put that on the table.

Even if he deserves it, even if it's his own damn fault...

I can't bring myself to say it.

Swallowing to keep the magic words down, I push against his chest, but he doesn't budge. "Stop, Landon."

He doesn't stop. He nips at my jaw, and then his rough kisses travel dangerously close to my mouth.

"Stop it!" I turn my head, but he just follows the movement and keeps working his way along my jaw. "I don't *want* you to kiss me. You're drunk and you're mean to me, and—"

He grabs my jaw, startling me as he pushes my head back against the wall so he has better access. "I don't care," he says distinctly, before attacking my neck with his rough mouth.

"Landon." I struggle to get away, shoving at his chest again. I can't move him, so I try to squeeze past him, but as soon as I gain a little ground, he grabs me by the hair and pulls me back. "Get off of me." I shove him hard in the chest, but he just smirks like he finds my efforts amusing. "You need to spend less time in the gym and more time in a therapist's office," I snap.

"And you need to spend less time running your mouth and more time opening it."

My eyes widen at the implication, then he pushes on my shoulders.

Is he crazy?

"I am not getting on my knees for you."

"Oh, I bet you will."

"Let go of my hair and get the fuck away from me, Landon. I'm serious. I'm done with this. I don't want to play with you tonight."

"Who's playing?"

"We need to go back to the party. Your... *Brittany* is probably looking for you," I snap, not knowing what else to call her.

"Anae said you made the guest list for tonight. Imagine my initial surprise." He smirks at the annoyance etched across my face. "I don't know if it was sweet of you to extend an invite to my latest toy, or if you thought her presence here would make you safer." His lips tug up in a smirk that makes me want to smack him.

"Thought *I* was your toy?" I say sarcastically.

"You're my *favorite* toy. The one I could break a hundred times and have to stitch back together so I could do it all over again. She's a throwaway."

Ugh, I hate him so much right now. "I was right. You *are* Satan."

He cocks an eyebrow, and I give his chest a good hard shove to get him away from me.

He doesn't budge, and he doesn't let go of my hair as he pushes me down to my knees. I fight him, but he's too strong, and he's right—he's not playing this time.

Fear shoots down my spine as I look up at him.

A dark smile tugs at his lips as he looks down at me. "I've been waiting for this for a long fucking time."

Guess you'll have to keep waiting, asshole.

He lets go of my hair to unzip his pants and take his cock out. I take advantage of the freedom to crawl away. I stumble on my way to my feet, but before I can stand, he grabs me by the hair and pulls me right back.

"Not so fucking fast. We're not done here."

"Fuck you," I cry grabbing the hair in his hand and trying to rip it free. "Get your hands off me, Landon."

"I'm gonna have a lot more than my hands on you, Parker." He yanks me back against his legs like I weigh nothing, my scalp screaming in pain since that's what he's using to control me. "I'm gonna have my cock in every fucking one of your holes. I will own you," he says, reaching his other hand down to caress my face as he spews his depraved words. "Be a good girl and I'll make it good for you."

Tears well up in my eyes.

This is what I was afraid of when he broke into my house, but this time there's no door between us.

I could scream, but I doubt anyone downstairs would hear me over the loud music.

I still have my purse. I could call someone for help, but not if I can't get away from him. It's not like he'll wait patiently while I text someone to come save me, and as soon as I grab my phone, he'll take it from me.

I need a door between us.

I look down the hall. There are plenty of doors in this hallway. We're just steps away from Hannah's old bedroom. There's a lock on her door. All I need is enough time to get to it.

He's faster than I am, though. Landon is an athlete and I'm definitely not. Do I really want to lead him into a bedroom with a locked door?

Every move I could make has bad odds.

I'm still on my knees pulled back against his legs, but I'm jarred from my thoughts when Landon starts moving me. I try to get my feet under me, but he shoves me back before I can, then follows me down on the ground, pinning me to the floor.

No.

"Landon," I say, my voice shaky as he releases my hair and slides his hands up the backs of my thighs. I wore a stupid dress tonight, so his hands find my ass with ease, nothing but the thin barrier of my panties protecting me.

He pushes my legs apart and moves between them, then grabs my hips and holds onto me so he can grind his cock against me.

"Do you know how fucking annoying it is that I want you?" he asks. "You're the biggest pain in the ass I've ever met. I can't stand you, and yet I want my cock inside you enough to commit fucking crimes to accomplish it."

My heart is in my throat as I push his hands away, but it's a maddening waste of effort. I push them off, and then he's touching me again somewhere else.

Tiring of my resistance, he uses one hand to restrain mine above my head like he did when he had me against the wall, and the other to shove my dress up until he can see my panties.

"No," I cry, seeing his intentions a moment before he places a hand on my belly, then slides it down into my panties. "No. Landon, please. Please stop."

I'm horrified by my own begging, but it gives him pause. His hand is hot and possessive over my pelvic bone, but it doesn't slide lower to actually violate me. Not yet, anyway.

"What are you willing to offer me?" he murmurs.

I'm too afraid to immediately comprehend. "What?"

"You don't want me to play with your pussy? Then you had better make a counteroffer that I find attractive."

"I don't... I don't know what you want."

He holds my gaze. "Sure you do."

When I don't immediately speak, his fingers inch lower. "Wait," I cry, my heart hammering in my chest, panic making my brain blank so I can't think of anything to offer. "I... I... I'll..."

"You'll kiss me," he suggests, since I'm struggling to generate any ideas.

I nod, though my stomach sinks. I still haven't kissed anyone yet. I've tried, but Landon doesn't let me date. He has never told *me* I'm not allowed to date, but the only guys I've ever agreed to go out with have mysteriously changed their minds after having run-ins with him. It's not hard to piece together what happened.

I did once, but now I don't want it to be him.

He's not leaving me much room to negotiate, though.

"You better make it convincing," he says as he leans in close.

I feel sick to my stomach and fluttery at the same time. I reach up tentatively and touch his face. It's not the first kiss I want, but it's the one I'm getting, so I might as well at least make it good for myself.

My heart slams to a halt, then flies into overdrive when his lips meet mine. His lips are soft and full and perfect. He could be mean and forceful, but he's not. He kisses me like we're lovers, making my fool heart flutter like it would have if he'd kissed me this way years ago.

Maybe it's the intoxicating kiss and the potent chaser of fear, maybe it's that he still has a hand down my panties, but I feel a stirring of arousal that I fight to crush down so I never have to think about it again.

His tongue pushes between my lips. I gasp, not wanting to let him in, but he goes anyway. He grabs a fistful of my hair and angles my head. His mouth crushes mine, his tongue sweeping in and dominating like a general at war, finding and marking every inch of land he touches as his.

My body arches off the floor as his hand leaves my hair and he squeezes my tit through the fabric of my dress. That was more than I put on the table, so I try to break away from the kiss, but his mouth recaptures mine easily. He doesn't let up, doesn't even let me breathe.

Then his other hand slides lower, his middle finger teasing my entrance.

"No." I shove at him, trying like hell to squeeze my thighs together, but it's impossible with him planted between them. "You said you'd stop if I kissed you."

"No, I didn't."

I stare up at him, wide-eyed. "What?"

He shakes his head, a smirk tugging at his mouth. "I just said make me an offer. We didn't strike any kind of agreement."

You cheating bastard.

"Get off me," I say, shoving with both hands and managing to push him back enough that I can maneuver my body out from under his. I grab my purse off the floor, launching up and taking off down the hall as fast as my legs can carry me.

"You can run, but you can't hide," he calls rather lightly, given our circumstances.

Wanna bet?

I tear open Hannah's door and hurl myself inside, slamming it shut and quickly turning the lock.

The last door barely held him.

I don't know if this one will.

But at least now, there's a door between us.

At least now, I stand a chance.

CHAPTER 12
PARKER

I WASTE no time fumbling with my bag to get my phone out. My hands shake as I navigate to Hannah's text chain, but I wait until I'm sure Landon is on the other side of the door before I text her for help.

His voice is calm this time, not like last time there was a door between us. "Open the goddamn door, Parker."

"Leave me alone," I tell him.

"I don't know. That kiss didn't feel like you wanted me to leave you alone."

My whole body is still flushed from that kiss. But my whole body is still flushed from the struggle, too, so maybe it wasn't the kiss at all. "You told me to make it convincing, so I did."

"Then you're one hell of an actress," he states. "Is that why your pussy was wet, too?"

I gasp, horrified. "It was not!"

"Lie to yourself all you want. I felt it."

I shake my head, pushed far past my limit. I text Hannah, "Get Malek and come upstairs to get Landon, please. He has me trapped in your old bedroom."

"AGAIN?" she texts back. "Are you okay?"

"I'm fine, I just want him to get the hell away from me and he won't listen."

"I'll be right there," she answers.

I feel safer with a door between us, since he's not trying to break it down this time. "Malek is coming upstairs to get you."

"You sure you don't want to call the cops on me again?"

"Maybe later."

Hannah must have grabbed Malek and sprinted up the stairs because before another word can be said, I hear the low rumble of Malek's voice asking Landon if he wants to get his dumb ass arrested chasing this pussy again.

A charmer, that Malek.

I wait for Hannah to say, "He's gone," then I unlock the door and let her in.

Her shoulders drop with relief when she sees me all in one piece, but she quickly looks me over just to make sure. "Are you all right?"

I nod, feeling... I don't actually know how I'm feeling. A little amped up, definitely embarrassed. "Sorry to drag you into it. I just didn't want things to escalate."

"You never have to apologize for asking for my help with these troublesome Baymont boys. There must be something in the water here, I swear."

I crack a smile. "Troublesome is a word. I might have gone for a stronger one."

"We shouldn't have invited him."

I shrug. "We had to. Not inviting him would have... If I work too hard to keep him off Anae's radar, that will just put him *on* her radar. Knowing him, he'd hook up with her just to piss me off, not fully realizing or caring that she's an unhinged lunatic. I may not like Brittany, but I prefer her to Anae ten out of ten times."

"That's true," Hannah murmurs. "After Dare, I'm not sure

Anae has the patience for competition, either. I can't handle her trying to kill *all* of my friends."

I crack a smile. "Yeah, and I don't think I have the temperament to escape a kidnapping unscathed. If she comes for me, it was nice knowing you."

"I'll plant some flowers in the garden in your honor," she promises.

I shake my head, but then I catch Hannah's gaze drifting to my mouth and jaw in a weird way, and I realize this is a lipstick party. "There's lipstick all over my face, isn't there?"

Hannah nods. "You look like a Smurf."

"Great." I walk over to her old dresser and cringe at the blue smeared along my jawline and down my neck. My lips have turned from yellow to green.

So much evidence of Landon's mauling.

Hannah follows me, inspecting the damage. "They're novelty lipsticks so they're not exactly high-quality. It smeared everywhere."

"I cannot go home like this. I need some makeup remover."

"I can grab you some."

"Landon is supposed to be going home after the party. Mom will wait up for me, but once I'm home, she'll go to bed. If he doesn't come home until later..."

I need to put a deadbolt on my door.

... Or not go home.

I turn around, looking at the lonely bed on the other side of the room.

When Hannah slept in here, the room was full of her stuff, but since her stepmom unceremoniously kicked her out of it last year and sold most of Hannah's stuff, it's barren now. Just a big, fancy bed in the middle of a huge, empty room.

The bedding is still on it, though.

I look back at Hannah. "Do you think Jackie would freak if I stayed over tonight?"

"There's not really room on my twin bed in the attic," she says, also glancing at her old bed. Her gaze is more haunted than mine, though. I suppose it must be odd to look at the place that used to be hers and not be allowed to occupy it anymore.

"I hate that woman," I state.

I don't have to say who. Hannah knows, and she nods sadly. She doesn't allow that feeling to linger, though. I can practically see her shove it away, and her face transforms with a mischievous, dimpled smile. "You know what? She's not here tonight because of the party. We can totally sneak in here if you want to. We'll just have to be quiet so Anae doesn't hear us."

Would I rather dodge Anae tonight, or Landon?

Anae is probably safer in this particular instance.

"Let's do it. Can I just stay in here now? I don't really want to go back to the party."

Hannah nods. "I'll grab you some makeup remover, a phone charger, and some snacks. Do you need me to bring up anything else?"

I shake my head. "I think I'm good. Thanks, Hannah."

"Of course." She pulls the door closed on her way out, but looks back at me before shutting it completely. "Lock this door in case he finds his way back up here. I'll knock when I need you to open it."

* * *

ONCE HANNAH CLEARS the last guest from the house, I go downstairs to help her clean up the mess from the party.

I can see she's exhausted, so I tell her, "Why don't you go take a shower? Let me finish up down here. That way you can get to bed sooner."

Hannah shakes her head, sweeping up spiced jackfruit someone carelessly dropped out of their taco earlier. "It's okay. Not like I'll be able to fall asleep, anyway."

I start to ask why, but when I turn, she's heading for the kitchen.

Finally, every surface is sparkling and we're able to head upstairs. Anae has been asleep for hours, so Hannah and I shower in separate bathrooms so we can get to bed sooner.

When I make it back to her old bedroom and climb beneath the covers, Hannah is still in her old bathroom. She comes out after brushing her teeth with her hair loosely braided and a few blonde tendrils hanging loose around her face. She's wearing a pale blue tank top and a pair of white sleep shorts. She flashes me a smile as she hops on the bed and slides her legs beneath the blanket.

"This bed is so much more comfortable than mine," she states.

"I mean, it *is* your bed."

"Not anymore," she singsongs rather lightly as she pumps some lotion into her palm, then offers some to me.

I take a pump, my gaze locked on her face. "Did Jackie ever tell you why she was evicting you?"

Hannah shakes her head as she rubs the lotion into her skin. "She didn't need to. I don't want to talk about that." Her gaze drifts to my jawline, no longer smeared with cheap blue lipstick, but her mind obviously replaying when it was. "I *do* want to talk about what happened between you and Landon earlier."

"And *I* want you to finish telling me about Dare. You didn't get to before the stupid party started."

She doesn't look excited by the prospect, but she nods. "You go first."

I feel a strange burst of shyness over confessing what actually happened. I don't even know how much I want to tell her.

Despite knowing Hannah isn't bossy and she would never judge me, I can't help knowing if the roles were reversed, I would have a lot of opinions about what happened and what she should do next. I would be afraid for her and want to keep her safe, and I know Hannah may have the same desires...

But I also don't think she'll try to interfere.

It was unusual last year when she tried so hard to pull Aubrey away from Dare. Evidence of how dangerous she must truly consider him, because usually Hannah might advise a friend if she believed the guy she was with wasn't any good, but she wouldn't put herself in the middle of it.

Hannah gives excellent advice to those who want it, but she won't try forcing anyone to take it.

That's me. I would do that.

She may have determined Aubrey needed more help than most people, but Hannah knows me. She has been my best friend for years, so she knows I'm more than capable of deciding for myself how to handle my hostile housemate.

I don't have to worry about her telling my mom or confronting Landon about his behavior. If there's anyone in the world I can confide in without fear of it coming back to bite me, it's Hannah.

Finally, I take a deep breath, then let it out. I start to rub in the squeeze of lotion she gave me so my hands have something to do, then I blurt, "Landon and I kissed."

Her eyes widen and her jaw falls open. "Consensually?"

"It wasn't—I mean, I didn't *want* to kiss him, but he was being exceptionally rapey and I was trying to negotiate the release of my body."

"That is the most Parker way of putting that I could possibly imagine."

"We made a deal, but then he reneged on it."

"Typical."

"He said all this crazy stuff about how he wants to bang me, even though he doesn't even like me. I think he said more to me tonight than he has in all the years we've known each other. It was lunacy."

"Everyone knows he wants to bang you, Parker."

"That's not true."

She raises her eyebrows. "He won't let you date. There aren't a lot of reasons for that beyond wanting you for himself."

"There are other possible reasons."

Ignoring my attempt to deflect, she asks, "So, how was it? Did you enjoy it, or...?"

"I..." I would really like to say no here, but I don't want to lie to her. "It was surprising. When he cornered me at the party before, I felt no stirring of interest, and I actually *liked* him back then. This time, I definitely..." I rub the lotion once more, but it may just be an excuse to wring my hands. "I don't know. It was intense."

She smiles mischievously. "Do you think you'll kiss him again?"

"What? No, of course not. We still don't like each other, just our mouths seemed to."

"Stupid mouths."

"They have no sense of judgment whatsoever," I agree. "Speaking of poor judgment, talking to Anae about Dare?" Now it's my turn to hike up *my* eyebrows. "Maybe something you should avoid doing at all costs."

Hannah sighs. "I know. I didn't mean to, she just caught me off guard. I've made a concerted effort not to look at pictures of Dare and Aubrey. I don't creep on his profile, of course, but I follow Aubrey and she posts pictures of him a lot. I never even paid attention to his tattoos, though."

"Well, yeah, because you're not obsessed with him. But Anae is, and you don't want her linking you to him that way. It's dangerous. Besides, that clock tattoo could mean a million things that have nothing to do with you."

She nods, but appears troubled. "Yeah. You're right, it could."

I watch her and my face pulls into a frown. "But you think it *is* for you?"

"I think... he made a point to call me Cinderella on prom night, and in that text to Anae. And she's right about him not blocking her. That's weird. Why wouldn't he block her? Even if only to keep Aubrey safe, I would think he wouldn't want her to be able to keep such close tabs on him. I hate to agree with her, but it does seem like he wanted Anae to see his tattoos."

"Maybe he just forgot to block her."

She shakes her head. "No way. Dare is meticulous. He wouldn't forget something like that."

"I thought you and Dare hated each other."

"We do."

"Then why would he get a tattoo for you? That doesn't make any sense."

Hannah shrugs uneasily, but I can't help feeling she's not as puzzled by the notion as I am. "Dare is methodical. I don't know what it is, but he has a reason. It *was* originally Anae's nickname for me, so he knew that tattoo would make her think of me."

"You seriously think he got a tattoo permanently inked into his skin just to incite Anae's wrath against you?"

"It wouldn't be the craziest thing he's ever done."

That's true.

"It could be something else, though," she adds. "Something more personal."

"Like what?"

She looks over at me. "You'll think I'm crazy if I tell you."

"I already think everyone involved with Dare is crazy," I tell her lightly. "Might as well share."

She fidgets with her fingers, looking at them instead of me. "I think Dare might become a serial killer."

My eyes widen and my heart sinks. Whatever I expected her to say, it was *not* that. "What?"

Her haunted gaze darts to mine. "I've had a lot of sleepless nights to think about this, and I think what he pulled last year with Aubrey was his trial run. He got to plan and almost execute a murder to evaluate his performance, see what he nailed and what he needed to improve upon."

"Hannah..." I trail off uneasily.

"I know it sounds crazy, but I have this weird connection with him. I don't know what it is, but it's like I can see him clearly and he fogs everyone else. You know how Harry Potter and Voldemort were linked? It's kinda like that."

"He's your Voldemort," I repeat flatly.

She shrugs. "Maybe. All I know is I can see things he doesn't want me to, things other people don't notice. People see him as such a mystery, but he's not to me. Not really. I can see the moves he makes pretty clearly. I can see through his bullshit." She pauses. "And sometimes I think I can feel his intentions, and sometimes those intentions..."

I wait, but she just sits there unwilling to verbalize whatever she's thinking. "Come on," I say, my eyes widening. "You can't leave me hanging like that."

Her gaze is so solemn it scares me. "I think he's going to kill me, Parker."

My heart nearly stops.

I shake my head without thought—a denial, a refusal to accept what she's saying. I mean, it's objectively crazy to predict something like that. Yeah, Dare is dangerous, but...

"I feel it," she says softly.

Dread dances down my spine. I wish I could dismiss this as paranoia or her being dramatic, but Hannah has never been one to overreact. And I guess after the stuff he pulled last year, it's not such a stretch to imagine him murdering someone.

It's certainly not a stretch to imagine if he *were* capable of murder, Hannah would be his chosen target.

"Is that what he threatened to do?" I ask softly.

She shakes her head. "No. But he didn't hate me as much then as he did by the end. Realistically, he'd probably even do that first. I think some part of him wanted to. I've had dreams about it." She looks down. "But I think he lied to Aubrey about needing her to cover for him to keep him out of jail. I think he only wanted Anae locked up for as long as he and Aubrey were around. It seems pretty convenient that she would be locked up only until they were gone, doesn't it? I think he *wanted* her out this year so he could sic her on me."

"How could he have possibly predicted she would even be willing to do anything for him? If some guy got my ass locked up in a mental institution for a year, I'd want his dick on a skewer roasting over an open flame."

Hannah smiles without humor. "He didn't leave it to chance. He tossed her a couple of bones. You heard Anae. Whether I'm right and he did or not, she's convinced herself he worked out that deal so she wouldn't spend much time locked up. The picture at prom made it feel like he was still on her side, and I was their common enemy. Even the crown tattoo. Maybe Anae's right and it is for her, but even if it isn't, he may have meant for her to think it is. Not blocking her so she could creep on his profile. He left enough openings for her to grasp onto and imagine he's still interested in playing with her. He's not into her romantically, but he could definitely be using her and stringing her along. Turning the queen into his pawn. Playing with her until she's no longer of use to him."

"That seems like a dangerous move when she just tried to kill his girlfriend last year."

"I know. I don't know what he's thinking. Looking at the pictures, it doesn't seem like there's any weight to Anae's hope that he's bored with Aubrey, but Dare is also very aware of the importance of appearances. She told me last year he strategically liked and posted things on social media to portray things in a certain light because he was lining things up to look that way after the kidnapping. If he wants to come off as the loving, devoted boyfriend and then his lunatic ex—who already tried to kill her once—comes back to finish the job? I mean, it's absolutely believable, and he looks totally innocent. Only Anae would go down for it. His hands would be completely clean this time. And if she tried to defend herself saying crazy things like 'he wanted me to find breadcrumbs in his social media posts!' she would look like a raving lunatic, even if it's actually what happened."

"Yikes. That's diabolical, Hannah."

"And maybe that's not why, maybe he only wants Anae out to torture me and he just thinks he can control the chaos and keep Aubrey safe, but he's definitely siccing her on me. There's no other reason for him to do these things."

"But what's his end game?"

"I don't know. I feel like he wants to kill me himself, but maybe he knows Aubrey would never forgive him, so he's trying to outsource the job? The feeling isn't a conveniently shared google doc; I can't read his mind, I just have this sense that he wants to kill me. And I have these horrific dreams." She shakes her head, probably not wanting to think about them right before we go to sleep. "I don't know, Parker. But I know there's violence in him, and I don't think we've seen the worst of it yet. I think he's capable of truly catastrophic damage, and I really don't feel like he's done with me."

"Well, if you seriously think he would kill you, that's even more incentive to stay out of it. I'm serious, Hannah. Just let him be gone. Block *him*. Block her if you have to. Sever all contact and just move on with your life. Maybe then he'll... back off."

"I've thought about it, but... I'm afraid he could hurt her, too. Aubrey believes him when he says he'd never hurt her, but I don't. I think he lies to her. She doesn't believe he does, but I don't trust him. You've never encountered him. You don't understand how scary he can be, how *remorseless* he is. He isn't a normal guy, Parker. He does not have the limits a typical person has."

This all makes me feel sick. The idea of anyone hurting Hannah literally makes me nauseous. "There has to be something we can do. He has done so much illegal shit. Isn't there something we can nail him for?"

Hannah shakes her head sadly. "Aubrey would have to testify against him, and she'd never do it."

"Maybe I could talk to Hayden and get some ideas." I frown. "Oh. Never mind. Hayden is Dare's lawyer, he can't help."

"Anae could testify, but she wouldn't do it, either. He inspires this weird, boundless loyalty in his lovers even though I don't believe he has any to them. It's wild, but he's very persuasive. It's like he substitutes their reality with his own doctored version of it. He made a comment once about how he makes people sick. I don't know, maybe it was more than his ego talking. Maybe he *does* corrupt people, but that just makes me even more scared for Aubrey. I love her to death, but she doesn't have a strong enough mind to keep him out without help. Even with my help, I couldn't get her to turn on him. Maybe I could have if I could have gotten her away from him for a while, but any clarity I give her, he fogs right back up as soon as he sees her again, and now they live together. There's no way I can get a good enough grip on her, and there's no way anyone else will, either. He won't let her have any other friends. He keeps her isolated so no one else can get close enough to see what I saw and try to help her."

I shake my head. "He is so toxic. I know you care about Aubrey, but you *have* to stay out of it, Hannah. I love *you*, and if this bastard murders you, I'll have to go all Veronica Mars on his ass. It will really disrupt my future plans."

She cracks a little smile. "I'm so sorry to be such an inconvenience."

I nod with playful solemnity. "I appreciate that."

Hannah sighs. "I guess we should try to get some sleep."

"I'm sure we'll both have amazing dreams now," I say sarcastically.

"Sorry," she says sheepishly.

CHAPTER 13

PARKER

AS SOON AS I step through the front door of the Atwater mansion, I can tell something is wrong.

My mind goes to all the worst places, but I tell myself Mom would have reached out to me if something truly catastrophic had happened.

I look for Mom and Hayden out by the pool and in all the communal areas, but I don't find them. I'm hesitant to check their bedroom, but since the door is closed, I knock to see if anyone answers.

Hayden's voice calls back, "Who is it?"

"It's Parker," I answer uncertainly.

A moment later, the door opens.

Mom's eyes are puffy, confirming the bad vibes in the house.

My stomach sinks. "What's wrong?"

Mom hugs me, her tone wobbly when she asks, "Why didn't you come home last night?"

I'm confused because I texted her to tell her I was staying over at Hannah's to help her clean up after the party. Since it would be late, I told her it made the most sense to just sleep there and come home in the morning.

My story was airtight. There's no way she should have suspected it wasn't true.

She looks me over like she doesn't believe me, and she needs to take stock of my well-being herself.

"I'm fine," I assure her.

Hayden approaches us, putting a grounding hand on Mom's shoulder. "I told you she was fine."

Mom shakes her head, her nose red. "You don't have maternal instincts. Men don't know anything."

I barely manage to bite back a burst of laughter.

Then Mom says, "I think we should go stay at the old house for a week or two. Moving in was too much all at once. We should have taken this slower."

I am no longer amused.

On one hand, I would really *like* to go back to our old house. Yeah, the Atwater place is bigger and it comes with cool stuff and a part-time staff, but I preferred the place that felt like home.

Hayden represents the other hand when he objects. "Gemma, that isn't necessary. I told you, I will do whatever it takes to keep Parker safe. She was at her friend's house. There's nothing more to it. You're sensitive about this, sweetheart," he says, turning her toward him, "because of what Landon pulled over the summer. I completely understand, but it has made you hypervigilant. You're seeing danger where none exists. If Parker felt unsafe in this house, she would tell us." His gaze flickers to me. "Wouldn't you, Parker?"

I swallow and nod. I hate lying to my mom. We didn't have this kind of relationship before. Sure, there was stuff I didn't tell her, but it wasn't on this level, where every single day of my life was covered by a blanket of deception.

Mom shakes her head, looking away from me. "I have to get

ready for work, but we need to talk just the two of us when I get home."

I nod, feeling about three inches tall as I turn and head down the hall toward my bedroom.

I'm not in there for long before there's a knock on my door. I tense up, but then he says, "It's Hayden."

I ease open the door and peer out, still a bit uncertain.

"You don't have plans tonight, do you?"

I shake my head.

He nods like that's the answer he hoped for. "Good. Don't make any. I have to make a quick phone call, but would you mind meeting me downstairs in my study? We need to talk."

IT HAS ONLY BEEN a week since I last stepped foot into this room, but it feels like longer.

Our box of photo albums has been unpacked, but I don't know where they've been moved to.

I consider having to repack all the things we just finished unpacking, but that's not the worst part of a proposed move home.

Before I can ponder that any further, Hayden enters the room behind me. I turn, startled by his presence, even though I was expecting him. He's wearing a nice suit like he would on a workday. I don't know if he went in this morning, or if he's planning to go in now that Mom's at work.

He flashes me a faint smile in passing, then approaches his mahogany desk. I follow him and take a seat in one of the chairs across from it.

"How are you doing?" he asks seriously.

"Um, good."

I fidget with the hem of yesterday's dress, trying to clear my mind of the memory of his son tugging it up and sliding his hand down the front of my panties just last night.

"I know this has probably been a difficult week for you. We all knew this would be an adjustment. I just wanted to check in, see where you're at, how you're feeling."

I don't know what to say. I'm not even completely sure what he's asking, and I have a rocking, fluttery feeling in my tummy at the prospect of having to tell more lies.

"Honestly," he adds, as if he can hear my intentions. "You don't have to bullshit me. I won't tell your mom. This conversation is... consider it attorney-client privilege," he says a bit dryly.

I crack a smile. "Don't I have to give you a dollar for that?"

He reciprocates the smile, but it's a calculated action to get me where he wants me.

I don't mind. I know Hayden better now than I did last time he pulled me aside for one of these. I know it's like Landon said—he's driven and determined to have his way, and currently, I am one of the tools at his disposal. Arguably one of the most effective if what he wants is to convince my mom not to leave.

We want the same thing, and he's just slicing through the bullshit to communicate that.

I feel my shoulders relax as I ease back a bit in the chair. "Honestly? I'm a bit overwhelmed."

Hayden nods, his intelligent eyes locked on me. Making notes, calculating. Waiting for more data.

"I... don't want to move back home. I mean, some part of me does, but we can't. If we have to move out after a single week of living here, I think that would be catastrophic. I don't know how easy it would be to ever get her back here."

Hayden nods, his expression grim. "Yes, that was my thought as well. That's very early to fail. Makes the whole thing seem like it was a bad idea—and not one you'd reconsider later."

To be fair, it was.

I don't say that.

Instead, I clear my throat and consider how to approach the rest.

He helps me along by asking a question to guide me. "How are things with Landon?"

"He's challenging," I say, quite diplomatically, if I do say so myself.

"Yes," Hayden agrees dryly. "But has he done anything to make you feel unsafe?"

"His existence makes me feel unsafe," I say, more honest than I expected to be with his father. "But I'm managing it."

"Did he do anything to upset you at the party last night?"

I drop my gaze, my heart kicking up a few speeds. Hayden may be requesting honesty, but I don't see how I could be *that* honest. There are so many layers to it. Now, it's not even as simple as, "yeah, the jerk pounces on me every chance he gets so I have to do an increasingly difficult sequence of diligence to ensure he never gets me alone—and it has only been *one week*."

Even if he only knew Landon kissed me last night, wouldn't he be extremely weirded out? I mean, he is marrying my mother. I can't physically bring myself to speak the word, but if all goes according to plan, Landon *will* become my stepbrother at the end of all this.

This is so fucked up.

I haven't allowed myself to think it that clearly before, and I don't like it.

But it is what I signed up for, and it's inevitable if Mom and Hayden are going to be married.

Sighing, I say, "Wherefore art thou Hayden Atwater?"

His lips tug up. "I'm afraid a rose by any other name would still be Landon's father. The party," he nudges.

I don't want to talk about the party. I'm tired just thinking about it, and there's no way to admit what happened even under Hayden's veil of confidence. Something like *that* he would have to tell my mom, jokes about attorney-client privilege aside.

"He had a few drinks at the party," I admit reluctantly, my cheeks instantly heating with the sense of being a total narc. "Please don't tell him I told you that. You can't punish him. I know he's not allowed," I add quickly, "but if he thinks I'm tattling to you, that will just make things worse for me."

Hayden nods his understanding. "I assumed as much when Malek texted that he'd just bring him home in the morning."

"Obviously, when he drinks, he turns into red kryptonite Clark and does dumb shit, so he did some dumb shit, but I'd prefer not to get into the specifics. The point is... yes, last night was a bit rough."

His head continues to nod almost absently, his gaze fixed on a spot across the room as he considers it. "Your mom could sense it. It was the most peculiar thing. She wasn't there, she had no reason to believe..."

I nod, too. "She's been really dialed in since the break-in. I think it's her guilt for missing all the calls and texts. She feels like she should have sensed something was wrong and gotten there earlier, but she was distracted."

"By me," he says grimly.

"Yes."

Hayden sighs, pinching the bridge of his nose. After a moment, he says, "Parker, I understand your desire to shield your mother. I know what happened over the summer was very traumatizing for both of you. But I'm going to be as clear as I can be: if anything like that happens to you again, under my roof, your mother will *never* forgive me."

I nod grimly, briefly glancing at my lap before returning my gaze to him. "I know. I'm doing my best here. I'm on your team, I'm just... Your son isn't," I say honestly. "He's working against me every step of the way."

"Landon and I have a complicated relationship. Ever since his mother died..." He trails off, then restarts and summarizes in a firm way that urges not to pry. "I probably could have handled it better."

I shrug one shoulder with awkward sympathy. "It's a difficult situation to navigate. I'm sure you never thought you would have to handle something like that when he was so young."

"No. And a loss like that isn't something I intend to endure again in my lifetime, so hopefully it's nothing I have to muddle my way through again. But it happened, the damage is done. Obviously, it runs very deep, and to be honest," he sighs, "I don't have a single clue how to fix it. He's so angry, so closed off. He doesn't *want* to repair the relationship, and he certainly doesn't want me to marry your mother. Historically, when Landon doesn't want something, there isn't any length he'll avoid if it means getting his way. Historically, I don't *let* things get in my way, but..."

"He's your son. Least ideal opponent because he's the one you can't strike back at."

He nods grimly. "Precisely."

I'm quiet for a moment, unsure he'll appreciate my two cents, but I decide it can't hurt to give it. "I think Landon has a lot of hurt buried underneath all that anger. I think maybe he doesn't feel... supported by you, or included. Maybe it's more... he doesn't feel like you *want* him here. And I get it, because the person he has become is very difficult, and sometimes even dangerous. You're obviously right to try to protect me from harm, and it's *his fault* he became the harm. He didn't have to give in to all his worst impulses, he could have put effort into rising above it, but assigning blame isn't going to fix anything here. It doesn't matter who is at fault for what. I can say with absolute certainty that he does not see me or my mom as 'part of the family' and for any of this to work, it seems crucial we fix that. I assure you, I am exhibiting the patience of an absolute saint in my efforts to push things that way, but I can't do this alone. I can't fix him. There's too much damage, and I didn't cause any of it."

"I did make him go to therapy when his mother first passed, but it didn't do any good. He wouldn't say a word to her."

That doesn't surprise me.

"Now, with the drinking." He shakes his head. "I don't know. I don't know if he needs rehab. I don't know what he needs."

"I don't either, but as long as we care, that's a step in the right direction, isn't it?"

Hayden's gaze shifts back to me.

"Why don't we start with something easy? I thought family dinner might be that, but it wasn't. We should stay in this time. Mom and I have always enjoyed having movie nights at home. We eat junk food and watch movies, and the best part is, nobody has to do much talking, but we're all together. Seems like it could be a good first step, and something Landon might actually be able to get through without exploding or... running off and committing various lowkey crimes."

Hayden cracks a smile. "Sounds inexpensive. I like it."

I nod, initially caught up in the approval of my plan, but that quickly wears off when I realize I'll have to watch a movie with Landon in front of both of our parents, and there are probably a lot of ways that can go wrong.

But Hayden is already set on a course, so he sits forward. "We'll do it tomorrow." He opens his desk drawer, very businesslike, and extracts a set of keys. He holds them out for me.

Wide-eyed, I put my hand out, and he gives them to me. "What is this?" I ask cautiously.

"The keys to your new car. I bought you the Prius you looked at with your mother. Very highly rated. Excellent choice."

"Um... Hayden, you didn't have to buy me a car."

He waves me off, as if he bought me a new purse or something. "You needed one. Now you have one. I won't be able to get you a reserved spot at the school as those have already been claimed for the year, unfortunately. If it's important to you, I can make some calls, but it may take a little time to free one up."

I shake my head. "It's not. Thank you, but... I can park in the lot like everyone else."

"If your mother asks..."

"I will tell her you offered."

A perfunctory nod. I try to bite back a faint smile, but I fail.

"I think you could both use a reset and a little break from the house. I've booked you a room at a spa resort on the beach for the night. Gemma wants to leave, and the best thing is to let her so she doesn't dig in, but not a move, just a break. You'll have a nice dinner on a beautiful beachfront terrace, enjoy spa treatments to relax your bodies; have a little girl time, maybe hit the beach. Just relax and unwind, that way tomorrow you're both fresh and ready for our movie night. Maybe once your mom has had more one-on-one time with you like she did before you guys moved in, she will feel better about things."

"I think that sounds lovely, Hayden. Thank you."

"I believe the dealership closes early today, but I had the keys delivered so we could pick it up, anyway. As soon as your mom gets off work, I'll give you girls a ride to pick up the car, and you can drive that to the spa. I'd prefer giving both of you a full day off from Landon, so if you wouldn't mind packing an overnight bag for her while she's gone..."

"Sure, I can do that."

"Perfect. Pack one for yourself as well, and we'll meet her at the door and whisk her off as soon as she pulls in."

"Okay. Sounds good."

"I appreciate your help with all this, Parker. And your discretion. I know we both want to protect your mother, but please make sure you're taking care of yourself as well. If you ever need *anything*, all you have to do is ask. I don't ever want you to feel that you're alone in this. Like you said, we're on the same team, and we both seem to have a pretty realistic idea of what we're up against."

You can say that again.

"And thank you for the movie night suggestion. If you ever have any more ideas about how to make this merger go any easier, feel free to share. I'm always happy to have your input."

I meet his gaze, amused. "It may help not to refer to this as a merger when you're talking to my mom."

"Of course." He smiles faintly. "But right now, I'm talking to you."

HAYDEN BOOKED us a junior suite at the Baymont Beach Resort, which is a fancy way of saying he booked us a whole apartment.

I don't know what a step up from a junior suite is because this room is incredible.

There's a stocked bar, a living room, a dining area inside and another one out on the balcony. Every room has a view of the ocean, and with the sliding doors open, you can hear the waves hitting the shore and feel the salty ocean breeze against your skin.

This place is perfect.

"Can we live here?" I joke to Mom, standing on the balcony and watching the ocean.

Mom slides her arm around my shoulder and leans her head against mine. "I wish. This is the first time I've felt like I could breathe since you left for that party last night." She looks over at me, her gaze probing, but her tone gentle. "I just had a bad feeling."

I've had enough time to decompress, and Hayden was right; being here is helping. I don't feel stressed or stretched thin or even like I'm lying—even though I know I am—when I tell her, "The party was fine, Mom. Everything is fine."

"You'd tell me if it wasn't, right?"

"Of course."

It doesn't feel like a lie because, of course, I *would* tell her if there was something I couldn't handle.

Last night may have been a close call, but I handled it.

And besides, I did talk to one adult about it. Just not her.

Mom has always been a touch overprotective, but Hayden is more willing to trust my judgement. He's willing to actually listen to what I think and let me take the chances I feel comfortable with.

Mom is much more risk averse.

I don't think she'd like hearing that I'd rather talk about this stuff with him. She may be marrying the guy, but I'm practically full grown. I don't think she considered that she'd have to share parenting responsibilities with him.

"Listen, I know living with Landon isn't the easiest thing in the world. We knew it wouldn't be," I remind her. "But we resolved to be open-minded about it, and leaving after one week would not be giving it a real shot."

"Open-minded, yes. But only up to the point that you're in any kind of danger. That shuts it all right down."

"I'm not in any danger, Mom. I have it under control."

Mom gives me a knowing look as she shakes her head. "Honey, I know you think you do, but in the week we've been here, all I've seen is that Landon is a loose cannon. I'm not going to wait for him to blow you up to leave. The way Hayden talked about it, I expected Landon to at least try in the beginning to be civil, but he has made no effort whatsoever. If this is him on his best behavior, I do not want to see his worst—and I certainly don't want *you* to see it."

I nod. "I agree that he isn't trying to make this any easier on us, but I don't think it's easy on him, either. It's not your fault, but I do think his dad moving some woman he doesn't know into the house... I think it bothers him."

Mom doesn't say anything, so I take that as progress.

"I told Hayden that I think we should do some stuff together."

"Like family dinner?" she asks dryly.

"Family dinner didn't go to plan," I acknowledge. "I suggested a movie night. Tomorrow when we go home. Something normal families do, where there is no access to alcohol—stolen or otherwise—and we can just do something together that doesn't crash and burn. That's what we need. One successful interaction. We need a win. Maybe if Landon can have a successful experience in this new family unit and realize it's not all bad and something he needs to destroy... maybe he'll stop being such an asshole. Maybe then *he* will be more open-minded. But the first step is giving him a successful family event. Giving *all of us* a successful family event."

Mom regards me skeptically. "And you think movie night will do it?"

I shrug. "It can't hurt that we're doing something where we're all in the same room, but not even talking through most of it. Seems like there will be less opportunity for things to go wrong."

Mom cracks a smile. "How hope-forming. As long as we all stay quiet, we might be able to get along."

"After this, we'll try charades," I joke.

"Maybe we can all attend mime school together," she suggests primly.

"Family naps. Who doesn't love a good nap?"

Mom smiles, and I can tell from the softness on her face I've convinced her. "All right. If you're sure you're comfortable, and you *promise me* you will tell me if that changes."

I have to swallow down the lump that forms in my throat. Bending the truth is one thing, breaking a promise feels like another.

But I tell myself there's a lot of wiggle room in the language here. My comfort level is open to interpretation, isn't it? Comfortable compared to what? Sleeping on a bed of nails? Yes, I'm totally comfortable compared to that.

I know it's a loophole, but I also know what I can handle, and so far, I've handled Landon just fine on my own. Is it a low-risk system? No. Is there a probability of things getting much worse? Sure.

But there's also a chance they get better, and I truly believe what I've said to her. I truly believe a success could nudge Landon in a different direction. We haven't had time or the opportunity (to be fair, because he has refused to give us the opportunity) to show him why us all living together could be a good experience for him.

Well, aside from him having more opportunities to torture

me, but my hope is that will die down once he realizes us all being a family together isn't the worst thing that could have happened to him.

"Of course I would," I tell her. I don't want to linger on this point too long since it makes me feel guilty, so I take one last look at the ocean and sigh. "We should probably head downstairs now. I want to try the assortment of weird spa waters before our massages."

"I've never understood putting fruit in water. Water is delicious as is, there's just no need for it."

"Especially when the cup's packed full of ice. Mmm."

Mom wraps an arm around my shoulders and gives me a little hug, then we head back inside so we can get ready for our evening of pampering.

"TRY NOT to do anything stupid this time."

I look over at my cousin, smiling crookedly as he gives me advice he knows I'm not going to take. "Try not to get caught, you mean."

Malek shakes his head. "I will never understand what you see in that girl."

"That's why we get along so well," I half-joke as I open the car door and let myself out of his gleaming white Aperta. The door opens out and up, so I raise my hand in a half-assed wave goodbye before pushing the door closed.

He doesn't wait for me to make it up the driveway. I hear him take off down the road behind me as I sling my duffel bag over my shoulder and make my way up the driveway toward the house.

I'm not surprised when I smell food cooking as soon as I open the door. It's around dinnertime, and I'm sure Dad and his new little family are hyped to hang out.

I roll my eyes at my own thoughts as I start to take the first set of stairs on the right so I don't have to deal with all that, but I stop when I hear Antonia call out for me.

Frowning, I make my way to the kitchen.

"There you are," she says, flashing me a warm smile. "Your father wanted me to catch you when you came in. I'll only be making dinner for you tonight, so I'm making your favorite."

"I'm eating alone?"

"Your father's going out for the evening. He'd like to speak with you in his study before he leaves."

Scowling, I ask, "Where are the girls?"

Antonia shrugs. "I don't know. Your father asked if I could come in and I was free, so here I am."

Gemma's car is in the driveway, so I expected them to be here. I suppose Parker could still be hiding out at Hannah's, but something definitely feels off.

Dad's study door is closed. I bang on it before I walk in, so he's looking up when I enter, his expression grim.

"What's going on? Gemma get sick of cooking already? Why's Antonia here on a Saturday?"

Dad motions for me to sit in the seat across from his desk.

I've always hated this fucking seat.

Even as a kid, he'd bring me to his office to scold me when he was the one doing the scolding. Mom had a different approach. Less confrontational. I preferred her handling things like this.

I sit down because I want to know what's going on, but I drop my duffel with a loud thunk and cross my arms over my chest so he knows I'm not happy to be here.

I wait for him to say something, but he just sits there, watching me.

"What?" I snap.

"You've made it very clear you don't want the girls living here. I just thought I should congratulate you on getting your way yet again. Gemma has decided that moving in here was a mistake, and she and Parker should move back into their old house."

My heart stops beating for a second. I don't want to look too fucking alarmed, but… "It's been one week."

"Yep." He nods grimly.

"What did Parker say I did?"

His gaze is already cool, but it drops several degrees when I ask that. "Parker didn't tell anybody you did anything to her. Should she have?"

"Then why are they leaving?"

"You know why they're leaving. In fact, I would say you probably have a more accurate idea than I do. Anyway, it's as good as done. I just thought you should know."

"So, what? The engagement's off? Gemma's car is still parked outside."

"It was an emotional day. Gemma and Parker both needed a breather. I sent them to a spa resort for the night because I'm trying to change Gemma's mind, but I don't think I'll be able to. Gemma is a sweet, confrontation-hating soul, but there is nothing she wouldn't do to protect her daughter. If that means not marrying me, then… that's what it means."

For all his coolness, the temperature in the room seems to be rising judging from the heat beneath my skin. "So, what? You're going to let her go, just like that? I thought this dancer chick was the next coming of Christ as far as you're concerned. You proposed after like two minutes, and now you're just going to let her move out and be done?"

"Well, obviously it's not what I want, Landon, but it's not as if I can keep her captive," he says dryly.

Sounds like quitter talk to me, but I don't say that.

"I tried reassuring her, but she doesn't believe me. I had to make a lot of hollow promises to get her to move in to begin with, and I didn't follow through, so I don't have much leverage. You've rejected every attempt made to bring you into the fold, and you've made trouble every chance you got. I can't tell her things will get better. She doesn't believe me anymore. What else would you have me do?" he asks, sounding like he's all but given up already.

Un-fucking-believable.

"When did you turn into such a pussy?" I ask him. His eyes flash, but I don't give him a chance to respond. "I, personally, don't give a fuck about Gemma, but if you like her enough to *marry her* after years of not even dating, I would assume you fucking do. So, you do whatever you have to do to keep her here. Burn her fucking house down. Then she doesn't have anything to go back to."

Dad stares at me. "That's illegal."

I roll my eyes. "Right, sorry. Hire someone *else* to burn her fucking house down. Make sure you're with her so she knows it wasn't you."

Despite himself, a faint smile tugs at his lips. "I suppose that's one way of doing things—if I'm not worried about starting a wildfire."

"I refuse to believe that *you* can't control a fucking ballerina. We're talking about the same woman, right? About five feet tall, weighs three pounds, has the intimidation factor of a fucking country mouse? I swear I saw a spider walk in front of her and do a little dance because it was so unafraid."

Dad cracks a smile. "Her gentleness is one of my favorite things about her."

"So, use it. You're far from gentle. Unleash the beast. What the fuck are you waiting for?"

"I suppose there are a couple of things I haven't tried."

"So try them," I say, wide-eyed. "Jesus Christ. It's not rocket science."

As soon as the words are out, I hear them.

I look at him sitting there, not looking one bit panicked for a man supposedly on the brink of losing his newest high-value prize.

He caught me off-guard and I had no reason to suspect him of pulling any of the Machiavellian bulltshit he's pulled in the past, but now I'm realizing... the suit's not rumpled. Not a hair out of place. No obvious signs of distress like I would expect if he actually thought for one second his bride-to-be was walking out on him.

"They're not leaving."

He doesn't answer, just continues to watch me.

"You would have come up with something. Your first move isn't to accept defeat and move on."

His lips curve up faintly.

I shake my head, realizing I walked right into a fucking trap. "You just wanted to see if I'd care."

"I won't lie, I'm relieved to see you do."

Now I'm pissed. "Yeah, I bet you fucking are."

"It wasn't entirely a drill," he says, dropping his sad sack act and sitting forward, steepling his hands atop his desk. "Gemma *did* tell me earlier today she wanted to move out. It took some work, but Parker and I managed to talk her down. *This time.* But this *is* how she feels, Landon. We can't continue as we have this week. If we do, I promise you, even my best efforts won't keep them here."

I glare at him, arms still crossed.

"If we're going to convince them to stay, I need your help."

He seems genuine. I can't remember the last time my dad asked for my help with anything. I guess he doesn't expect I'd give it to him, but he's already done his manipulative bullshit to make sure we have a common interest.

"Unless you truly want Parker and her mother to move out in the next week or two, you have to start making more of an effort."

"What I'm hearing is, burn their old house down so they don't have a choice and they have to stay."

He stares at me flatly, but, realizing I may be serious, his tone turns firm. "I am absolutely not telling you to do that."

"I don't know, sounds like something a guy would say to keep his hands clean." I wink at him. "Don't worry. I *won't do it.*"

"Landon."

I can't help laughing a little. "I won't burn the fucking house down. Yet. But you better keep Gemma happy, because the thought's crossed my mind now, so..."

He gazes at me, still unimpressed, but he continues on. "Parker suggested we do something as a family."

"Yeah, that went well last time."

His gaze narrows on me. "Yes, and whose fault was that?"

I roll my eyes.

"She wants to do a movie night this time. The girls won't be home tonight, they're spending the night at the resort so they can recharge and come home fresh, but I need you to make an effort tomorrow, Landon. Please be nice to Gemma. Watch the movie with us, and then you can go to your room and ignore us if you want, but I need for Gemma to have a good experience. Something to renew her hope that this can all work out. I'm not asking you to make her a friendship bracelet and braid her hair, but please, for one night, do not make trouble."

I smirk as I lean forward and grab my duffel, then I stand. "Don't worry. I'll make sure I'm on my best behavior."

My sarcastic tone must not offer him enough reassurance, because as I head for the door, he says, "I hope so. There's a lot at stake here, Landon, and some damage can't be undone."

I can't help but laugh bitterly at *him* telling *me* that. "Yeah, Dad. I know."

CHAPTER 15

PARKER

ONCE THE POPCORN is salted and evenly distributed between two bowls, the candy open and waiting on the coffee table, and a bevy of beverages lined up and waiting for our greedy consumption, we are finally ready for family movie night to begin.

Well, mostly.

Landon isn't here.

He was supposed to be, of course.

His attendance was the single most important part of family movie night.

But we've waited twenty minutes past when the movie was supposed to start, and he still isn't here.

I wish I could say I'm surprised.

Mom isn't surprised, either, but she isn't as disappointed as Hayden and I are. Now we can all have a relaxing night and not have to worry about Landon's antics.

"What are we watching?" I ask, sinking back into the comfy couch cushions with my green bowl of popcorn.

Mom and Hayden are on the middle couch together with their blue bowl. "I'm not sure yet," Mom says, glancing at Hayden.

Hayden checks his phone one more time, then sighs. "I hadn't decided yet. I was going to ask Landon what he wanted to watch. Since it's just us, I suppose you girls will have to weigh in. I've narrowed it down to *Goodfellas* or *The Departed*."

"Oh, good choices," Mom says, impressed.

I grab a couple of pieces of popcorn. "I've heard of the first, but not that second one."

"Really?" Hayden asks, eyebrows rising. "Well, that's what we're watching, then. I have to educate you."

"What's it about?"

"Illegal things," Mom answers.

"Don't get enough of that at work, huh?" I tease.

"I'm a man of many interests. Illicit activities happen to be among them."

Like father, like son, I guess.

I smile faintly as Hayden fires up the massive television in the living room. "I still think we should do this in the media room. That's literally what it's for," he says.

That was the original plan, but we were waiting for Landon downstairs on the couch. We waited so long, Mom suggested we just stay down here to watch the movie.

"It's weird that you have a movie theater in your house," Mom states. "If we can go to the movies here, why do we ever need to actually *go* to the movies again? It's supposed to be a special outing. Family movie nights should take place in the living room."

"But the media room has surround sound and a bigger TV."

"And comfy theater recliners," I add, on Hayden's side in this matter.

"And it's dark," Hayden says. "Movies are better in the dark."

"We can turn the lights off in the living room," Mom says

primly, unwilling to budge. "Family movie night is happening here, whether you two gang up on me or not."

Hayden sighs dramatically. I'm smiling at the fun novelty of family bickering, but my smile drops and my heart falls when I hear the front door open and close.

There's only one person that can be.

"Nice of you to finally show up," Hayden remarks dryly.

"Yup," Landon answers succinctly, glancing at the TV and seeing it turned on. "Being nice. It's what I'm known for."

"We were just about to pick a movie."

"And then watch it with all the lights on, like psychopaths?"

Hayden cracks a smile. "I was just about to get up and turn the lights off, actually. You can do it since you're still standing."

Landon hits the light and suddenly the room is much darker. There's still a bit of light sneaking in from the kitchen around the corner and coming in through the wall of windows to our right. Hayden presses a button on the control and a faint mechanical sound snags my attention. I turn my head and watch blinds automatically lower to block out the moonlight and make this room darker.

I usually prefer a dark room when I'm watching movies, too, but due to every interaction we've ever had in one, being in a dark room with Landon unsettles me.

I tell myself it will be okay because our parents are in this one with us, but when the distance between us shrinks, my lungs seem to as well.

He saunters over and eyes up the empty couch we saved for him. Instead of taking a seat on it, he drops onto the couch right beside *me*.

My stomach rocks with nerves, but I try to keep the apprehension off my face as I sit up straighter. "Um... What are you doing?"

"Family movie night, apparently," he says, his tone mocking. "I'm surprised you don't know that. It was your idea, wasn't it?"

"There's a whole empty couch right over there," I point out, gesturing to the seat we saved for him.

"Ah, but you have the popcorn."

I look back at him, inches away from me, and he smiles, his green eyes dancing with mischief.

He reaches past me, deliberately brushing my arm, and grabs a few pieces of popcorn to stuff into his mouth.

"Yummy," he says, just to taunt me.

My heart sinks when I catch the scent of alcohol on his breath.

Oh no.

Any hope I had of this going well tries hard to fly out the window, but I grab a hammer and nails and anchor as many fragments as I can catch to the ground.

This *has* to go well. It has to. I'm running out of chances to change Mom's mind about him.

"Fine," I say, as if unperturbed. "I couldn't have eaten all this, anyway. Have as much as you'd like."

"Oh, I will," he assures me, grabbing another greedy handful.

I have a bad feeling he isn't talking about popcorn.

Hayden tries to steer this potential wreck back on course. "I guess we'll stick with *The Departed*, then."

"Works for me," Landon says.

I can feel our parents watching to make sure I'm okay with him sitting here, so I try to ignore the discomfort of having him so close and turn back to face the television.

It is *impossible.*

I can already feel him shifting and moving just to make me nervous that he's getting too close. I think about giving him the popcorn so he won't have to keep reaching for it, but Mom will know something's up if I don't have an appetite anymore. I've been talking about popcorn nonstop since we started getting stuff ready for movie night.

Hayden starts the movie, and Landon shifts his position so he can drape his arm over the back of the couch behind me.

My whole body tenses having his arm wrapped almost around me, but I keep telling myself he won't do anything crazy in front of our parents. He's crazy, but not *that* crazy.

Well, at least when he's sober, he's not that crazy.

Which he isn't right now.

It's fine. This is fine. Everything will be fine.

I try hard to believe it, but before the credits have even stopped flashing across the screen, I feel his fingers at the nape of my neck. Ever so lightly, he runs his fingertips across the sensitive spot, sending shivers straight down my spine.

I suck in a slow, steady breath, careful not to draw attention. Attempting subtlety, I shift my shoulder blades and my posture, trying to knock his hand away from me.

All that does is make him move his hand down my back.

His fingers move to my bra strap and he traces it down to the strip of fabric across my back. I try moving in different ways to get his hand off me without alerting our parents to what he's doing, but the bastard is shameless and gets his fingers underneath the clasp.

Before he can unhook it, I put the bowl on his lap and abruptly stand. "I just realized we didn't get Landon a drink. You seem thirsty," I say.

He smirks. "Do I? What a good girl you are, paying such close attention to my needs. How about a nice, cold glass of lemonade?"

He needs something cold, all right—maybe a shower.

"There's none in the fridge," I state since I just went to get some for dinner and noticed the pitcher was gone.

"Then make me some."

My hands curl into fists at my sides, but I can feel my mom about to jump in and I don't want her to. He already doesn't like her without a single good reason. It's not that big of a deal, just, you know, *horrifying* for my pride.

To take the sting out of it, I glance at Mom and Hayden. "Lemonade sounds good, actually. Anyone else want some?"

Hayden is watching his son warily. "Parker isn't your maid, Landon. How about some manners?"

He has weaponized the word please at this point, so I actually prefer never to hear him say it again. I expect him to since he's taunted me with it before, but when Landon looks back at me, he says, "Aw, shit. I wouldn't want to have bad manners. Want me to come to the kitchen with you and give you a hand?"

"No," I say flatly. "I think I can handle making lemonade on my own." My gaze flickers to Mom and Hayden. "I'll just be a minute."

While I'm whipping up a fresh pitcher of lemonade, I text Hannah to vent about Landon thinking I'm *his* personal Cinderella. I also keep an eye out to make sure he doesn't really come in here. He'd give me a hand, all right, but I don't think that hand would be anywhere I want it.

"Ugh, that sucks, I'm sorry," she texts back sympathetically.

"He showed up late and he has been drinking. He has no lack of audacity, and I'm kind of worried about it."

"As a responsible friend, I have to say this. Maybe you should tell your mom about what happened at the party."

I dismiss her suggestion without even considering it. "I can't do that. But it would make me feel better if I didn't have to worry about him slipping into my bedroom once this movie is over and our parents go to bed. Any chance you can sleep over since there's no school tomorrow?"

It takes her a minute to respond, so I grab two glasses out of the top cupboard.

Finally, she texts back, "I might be able to, but not until I'm done with my chores. And if I won't be here in the morning to make them breakfast, I'll need to make something tonight before I leave. Muffins or egg cups or something."

"Well, that's okay. We've just started The Departed anyway, so you have plenty of time."

I head back to the living room with my phone tucked in my pocket and two glasses of lemonade. I'm tempted to sit down on the empty couch, but I can see how anxious Mom is and I don't want her to think I'm uncomfortable just because I am.

When I sit down, I sit on the same couch Landon is on, but I sit a couple of cushions away so he can't keep touching me.

"Everyone good now?" Hayden asks.

Landon takes a sip of his lemonade. "Mm. Delicious." Then, just to taunt me, he says, "Thank you, Parker."

Just the sound of his voice saying something normal sets me on edge, so before we get into the movie, I seek to assure myself there will be sanctuary at the end of all this.

I draw out my phone and ask Mom, "Is it okay if Hannah comes over to spend the night after we watch the movie?"

"Oh. Well, sure, but it will be pretty late by then. This movie is two and a half hours long."

Of course it is.

"I know," I say, since it doesn't matter for my purposes. "She hasn't been sleeping well crammed on a twin bed up in the attic, and I haven't shown her my room here yet. I thought it would be nice to have her over tonight since there's no school tomorrow and she can sleep in, even if she only gets here in time to sleep."

Hayden frowns. "Why is she sleeping on a twin bed in an attic?"

"It's a long story."

"She messed around with her stepsister's boyfriend and got caught, so she punished her for it," Landon says.

My gaze flashes to him, my eyes wide and my skin suddenly hot with anger. "She did *not*. Where did you even hear that?"

Landon shrugs, popping a few more pieces of popcorn into his stupid mouth. "Everyone knows."

I guffaw in disbelief. "Oh, you mean like everyone knows I invited you over to my house and then called the cops to frame you for breaking in?"

He smirks, his eyes dancing with amusement. "Yeah, just like that."

I want to yell at him or dump the popcorn bowl on his head —something to make me feel better, but our parents are right here, so I have to rein in my temper and keep things friendly.

Turning back to Hayden, I say firmly, "She didn't do *anything* to get kicked out of her old room. She's the one I told you about before, she lives with Anae Richards. That's the stepsister Landon is referencing."

"Ah," he murmurs, looking much less excited. "Then I presume Chase Darington is the boyfriend in question."

"Yes, but that didn't happen. That's not a thing. She was friends with his girlfriend—not Anae, his new girlfriend that Anae hated. Like I said, it's a long story." I look at Mom. "So, she can spend the night?"

"Sure. I don't see why not."

Hayden waits for me to text Hannah and put my phone away, then he unpauses the movie.

The first half passes uneventfully. I get into the story and the characters, and Landon is far enough away that he can't touch me.

Then Landon gets up to hit the bathroom and we have to pause the movie. When he comes back, he sits closer to me on the couch, so getting up may have just been a ploy to move.

I don't care at that point. We're at a tense part of the movie and I can't worry about his proximity. I need to know what happens next.

"He's back. Unpause," I say impatiently, since both parents are looking over here to make sure everything is okay.

Hayden smirks. "I take it you're enjoying the movie?"

"You have excellent taste," I confirm. "Now, make with the clicking."

Hayden chuckles and unpauses the movie.

Landon pulls me back so my body is pressed against his on the couch, but I don't fight it because he probably wants me to. I don't want to feed him; I want to watch the damn movie.

Mercifully, he seems to be satisfied with our bodies making contact because he lets me enjoy the rest of the film without distractions.

I'm pumped when the movie ends. I want to scour Hayden's more experienced movie brain for other gems just like it so we can watch another one, but Mom yawns, and that reminds me they'll be going to bed soon.

"We should do this again next weekend," I propose, pulling my phone out so I can text Hannah and see if she's leaving soon.

"Definitely," Mom says with a smile.

"Hayden can pick the next movie, too," I say.

Hayden smirks. "We can do that. Saturday night?"

"Works for me." I look over at Landon.

He cocks an eyebrow. "I have to be present for this, too?"

"You do," I confirm, tucking my phone in my pocket as I stand. I collect Mom and Hayden's empty popcorn bowl and stack it in mine, then I do the same with our drink glasses so I can take all the dishes to the kitchen in one trip.

I rinse everything in the sink and unstack it, but when I turn around, I'm startled to find Landon holding a half-empty bag of Twizzlers and some of the other snacks we had out for the movie.

You're helping? nearly bursts out of me, but I hold it in and offer a much nicer, "Thank you for your help."

He drops the snacks on the counter without a word.

"Did you like the movie?" I ask, trying to keep things friendly.

He grabs a Ziploc bag out of the cupboard and puts the Twizzlers in it. "I've seen it before. I knew I liked it."

I grab the M&M box and tuck the tab in the little slot to close it. "Oh. Right, that makes sense. I suppose if your dad likes the movie…"

"What'd Hannah say?"

"She's on her way."

His mouth tugs up at the corners. "Of course she is." He shakes his head as he slides another bag closed. "I can't believe you called a chaperone."

Ignoring the implication, I reiterate the excuse I gave to Mom and Hayden. "Hannah hasn't seen my new room yet, and I thought—"

He cuts me off. "You can save the bullshit for someone who might believe it." He drops the bagged candy on the counter and turns toward me. On impulse, as he moves toward me, my eyes widen and I back away. "We both know why you want Hannah in your bed tonight."

I swallow, my gaze darting to the opening of the kitchen.

Our parents aren't there, but they could be any second. I

can't play his stupid intimidation games right now. The night may not have been a total success, but it wasn't a total failure, either. He could change all that right now.

I sidestep him, and thankfully, the kitchen is big enough that I have plenty of room to get around him.

It helps that he doesn't try to chase me.

My heart still pounds, my mind half-expecting him to grab me around the waist and yank me back against him, but then the doorbell rings, and relief floods my body.

Hannah's here.

"I got it," I call out cheerfully, quickly making my way to the door.

Hannah's waiting on the other side with her hair down and a large tote purse slung over her shoulder, likely with tomorrow's clothes inside.

"Hey," I greet her cheerfully. "Perfect timing."

"Movie just end?" she guesses as she steps inside. "I looked it up online and saw how long it was, so I tried to time my arrival right when it ended."

I nod. "We were just cleaning up. Have you ever seen the movie? It was really good."

"I have not."

"We'll have to watch it someday." I stop at the end of the cavernous hall since Mom and Hayden are standing in the living room. "Hannah, this is Landon's dad, Hayden Atwater. Hayden, this is my best friend, Hannah Dupont."

Hannah offers a friendly smile, and Hayden offers one back. "It's a pleasure to meet you, Hannah. I've already heard so much about you."

"Some of it was even true," I say lightly as Landon saunters out of the kitchen. Back to the parents, I say, "We're gonna go upstairs."

"Have fun," Mom says as I start up the stairs.

I hear Hannah's light footsteps behind me, but I hear Landon's heavier footfalls, too. I'm not worried about him following me up these stairs tonight even if he has been drinking because Hannah is between us, and I know he won't mess with her. It's only me he messes with.

CHAPTER 16
LANDON

"SO, how is it having a new stepsister?" Arden asks.

His tone is knowing and fucking obnoxious because he knows as well as I do that no matter what happens between her mom and my dad, I'll never see Parker as anything like a sister.

"Fantastic," I say sarcastically, tipping back my beer bottle and taking a swig. "For me, not so much for her."

Arden smirks. "I'll bet. She's got a lot of sass. Needs someone to show her how to use that mouth."

My eyes flash and I slide him a dark look. "Watch it, fucker."

He holds up his hands in mocking surrender. "Hey, I wasn't volunteering for the job."

Sure he fucking wasn't.

It's not like it would matter if he did. Even if he didn't slightly fear me and he could pull out all the stops going after her, Parker would never give that asshole the time of day. He's not her type.

Not that there's any way of knowing what her type is, I guess.

The truth is, it doesn't matter.

Her type is me, whether she likes it or not.

The reminder of Aladdin surfaces unpleasantly, and not for the first time since that fucking dinner, I look toward the road, my thoughts on heading back to the country club to finish what I started.

Of course, my dad warned me to stay away unless I was there with them—and to be on my best behavior, in that case—but he knows I won't fucking listen, and the truth is, he doesn't care. He's only making this powerful show of wanting to parent me all of a sudden because he thinks Gemma's into it.

And, annoyingly, he's right.

He couldn't have just picked up some generic bimbo who didn't give a fuck, could he? What's wrong with him? Doesn't he know he's supposed to date someone half his age who cares more about purses and grabbing cocktails with the girls than his relationship with his son from a previous marriage? What kind of man at his age with his bank account picks an actual adult woman with a teenage daughter of her own for his second chance at a happy little family?

It's sick, that's what it is.

He never does anything right.

Well, I guess he's the one who convinced Parker to live under the same roof as me.

Fine, one thing.

I smirk, draining the last of the beer in my bottle as I remember the way she used to hide from me when we only went to school together.

Little fucking coward.

Which is ironic since she's an emerald.

The house of the courageous—except when it comes to me.

I run my hand along the sleek curve of my emerald green Jaguar, then I glance up toward the house. It's late. I'm sure she and Hannah are fast asleep, dreaming of rainbows and unicorns or whatever the fuck girls like them dream about.

I'm gonna wake her up.

I want company.

Sure, I have these fuckers out here, but they're not the company I want.

"What are you doing?" Malek asks as my self-appointed playground monitor, watching me drop into the driver's seat. "You are not driving that fucking thing. The last thing I need is—"

He's a pain in my ass, so I smirk at his annoyance as I fire up the engine, the noisy-ass motor cutting him off so I don't have to.

My attention drifts away from him and I focus instead on the dark windows on the top floor of the house. I don't expect Parker will turn on any lights. It's late, and she's too considerate for her own good, so she won't want to wake anyone up.

But she won't want me waking anyone else up, either.

Not this late.

Not when I've been drinking.

And she knows I was earlier. Before I came into the house, I made sure to take a swig out of one of the little bottles I snatched from Hannah's house so she'd smell it on me and know she had damage control to do.

With the car still in park, I press my foot down on the gas.

This car is very nice to look at, but it's noisy as all fucking hell.

I rev it again, and again.

Arden smirks, and Malek shakes his head. They know what I'm doing.

And I keep fucking doing it until I get what I want.

IT'S STILL DARK when I wake up.

I'm not initially sure what woke me. A noise, I think. Something outside.

Typically, I'm not afraid of the dark, but when I was trying to fall asleep last night, I was keenly aware of Hannah not sleeping beside me. That made me think of the nightmares she keeps having, and I guess that triggered a sympathy nightmare of my own.

So, when I push back the covers and climb out of bed in the middle of the night, my mind is caught in a land where evil men can't be kept from the things they want by doors or walls—no matter how expensive or impressive those well-meaning barriers may be.

Nobody's here.

I tell myself that as I creep toward my bedroom door. I only intend to go down the hall until I get to a window with a view of the driveway. But then I hear a revving engine outside, and that's too brazen to be anyone trying to creep around the property.

I don't bother going to the window when I hear it again.

I know some asshats who would rev engines in the

driveway in the middle of the night without caring who they woke up. A whole group of them, actually.

I glance back at the bed to make sure Hannah is still sleeping before I slip out of my bedroom.

It occurs to me I probably should have grabbed my phone or at least a robe. I'm wearing a pair of grey sleep shorts and an olive green tank top with no bra underneath. Not exactly an ideal uniform for dealing with Landon and his debauched friends.

I slip on a pair of sandals and head outside to see what's going on.

Tonight, court is apparently convened in the middle of the driveway.

Arden Prince leans against the door of a sleek, sexy red Camaro. It's a new model, not a classic. It's a gorgeous car, pretty and showy like he is, but somehow it doesn't quite suit him. It's probably too cheap for one of Baymont's wealthiest heirs.

He seems to agree. Arden's gaze is locked on Malek's car, some crazy-expensive limited-edition Ferrari he doesn't even care about. His dad has so many cars that he famously gave Malek this one last year for his birthday when it's rumored he completely forgot about it and had to scramble for a present. Maybe it's because of the thoughtlessness of the gift, but Malek has quietly loathed his three-million-dollar ride from the moment he got the keys.

He's not even standing by the coveted car now. Instead, he hangs off to the side with Jordan Brewer.

Landon is behind the wheel of his Jag. I'm guessing he was the one revving his noisy ass engine.

Of course he was.

"Well, well, well, it looks like we have company," Arden observes as I come down the stairs.

Landon has the roof up but the windows down. He looks at me through the passenger window hole, and he does *not* look happy to see me.

"What the hell are you wearing?"

Eyes wide, I stare at him. "Clothes."

"Barely," he snaps. "Those shorts are practically fucking underwear."

Logically, I know he is completely insane.

Illogically, his comments make me feel like these are shorter than I realized and maybe I shouldn't be leaning over the car door with all these creeps around to stare at my ass.

I can't let Landon know his criticism bothers me, though, so I resist the urge to tug at my shorts to try to cover more of my thighs and toss back a biting comment. "Yeah, I know. I don't know how Hannah's keeping her hands off me with all the sexiness I'm exuding right now."

Landon glares at me, but my attention is pulled away by the voice behind me.

"Hannah's inside?" That gets Arden's attention. He glances back at the house with interest.

Ignoring him, I look back at Landon. "I would be in bed sleeping, but some inconsiderate asshole woke me up with his noisy ass car. Have you seen anyone like that around here?"

Jordan laughs but Malek doesn't. He hates me, too, he just isn't as interested in letting me know it all the time.

Landon doesn't smile. His gaze drops to my chest and makes me self-conscious, so I cross my arms to cover my breasts.

"Get back inside," he tells me.

Even if I wanted to, I can't now because he just ordered me to and his stupid buddies make "ooh," noises in the background that saddle me with a pair of cement shoes.

"I'm not going anywhere without your keys. You've been drinking, and I don't trust you not to drive off a cliff."

"Like you would care," he mutters.

"I would obviously care if you drove off a cliff, Landon. I would care if almost anyone drove off a cliff. The list of people who can do that and I wouldn't care is short, and try as you might to get on it, you haven't yet."

"Yet, she says," Arden comments. "Give him time, he'll get there." Ready for a change of scenery, apparently, he adds, "She's right, though. You shouldn't drive. Why don't we go inside? I'm thirsty. I could use a drink. Is Cinderella awake, too?"

"Don't call her that," I say, not at all amused. "She's sleeping, and she's not your maid regardless."

He smirks at me. "Not yet. The way that stepmother and stepsister of hers bleed money, I bet they'd sell her to me if I made a good enough offer."

He's repugnant and I can't believe I'm literally losing sleep talking to him.

I know Landon is too difficult to let me rein him in with his friends as witnesses, so I take a softer path to the same destination since I'm tired and I know it's likely to get me there quicker.

Leaning farther into Landon's car, I say more softly, "It's really late and you're not supposed to be doing stuff like this. Why don't you kick these guys out and go to bed before you wake someone else up?"

He smirks and leans closer. "I will if you come with me."

I maintain an even, dead-eyed look. "Pass."

He shrugs. "Then I guess I'm not coming inside."

I sigh. "What are you even doing out here?"

"Arden's looking for a new ride, so we were comparing cars. He's trying to convince Malek to sell him the Aperta."

"You guys can play with your cars when it's not three in the morning," I tell him.

"We could, but we're already here, so..."

"What do you think your dad's going to say if you wake him up like you woke me? For that matter, when he realizes you've been drinking and you're behind the wheel."

"I don't care," he states.

I sigh, totally unable to relate to his rebelliousness. "Please just come inside, Landon. It's the middle of the night."

He watches me for a moment, then surprises me by turning off the engine and opening the door. I'm even more surprised when he climbs out.

Is he actually listening to me?

I look overhead to see if pigs are flying, but all I see is a clear night sky.

"You guys are gonna have to hit the road," Landon tells his friends. "Parker here has other 3 AM activities in mind, and I'm afraid she has nicer tits than any of you, so..."

Oh. My. God.

Arden smirks, Malek rolls his eyes, and I glare at Landon, hard.

I stiffen when he walks over and slings an arm around my neck to pull me close, but I don't fight him.

He's the worst, but I don't bother denying it, either. Anyone with half a brain could see I'm not in the mood to fuck him, but at least Jordan seems to believe him, judging by his smirk.

I guess possessing at least half of a brain was too great an expectation.

I would never sleep with any of these guys, anyway, so I really don't care what they think.

Arden pushes off his car first. "All right, man, we'll see you tomorrow."

The other two follow suit, getting into Malek's sleek white sports car. I flinch when he fires up the engine.

"Why are your cars so loud?" I complain.

My Prius is much more polite than their dumb sports cars.

"To match the owners," Landon says glibly, his arm still locked around my neck to keep me close even as he hauls me toward the stairs.

"You can let go now," I say, trying to pull away from him.

"I could," he agrees, but his tight grip doesn't ease.

I'm realizing a bit belatedly that I just dismissed all the witnesses, and now I have to walk into the house with him alone.

My brain was too foggy from just waking up to think through what I was doing when I came downstairs. I thought about the possibility of him waking up everybody else and getting in trouble, and I acted without further thought.

But I should have given it further thought.

Seeking a distraction, I ask, "Are you hungry? I might make a snack while I'm downstairs."

"Nope. You better help me to my room. I may not be sober enough to make it all by myself."

I roll my eyes as he flashes me a puppy dog face that *should not work at all*, but does shamefully make my stomach sink. "You are *not* that drunk."

"You don't know how drunk I am."

I'm uneasy as I'm forced to walk up the steps with him or risk falling down them.

When we get to the top, I see him glance up at the security camera on the front door. It would be nice if that reminded him to act right, but it doesn't. He seems supremely unconcerned as he opens the door and hauls me inside.

"Let go of me," I say, trying to move away from him once we're in the foyer.

He keeps me close as he kicks the door shut, then falls back

—hauling me with him—to lock the door. "Gotta make sure no one steals you."

Maybe he *is* drunk. That doesn't strike me as something he would say sober, even if he is joking.

He's obviously stronger than I am, so he controls the path we take. We weave to the right toward the staircase leading upstairs that opens up to just outside the master suite. You can get to my room that way, too, if you go left and keep walking past the empty spare room, but he knows Hannah is in my room.

Just when we get near the stairs, he drags me to the left, away from them. "Nope, can't go that way, huh?" Leaning in, he whispers conspiratorially, "Might wake up the parents."

"You should get a bottle of water to take to bed," I tell him.

"Aw. Are you worried about me?" he mocks.

I roll my eyes, trying to pry his arm off my neck. "Yes, I'm very worried you're about to lose a limb."

He chuckles. "I've seen you struggle to carry a couple of boxes. I'm not worried about your capacity to wound me."

"Maybe you should be," I say primly. "It's always the ones you least suspect."

"Yeah?" He lets go of my neck, but before I can feel too victorious, he grabs my hips and walks me back against his dad's study door.

My heart slams forward in my chest as he cages me in, moving in close.

"Fight me off, then. Let's see what you got."

"Landon." My gaze darts to the nearest staircase. If his dad or my mom heard something and wanted to come downstairs to check, that's the way they would come. "This is not the time and definitely not the place for this."

Rather than heed my objections, he slides his hand up underneath my tank top. My heart falters when his fingertips graze my waist. His hand slides higher and a kaleidoscope of butterflies burst free inside my stomach. Then he grips my side to keep me in place while his other hand slides up to grab my bare breast.

Panic scares off all the butterflies. I try to shove his hand away, but he easily locks an arm around my back and pulls me close, flattening me against the front of his hard body while his hand possessively squeezes my breast.

"Landon, stop."

I feel his hot breath against my neck, the devious way his fingers graze the underside of my bare breast beneath my shirt. The panic makes it hard to think as my blood runs hot and cold through my veins. My mind and body are at war as his lips graze my neck, and combined with him palming my breast the way he is, it triggers a confusing sensation low in my belly.

"Make me."

I need to get away from him.

I need to get away from him right now.

I shove at his chest, but I may as well be trying to push down a wall. My gaze darts to the staircase. I lick my lips, the desperation to get him to stop tempting me to do whatever I have to do.

I know if I scream, someone will come.

Mom and Hayden are right at the top of those steps.

Hannah is just down the hall from them.

It's like a bad dream I can't wake myself up from.

Help is just a cry away, but I can't seem to open my mouth.

LANDON'S THUMB slides across my beaded nipple, triggering a shock of sensation that rips me from my thoughts about an external savior.

The only person who can get me out of this situation without throwing the entire household into chaos is me, so I try to generate an idea.

Knee him in the balls.

I try to lift my knee, but he anticipates the move and drops a hand to block my attempt. Then he chuckles, looking down at me with dark amusement splashed across his handsome face. "Nice try, baby." Palming my raised knee with one hand, he drops the other from my breast.

My relief is short-lived. It occurs to me belatedly that by raising my knee, I gave him easier access. I try to free my leg, but he already has my knee in a firm grip. His hand slides between my legs, and I can't even stop him.

"I said *no*," I growl, aggravated and hot all over from struggling against his brute strength. I can't think of a single thing else to do, so when his palm comes to cover my pussy through the thin fabric of my gray sleep shorts, I slap him right across the face.

He freezes, and I do too. My heart drops like a rock and I stare up at him wide-eyed as he slowly turns his head and locks gazes with me. Even here in the shadows, I can see his eyes are burning like two emeralds tossed on a pyre.

I know I only have a split second before he recovers from the shock, so I take advantage of it and shove him. He falls back, not braced for it, and I run like hell toward the staircase on my left.

"Oh, I don't fucking think so," he says, making my heart pound when I hear him come after me. I only make it a few feet before he grabs me around the waist, yanking me back against him so roughly, it knocks air out of my lungs. "You want to play rough, huh?" he murmurs, his hot breath hitting my ear. "I can play rough."

"Landon, please."

My breath catches in my throat as he ignores the pleas he tried so hard to get out of me the night he broke into my house and drags me toward the sunken living room. I'm trying to fight his bruising grip and push back to keep him from taking me wherever he's taking me, but all I end up with is a stubbed toe. I nearly fall on the step down, but Landon's arm is locked around me so tight, he keeps me up even when both of my feet leave the floor.

"Please," I say again, my desperation growing as he hauls me toward the couch. "Landon, let me go. Let me *go*."

And then he does, but not so I can run away.

So he can shove me over the arm of the couch.

At first, I think he's just trying to get me on the couch so he can climb on top of me and trap me underneath him, but instead of shoving me forward onto the cushions, he grabs my hips and adjusts my position so I'm still hanging over the arm.

Then he wrenches my thighs apart and I realize he's not

trying to shove me anywhere—I'm already *in* the position he wants me in.

"Stop!"

I try to look back at him and kick him away, but he grabs the back of my skull and pushes my face into the couch cushion. I panic when he holds it there, then icy fear slides down my spine when he says, "You lost the privilege of looking at me when you hit me. You want to play rough, we'll play rough. But don't expect fucking kisses and eye contact."

My body is stuck in fight-or-flight mode, but I can't breathe shoved into the couch cushion like this, so I try to calm down and stop fighting him. As soon as I stop, his grip eases slightly so I can breathe even though my face is smashed against the couch cushion.

As soon as I stop fighting, he releases my skull, then both hands return to my hips. "Now, keep that pretty mouth shut and put your ass up like a good girl."

I gasp, grabbing the edge of the couch cushion as he rams his hips forward and shoves his hardness against my entrance. There are four layers of clothing between us, but it feels like an inadequate barrier as he grips my hips tighter and forces himself against me. He grinds his hardness into my soft parts, making my heart pound so fast it's all I can hear, and leaving my stomach a jumbled mess.

"You like that?" he asks roughly, grinding his cock against me so hard it hurts. Rubbing it up and down, up and down.

"Landon." My voice comes out a ragged whisper. He keeps thrusting against me. I hold tight to the edge of the couch as he uses my body to satisfy his. His bulge grows bigger and harder as he rubs it against me. Even through the layers of clothing, I can feel his dick pressing into me.

His voice turns gravelly as he says, "Fuck, Parker."

I can feel his swollen head prodding my pussy. He pushes against me harder, faster. My breaths come in short, fast bursts as my body is bounced back and forth against his dick. The friction lights my blood on fire. I'm so hot as I hold on to the couch, feeling my pussy part to take him as he shoves against it. Feeling a desperate need building from the friction of him rubbing against me.

No!

I try to get over the arm so I can crawl away from him, but he doesn't let me. As soon as he feels me trying to crawl away, he drags me back, driving forward and grinding his cock into me harder, holding it there so I can feel the threat of penetration more keenly.

"Keep trying to get away from me, and I'll take your fucking mouth instead."

His words paralyze me.

I don't want *this*, but I don't want *that* more.

It shouldn't feel worse being given a choice—*if you can consider that being given a choice*—but it does. It makes me feel complicit in this filthy act that he literally forced me into. It's not fair, but he doesn't care about that. He's telling me my options—let him use me to get off and he won't penetrate me, or fight him and he makes it ten times worse.

I don't doubt his ability to do it. I don't doubt the likelihood of him following through, either.

So, I know my odds, and I'm not willing to gamble with the outcome.

My stomach rocks as my nails sink into the soft fabric covering the couch. I squeeze my eyes shut and tell myself it can't last forever. It will be over soon. I just have to get through it and then he'll let me go.

"Good girl," he murmurs almost soothingly as his hand

caresses my ass. It's a fleeting, depraved gesture of comfort that makes my heart sink, then I hear his zipper.

Panicked, I start to raise up off the couch. "You said—"

He pushes my face back down into the cushions. Panic seizes me and I start to fight again, but his previous words rush in and I manage to override the instinct.

I don't know if Landon's word means anything. He tricked me at the party when he made me bargain with him and then after I kissed him, he still went for more.

But realistically, I'm at his mercy.

He'll take whatever he wants to take because he knows I won't fucking scream, and I certainly don't possess the physical strength to fight him off.

I have to *hope* his word means something and vow to never let him get me alone like this again.

Reality whispers across my mind, determined to dash my hopes with the solemn reminder that this is only the second week of senior year. The *beginning* of the second week.

It feels different this time when he pushes himself against me. I don't have to look to know he's taken his cock out. My shorts and panties are still on, but I no longer have the barrier of *his* fabric to protect me.

"Next time you think about wearing these shorts in public," he murmurs, rubbing his cock against the soft fabric, *"Don't."*

Next time you think about being a rapey asshole, don't, I think, but I keep my mouth shut since it's likely to only get me in more trouble.

He simulates fucking me through my clothing for several more minutes, but I don't start to fight until he peels my shorts down, exposing my ass in just my underwear. He squeezes until it hurts, then slides his fingers down to rub my pussy through the thin fabric.

My muscles are trembling from the strain of this position and holding back all the noises that tried to escape me as he rubbed his cock against me. I know it's physiological and I can't control it, but I refuse to let him get me off. I tell myself that will only make him feel better about what he's doing, but I don't know if he feels any shame over it. I don't know how far gone he is.

Flashbacks from the night he broke into my house replay in my head as he fingers me through my panties. I wiggle my hips to try to get him to stop.

Then I gasp, a warm, wet sensation hitting my ass and leaking down to reach my pussy as he groans, pushing forward with one slower, longer stroke.

My heart pounds and I can scarcely breathe as I lay there motionless. The wetness trickles down my left thigh, and my skin feels so hot I think I may explode.

He sighs, a heavy sigh of relief.

I draw several loud, hitching breaths and try to ignore the reality that he just *came on me*.

Once he recovers enough to regain his strength, he pulls my shorts back up to cover my ass. I can still feel his cum on my panties, pressed against my skin.

Horror swells up inside me, my muscles shaking as I crawl forward and climb off the couch. I can't look at him as I stumble. He reaches out to grab me on instinct so I don't fall, but I swat his hand away and dart around him.

I don't know what to feel as I race up the stairs and make my way to my room. I close the door behind me and press my back against it, then I slide down until I'm hugging my knees to my chest.

My mind is blessedly blank. I can feel chaos beneath the blanket of blackness covering everything, but I don't have the energy to deal with it right now.

I'm drained.

Defeated.

I thought I had arranged for safety tonight, but then I let him lure me right out of it.

When my muscles stop shaking, I push up off the floor. I have to get out of this soiled clothing. Before I climb into my bed, I need to clean him off me, too.

I check to make sure Hannah is sleeping, then I walk softly into my bathroom. I turn on the shower, and robotically, I undress.

I stand and look at myself in the mirror completely naked. The same pale, freckled complexion looks back at me.

But I feel different.

I try to shake it off, tell myself I'll feel better in the morning. I just need a shower and some sleep.

I'll be fine.

I step under the hot spray. Normally, my brain works over-time when I'm showering, but tonight it has enough compassion to be quiet.

When I've run out all the hot water and scrubbed my skin until it's red and blotchy, I finally get out.

I pull on a long-sleeved shirt and pants because despite the hot shower, my body feels cold.

Finally, I climb into bed, careful not to wake Hannah.

I imagine her waking up and noticing I changed clothes. I imagine having to tell her what just happened, but I don't even know how I would explain it.

I know what her face would look like. I know what her hug would feel like when she wrapped her arms around me protec-tively. I can even guess what the tears she might shed for me would feel like when they inevitably dropped off her face and hit my skin.

And I know this time, if I still wouldn't tell my mom, there's a good chance she would.

Hannah is an amazing friend. Because of that, if she knew the line Landon just crossed, she might feel compelled to intervene on my behalf.

She hasn't before because I assured her I could handle it, and she believed me.

But it does not feel like I just handled anything.

I *was* handled.

By a fucking meathead jock who couldn't think his way out of a paper bag.

It's perhaps the meanest thought I've ever had about Landon, but as the shock is wearing off, anger is setting in.

He had *no fucking right*.

I know the anger will only keep me awake and what I desperately want to do is sleep, so for now, I try to shelf it. I think of the beach, the waves hitting the shore. I think of the pool, and the peaceful contentment I feel when I'm floating in it with my eyes closed and my arms spread in the rare moment I *don't* have to worry about Landon.

My recaptured peace wavers when the thought of him creeps in, but I shut it down. I achieved peace, and he's not going to ruin it.

My muscles have relaxed, and my body feels heavy.

Tomorrow feels daunting, so I remind myself it won't be. Hannah's here, and tomorrow she'll be awake. He won't be able to get me alone (if he even tries to), and as long as I commit to that course and stop letting him get me alone... we can keep living here.

It's not a *comfortable* thought. I want that less now than I have at any other point.

Unfortunately, nothing else has changed.

I feel my peace beginning to slip away, so I tamp down all my thoughts and picture the beach again.

Tomorrow I can regroup and make a better plan going forward.

Tonight, I need to sleep.

WHEN I ROLL out of bed the following morning, I seem to have aged 64 years.

I'm hunched over like a wart-faced Disney villain and I can't seem to straighten up.

Fantastic.

Annoyance thickens around my heart when I make my way to the bathroom and, even after peeing and washing my hands, I can't straighten to my appropriate height.

I planned to get dressed before I went downstairs on the off chance that Hannah didn't notice I'd changed clothes in the middle of the night. She's not in my bed, so I'm guessing she went downstairs. But with my back like this, I'm not sure I can.

Grouchy and in slight pain, I unplug the charger from my phone so I can take it downstairs with me. I see the display light up with a missed text from Mom.

"Morning honey! Since Hannah is still at the house, I have a few errands to run while Hayden is at work. Don't let her leave until I get back."

No worries there.

I text back that I won't, but most of my focus is on keeping my mind straight in case I walk down those stairs and have to see Landon. Since both parents are out, I don't really have to be nice to him, but Hannah is here, and if I don't want to tell her what happened last night, then I will still have to keep a lid on it.

As soon as I open the door, I can smell food cooking. Delicious food, if my watering mouth is any indication.

Bless you, Hannah.

I'm even more relieved when I make it to the kitchen without seeing Landon.

"Good morning, beautiful breakfast maker."

Hannah cracks a smile and glances my way. "Hey."

"You didn't have to cook."

She shrugs. "It's part of my daily routine. Feels strange not to, honestly." Her gaze flickers in my direction again, quickly taking note of my outfit. "That's not what you were wearing when we went to sleep, right?"

I shake my head, walking to the fridge so I don't have to make eye contact while I lie to her. "I woke up and I was a little chilly, so I changed." Opening the massive fridge door, I ask, "What do you want to drink?"

"I'll have orange juice," she tells me.

I reach in to grab the carton, but my whole body freezes when she speaks again.

"I made enough for us and Landon, but I think he's still sleeping. Should we call him down?"

"No," I say flatly. "He does not get breakfast. You can split his portion between us."

Her eyebrows rise in surprise, but she nods without arguing. "Okay."

I've never been more appreciative of Hannah's easygoing nature than I am in this moment. The tension that developed quickly when I thought I might have to explain eases, and I walk over to the cupboard to grab two glasses. "Can you stay for a while, or do you have to get right back?"

"Anae's going shopping with the girls, so she'll probably grab lunch while she's out. Jackie had a meeting this afternoon, so she'll probably eat out, too. I should be free for a while."

"Good. This house has some serious amenities, but since I live with Satan, I usually don't get to enjoy them. We might as well enjoy them together today in case this is the last week we live here."

Hannah's eyebrows rise again. "Have things gotten worse with him?"

"I *really* don't want to talk about him. I was mostly joking, anyway. I'll show you the pool house after we eat."

Hannah nods, but then she notices the way I'm walking and frowns. "Are you okay?"

I nod. "I think I twisted my back the wrong way or something. I need to stretch it out. Maybe we can do yoga in the gym in the basement. You can borrow Mom's mat."

"Sure. I can give you a massage if you need one, too." She pushes the eggs in the skillet before turning off the heat. "Should we do yoga in the basement or on the beach?"

"With my old crone's disease today, I'm not sure I can make it down to the beach."

Hannah smiles faintly. "Maybe next time."

***

AFTER BREAKFAST, I lend Hannah some athletic wear and carefully change into some myself, then we head down to the basement gym to do a yoga routine.

Hannah's a really gentle, peaceful yoga teacher, and that's just what I need today, so I let her take the lead and guide me to letting go of my troubles so I can be present with her for a while. I can feel weight coming off my shoulders as she talks me through the first several poses.

I'm feeling significantly better when we're done. I didn't think it was possible, but I'm practically radiating peace and tranquility as I lay on the mat, my body no longer aching and hunched.

"I love you," I tell her serenely.

Hannah laughs softly. "I love you, too."

"You need to move in here. I would have literally no problem living here if you lived here with me. I could relocate to any of the nine circles of hell, and if you were my roommate, I could be okay with it."

"Those must have been some stretches," she jokes.

"It's not the stretches. It's you. You're amazing." Reluctantly, I open my eyes and turn my head to look over at her lying on the mat beside me.

Smiling mischievously, she says, "Wait until after your massage. You'll really love me then."

"Move in," I drawl, my tone pleading. "All I have to do is tell Hayden it's what I need in order to live with his awful son and he will literally hire moving people to move you in tomorrow. You'd love it here. You wouldn't have to be anyone's maid —we have a housekeeper who comes as often as we need her to. And you'd be safer. I know you worry about Voldemort coming back for you, but we have security cameras on every entrance, and if Dare shows his stupid face here, I'll stake him in the heart like the soulless bloodsucker he is."

"Wow. Strong opinions about someone you've never met."

"I have all the information I require to know he's a jerkface and he would deserve it."

She nods, looking up at the ceiling. "I can't argue that."

"So, it's decided. You're moving in."

She cracks a smile. "I appreciate the offer—"

"Plea," I correct. "I'll bribe you if need be."

Her smile widens slightly. "But I can't. That was my mom's dream home. My dad had it built for her. I know it's just a house, but that house is all I have left of them. Every memory lives there. The flowers my mom planted with her own hands still grow in that garden. I can't just… give it up to those awful people," she says, shaking her head. "I know that legally, it will never be mine again, but I have to be its caretaker for as long as I'm able. It would kill me to leave and watch them destroy it with their careless ways and unquenchable greed. They would… they would kill the last living parts of my parents, and I just can't let that happen."

I sigh. It's not like it's news to me that Hannah still associates her house with her dead parents and clings to the remnants of the life they had together, but someday when I ask, I still hope she says yes. "You deserve more than memories, Hannah."

"I know," she says softly. "And someday I'll have more than that. But in the meantime, I'm perfectly content with my choices."

"Well, wherever I live, you can always come there if you ever change your mind."

"Thank you. I appreciate it."

"I guess we should get up now," I say sadly.

"I guess so."

"How do you feel about saunas? I haven't seen it yet," I say as I reluctantly rise and climb to my feet. "But allegedly there's a spa room down the hall with a sauna."

"A spa room?" she asks with interest. "What does that even entail?"

"I don't know." I walk over to the mini fridge in here and grab us two waters, passing one to Hannah. "Why don't we go find out?"

Turns out, I didn't need to grab us waters in the gym; there's a mini fridge in here, too. There's also a juice bar, a massage table, and an in-ground hot tub.

Hannah insists on giving me a massage even though my back is feeling better just in case it's not "all the way better," and this will be my second massage this long weekend—which is two more than I've had in my whole life prior.

I joke about my new rich girl life and Hannah points me toward a bathroom and tells me to strip down to my comfort level and then we can get started.

Undressing in the spa bathroom provides a different experience than quickly pulling clothes on in my walk-in closet upstairs so we could come down to do yoga.

Here, I can see bruises the size of Landon's fingerprints all over. I'm fair-skinned, so I bruise *very* easily, but the story my skin is telling is one that feels much more dramatic than what actually happened.

If I let Hannah give me a massage, she'll be focusing on working different parts of my body. It's hard to imagine she wouldn't see a lot of these bruises. The massage would even give her an opportunity to study them closely before she even brought them up to me.

Shit.

I can't let her get that close.

Licking my dry lips, I try to ignore my racing heartbeat and look around the room for inspiration.

Big, white fluffy towels are folded neatly on the counter for anyone who wants to enjoy the sauna and get the maximum benefit.

On impulse, I take off my panties and wrap a towel around my body. I know the sauna room is darker anyway, and it will be steamy. Hannah won't be looking at my body the way she would for a massage, and the towel is huge so it covers most of it if I wrap it right.

Yep, this will work.

I take my hair down and put it back up more tightly, then I wash my hands and head back to the spa room.

"New idea. My back feels fine now. Let's skip ahead to the sauna."

"Are you sure?"

I nod. "As tempting as it is, I just had a massage when Mom and I went to the beach resort. I probably shouldn't mislead my body into thinking my new rich girl life comes with multiple massages each week."

Hannah cracks a smile and walks over to put back the lotion she picked out. "All right. I'll go change."

I smile until I see her off, then my smile drops and I sigh heavily.

I'm growing tired of lying to the people I love, and this is only the second week.

My serenity from yoga is slipping away, so I try to reclaim it, clearing my thoughts of Landon and everything associated with him.

I haven't checked my phone in a while, so while Hannah is in the bathroom, I take it off the folded stack of yoga clothes I sat on the table in front of the white couch facing the hot tub area and check my notifications. Some social media stuff I don't care about, but there's a text from my mom that just came through two minutes ago.

"Hey honey, how's your day with Hannah going?"

"Amazing," I text back. "She's an angel on earth and we don't deserve her. How are errands going?"

"Good," she texts back. "You know Kara, Kayleigh's mom from the 8-9 ballet class? She's a member at the club, too, and I ran into her at the store. She invited me to play tennis with her.

I was thinking maybe you could bring Hannah as your guest and we could all play together, then maybe we could have some lunch before Hannah has to go home."

"That's a great idea," I tell her, remembering what Hannah said about the rest of her household likely eating while she's out.

"Hannah can borrow something of mine if she needs a tennis outfit. Tell her to take whatever she likes."

"We were just about to hop in the sauna and then probably take showers. Do you think we have time?"

"Sure, just make them quick showers, lol. Kara and I will have a cocktail and catch up while we wait for you."

"Perfect. I'll run it by Hannah, but I'm sure she'll—"

Before I can finish my message, I hear the bathroom door open and Hannah emerges in a white fluffy towel like mine and a stack of yoga clothes in her hand.

"Hey, perfect timing. After the sauna, do you want to meet my mom at the country club for some tennis and lunch? One of the dance moms wants to play, so I think it would be us vs. them."

"Sure," she says, bending gracefully to drop the stack of clothing on the table next to mine. "I haven't played tennis in a long time, though. I may be rusty."

"That's okay," I say, quickly tapping out a message to Mom while I talk. "Mom said you can raid her closet for tennis clothes, and she has some really cute club outfits. We can take my car if you're coming back here, or we can take yours and then I can get a ride home from Mom if you have to leave."

"We can take my car. I haven't started any of my weekend homework, so I should probably go home and take advantage of no one else being there for a while."

I nod. "I kinda figured. I wish we could do sleepovers more often, even if just to get you more breaks."

She nods, her pretty face tugged into an expression of regret. "They're kind of hard to arrange. I have round-the-clock duties and they're not used to doing anything for themselves."

Irritation flares up again, but I force it away from me. We are being relaxed. Peaceful. Serene. We will not give up our peace to all the evil forces at work in this godforsaken town.

"Oh! Maybe Javi will be working and you can meet him, too."

Hannah's eyes widen slightly, then her expression turns conspiratorial. "Who's Javi?"

"Oh, just this super-hot valet that Landon now hates with every fiber of his being," I say innocently as I drop my phone back atop the clothing stack. "He reads, too."

Hannah makes a show of dropping her jaw. "Oh my god, does Parker Johansson like a boy?"

"I don't know," I say, feeling my face flush and almost regretting bringing it up. "We haven't talked much or anything, but he *is* very cute, and he seems really nice."

Hannah clasps her hands together. "Aww. I love that. There aren't enough nice boys."

I laugh. "Ain't that the truth." Feeling much more hopeful, I approach the sauna and open the glass door for her. "After you."

AFTER SOUNDLY DEFEATING Mom and Kara at a game of tennis, Hannah and I head inside to get a table for lunch while Mom says her goodbyes to the dance mom.

Hannah's stepmom has a membership here, but I don't know if Hannah has ever been. We're allowed to bring a guest on a day pass, but bringing her along doesn't seem like something Jackie would do. Like Anae, she seems to get more joy out of excluding Hannah from things.

"Well, well, well. Look who it is."

As if I summoned dark forces by thinking about them, I hear the smug sound of Arden Prince's voice and sigh, turning to face him.

He's not looking at me, though. His appreciative gaze is moving down Hannah's body, admiring the way she looks in my mom's white top and tennis skirt. Because Hannah wore a sweater to my house last night and she's going home after this, she wanted to bring her clothes inside to change into before she left. Her soft blue wool-blend cardigan is draped over her shoulders, her leggings unseen in her purse, and I have to admit, she looks exactly like the type of person who belongs here.

So does he, but it's because he does. He's wearing white trousers and a beige polo with a watch that probably cost more than my car. Classic old money, but then, he is.

I feel like the odd one out, because I am. Looking at the three of us, you can very easily guess I am the one who owns a pink yoga mat that says, "after this, we are so getting pizza."

"Oh, sorry," I say to Arden, pulling a fake grimace. "We have a strict no troublemakers allowed policy."

He smirks, ignoring me to watch Hannah. "If there were two girls in Baymont I wouldn't have expected to see here today, they would definitely be the maid and the upstart."

Even Hannah gives him a cool look. "Hello, Arden."

He takes her hand and kisses it because he is *the biggest asshole* in the known universe. "Cinderella," he murmurs, expertly straddling the line between teasing and an outright taunt.

Her eyes narrow slightly and she takes back her hand.

Since we're in public, he lets it go.

And since I just saw him in my driveway last night and Hannah doesn't know about it, I am eager to get the hell away from him.

Well, I'm always eager to get the hell away from him because he's the worst, but I am currently *more* motivated than usual.

"Anyway, we're meeting my mom here, so..." I trail off in hopes that the mention of a parental figure will encourage him to fuck off.

"Yeah? Moms love me. Maybe I'll hang around."

"Mine won't," I assure him with a fake smile.

His smile widens, his eyes glinting knowingly. "Parker, if I didn't know any better, I'd think you were trying to get rid of me."

"*Do* you know better?" I ask, cocking my head.

He's not a guy accustomed to rejection, even from someone he doesn't care about, so he smiles at me coolly and asks, "How's Landon this morning? I thought you two might sleep in today."

My heart sinks, but mercifully, before I have to respond, the hostess comes over and says, "Your table's ready," as she grabs menus and plasters on a polite smile. "If you'll just follow me."

Thank god for customer service workers.

Without another word to *Satan: The Sequel,* I grab Hannah's hand and haul her with me to the table by the windows. We have a nice view of the ocean but also air conditioning since it's getting hot outside. It's the best of both worlds.

"What was he talking about?" Hannah asks as she takes her seat.

"Who knows? You know Arden, he loves to cause trouble."

She frowns slightly, probably because that explanation doesn't entirely make sense, but the universe must be on my side today because before she can press me, Mom comes walking over.

"Hey, girls," she says warmly as she takes her seat at the table. "Sorry, Kara's a talker."

"No worries," I say, flashing her a smile and grabbing my menu. Looking across at Hannah, I tell her, "I highly recommend the sunset lemonade if you're looking for something delicious to drink."

"They have a juice bar, too," Mom adds. "So you can get juices. Even juice shots."

"And a real bar in case you want to steal from it and maybe frame a valet."

Hannah nods as if not at all thrown off as she looks over her menu. "It's nice to have options."

We look over the menu so we'll be ready when the waitress

comes over like you're *supposed* to do as a considerate human being dining out.

All these underhanded thoughts of Landon that are trickling in bring my mind back to the thing I've been running from all day.

Hannah has been an excellent shield, so the fact that they're getting in even with her and Mom sitting at the table worries me about what it will be like when she leaves.

And that encourages me to find a way to replicate these circumstances to the best of my ability using a method that isn't Hannah-dependent, since I can't use my best friend to avoid Landon forever.

By the time the waitress has brought our drinks around and taken our lunch order, I have a solid plan that I feel pretty good about.

"So, Mom."

Mom looks at me, taking note of my business-like tone. "Yes?" she asks cautiously.

"You know how during the summer I sometimes help out at the dance studio for extra money?"

Mom nods.

"I'd like to start doing that again." Anticipating reluctance, I make quick work of bolstering my argument before she can rule against it. "Hayden bought me this new car, and that's amazing, but I'll need to pay for insurance for it and keep gas in the tank. There will be maintenance costs, too."

As I feared, Mom is already waving me off before I've finished. "Oh, honey, you don't have to worry about all that. We'll pay for any upkeep on the car."

"I know you would, but isn't it good for me to start practicing responsibility?"

Mom and Hannah both slide me dry looks, and Mom says, "You've been responsible since you were five years old."

Okay, that was a bad argument, but I'm desperate to make this plan work. "Fine, but I'd like to have my own spending money for other things. Maybe I want to go shopping with Hannah or catch a movie or something."

"I can talk to Hayden about getting you a credit card. Not the one you have for emergencies, but one you can freely charge on whenever you want something."

I should have known she would shoot down my hastily made argument with her supportiveness. "I just think it would be nice to earn my own money."

"I understand that, but trust me, honey, you'll have the rest of your life to earn your own money. This is your senior year, and I want you to have adequate time to devote to your studies. Baymont is a very challenging school with rigorous coursework. I also want you to have down time to spend with your friends and with us at home. You don't *need* to work. This is the last time in your life that may be true, so while I understand your eagerness, it's a no. I don't pull this card often, but you will understand when you're older. In this case, mother knows best."

My shoulders slump with disappointment, but Mom simply averts her gaze and uses her straw to stir the ice in her cup. I know Mom, and she doesn't dig in often, but when she does...

I'm not getting a job at the dance studio.

I'm disappointed because I most certainly will still get a job, but I really wanted my old job at the studio. It would mean spending more time with Mom, while getting a job elsewhere will mean spending less time with her.

I also risk making Mom mad when she finds out I went against her wishes. Which also increases the risk of her wanting to know why I'm so desperate to work, which may lead her down the path of realizing I'm just trying to avoid being at home...

All the risks went up. I wish she would have just given me what I asked for. It would have made things so much easier.

When lunch is over, Mom waits at the table to pay the bill. I tell her I'm going to wait with Hannah while the valet gets her car, and Mom says, "Oh! Just a minute," and grabs her purse.

Then she slips Hannah a fifty, which Hannah stares at wide-eyed. "What's this for?"

"Spending the day with Parker."

Hannah opens her mouth, shuts it, then opens it again, saying with a faint smile, "I wasn't babysitting. She's my friend, we were just hanging out."

"I know, but... well, I appreciate it. It gave me peace of mind knowing you were there. Anyway, I know Jackie cut your allowance, so just take it. Use it for gas or buy something for yourself."

Hannah still seems uncertain about accepting money to hang out with me, but she must really need it, because in the end, she relents. "Thank you."

"Of course."

Hannah puts the money in her purse as we walk away, then she looks at me uncertainly. "I didn't know what to do..."

I wave her off. "Please. I don't care. If you can get paid for hanging out with me, do it."

"It's just, Jackie didn't give me extra money in the household account to buy groceries for Anae's party, so I was already short for the week."

"Hannah, you do *not* have to explain. I truly do not care. If my mom's going to marry Daddy Warbucks and can afford to give you money, then that's a win as far as I'm concerned. Hell, when I get a job—if I can find one—I'm already planning to treat you like my sugar baby every time we do anything."

Hannah cracks a smile and rolls her eyes. "I appreciate the sentiment, but I can pay my own way. Funding a sugar baby that doesn't give you any sugar doesn't seem like a fair exchange."

"No exchange required. I *enjoy* providing for you. I don't know why. Maybe it's your domestic goddess energy. You deserve it so much, you just make people want to take care of you."

"I'm not sure that's true," she murmurs. "I live with people who certainly don't have the drive to take care of me *or* appreciate me in any capacity."

"No, you live with parasites. I said *people*," I say, exaggerating the pronunciation just to make her smile.

"Ah, of course. My mistake."

"I wish I were into girls and we were into each other because I know life with you would be—" I stop talking to kiss my fingers in the universal gesture of a chef's kiss.

"At a glance, it does seem the answer to many of life's problems."

"I would always be full of delicious muffins and smoothies. I would buy you all the things and tell you how amazing you are every day. It would be perfect."

Hannah nods along. "So perfect. And then Landon would hate me as much as Dare does. They could team up and plan my murder together."

"Hey, they should be mad at themselves. You wouldn't be able to steal their girls if they were doing their part." I stop, frozen in horror, and look over at her. "Oh my god, I did not mean—Ew. Obviously, I am not Landon's girl. Those are different relationship types. Not even relationships because Landon and I don't have a relationship. We are just hostile housemates who hate each other and... there is no relationship to speak of."

"Are you getting paid every time you say the word relationship?"

"Yes. It's my new job. You'll be rolling in Manolos in no time."

Hannah cracks a smile, then wraps an arm around my shoulder to bring me in for a little reassuring hug. "It's okay. Nobody heard you. My lips are sealed."

"Thank you."

"Speaking of Manolos, I have my sights set on this really cute pair of white mules with silver buckles. *So* cute. My girlfriends would be so jealous."

I look over at her and she gives me a mischievous little smile and a wink.

I feel instantly better. My smile comes easy as I wrap my arm around her and squeeze her back. Distancing myself from ugly reality, I go back to the fantasy world where I'm her sugar daddy and tell her, "Don't worry, baby. We'll go shopping soon."

I don't think about how close we are to the valet stand or about the possibility of anyone around actually hearing us because it is *very* easy to get lost in your own little world when you're with Hannah, but when Javi spins around with a raised eyebrow, clearly having overheard the last part of our exchange, I quickly drop my arm and put a little space between us before he gets the wrong idea.

Javi wasn't here when we got here, so I didn't expect to see him now.

"We were joking," I state, even though he doesn't ask.

Raising his hands, he says, "Hey, I'm not here to judge."

"We're just friends. She's not a golddigger or a sugar baby."

Amused, he nods. "Got it."

"Definitely not mine."

"Weird. I was sure you were a rich old white man. Thanks for clearing that up."

Hannah puts her hand out to gently interrupt my awkward rambling explanation. "Hannah Dupont. You must be Javi."

Javi smirks, glancing at me as he shakes her hand. "Have I been mentioned?"

"What? No. I don't even know your name. What is it again? John?"

"So close." His smirk grows, making him even cuter, and I decide we should probably end this interaction before I make things worse.

I hand him the parking ticket, my expression solemn. "I apologize for the entirety of this interaction. Please bring my princess her pumpkin car."

Still smirking, he takes the ticket.

Then he reaches under the valet counter and pulls out a business card. I'm confused as he jots something down on the back of it, and wide-eyed when he hands it to me and it has his phone number on it.

I can't speak. I can hardly breathe as I look up at him.

"The club's hiring," he says, making me realize he heard more of the exchange than I realized. "The whole application process is online. Website address is on the front of the card. My number's on the back in case you have any questions." Then, he adds, "Or in case you want it for any other reason."

I am milliseconds from actually *exploding* with a kind of giddiness I have not felt in years, so I barely manage a nod before I turn and hustle over to sit on the bench before I have an actual heart attack.

Oh my god oh my god oh my god.

Hannah hurries over and sits beside me, eyes wide and dancing with glee. "Oh my god," she whispers. "He totally likes you."

"But why? Is that a red flag? I have only ever been an awkward, dorky mess in his presence. Why would he like me?"

Hannah laughs and puts her purse on her lap. "Because he has excellent taste, obviously."

It takes a couple of minutes for my pulse to stop pounding as if I'm being chased by a hungry lion. I still feel jittery and excited as I look down at his neat, masculine writing on the back of this card.

I haven't liked a guy since I liked Landon, but I think I like Javi.

It's just disheartening, because right on the heels of that admission is the part I don't want to admit, even to myself.

I'm afraid to act on it. Not because I'm afraid I'll be awkward—*I will, but he knows that by now*—or even because I've never gone on a date before and I'm nervous about it.

Because deep down, I know Landon will never let me have this.

I haven't faced him since last night, but every instinct I possess tells me that will make it worse, not better. He very literally *marked his fucking territory* because I wore shorts he deemed too short in front of *his friends* who he knows I could not be less interested in if they were actual frogs.

He already knows I might be interested in Javi, it's why he pulled the "prank" where he casually tried to get him fired.

What will he do if he finds out I'm talking to him?

On the flip side, Javi clearly knows the risks. He already knows Landon tried to frame him for stealing alcohol, and given the way Landon was behaving in front of him that night, he probably has some idea of why. Since Javi knew I was looking for a job, he also overheard some of what I was saying to Hannah as we walked toward the valet station, and while I can't remember the order of everything, I know my awkward *relationship* ramble came at the end. If he heard I was looking for a job, he definitely heard that.

And he still gave me his number.

So, clearly, he is at least somewhat aware of the risks.

I've never been in this position before. I've never made it past The Landon Factor with the guys who asked me out previously. If Javi is already aware of The Landon Factor and he's still interested...

Maybe...

Maybe this could actually work.

TUESDAY MEANS BACK TO SCHOOL—AND it also means I am blessedly busy.

Our first official meeting of the school year for this community outreach club I'm in is on Friday, but I had an idea for a book drive that needed to be worked on before then. The faculty adviser said if I could get enough people on board to get it done, then we could do it.

No one else was as eager to get a jumpstart on projects before the first club meeting has even happened, so I volunteered myself to handle everything.

Hannah is in the club with me so she said she would help if I needed it, but unlike me, she doesn't have *enough* time to do all her own stuff, so I told her I didn't need help. I'm perfectly capable of making all the arrangements, flyers, and sending all the emails myself.

It's the perfect distraction. During the first class I have with Landon, I don't look at him once. I'm on my phone composing emails until the bell rings, and then as soon as class is over, I'm out the door because there's no time to waste.

Being busy is definitely the answer.

I thought after the party this weekend, Anae would have

mingled with enough people that we wouldn't have to see her again, so imagine my surprise when she drops into the seat right next to me at lunch.

Hannah freezes with her sandwich halfway to her mouth, and I look over at Anae with my own expression that must convey *are you lost?*

Anae isn't looking at me, though. She's rooting around in her purse, next to mine on the seat between us. I blink as she takes out a bottle of hand sanitizer and makes quick work of sanitizing her own hands—of course, without offering any to me or Hannah.

"What?" she finally asks, staring back at me as she rubs her hands together.

"I just... didn't expect you to sit with us."

Didn't *want* her to sit with us, but I don't add that.

"I heard you were organizing some book drive thing. I want to help."

I continue to stare at her, wide-eyed. "You want to... help?"

She nods. "I want to join your little uprising club."

"Uplift."

"Whatever. Who cares? I want to join."

"Why?" When she cocks an eyebrow, I expand, "I mean, no offense, but you are aware the entire goal of the club is to help others, right? Doesn't really seem like your thing."

"Next year I'll be going to college, and I plan to join a sorority. I've been researching the top sororities at Dare's school, and they do a lot of philanthropy. So, next year, when I'm rushing, I figure it will help if they see I dabbled in stuff like that in high school. Thanks to Aubrey, I have a lot working against me now, so I need to rehab my public image a bit and control the narrative."

"Okay," I drawl, choosing not to deal with her delusional reasoning. "Well, I guess I could use a little help. We're putting this project together really quickly. The book drive is on Friday, so I need to really amplify the signal and get the word out so people know about it."

Anae nods. "I can definitely help with that. Why don't we meet up at your house after school to brainstorm and go over everything? You can show me what you've done so far and what still needs to be done. I'll do a video and upload a story about us organizing it today to bring a little awareness, and I can handle the social media to really amplify the signal, like you said you wanted to."

I'm reluctant to admit Anae had a good idea, but... "That could probably work. Why don't we meet at your house instead of mine, though?"

Anae shakes her head. "You live right on the beach. I'm considering a beach shot. I haven't decided yet, I'll have to see your place, but it's a good option. Plus," she adds, looking me over and appearing unimpressed, "you'll have to change into something more fashionable if you're going to show up on my feed, so proximity to your closet is important."

It's not worth arguing about, so I say, "All right, fine."

"Great," she chirps, clasping her hands together. "Hannah and I will head to our house after school to grab—wait, I assume you have a pool?"

I nod. "We do."

"Perfect. So we'll grab swimsuits in case we want to go for a swim or get a little sun while we work, and then Hannah can drive me to your place."

Every cell in my body tells me it's a bad idea, but I can't think of a good reason to tell her no. I can't stop her from joining the club, and if I put up too much resistance over her coming to my house, she may wonder why.

I'VE NEVER HOPED Landon was out wasting Brittany's time before, but as I drive toward our house with my mind on preparing for Anae to come over, I am definitely hoping not to see his car in the driveway.

I breathe a sigh of relief when I pull in, but the feeling is short-lived. I still have to host Anae Richards at my house, and that was not on my senior year bingo card.

I'm not sure if she was serious about me changing clothes to hang out with her, but just in case, I head upstairs to my bedroom to unload my school bag and change my outfit. She did mention perhaps swimming. If Landon doesn't get home soon, I might not be opposed to the idea, so I put a one-piece swimsuit on underneath a pale blue dress that will be easy enough to peel off. I tug on a white sweater over it for added coverage, then I grab my purse and head back downstairs.

I should probably have something to offer them to drink, so I check the fridge. On impulse, I make a pitcher of lemonade.

Before long, I hear a car pull in. I'm slightly anxious and unsure what to do with myself, so I stand awkwardly in the foyer waiting for them to come to the door.

Anae walks in first. She plucks the stylish sunglasses off her face and walks right past me toward the living room, leaving a faint scent of perfume in her wake.

Hannah trails behind her carrying a tote bag and her purse. I close the door behind them. When I turn back around, Hannah does a little spin, strikes a pose, then puts her legs out and flexes her ankle to draw my attention to her feet, apparently.

She's not wearing the shoes she wore to school. Instead, she's wearing a pair of heeled white sandals with glittery silver buckles.

"Pretty," I say with a polite smile.

Her eyes widen. "I'll say. You're officially not allowed to get me a birthday present now. These were so expensive, Parker. You're crazy, but they're *so* pretty. Even prettier than they were in the store. Thank you so much."

I'm... confused.

Before I can say as much, Hannah looks down to admire the pretty, obviously already loved shoe and asks off-handedly, "I guess your mom gave you that spending money credit card, huh?"

"Um... no. I mean, Hayden said he's ordering one, but it will probably take a few days to come in the mail."

Since I'm frowning when Hannah looks up at me, she loses her smile. "You didn't buy them?" she says slowly.

My eyebrows rise in surprise. "What? No. You know I'm not a heel girl, I wouldn't know how to pick them out for someone else."

Hannah stares at me blankly. "Then who are they from?"

I shrug helplessly. "I have literally no idea. Why did you think they were from me?"

She swallows, looking down at the shoes with a more cautious awareness. "I don't know," she says softly. "They were delivered to my house, but the note didn't say... I thought... because of the sugar daddy jokes yesterday, and I was only joking, but I told you about these shoes—"

Speaking of shoes, Anae's heels click as she makes her way back down the hall to retrieve us, apparently having acquainted herself with this level of the house. "Next time you buy her a present, make it a purse," Anae says. "Her feet are freakishly small, so I can't borrow her shoes." Looking from Hannah to me, she says, "Are we going to work, or—" Then she grimaces, looking at my clothes. "Jesus Christ, Parker, who told you that you could pull off white?"

"What?" I look down at my clothes, protectively pulling the sweater around myself.

"And that pale blue. Ugh, no. No. Take me to your room, I'll find you something else to wear. And throw away everything you own in both of those colors. They wash you out and make you look sickly. Are you a long-suffering heroine in a Brontë novel? Because it certainly looks like you are."

She has only been here for thirty seconds and already Hannah and I are both frowning as we head upstairs.

This was *definitely* a bad idea.

I show Anae to my bedroom against my better judgment. Hannah tenses up as soon as we step foot inside and her gaze darts to the jewelry box on my dresser.

That's where the necklace is stashed. I didn't even think about it when I was up here, or I would have moved it before they got here.

Hannah and I exchange glances, then I haul only Anae into my walk-in closet to help me find a new outfit. I hang back by the door while she goes through all my things. When she finds a gray jersey dress and says, "I guess this will work," I stall a bit by asking if I should change shoes, too.

When we emerge from my closet, Hannah is sitting on the edge of my bed and the jewelry box is gone.

Phew.

"You need a bracelet or something cute. Maybe an anklet. Where's your jewelry?"

"I haven't unpacked it yet," I lie. "We just moved in, so..."

Anae rolls her eyes and shoves the dress at me. "Go change. Hannah, do something with her hair while you're in there." Sighing, she drops onto the couch and puts her purse on her lap. When we still haven't done as she ordered, her eyes widen and she uses her hand to shoo us along. "Come on. We don't have all day."

Hannah and I go in my bathroom and shut the door. I shoot her wide eyes, and she leans in to whisper, "I moved the jewelry box to your bottom desk drawer, but we better hurry in case she snoops."

I sigh. "This is not how I want to spend any of my days."

Hannah nods her agreement, keeping her voice whisper soft. "Let's just get this over with."

I'm uneasy leaving Anae in my bedroom unattended, so I change dresses as quickly as possible and Hannah makes quick work of pulling half my hair back and securing it with a cute clip. I shoo Hannah back to the bedroom so we can get back as quickly as possible and step into the low white heeled sandals she found for me. They're not nearly as cute or as fancy as Hannah's, but other than maybe a wedding, there is no reason I would *ever* wear the shoes on Hannah's feet.

When we emerge, much to my relief, Anae is still sitting on the couch. Her gaze rakes over me and she nods, though she only looks barely satisfied. "That will do." Standing, she slides her purse on her shoulder and leads us out of my bedroom. "What's the aesthetic of this club?"

"What?"

"Is there a color scheme? What does the logo look like?"

"A color scheme?"

What is she talking about?

"We need to brand it. Make it cool. Exclusive. Something people actually *want* to join. Does the club have a social media presence?"

"No?"

"That's lame. We're going to set one up. I'm thinking a cool black and white aesthetic, kind of a callback to photojournalism, but with classy pops of color. If there's not a logo, we'll have one made. Something stylish and wistful blended with a more solid, grounded font. I'm thinking that will be the vibe of the club. Doing good while looking good. Casual elegance."

She says all of this as if she's pitching people who will actually respond to it.

Immediately, she realizes, "My ideas are wasted on you, aren't they? It doesn't matter. Just leave the branding and social media presence to me. Those can be my areas of expertise. You guys can handle all the real do-gooder stuff. I'll participate, of course. Mostly to cover the events and make sure we have a lot of candid-looking evidence of all our hard work. When colleges look into this club, I want it to have a *presence*. It will help you, too, honestly."

Her idea isn't terrible, I just hate everything about it. "This club isn't about looking good, Anae. It's about doing good."

"Right, but why not do both? There are no downsides to this. It can only be helpful and more attractive to colleges. You guys may not have to work extra hard to get into the good places next year, but I do. So, yay for you. You get to benefit from my efforts. You're welcome." She misses a beat, then she says, "Why don't we set up out by the pool? I want to get some sun and get a feel for potential photo ops. You girls grab some drinks and meet me out there."

I sigh, standing at the foot of the stairs and watching Anae dismiss us like her hired help as she makes her way out to my pool like she's on vacation.

"I do not enjoy her," I tell Hannah as the sliding door closes behind Anae.

Hannah shakes her head. "Nope. But it's easier to just do what she wants. I'll go chill some drink glasses."

"I made lemonade," I volunteer.

"Sugar-free?"

I shake my head no.

Hannah nods, her mind clearly on her next task. "We should take out bottles of water, too."

———

ANAE SUCKS ALL the energy out of me while she's over, so there's none left to deal with Landon when he comes home.

I head upstairs as soon as I hear his car pull in.

Mom's at work, so I text her and ask if she could stop by my favorite deli and grab me a turkey sandwich for dinner. I tell her I have a lot of homework and club stuff to do so I don't really want to take time to have an actual dinner.

I really *do* have homework, so I kneel on the floor by my backpack and start unloading books. In the middle of prioritizing which subject to start working on first, I realize the card with Javi's number isn't in my statistics folder where I left it. Panic floods my veins and I start ripping through my bag.

Oh my god, where is it?

I took the card with me to school because I was afraid of Landon finding it if I left it in my room. He's not even supposed to be in my room, but he does a lot of shit he's not supposed to do.

I didn't take it out, right? I know it was in this backpack, I remember looking at it fondly before one of my classes started. Oh my god, what if it fell out *at school*?

Oh my god, if Landon finds that card...

Just before I completely melt down, my finger touches glossy cardstock. I pull out the card, and my shoulders slump with relief when I turn it over to see Javi's writing on the back.

I place my hand and the card over my chest and breathe a sigh of relief, then I set it aside and get out the rest of my books.

By the time I lay out my books and notes on the desk and I'm *still* thinking about the card, I realize I don't feel entirely safe having it around. I don't want to get rid of it just in case this thing with Javi really turns into something. For sentimental reasons, I may want to have the card he first gave me his number on.

But I can't have it out where someone could see it, either.

Setting the card down on the desk, I open the drawer and carefully draw out my jewelry box. I open the bottom drawer to make sure Hannah's stuff is still safely tucked away, and when I see it is, I decide to add Javi's card to it.

But, just in case I get up the nerve to text him, I better save it in my phone first.

My hands are clammy and a bit shaky as I create a new contact and type in Javi's name. I type in his number, then double check against the card that I put it in right.

Once I confirm I did, I slide the card in the bottom drawer alone with Hannah's stuff, then I put the jewelry box back in its regular spot.

But now that his number is actually saved in my phone, it feels like a deliberate choice not to use it.

Maybe I should send him a quick text just to say hi and triple check I saved the number correctly. Yeah, that's a good reason. Accuracy. I love accuracy.

My stomach is an absolute wreck as I try to think what to type. I've talked to guys on social media messengers and stuff, but I've never actually texted with a guy I had romantic interest in.

"This is so stupid," I mutter to myself. "You're making a big deal out of nothing. Just say hello."

My fingers protest by not working, but I force myself to compose a simple first text message.

"Hey! Just wanted to say hi so you had my number, too." I add a quick smiley face, then backspace, then re-add the smiley face because I'm being ridiculous.

I press send quickly before I can change my mind.

Then I feel like I have a whole vat of acid in my stomach as I stare at the screen, waiting for a response.

He's probably working. Or hanging out with friends. Or... doing literally anything, but there's no reason to expect he'll answer right—

He's typing.

I stare, wide-eyed, at the three gray bubbles dancing on the bottom of my phone screen.

"It's about time," he texts back with a winky emoji.

I break into a ridiculous grin. "I know, you gave me your number YESTERDAY. I'm surprised you didn't die waiting."

"It's fortunate for both of us," he replies. "What are you up to?"

I sigh, giving up on studying for the moment and hopping up on my bed so I can relax on it while I text him. "Not much. I just finished up a sort of club meeting with the best and worst girls at my school. Now I'm about to do some homework while I wait for my mom to bring me dinner."

"Sounds fun."

"Oh yeah. Too much fun. Should be illegal. What about you? What are you doing?"

"Thinking about you," he says, with an added wink.

A stupid grin reclaims my lips. "Well, I certainly hope so. If you're talking to me and thinking about somebody else, we may be on the wrong track."

"Oh yeah? What track are you hoping we're on?"

My eyes widen. That's... aggressive. Or is it? Maybe not. Maybe I'm just so new to this that it seems that way.

My suspicion is confirmed when I search my brain for a response, and all I can come up with is, "A good one?"

I do not type that.

I do not type anything.

Too much time passes and I start to panic, realizing I've let an awkward amount of time pass after a question like that.

Perspiration gathers along my forehead. I drop the phone on the mattress and shake out my hands, trying more desperately to come up with something cogent to say.

The bubbles dance.

I hold my breath.

"You there?"

Smacking my palm against my face, I groan. I grab the phone and try to think, but my brain won't work. Finally, I type out the only thing I can come up with.

The truth.

"Yeah, I'm here. Sorry, I didn't mean to... disappear. I should warn you, I'm really new to this."

"Texting?" he jokes.

"Yes. I've only had a phone for three days. Prior to this, I lived in an ocean cave with dolphins and a crab."

"Makes sense. I thought I smelled the beach on you."

I crack a smile. "No, but in all seriousness, the whole talking to a guy thing. I know that probably sounds lame, but I've literally never texted a guy before, so..."

"How old are you?" he messages back.

Oh boy.

He thinks it's weird.

Of course he thinks it's weird. It *is* weird.

"I'm 18," I answer.

"And you've never dated?"

I can't tell if he thinks that's horrifically weird, or he's just curious. Stupid toneless text.

Swallowing, I type back, "No, I haven't."

"Why? Never liked anyone?"

"I have, but... it's kind of a long story."

"I've got time."

I smile faintly, but with very little humor. "I also think it probably isn't the best idea to start off the first time we've ever texted by talking about another guy. Isn't that a dating etiquette rule or something?"

"Maybe, but I tend to think you should only obey rules as long as they serve you."

Of course he does.

I guess I have a type.

Another text comes through, one that is decidedly un-Landonlike.

"You can talk to me about anything you want."

I stare at those words on the screen for longer than I should without responding. It's hard to say exactly why they feel so reassuring. I guess because I believe them, and it's nice to have someone I can confide in.

"It's too messed up," I finally text back. "I don't want to bring you into it anymore than you already have been."

"Is it about that guy you came to dinner with? Your new stepbrother?"

I cringe seeing that word on the screen and knowing it's a reference to Landon. Licking my lips, I debate how much I want to share.

Then I glance at the time and realize it's getting late. Mom will be here soon, and I really do have a lot of homework.

"Hey Javi, I'm really not trying to be evasive or anything, but I just realized how late it's getting, and I still have a lot of homework to do..."

"No problem. We can talk more later."

"Thanks for understanding."

"Of course. Now go get that A so you can come back and talk to me."

I grin at the screen and type back, "Yes, sir."

He types back an ellipsis, then he says, "You wanna keep that up, or you wanna do your homework?"

I flush, chuckling to myself and trying to ignore the butterflies in my tummy. I guess I walked into that, but I didn't expect risqué texts so soon.

"Homework!" I text back. "Talk to you later," I add with a smiley, just so he knows I wasn't put off by the joke.

"In case I don't talk to you later, have sweet dreams."

"You too."

"Oh, I will."

Sighing heavily, I sink back against my pillows and cradle my phone against my chest. I can hear my heartbeat, feel the lingering aftershocks of excitement moving through my veins.

I don't know how this can possibly work with me living here, but for now, I'm not going to worry about it. For now, I'm just going to enjoy texting a great guy who seems to like me, and hope with all my heart that I'll be able to keep Landon from ruining it.

I WAKE up to a picture of the sun rising over the ocean—not out my window. I just missed it there. But Javi took a picture of it. He must have been on the beach early this morning, so he sent me the beautiful picture without a single word.

Peace fills me at the sight of it. I don't know if it's the picture so much as the message. The fact that he was thinking of me practically as soon as his eyes opened.

I was thinking of him until I went to sleep. I didn't message him because I wasn't sure of the dating rules. I thought about googling them, but I know it won't be that simple. I don't care about following rules for the sake of following rules, but rules usually exist for a reason. In this case, I imagine any particular rule I might follow would have more to do with not coming on too strong too fast and scaring him off. After all, I don't know him well yet, so I don't know how he operates.

"That's so pretty. Thanks for sharing," I text as soon as I wake up.

I lie there with my phone on my chest for a few minutes before he responds. "You finally wake up, bookworm?"

My stupid, impossible to tame smile immediately emerges.

"Yeah, I know, I'm such a slacker. Didn't even start my day on the beach."

"Lame."

"Do you live by the beach?"

"Yeah, pretty close. Sometimes I like to come down here for a morning run."

"Oooh. I only run if something is chasing me."

"Noted," he replies with a wink. "You get chased often?"

More often than you'd expect.

Along with that sobering thought of my own evil stepbrother, I get an actual wake-up call. My phone alarm goes off. I silence it quickly, but that means it's time to start getting ready for another day of school.

I put my phone down and stretch, then, reluctantly, pull myself from the comfy sanctuary of bed.

"I don't want to wake up," I text Javi. "Are you a morning person?"

"Nah, I just don't sleep much. I stay up late, too."

"That's not healthy."

"The run makes up for it," he teases.

I laugh, walking into my bathroom. "No, it does not."

My phone lights up again when I'm brushing my teeth. "You know, I sent you a picture of my view..."

"Mine's nothing to get excited about," I assure him. "I'm brushing my teeth."

"Maybe I'm really into teeth."

I laugh again, then decide what the hell. I am certain whatever introductory dating rules exist, this violates each and every one of them, but I aim my phone at the mirror and take the least sexy picture of myself ever: me literally brushing my teeth. I shake my head at the dumb picture, but I push send before I can overthink it.

"Sexy, right?" I joke.

"I can think of a few other things I'd like to put in that mouth."

My stomach drops, but it's more with excitement than fear—which is a nice change. "A few? How many dicks do you have?"

"Four. I hope that's not a dealbreaker."

I shake my head, sighing once I'm done laughing as I rinse out my toothbrush. I expected Javi would be smart and funny from the few interactions we've had, but I think he's even better than I thought he'd be.

I'm light as a cloud as I float downstairs. Smiling is so easy, I can't really stop.

It would be nice if Mom were in the kitchen when I get there so she could witness me being so happy, but she must still be upstairs getting ready. I am downstairs a little earlier than usual since I woke up before my alarm and I was extra energized from texting Javi.

Speaking of...

Since I'm the only one in the kitchen, I sit down at the island counter and drop my backpack on the floor by my feet. I pull out my phone and open my text with Javi, smiling fondly at the text on the screen. I start to type out another message, but before I can finish it, Landon appears so close behind me, I can feel the heat rolling off his chest when he leans in to whisper, "Who are you texting?"

Fear jumpstarts my heart. I drop the phone, startled, then fumble to pick it back up and darken the screen before he can see. "What? No one. Nothing. Hannah. Mind your business," I blurt, feeling heat explode beneath my skin.

Landon looks at me oddly, his dark brows pulled together as he drops onto the seat beside me. "Yeah, that sounded like the truth."

I glare at him and shove my phone into my backpack. "It's

none of your business who I'm texting. Nothing I do is any of your business."

He shrugs. "Guess we'll have to agree to disagree."

I roll my eyes, utterly uninterested in his bullshit. I'm not going to sit here at the counter with him, though, so I get up and start making myself a smoothie.

"Arden says he ran into you at the club."

Fucking Arden.

"Yep. Hannah and I played tennis and had lunch with my mom."

"You run into Aladdin while you were there?"

I turn around to meet his gaze. "You know Javi is Hispanic, right?"

"You know he's also a poor asshole in a vest trying to trick some sheltered rich girl into liking him, right?"

My cheeks flush with heat. "I am not rich. I'm middle class at best. You're the one with money."

"Which you have access to now. You live in my house. You met him at a *country club*, Parker. You think he looks at you and sees middle class?"

I sigh at him, then shake my head and focus on putting fruit in the blender. "Whatever. He wasn't even working, so no, we didn't see him. Again, not that it is *any* of your business."

Landon nods at the fruit bowl. "Get me an apple."

"Get it yourself."

I spoke without thought because I'm so annoyed at him, but when he actually gets up and saunters over toward me, my heartbeat accelerates like it's auditioning for *The Fast and the Furious*, and I find myself wishing I'd have just handed him the damn apple.

I swallow, trying my very best to ignore him as he comes up behind me. He looms deliberately, caging me in from behind, placing his hands on the counter on either side of me. I gasp as his heat hits my back, stiffen when he lets go of the counter to reach for the apple.

His breath tickles my ear as he murmurs, "Guess I didn't ask very nicely, huh?"

My heart ticks erratically and suddenly I can't breathe. It's not fear, though. His words aren't mean, they're almost teasing. Lighthearted despite his threatening position behind me. It feels... different. Almost intimate.

Snatching his apple, he steps back, and in a split second, the moment has passed. He isn't so close, and I can breathe again.

I brace my hands on the counter and try to steady my breathing and my racing heart so he doesn't notice when he sits down, but he doesn't sit down. When I look over, he's gone, already on his way out the door.

I should feel relieved. I do, but some strange part of me feels bereft, too.

I shake off that insanity and get back to my smoothie. I can't stop thinking about that brief interaction, though. I have literally been dreading it since he bent me over the couch and did what he did to me that night. The dread had built up and hardened because I had no idea what to expect of our next interaction. But that... that wasn't so bad.

"Hey, honey."

My gaze jumps over to Mom, putting her purse on the counter.

"Hey, Mom."

She comes over to give me a kiss on the temple. "Did you sleep well?"

I nod, flashing her a smile. "Yeah, I did. You?"

Hayden comes around the corner, already dressed for work with his briefcase in hand. Mom glances at him, then smiles softly as she nods, but she doesn't say a word.

It's a bittersweet smile, one that feels as true as the mountain of lies I've told since moving in with the Atwaters.

We never used to lie to each other before them.

At least I know if she lost any sleep—*for a bad reason, anyway*—it wasn't because of Hayden. It was the younger Atwater and concern for me keeping her up at night.

Last night may have been the first night since we moved in that was entirely unwarranted, though. I was so distracted by Javi, I didn't think of Landon once.

Okay, not more than once.

Okay, not more than a couple of times.

The point is, I thought about him less, and even when I did, the thoughts weren't as potent.

Until he cornered you in the kitchen and you couldn't breathe because he was standing so close.

I scowl at my own unhelpful thought and the bite of guilt that comes with it. I know I've only been texting Javi for less than a day, but I've enjoyed it so much. I *like* him, so Landon's inconveniently dominant physical presence shouldn't still work like that, should it?

I'm probably being unreasonable. The thing with Javi is new. The thing with Landon is very old. Even if it does turn into something with Javi, I'm sure it will take a little time before Landon becomes utterly powerless over me. Old habits die hard and all that, right?

I'm in new territory and lacking a roadmap, so I pour my smoothie into a to-go cup and decide to do what I always do when there's something I don't thoroughly understand.

Research it.

I ONLY HAVE a little time to hit up the school library before my first class, but I'm able to grab a couple of books to check out and take with me.

Andreas Capellanus wrote a book codifying the rules of courtly love in the twelfth century, and because I'm thorough, I decide that's a good place to start.

Having a book to bury my nose in makes it easier to ignore Landon in the classes we have together, too. I read it until the bell rings, and then, like yesterday, I'm out the door.

I'm still reading at lunch. Hannah is sitting with me, but she doesn't mind. She scrolls on her phone while I read, and I pop my head up when I want her input.

"Do you think it's possible to like two people at once?"

Her eyebrows rise, then draw together as she thinks about it. "I don't know," she says after a few seconds. "Possibly. I've never tried."

"Capellanus is pretty firmly against the idea."

Hannah shrugs. "Different folks, different strokes. Also different times, but I don't have to tell you that." She nods at the book. "What's with the side project?"

"I started texting Javi last night," I confess.

Her eyes widen. "Oh yeah? How's it going?"

"Good. Great. I don't know. *He's* great. I'm immensely enjoying talking to him. But then this morning Landon and I were alone in the kitchen, and..." I trail off, not even sure how to describe it.

I don't have to. Hannah seems to understand. "You've had a crush on Landon for a long time," she says gently. "Even if Javi is the greatest, healthiest guy in the world, you're not the kind of person who can jump in and out of things quickly. You are reading a book trying to make sense of your feelings about a situation you've been encountering for *hours*. When you commit to things, you commit with your whole heart."

Frowning poutily, I say, "I do not have a crush on Landon."

"Whether you do now or not, you have, and it made a profound impact on you. And whether it's fair or not, he *is* part of the fabric of your romantic history. He has literally stopped you from dating for years. That's bound to make an impression."

"That is such bullshit. He has done literally nothing to deserve making any kind of impression on me, ever."

She nods sympathetically. "Unfortunately, whether they deserve it seldom has any bearing on who leaves an impression on us. Sometimes I think the worse they are, the greater chance they have at leaving an impression since they'll sink to lows a more principled person wouldn't. Tends to be memorable."

I shake my head. "That's so annoying."

She nods her agreement.

I look across the lunchroom where Landon always sits and find him looking right at me. I narrow my eyes, and he smirks, his eyes dancing with amusement.

Sighing, I look back at Hannah. "I have a psycho ex-boyfriend and I never even dated him."

Hannah cracks a faint smile. "If you want my honest opinion?"

"Of course."

Her smile shifts faintly, like she knows she's about to tell me something I won't want to hear. "Even if it's theoretically possible to like two people at once, I don't think it's possible *for you*. You'd have to end one thing before you could start another. If you really like Javi and don't want to ruin things with him... you might want to handle your Landon stuff first."

HANNAH'S WORDS weigh on me all afternoon, so I don't text Javi.

I don't *want* her to be right because I have enjoyed the temporary escape of talking to him and I don't want it to end, but I think she is.

The problem is, I don't know *how* to handle my Landon stuff. It's not like I can just politely ask him to stop tormenting me. Parental intervention is off the table unless I admit defeat and convince myself I've tried literally everything else first, and I know myself well enough to admit that's unlikely.

Realistically, I just always assumed I would have to deal with this through high school, then I would go to college and be free of him. I had made my peace with that.

But now there's someone I could have an actual connection with, and I want to explore it, but Landon is standing directly in my way.

So, the circumstances have changed. Even if it was fine to deal with his bullshit when it wasn't hurting me, that's no longer the case.

My latest idea is my craziest: I want to have an honest, straightforward conversation with him about this.

I'm just not sure how I could arrange it safely since I'm committed to not being alone with him. I could probably ask Hannah to come over and linger close enough to keep me safe while I talked to him, but it would need to be when Mom and Hayden weren't around since I couldn't risk them overhearing.

I think about trying to do it tonight, but before I can get up the nerve, Landon leaves to go hang out at Malek's house.

As eager as I am to get this issue settled now that I've decided there is one, I am much more excited about having Landon out of the house. I think about texting Javi just to say hi since I don't have to worry about getting caught, but turns out, I don't have to. He texts me.

I bite my bottom lip as I swipe the screen to see the picture he sent me.

It's a picture from behind the valet stand.

His view.

I'm a fast learner and we've already done this once, so I stretch my legs out on the bed and reposition the open textbook on my lap before taking a quick picture to send him.

"The weather's this beautiful and you're inside? Come on now."

I smile and type back, "I'm studying. You want me to deal with laptop glare outside? What are you, a psychopath?"

"You can study later. You live in one of those hilltop mansions, don't you? Go for a swim."

"I feel like that's a really sneaky way of trying to get a bikini pic," I joke.

"It wasn't, but hey, if you want to send one, I won't say no."

"Sorry, pal. I don't even wear bikinis."

"Bullshit."

"I don't! I have the complexion of a friendly ghost, so if I even think about the sun without sunscreen on, I burn. If I could swim fully clothed, I would."

"You can jump in the pool fully clothed and then climb out and send me a picture. I'm cool with that."

"I bet you are." I shake my head, trying to stop smiling so much because it's absurd. "Anyway, I am supposed to be studying and you are distracting me."

"Good. Get your ass outside and study later."

"So bossy," I tease, but honestly, I don't hate it.

I refuse to ignore my studies and spend the whole night talking to him, though, so I exercise some restraint and plug my phone in to charge so I won't be tempted.

Just when I get back into a groove working, there's a knock at my bedroom door.

"It's open," I call back.

Mom pops her head inside. "Hey, honey." Her gaze flickers from my laptop back to my face. "Doing school stuff?"

I nod. "Working on some club stuff. It's not super important if you need me for something."

"Oh, no." Mom waves me off. "I just wanted to let you know we were going out. Since Landon won't be around this evening, Hayden and I thought we would take advantage and have a little impromptu date night."

"Sounds good." I flash her a smile. "Have fun."

She smiles back. "We will. Antonia is downstairs. She'll make you dinner tonight, so just let her know whenever you get hungry."

Mom leaves and I spend a few more minutes working, but it's a struggle. My focus is being pulled away by the knowledge that I have the house to myself. That never happens, so I can't help thinking I should take advantage of it.

Like Javi said, I can finish my homework later when everyone is back and I need to be holed up in my room, anyway.

I change into my swimsuit and pull on a loose dress over it, then I head downstairs. Antonia is wiping down the already gleaming countertop when I come down.

"Hey, Antonia."

"Hello, Miss Parker. Hungry?"

I bite my lip, glancing out at the pool. It's calling my name. "Not just yet, but I have a request. If this is not something you do, please tell me, I don't want to like give you extra chores..."

She waves me off. "What would you like?"

Flinching at the awkwardness of placing an order with someone *not* working a drive-thru or carrying a notepad around a restaurant, I say, "I was wondering if you make strawberry banana smoothies?"

"Of course. With chia seeds or without?"

My eyes brighten. "Without. Oh, the blender may be dirty," I warn her, grimacing. "I had one this morning for breakfast, but it was so good. There's no rule that you can't have two smoothies in one day, right?"

"If there is, it's a dumb rule."

I crack a smile. "Thank you, Antonia."

She flashes me a smile, setting her cleaning cloth aside. "Of course. I'll wash up and make that for you now. Are you heading out to the pool? I can bring it out for you."

"That would be amazing. Thank you so much."

I sigh happily as I slide open the door leading out to the pool area. The water ripples welcomingly, and the weather is perfect. I peel my dress off and toss it on the lounger positioned by a little table so Antonia will know where to set the smoothie, then I make my way into the pool.

Peace washes over me as I swim, refueling me, shoring me up for the battles ahead. I never want to get out.

I tell myself I should so my smoothie doesn't melt in the heat, but I haven't actually seen Antonia bring it out. She should have by now, right? How long does it take to make a smoothie?

That might be terrible. I feel guilty even asking her to serve me—let alone rushing her. Maybe she got busy doing something else. Maybe she hadn't done the dishes yet and needed to clean the blender first.

I consider going inside—maybe she just forgot to bring it out?—but if I walk in there looking for a smoothie and she hasn't made it yet, I don't want her to feel bad.

I am thirsty, though, and since I don't have a smoothie and I'm now afraid walking back into the house for any reason could be taken as impoliteness, I go to the pool house to grab a bottle of water.

When I return, there is still no smoothie, so I pull my dress back on over my wet swimsuit and relax on the lounger while I wait for it. It's peaceful out here when I know I'm not being watched.

I end up getting so relaxed, I feel myself getting drowsy. I try to listen for the door to slide open behind me, but I must doze off for a minute. The next thing I know, I'm jolted awake. I look at the end table and see my smoothie has just been delivered.

"Oh, thank you, Antonia." I shift my position on the lounger and reach for the drink, but my blood freezes when I glance behind the table where she should be standing and catch sight of denim.

Antonia wasn't wearing jeans.

My gaze darts up and I see Landon standing over me.

My heart sinks and then somersaults. Adrenaline shoots through my veins like a shot of heroin, and I start to push myself up off the lounger.

"No," he says simply, shaking his head. Before I can stand, he sits on the edge of the lounger, casually planting his hand near my hip to keep me from being able to get up. "Stay put. Enjoy your drink."

I don't really want to drink it now.

"What are you doing here? Where's Antonia?" I ask uncertainly.

"I told her she could go home," he says, his mouth tugging up at the corners as his eyes dance with satisfaction. "Told her we were going to order in tonight."

I lick my lips, trying to subtly sniff the air to see if I smell alcohol on his breath. I don't smell anything, but maybe he's just not close enough. "I thought you were going to be at Malek's."

"Yeah." He reaches out and runs a knuckle under my chin. I suck in a breath and draw away from his touch. "So do our parents. That's why they're gone."

"You know my mom. She's paranoid. She'll probably check the security feed even though she didn't expect you'd be here."

And even though I was in my room, and Antonia was supposed to be here...

If ever there was a night Mom may *not* feel the need to check the security feed to make sure I'm safe, this is it.

Landon smirks, then he reaches into his pocket and draws out a little black wire frayed at both ends. "Oops. I don't think the pool camera's working."

Shit.

All my excuses have dried up, and I'm starting to feel the onset of panic creeping in. My mouth feels dry and my pulse starts to race. My ribcage seems to be shrinking around my lungs, and the tiny hairs at the back of my neck are on alert.

I know he's faster and stronger than I am, and I know I am already at a disadvantage. I have no shoes on, I am lying on a fucking pool lounger, and he caught me off-guard. There is literally no fucking way I can run away from him right now. He trapped me before I even knew there was a threat I needed to run from.

With the flight option off the table, all that leaves is fight, but I don't want to be the first to swing, either. It feels farfetched right now, like a legitimate fucking fantasy, but maybe he isn't going to do anything to me. Maybe he's just pushing me around to show me he can. Maybe he only wants to scare me.

Each time he has attacked me before, he has been drinking, and I don't smell any alcohol on his breath right now. I think he's sober.

He did push me up beside the lockers at school when he was sober, though.

There were people around then, and I still wasn't sure what was going to happen. What might have happened if Malek hadn't intervened.

Malek.

He said he was going to Malek's, but that was obviously a lie.

I need to get my phone or Landon's phone. Somebody's phone. I can't call the police this time, but if I can get away from Landon long enough to make a call…

Malek will come. Not for me, but to save his cousin from doing something stupid. I don't care about his bullshit motivation, I only care that he intervenes.

While my mind is racing for a way out, Landon sits there watching me. He notices my tongue dart out to wet my dry lips.

"Thirsty?" He grabs the smoothie, pushes the straw to my side of the cup, then guides it to my lips.

I seal them.

"Oh, come on. Antonia went to all the trouble of making it for you. Seems a shame for it to go to waste."

Still, I keep my lips closed.

His gaze hardens. "Open your fucking mouth, Parker, before I open it for you."

My heart sinks. I swallow past the lump in my throat and tentatively take the straw between my lips.

I hate him watching me take a sip.

And when the flavor hits my tongue, it's off.

My heart starts to pound harder. What did he put in my drink? I wouldn't accept a drink at a party from him, so I probably shouldn't take another drink from this smoothie, either.

Panic begins to shut down my brain, but I fight to keep it working for me. My brain is the only advantage I have over him. Physically, all the odds are in his favor.

Where should we order in from?

I can't speak, but my brain tells me to say it.

Take control of the conversation. Guide him away from whatever he wants to do. That's probably bad, so push him elsewhere like you did at the club.

But I can't move. I'm too fucking afraid, and all I can think about is what's in the smoothie? Why did he need to put something in my smoothie? If I ask, will he tell me?

I only took one sip, so I should be okay, right? It would take more than one sip...

Before my panic can overwhelm me, Landon pulls the straw to the side of the cup nearest him and takes a draw.

I sag against the lounger with relief. He's not going to drug *himself.*

Amusement tugs at his full lips when he notices my relief. "Needed a little rum," he says lightly. Setting the drink back down on the table, he says conversationally, "What, were you afraid I was going to drug you?"

I don't answer, and he doesn't seem to mind.

He shakes his head, answering me anyway. "I wouldn't do that." For the briefest blip of a heartbeat, I think he's saying something decent, but then he adds, "I'd want you to be awake and completely conscious to experience whatever I'm doing to you."

Wow.

It's hard to take that more than one way.

My plan to call Malek starts to slip from my fingers, every system in my body working overtime to convey just one message: run.

It still doesn't feel like the right move, but right now, I'm a sitting duck.

Run.

Don't run.

I don't know what to do. We're in the eye of the storm. Any move I make in any direction will put us right in it, but I can't just sit here waiting for him to pounce on me.

My muscles feel jittery and unreliable as I swiftly bring my hand to the side, chopping his wrist and shoving him back, then launching off the side of the lounger he's not sitting on.

My heart thuds like a judge's gavel deciding my fate, and as I run barefoot across the expensive tile, I hear his faster, heavier footfalls behind me.

It was the wrong move.

It was the only move I had.

Both things are true.

Neither thought is helpful.

Landon grabs me around the waist, ripping me off my path to the poolhouse and pulling me back against him.

"No," I cry, thrashing and digging my nails into his arm, trying to make him let go.

My heart is racing, my lungs working to draw breath. His voice is low, but I can still hear him over the ruckus in my body. "You think I'm gonna let you get a door between us this time, Parker? I don't fucking think so."

"Let me go," I cry angrily, fearfully. "Get your hands off me, Landon!"

He doesn't let go, and his steely grip doesn't ease. Instead, he tightens it, forcing me even closer to his body as he waits out my thrashing. "You go ahead and tire yourself out," he taunts. "I'll wait."

Furious tears gather at the corner of my eyes. *This isn't fair.*

I can already feel my muscles tiring out. The flood of adrenaline allowed me to fight harder than I would usually be able to, but even that wasn't enough. My skin is on fire and I feel on the verge of collapse, while Landon doesn't even seem to be winded.

His head is close enough that I reach back and grab a fistful of his hair. I want to hurt him, to make him let me go, so I pull it as hard as I can. He lets me pull until his face is next to mine, but as soon as he wants to, he stops me. I watch the muscles chord in his neck. My body must be intensely confused by all the different stimulation, because a wire seems to cross in my brain and I feel an answering wave of heat between my thighs at the sight of it.

"Aren't you getting tired yet?" I ask him.

Landon's green eyes dance with amusement. "No," he murmurs.

"Fuck. That really sucks."

He smirks. "You might want to start doing a little cardio, Johansson."

"You might want to start doing a little less."

"Nah. I like being able to throw you around." He loosens his grip on my waist, and I let go of his hair, thinking this is my chance to... speedwalk away while panting because I don't think I can run right now.

Unfortunately, rather than let me escape, he scoops me up bridal style and carries me over to the nearest lounger.

I don't want to do this again.

It did not work very well last time.

I let him exert his stupid muscles putting me down on the lounger, and I don't try to flee this time. I look up at him and watch, my heart in my throat, as he unbuttons his jeans.

Oh my god oh my god oh my god.

Nope, it's not going to happen. I'm going to figure out a way to avoid it. I just have to... think.

I am incredibly distracted when he unzips his pants and slides up his gray T-shirt. I see a flash of his abs, but it's the waistband of his underwear I shouldn't be seeing. It's black and stretched over taut muscles. The fabric beneath the black band is gray.

I wait for him to take his pants all the way off, but he doesn't. Once they're unbuttoned, he straddles me on the lounger, trapping me beneath his weight.

My pulse pounds *everywhere*. I can hear it, feel it. I'm surprised I can't taste it.

There's only one move I can think to make.

So, without hesitation, I grab Landon's hair and pull his face close. I kiss him, holding my breath at first, like I'm diving into the deep end of a pool without a marked depth. I don't know if I'll crash into something hard that will break me, but I know it's a distinct possibility.

His body tenses at first, obviously surprised by my aggression, by the feeling of my lips pressed willingly against his. But it only takes a split second for him to respond. He knows I don't know what I'm doing, and he does, so he pushes a hand into my hair and cradles my skull, pulling me close as his mouth dominates mine. I'm breathless for a completely different reason, forgetting what to do with my hands. Forgetting that I did this for a reason.

Slowly, the reason comes back to me. I gasp against his

mouth and angle my neck as he moves his rough kisses across my jaw and down the sensitive column. Even his kisses are scary and aggressive, so fucking hungry, like he's trying to suck my soul out through my skin. It hurts when he bites me. I shiver when he follows it up by dragging his hot tongue across my flesh.

Fuck.

It feels demented the way he marks me, but it kindles something inside me, too.

My stomach rocks with nerves as I remind myself I didn't kiss him to trigger a mauling. I kissed him to distract him.

Tentatively, I let my hand crawl over his muscular back. I skim his sides and let my hand settle at the waistband of his jeans. I know they're loose since he unzipped them, but I can't *see*. I don't want to reach into the wrong pocket of fabric and end up with his dick in my hand.

That is too far to go to distract him.

His body radiates heat that makes me sweat, and the nervousness doesn't help. I'm on fire as I tentatively slide my hand lower, keeping my touch as light as possible as I finger the fabric, trying to find the pocket where he keeps his phone.

I feel the hard edge of something and hold my breath, listening for any sound from him that might indicate my fingers are touching the wrong thing. I dig my fingers through his hair and angle my neck to keep his attention where I need it, and then I walk my fingers along the item's hard edge.

Relief rushes through me when I confirm it's a rounded, rectangular shape.

I went fishing in the right pocket.

As slowly and carefully as I can, I draw the phone out of his pocket. I moan and caress his scalp to keep him busy marking up my neck.

Dammit, the fucking phone is locked.

Of course it is.

There's no way I can convince him my skin feels like a screen and press his thumb against the damn thing, so I have to try something else.

The camera still works.

I touch it and turn the screen around. I snap a quick picture of him mauling me, then I touch edit and—

Nope.

Fuck.

I try to send it to Malek without the "help!" text written across my face as initially intended, but I can't send it with the phone locked, either.

I close out of the unhelpful picture and click emergency call. I don't know Malek's number. I saw Javi's written down recently, but I'm so used to texting names instead of numbers, I didn't pay close attention to it except when I was putting it in my phone.

I don't know anyone's number by heart except for Mom's and Hannah's.

I can't call Mom, so I tap out Hannah's phone number...

Only to be shut down when the stupid thing tells me "emergency calls only."

This is a fucking emergency call, you stupid piece of shit!

His phone is pissing me off so much I'm tempted to hurl the damned thing into the pool. Before I can, he startles me by grabbing my wrist.

"Drop it," he murmurs against my skin.

I swallow. "Drop what?"

He stops devouring my flesh for long enough to pull back and look me in the face. "Don't play dumb, Parker. You're not good at it."

I narrow my eyes at him. "Fine." I slide the cell phone back into his pocket.

"Next time you want something in my pants, just ask."

I glare at him, and he smirks at me.

Then, since I've calmed down some, I think clearly enough to say, "I need to pee."

His amusement fades, and he regards me skeptically.

My phone is charging upstairs and his is useless to me, so there are no more lifelines to reach for. I have to find my own way out of this.

I remember Hannah telling me about Anae that sometimes it's easier just to give her what she wants, but everything within me rebels at making such a compromise again. I compromised with Landon at the party and then he didn't bother playing by the rules. He wanted more and would have taken it, but I got a door between us and locked him out.

If I want to avoid further traumatizing myself, I'm going to have to get creative.

"I'm also hungry," I add, since he didn't outright reject my last request. "You better be planning to make me dinner if you sent the cook home, because if I don't get some food in my belly soon, I'm going to turn into a person you definitely don't want to spend the evening with."

He considers my requests/demands, then he eases back and climbs off me. Pointing to the pool house, he says, "There's a bathroom in there. One with a real flimsy lock. I'm going in the house to grab a couple of steaks. If you're still hiding out in that bathroom by the time they're done cooking, I'll break the door down and drag your little ass to the dinner table."

"I do not doubt this," I say, trying not to look too surprised by my victory as he lets me stand up. "I should run in the house real quick and grab my phone, too."

He grabs my wrist, halting me when I try to breeze by. "I don't think so. You need to pee, go pee, but you're not going in the house."

The look he gives me makes it clear I am still in captivity, I'm just a free-range captive for the moment with access to a bathroom and eating privileges. He's happy to ditch the plan to provide me what I've asked for and pounce on me instead if I want to push it.

So, I do not push it.

"All right," I say, and I turn around and head back toward the pool house.

IT TURNS out there are at least two things Landon excels at: causing an endless stream of chaos and grilling steaks.

The meat melts in my mouth when I take the first bite, and it's all I can do not to moan with pleasure. "Oh, my god. Yum."

Landon cocks an eyebrow at me from across the table before taking a bite of his own steak. "Yeah?"

"So good. So, so good." I shake my head in disbelief as I cut into another piece.

He even gave me a knife. He is so not a good captor.

Not that I'm in any danger of using it on him right now.

I wasn't positive he was serious about grabbing steaks when I went to use the pool house bathroom, but when I came back —*admittedly, I was in no rush*—there was a bowl of salad with a pair of tongs in it on the table, and Landon was standing at the grill cooking two of the juiciest steaks I have ever had the pleasure of consuming.

"Why is it so good?" I ask him. "I didn't even know you could cook."

He shrugs. "I'm not much of a cook, but I know how to season a steak. We used to grill out a lot. Mom was outdoorsy, couldn't keep her inside. If it was nice, she was out here. Some-times even when it wasn't."

I swallow, grabbing my spiked smoothie and taking a sip to reluctantly wash down the meat.

I don't know what to say. I didn't expect a real answer.

Clearing my throat subtly, I ask, "Did your dad teach you how to grill?"

He nods. "He doesn't do it much anymore, but he used to."

I try to picture Hayden standing in front of a grill, but I can't. I've probably never even met the Hayden Landon remembers.

I know he loves my mom a lot, but maybe you love different people in different ways. He started a family with Sally. They had an entirely different life.

"She used to make this vegetable salad with it. Not this kind of salad," he says, nodding toward the big bowl of greens. "It was just a big bowl of vegetables tossed with some kind of sauce. I don't know how she made it. It was something she came up with one day when she needed a side for dinner and felt bored at the idea of steamed veggies, so the recipe died with her, but damn, was it good."

I crack a smile. "Maybe you could ask your dad."

He shakes his head, his jaw locking at the mere mention of Hayden. "He wouldn't know."

The sound of the sliding door being pulled open startles me, then Hayden comes striding out with my mom right behind him. His intelligent gaze quickly surveys the scene and his brow furrows with slight confusion. Mom is similarly uncertain when she steps around him.

"Hey," I say casually. "You guys are back early."

Hayden scowls up at the security camera that usually monitors the pool door, then his gaze drifts to his son. "Yeah.

Something seems to have happened to the security camera out here."

"Huh," Landon says, taking a bite of steak and looking at his dad over his shoulder as he chews. "Weird."

Mom's worried gaze lingers on me. "We wanted to come home just to make sure everything was okay."

As much as I was happy for them to get a date night, I am relieved they're home now. I bought time with my needs, but I wasn't sure how I was going to keep things going once we finished eating.

Now that the calvary is here, though, I see no need to confess there was ever an issue.

"Landon made us a couple of steaks and some salad for dinner. Are you guys hungry? Maybe Hayden could grill up a couple more and you could join us."

"Antonia made the salad," Landon grumbles, apparently annoyed at being given credit for something he didn't do. "It was already prepped and in the fridge."

"Well, the steak is amazing," I inform them before slicing off another bite.

"All right," Hayden says, accepting more readily that everything is okay than Mom. He glances over at her. "You want a steak?"

Mom is a bit slower to accept the reality that Landon is here alone with me and the sky didn't fall. "I thought you were going to Malek's tonight," she says.

"That was the plan. He wasn't home," Landon lies.

"Oh," she murmurs.

"Well, maybe it all worked out for the best," Hayden says. "I'll go prep the meat and get it on the grill. Gemma, honey, do you want to throw something together for dessert?"

Mom nods and gives me an uncertain little smile before she follows Hayden into the house.

As soon as the sliding door closes, Landon grabs his plate and his drinks and brings it around to my side.

I look up at him cautiously as he takes the seat next to me.

"Gotta make some room for the parents," he says.

Forget that Mom could have sat by me as easily as he is now.

My spine stiffens when, as soon as he sits down, he lays his massive palm over my thigh and gives it a squeeze.

"Remove your hand from my thigh, please."

"I don't think I will." He gives it another squeeze, then shoves his hand between my legs.

I squeeze them together a moment too late, my gaze darting to the house and then over at him, my eyes wide. "Are you crazy?" I ask, grabbing his wrist under the table and trying to pry it away from my leg without attracting attention. "Our parents are *right* there. Stop it, Landon."

"I wouldn't squirm too much unless you want to get caught," he says, grabbing his glass to take a drink as he casually glances at the sliding door. There's a clear view of the kitchen from here, and a clear view of us from where they're standing, but they can't see beneath the table where he's touching me.

My skin feels like it's on fire. I swallow, watching Mom grab something out of the fridge.

"Relax your legs," he demands.

"No," I bite out, letting my nails dig into his hand.

"That doesn't bother me," he says, his tone amused. Rather than give up, he forces his hand where he wants it and my stomach flips over when he roughly cups my pussy in his hand.

"Landon," I say, starting to sweat from the sheer audacity he's exhibiting right now.

"Relax your legs," he says again. "I'll hurt you if you don't. Let it feel good."

There's tension everywhere else in my body, but reluctantly, I let my legs relax.

Maybe if I give a little, he'll back off.

Maybe it's more a battle of wills than anything. A game of chicken. I don't mind losing that. Besides, there's fabric—

Landon's fingers slide *beneath* the fabric of my swimsuit and I gasp as he fingers my slit. "Landon."

"Take a bite of your steak."

His voice is steady as he rubs two fingers along my pussy with a sense of calm and confidence I can't fathom given the circumstances.

What's worse is the wetness that pools inside of me as he does it.

"Landon, please. They're going to—"

He rubs me. "Shh. Pick up your fork and take a bite of your steak, Parker."

I can scarcely sit still as his finger curls and the tip brushes my clit. I cry out sharply, gripping the edge of the table.

"Your face is too expressive, baby." He sounds completely unconcerned as he fingers me harder. "Take a bite to give it something to do."

Eating is the next to last thing I want to do right now, but getting caught tops the list. I grab my fork with unsteady fingers and stab a piece of juicy steak. My thighs tremble at the sensation of Landon rubbing my clit, and I grab his thigh with my other hand, needing something to hold on to.

"That's a good girl. Now, put it in your mouth."

I do as he commands, and this time when the juicy steak hits my tongue, his finger brushes my clit and a moan I can't hold back escapes my throat.

"Perfect." He teases my clit and my fingers clench more tightly around his thigh. "They're glancing our way. You better smile. We're having a nice evening, aren't we? Spending time together as a family, just the way you wanted us to."

It's sick to say something like that when his fingers are currently bringing me so close to climax, I want to die. "Landon," I murmur, trying to keep my face straight.

"Shh. Let it happen."

The pressure mounts as he teases that overly sensitive bundle. The nervousness of getting caught intensifies the unwanted sensation. This shouldn't be happening, but it is, and I can't stop him. All I can do is let it happen so he'll stop and then... and then...

A series of helpless noises escape my throat as he plays my pussy like an instrument he has spent his whole life studying. I can't sit still and come up off the seat, my legs and thighs spasming as ecstasy rips through me.

He keeps his fingers inside me as pleasure washes through me in waves.

When the tremors pass, I take a deep breath and look down at my plate. My face burns with shame as Landon withdraws his fingers from my body, but I don't have time to process what just happened. The sliding door opens and my stomach rocks.

With his fingers still pressed against my pussy, Landon leans over and murmurs, "You think you're safe when they're around. Maybe now you understand; you're only safe from me when I want you to be."

Landon's fingers slide out of my panties and briefly close possessively around my thigh. It's only for a second, then he lets go and uses that filthy, demented hand to grab his drink glass. I finally dare to look in his direction and watch him subtly dip his finger into the drink and swish it around. He gives me a wink, then takes a long, thirsty gulp.

I am mortified and... too many other things to name.

Mom takes a seat across from me and flashes me a smile.

I attempt to smile back, but it's a weak one.

"So, Landon makes a good steak, huh?" she asks, trying to be relaxed and friendly, since she believes he isn't being a menace tonight.

Landon smirks. I know it's for me, but he doesn't look my way. "Oh, yeah. And Parker loves a good piece of meat."

OF COURSE, Thursday is picture day, and I have a neck full of hickeys from Landon's mauling last night.

I bruise so easily, it looks like I was well and truly man-handled.

Well, I guess I was, but I don't want photographic evidence of it recorded in the yearbook.

Grabbing my phone, I frantically text Hannah. "I need help! Can you get to school a few minutes early and bring your makeup? I need you to cover up... I just need you to cover something," I finish, not wanting to commit it to text.

I finish brushing my teeth before she answers. "Any way you can meet me at my house? I'm running a little behind myself. If we're a little late, then we're a little late, but I'm not sure I'll make it to school early."

I don't do much to doll up on school picture day, so I suppose it would be easier for me to go to her. She's the one doing me the favor, after all. "Sure, I'll be there in a few," I text back.

I've tried to think as little about my situation and what happened with Landon as possible, but when I'm done texting Hannah, my gaze is drawn to the little blue arrow on the top left-hand side of my message screen. Beside it, a number one is in a blue bubble, indicating there's a message I haven't checked.

I know there is.

I saw the notification on my screen as soon as I woke up.

Javi's view on his morning run.

I've never had a reason to feel as dirty as I felt then, getting that text from him that I'm quickly coming to associate with a "thinking of you" gesture.

Meanwhile, I spent half the night awake because I couldn't stop reliving the feeling of Landon's fingers between my legs.

My heart sinks just thinking that. I tell myself I should read the message and send him a quick one back, but I know my heart won't be in it, so I don't.

Instead, I head downstairs and make myself some oatmeal since I can eat that quickly. I chop up a couple of strawberries to put on top, then I scarf it down so I can get out of here without encountering the other people in the house, mercifully still busy upstairs with their morning routines.

I shoot Mom a quick text on my way out the door to let her know I have to stop at Hannah's before school so she doesn't worry, then I book it to my car.

WHEN I GET to Hannah's house, everything is a bit chaotic.

Apparently, Anae hired a stylist to do her hair and makeup today. Judging by the way she's barking at them, I don't think they're doing a good job.

I'm not sure where Hannah gets ready anymore. It used to be her bathroom, but the night of the party is the only time I've slept here since she was moved to the attic. She doesn't have a bathroom up there, and there's certainly not enough light to do makeup.

Reluctant as I am to enter the lair of the beast, since I don't find Hannah and we're short on time, I poke my head into Anae's bedroom.

"Hey, do you know where Hannah is?"

"How should I know?" Anae snaps. "Probably scurrying around the basement with the rest of the rats."

Wow. Somebody woke up on the wrong side of the bed today.

"Allrighty then."

"Wait," she says sharply, slapping away the hand of the woman doing her hair and turning around in her spinny chair to face me. "Don't go anywhere until I'm done in here. I want to talk to you and Hannah together before I leave for school."

I frown, unsure what that's all about, but as the poor woman doing her hair looks near tears, I decide I should probably let them get back to... whatever they're doing.

Since I've looked everywhere else, I trudge up the closet steps in one of the guest rooms they don't use and find Hannah in the attic.

This room was never meant to be a bedroom. It's big enough to be a storage space, but not much else. Only the middle of the room is tall enough to stand up straight in. The roof slopes on both sides, rendering much of the space useless. They also *used* this as storage space prior to putting Hannah up here, so there are totes and boxes filling the narrow spaces on either side.

I can't be in this "room" without becoming enraged, so I focus my attention on Hannah, sitting on a little blue storage ottoman by the window since it's the best source of light. In front of her is a scratched accent table they used to have in the foyer, but they moved it up here when Jackie bought an expensive new one. Apparently, Hannah is using it as her vanity, because she's leaning over it now, applying mascara.

My problems fade away and my plan to turn the pool house into her place comes back full force. I got distracted with my own life, but I need to get back to that project. I'm convinced if I actually make the space habitable for her, maybe she'll change her mind about staying there. It's only a pool house, but it would be so much nicer than this fucking bullshit.

I know she loves this house, but I want to burn it down—with the Richards women still inside.

"Oh, you should have texted me that you were here," Hannah says, sitting back and popping the mascara wand back into the tube.

"They make you get ready in here? It's as dark as a dungeon. You can't even use your old bathroom? It's literally empty. Nobody's using it."

Hannah waves me off as she stands. "I'm sure I could sneak in there and get ready, but it's not worth it. They'd be so angry if they caught me. The whole point of putting me up here was to punish me, it wasn't because there wasn't space for me downstairs."

My eyes bug out. "You didn't *do* anything!"

Hannah shrugs, stepping into her shoes. "I displeased the king, and he likes to see me punished for it. Anyway, what do you need help with?"

"Right now, I need help with containing my temper because I want to go raise absolute hell with your stupid housemates."

Hannah lightly grabs my wrist and drags me over to the window so she can actually see. Then her eyes widen when she catches sight of the hickeys. "Are those...?"

I nod grimly.

"Landon?" she guesses.

I nod again, exaggerating my pout.

"Well, you've come to the right place. Have a seat over here by the window so I can see what I'm doing."

I glare out the window before sitting down with a huff. "If you don't move on your own soon, I swear to god, I may be tempted to kidnap you."

"It's not all bad," she says as she grabs her brushes and various makeup containers. "The view out this window is lovely. I can see the ocean. I didn't have that in my old bedroom."

All I want to do is rage and forcibly remove my best friend from her childhood home, so I force myself to keep quiet as she moves my hair and begins her task of covering all of Landon's handiwork.

It takes a while, but when she shows me a mirror after she's all done, I truly can't even tell there was ever a mark on my neck to begin with.

"Wow, thanks, Hannah. You did even better than I expected."

"No problem," she says, turning around to return her makeups to their correct spots on her makeshift vanity.

I'm definitely buying her a vanity for the pool house.

I stand and look out the window at this view she claims is so great. My house is literally right on the ocean now, so the view from here doesn't impress me, but it is nice.

On impulse, I pull my phone out of my purse and aim it out Hannah's window, then I snap a picture and send it to Javi.

Since I'm still standing at the window and there's not much space over here, Hannah is right on top of me when she turns around. Her gaze hits my phone almost without thinking about it, then she looks at me.

"He texted me earlier and I haven't answered," I explain. Then, because I don't want her to ask questions and I just noticed it in the picture, I look back out the window with a frown. "Isn't that Arden's house?"

Hannah follows my gaze to the palatial white mansion in the distance, towering over its nearest neighbors. "Yep." She points down the beach at another lavish mansion perched on a hilltop overlooking the ocean. "And that's where Dare lived before he went off to college."

"I guess your prison tower has a perfect view of all the royals," I say sourly.

Smiling mischievously, she says, "Lucky me, right? Come on, let's go downstairs. Did you have breakfast?"

"Yeah, I'm good," I say, walking down the stairs first so she can turn off the lights and grab her things.

We're in the hall about to head downstairs when Anae stops us. "You two. Come with me."

Hannah frowns slightly and looks over at me.

I roll my eyes and shrug, but then we follow her because... well, it's just easier that way.

Anae walks through the open double doors into her massive bedroom, and indignation fills me all over again. This bedroom is about the size of Hannah's old bedroom, and it's so unjust that Anae is living in a bigger room in *Hannah's house* while Hannah is stashed in the attic like a traumatized child in a V.C. Andrews novel.

"This is such bullshit."

Hannah shoots me a warning look at my muttering, but Anae hasn't even noticed. She opens the doors to her private terrace and walks out, expecting us to follow.

Her balcony overlooks the property and has a nice view of the pool. There's patio furniture and an umbrella for when she and her friends want to come enjoy the view, but the umbrella is closed and secured right now.

A couch, a loveseat, and two separate chairs await us. Anae

stops in front of the chairs, then points at them, indicating she wants one of us in each of them.

"What's this about, Anae? We need to get to school," Hannah says.

"Sit," she demands.

I sigh, dropping onto the cushioned seat and crossing my arms over my chest.

Hannah sighs, too, then takes a seat on the other chair.

Anae's eyes are cool as she looks us over one at a time. Then, apparently having seen too many movies, she begins to pace back and forth on the balcony. "You know, I think I've been really nice to you girls so far this year. Carter came in with her 'let's start fresh!' bullshit, and I think I did my part in accommodating that."

It takes me several seconds to realize she was talking about me. Unlocking my jaw, I say, "My name is *Parker*."

"Whatever. Your name has never mattered less to me than it does now."

"I don't know why you're mad at me," I state, not bothering to add that I also don't care.

"Don't you?" she asks, narrowing her eyes.

I shake my head, eyebrows rising with impatience. "Nope, and you have about ten seconds to tell me before I say fuck this and leave."

Her narrowed gaze drifts to Hannah, the scrutiny intensifying. "Then maybe it was you. *Cinderella*," she says with a feigned pout. "The poor, mistreated little orphan girl. Did you decide to fight back for once in your pathetic life? I bet you felt so brave setting out to spite me."

Hannah swallows, probably more accustomed to Anae's drama and ridicule than I am. "I don't know what you're talking about, Anae."

"*Someone* told Dare I was watching his social media accounts, and you two bitches are the only ones who knew."

Whatever I expected this to be about, *that* wasn't even on the list of possibilities.

"What makes you think anyone told him?" I ask, scowling.

"He blocked me," she bites out, her sharp gaze moving between me and Hannah. "So, which of you was it?"

Unease crawls down my spine, and heat suffuses my cheeks. "We don't talk to him, Anae. He probably just remembered to block you since you're out now—"

She shuts me down as quickly as Hannah did when I made the suggestion to her. "Dare isn't sloppy. He didn't *forget*. Blocking me now was his way of letting me know there's a rat in my midst." She scrutinizes me briefly, but her gaze lingers on Hannah the longest. "So, which one of you betrayed me?"

Hannah swallows, her face pale, her gaze aimed at the ground.

I don't want to believe she would do something as insane as actually contacting Dare, even if it was just to let him know he had left a window open for Anae, but I know *I'm* not the leak, and the way Hannah is looking...

She looks guilty.

Anae will *eviscerate* her.

"It was me," I lie.

Anae's gaze snaps to mine, her eyes narrowing with suspicion. "You? Why?"

I can feel Hannah's wide-eyed gaze on me, too. I know I'm poking a beast, but I'm not at her mercy the way Hannah is. "I reached out to Aubrey to let her know Dare had forgotten to block you. It seemed like an oversight. I believed it would be best for everyone if you just moved on, and I thought that might force you to."

"No, you didn't," Hannah says quickly. "She's lying to protect me, Anae. It was me. I messaged Dare."

My eyes are nearly as wide as Anae's, but Anae is significantly angrier.

"You and Dare *text?*"

Fear leaps in my stomach.

Hannah, what the hell are you thinking?

"No," Hannah says quickly. "I don't even have his phone number. I sent him a DM one night when I couldn't sleep. I just wanted to ask him if it was a Cinderella tattoo. That's all. Honestly, he hates me, so I didn't even expect him to respond. And I didn't do it to spite you, but I did mention that you noticed the tattoo in one of his pictures, so he knew you were looking at his profile. I thought maybe if the tattoo meant something else, he would tell me, and then we would know once and for all."

Anae still appears angry and skeptical, but she's too hungry for information about her former lover to pass up a chance at more. "What did he say?"

Hannah shrugs apologetically. "He's Dare. He didn't give me a straight answer."

"But what did he *say?* What else did you say to each other?" Losing her patience, her gaze drops to the phone in Hannah's hand and she holds out hers expectantly. "I want to see the message."

A frown flits across Hannah's brow and her grip on her phone tightens. "I—I deleted it."

"You deleted it?"

Hannah nods vigorously. "It was hardly a conversation, it didn't matter. I just asked him if it was a Cinderella tattoo, and he... he didn't give me a straight answer, so I still don't know."

"What did he say exactly? Word for word."

"I don't remember. Nothing important."

"I don't believe you. You slide into his DMs in the middle of the night like a thirsty little slut and then delete the message? I want to see your phone."

Hannah's grip on it tightens into something I would guess is much closer to a death grip. As hard as she tries to regulate her breathing, I can see her fear in the swift rise and fall of her chest. I'm guessing that means she *didn't* delete the message, and she knows whatever it says would likely set Anae off.

"I'm not going to show you my phone, Anae," Hannah says softly. "I told you what he said."

"You're leaving things out," Anae states, her fury and viciousness growing. "If you think you can form some kind of secret connection with him and push me out, I swear to god, Hannah..."

"What are you talking about?" Hannah cries desperately. "You know I don't even *like* talking to him. You were obsessing over the tattoo, and I thought maybe I could get an answer so you didn't have to keep digging."

"Bullshit," Anae seethes, her eyes flashing with anger. "Dare belongs to *me*. I'm the one who knows how to keep him, not you vanilla bitches. Soon, he will be with me again—and when he is, you will pay for your betrayal. I will let him take every bit of aggression he has toward you *out on you* before exterminating you like the little rat you are, and I will enjoy *every second* of it."

"I didn't betray you, Anae," Hannah says softly, but I can hear in her voice she knows her denial is useless.

"You messaged my fucking boyfriend behind my back."

"*Ex*-boyfriend," I put in gently, ill-at-ease with this demonstration of Anae's temper. Everything she's saying is so fucked up, I just want to grab Hannah and drag her away to safety.

But I also know she'll vent her fury now or later, and I'd

rather there be a witness so at least I can make sure none of Hannah's wounds from this lashing will be physical.

Anae looks at me, only just seeming to realize I'm still here. She was so lost in her rage fog, so zeroed in on Hannah, I think for a moment I ceased to exist to her.

"Yes," she says, visibly coming down from the heights of her rage. "For now. Because Dare likes games, and so do I."

It's sad that that's the story she's telling herself, but right now, I have no capacity for concern for Anae. My entire focus is on not letting her temper escalate again so I can get Hannah the hell out of here.

"And this is part of it," Anae says, refocusing on her mission. "It's my task to figure out what I'm supposed to do next. Maybe he blocked me so I would interrogate Hannah and consequently read the message he sent her. Maybe something he said in it was meant for me."

I keep my tone calm and rational. "He obviously has your phone number, Anae. If he wanted you to know he and Hannah exchanged a simple message about his stupid tattoo, he could have just sent you a screenshot."

Anae looks absolutely disgusted. "What kind of game is that, Parker? God, you're so clueless. Grilling Hannah is part of the fun. A screenshot is boring."

Out of the corner of my eye, I see the slightest movement from Hannah. Her hand. She's touching the screen of her phone.

My heart starts to pound faster.

She's deleting the message.

I don't know if there's any truth to Anae's seemingly crazy claim that Dare must have left a breadcrumb for her in that message, but even if there isn't, I think Anae may be delusional enough to invent one if she gets hold of it.

My guess is Hannah realizes that, too.

Currently, Hannah is the only one who has seen the message, and even if she has to risk incurring Anae's wrath, she's going to keep it that way.

I know that's probably for the best, but I know one other thing with absolute, startling certainty.

If Anae catches her in the act, Hannah is completely fucked.

ANAE'S HEAD starts to turn in Hannah's direction, and my heart nearly stops.

"Arden asked about you," I blurt, desperate for a way to distract her.

Anae's gaze snaps back to me. "What?"

"Remember, we talked about focusing on the present instead of dwelling on Dare? Well, I saw Arden the night of your party. We talked in the study. Another girl was blowing him, but you probably don't care about that."

"I don't—unless you got a good look at his dick while it was out? What's he working with?"

I shake my head. "It was shoved in the girl's mouth when I walked over, and I didn't look when she popped off. But whatever he's packing, he must be pretty good with it because he wasn't even nice to her, and she still wanted to please him."

She rocks her head from left to right in consideration. "That could be a good sign. Of course, she could just be pathetic like that Brittany girl and eager for whatever crumb is thrown at her."

I try to tamp down my eagerness that she's interested in my

bait. "Yeah, I'm not sure. Anyway, he said..." I pause, pretending to think. "What was it he said?"

I fight the urge to dart a look at Hannah because I know if I do, Anae might, too.

My brain generally works much faster than this, but my utter panic is slowing me down. I'm also hesitant to directly lie about the only thing he *did* say, which was about Hannah and not Anae at all.

Unfortunately, it's the only thing I can think of.

"He said you looked really pretty, and he made a—Actually, I should give you better context. Like I said, he was getting a blow job in the study. So, I told him the girl better swallow so they didn't make a mess since it was your house, not his, and then he made some obnoxious remark about how any girl lucky enough to have his cock in her mouth always swallowed. Then he said maybe he would show you firsthand one of these days. So, I guess it wasn't actually *asking* about you, more... making a lewd comment about you."

Anae stares at me. "You are shit at telling a story, Parker."

"I'm a woman of many talents. Apparently, storytelling is not among them."

Anae looks back at Hannah, so I'm free to as well. Relief trickles through me when I see Hannah doesn't look as anxious as she did before. Her shoulders are more relaxed, and the phone is cradled in her hand instead of at risk of being crushed. I guess I bought her enough time.

"Arden's family is super rich," I add, since dropping the topic all of a sudden would be suspicious. "I don't know if he's a puppet like you originally expressed interest in, but if you can handle someone as cocky and obnoxious as him, I really think he could be a good match for you."

This is my boldest lie to date. With Arden's resources and

Anae's ruthlessness, I think the two of them together would be a colossal disaster.

Anae ponders the idea. "Yeah, I had similar thoughts, but I didn't think he..." She stops before finishing whatever she was about to say. "Keep an ear open. If he mentions me again, make sure you let me know right away this time."

I nod obediently. "Yes, my queen," I joke.

Anae rolls her eyes, but I'm just happy to appease her for the moment. If there's one thing I know without a doubt can drive Anae to *literally* attempting homicide, it is the devil known as Chase Darington.

Focusing in on Hannah again, she says, "If you think your bestie's little distraction is going to make me forget about Dare, I'm afraid you're mistaken. Show me the message. I want to see exactly what was said."

Hannah shrugs apologetically, but still doesn't offer her phone. "I really did delete the message, Anae. I told you what was said. It was just a couple of sentences. There was no secret message he wanted you to see."

"I'll judge that for myself. Open the app."

Hannah sighs, but does as she's told.

"Go to his profile and click like you're going to send him a message. See if it comes back."

Hannah's fingers freeze and my stomach drops.

Will that bring the message back?

Hannah begins nervously, "I don't know if—"

"Just do it," Anae snaps.

Hannah takes a breath and taps the screen.

I hold my breath, my teeth sinking anxiously into my bottom lip.

Hannah lightens a bit, turning the phone screen to show Anae. "See? Nothing there."

Oh, thank God.

Anae narrows her gaze with dislike, but I see an out, and I don't hesitate to take it. "There you go. The message is gone and there's no getting it back." I stand, lightly grabbing Hannah's arm. "And you know what else we aren't getting back? Our perfect attendance records if we don't all get our asses to school ASAP."

Anae doesn't care about being tardy, but she must realize this conversation isn't going anywhere, either.

I don't give her the opportunity to delay our exit. I haul Hannah through Anae's bedroom and out into the hall, and I don't let go until we're about to walk down the stairs.

"That was a close call," Hannah murmurs as we head for the front door. "Thanks for having my back in there."

"You know I always have your back." I glance over at her. "But should I be worried that you are apparently exchanging scandalous enough messages with Dare in the middle of the night that you and I need to hurl ourselves into traffic to avoid Anae reading them?"

"No. Of course not," she says, shaking her head. "They weren't scandalous at all. The messages were completely harmless—to a sane person."

I cock an eyebrow.

"Honest. I would show them to *Aubrey*, just not Anae. You know how she is. She would read into every word and see things that aren't there."

I've never had a reason to doubt Hannah before, so I take her word for it, but I'm still a little uneasy. It's not her I don't trust. It's Dare. The effect he seems to have on people is, to say the least, frightening.

I know Hannah hates Dare, though. She probably didn't think about it being the middle of the night when she sent the message. She was probably worried about Aubrey since Anae is still hung up on Dare. If he doesn't know Anae is still a threat, he can't watch out for her, and not watching out for her could literally endanger Aubrey's life.

"Have you talked to Aubrey?" I ask.

Her lips press together and she shakes her head. "He still doesn't really let us talk. I like her stuff on social media from time to time, but I've been afraid to actually message her. He was pretty clear about not wanting me to."

"In this middle-of-the-night DM?"

Hannah shakes her head. "Before they moved. The tone of our message was actually surprisingly non-hateful. It was probably just because I caught him by surprise reaching out to him like that, but it actually made me wonder..." She trails off like she's not sure she wants to share.

I shake my head. "Nope. No saying potentially scary things concerning Dare and then trailing off. Spill."

"It's probably a pipe dream. Last time I asked, he was not at all receptive to the idea, but some time has passed, and we live on opposite ends of the country now. Maybe if I play nice, he'll let me talk to her. I may not even have the same fog-clearing effect on her from so far away, so maybe he could tolerate me being her friend now."

I shake my head. "It is *such* bullshit that she requires his *permission* to talk to her friends."

"He's very high-maintenance," she agrees. "But he's also the boss, so if I want any contact with her, I have to go through him to get it."

"That is so fucked up. I don't know how she tolerates him."

Hannah nods. "I know, but it's not her fault. It's hard to fight back against someone who plays as dirty as Dare does. She's armed with a water gun, and he has a tank—and a willingness to roll over anyone who gets in his way."

I nod, my lips pressed firmly together. "Speaking of his willingness to literally *take out* the competition. Remember when *we* had that little chat about how the smartest and safest thing for you to do is stay far, *far* away from Aubrey and let her battle her own demons?"

"I do. Remember when we had that little chat about *you* handling your Landon stuff so you could be free to talk to Javi?" Pointedly, she pushes my hair back over my shoulder to expose my neck that she just finished covering up for me.

"Touché. But—"

She holds up a hand to stop me. "No. I don't want to talk about this anymore. I know the risks, and I'm just as capable of making my own terrible decisions as you are."

I crack a smile. "I guess I can't argue with that."

SINCE WE WERE RUNNING LATE this morning and I was already at Hannah's house, I gave her a ride to school.

Since tonight is Mom's night to work late and Hayden is working late as well, I ask if she wants to come home with me to do homework and stay for dinner.

Last night was the closest thing to a win as we've had with Landon, but that family time win didn't come for free, and I'm the one who had to pay the very depraved cost.

I'm not feeling very spendy tonight, so I need my bestie to play shield for me.

When she was here last time, I also forgot to show her the pool house, so I decide I should finally do that now.

Landon's car is in the driveway, but I haven't seen him since we got here. He might be hanging out in his cave in the basement, or maybe he's in his room doing homework. I've never *seen* Landon do homework, but presumably he does since he hasn't been kicked out of school yet.

It's a nice evening, so when we first step outside, I'm sad I can't take advantage of it and go for a swim. Hannah touched up my makeup at lunchtime, but a swim in the pool would definitely wash it all off.

Then we step out onto the patio, and I see Landon's muscular arms slicing through the water. Guess I wouldn't have been able to go for a swim, anyway.

I knew Landon was on the swim team, so I assumed he spent time swimming in the off season, but this is the first time since we moved in I've actually caught him in the pool.

He's swimming away from us and I don't think he's seen us yet, so I grab Hannah's hand and make her walk faster with me toward the pool house's side door. Opening the main one is a whole thing and can't be done without drawing attention.

Hannah giggles, her eyes twinkling with mirth when we get inside.

"What?" I ask defensively.

"He'll never find us in here!" she teases, gesturing to the full wall of windows.

This edifice wasn't designed for privacy, so next to the half wall of windows, the front of the pool house has a glass, bifold door. You can fold it up and essentially open the front wall, making the pool house an extension of the pool area more than its own separate living space.

From the front, it literally looks like a glass house.

I realize that's not helping my case of convincing her to move in here.

"We can get curtains," I state. "I'm sure they make curtains for bifold doors, Hayden just doesn't have any because he has never needed them before."

"Uh-huh," she murmurs to placate me.

I roll my eyes at her tone and continue my planned tour. "Okay, so over here is the closet." I open the door next to the bathroom to show her inside. "I know it's a little small to use for clothes, but I figure you could keep sweaters, jackets, stuff like that in here. Then there's a little storage space up top, and you could even put a shoe rack or something here in the bottom."

Hannah nods, but I know she's just appeasing me.

I soldier on, undeterred. We enter the bathroom and I gesture for her to come inside with me. "Love the Coastal vibes in here. There's a nice big shower, plenty of storage space beneath the cabinets, and since this is really only used for changing into swimsuits or peeing when you're out by the pool, it's pretty empty," I say, opening the bottom cabinet door to show her. "You could fill it with your own things."

"I see."

We exit the bathroom and I take her over to the big open space in front of the bifold door. "A cute little living area here in front of the fireplace. And back here," I say, turning to face the back of the pool house, "is where I see your bedroom."

"More glass walls."

I nod. "We're going to buy so many curtains."

She cracks a smile and turns around, eyeing up the fishbowl I want her to live in. "Not so much as a privacy divider. So, anyone who happens by can watch me sleep."

"Not with all those curtains we're buying. And we could get a privacy divider to close off the bedroom area a bit if you want to. Right now, the space isn't set up to be lived in, but it could be modified that way easily."

"There's no kitchen. Not even a kitchenette."

"Well, no." I glance at the bar. "That's the closest thing, but you could use the kitchen in the house. You see how close it is," I point out, gesturing toward the sliding doors leading into the house. "And there is a mini fridge out here that we keep stocked with drinks," I add, pointing to the bar area. "I figured we could put a bed over here for you, a double or a full so you have space. Then we could put an armoire over here for your clothes—it may not be enough space, but you can keep stuff in the house, too. You've seen how massive my closet is. I don't have enough stuff to fill it. And the room Hayden set up as a media room was designed to serve as a bedroom if they ever wanted to convert it, so it has a bathroom and a whole walk-in closet no one uses. You could keep your stuff in there."

"It's very nice," Hannah says. "Thank you for thinking of me, but you don't have to change your pool house."

"I'm still gonna do it. I just have to clear it with Hayden first."

I turn around, and when I do, I see Landon climbing out of the pool.

"I love that you want to help me," Hannah says, by way of sweetly rejecting me. "But I'm really okay where I am."

She's not, but I'm too distracted to argue as I watch Landon towel-dry his hair, water dripping off his hard body and melting into the ground beneath his feet.

It's annoying that he looks so good wet.

It's also annoying that he's looking at me with that smirk on his face and that twinkle in his eye, like my thoughts are being broadcast right across my face.

"Got your chaperone around again today, I see."

I glare at him. "My *friend*. Yes, I have my *friend* here."

"You sticking around?" he asks, finally glancing at Hannah.

"Yep."

Landon smirks, shaking his head as he drops the towel. "I hope they're paying you for all this babysitting."

"I'm happy to do it pro bono," Hannah says, smiling sweetly.

"I bet you are." He slings the towel over his shoulder. "Well, since you girls are going to be hanging around while the parents are out, you want to do something?"

For a moment, I think I've hallucinated.

Then I wait for him to say something crude and gross so we can roll our eyes at him and head back inside the house.

Hannah, ever the peacekeeper, gives him the benefit of the doubt and responds as if he's making a serious suggestion. "Maybe. What did you have in mind?"

Landon shrugs, his gaze trained on me. "A movie?"

I blink, slowly coming to realize... he *is* making a serious suggestion.

"I could do a movie." Hannah looks over at me. "What do you think?"

I can't form words. I'm still partially waiting for him to rip the rug out from beneath my feet as soon as I express interest.

Finally, I muster a few. "You mean, *go* to a movie, or...?"

"I figured we could watch something in the media room, but we can go out if you want."

Oh my god, what?

I'm so confused.

"Personally, I would rather stay in," Hannah says. "I know Anae is going out, and I doubt it's to the movies, but I'd prefer not to run into her—especially looking like a third wheel. She doesn't need more ammunition for her 'jokes.'"

Landon cocks an eyebrow. "Anae tells jokes?"

"Not really. She's just mean, and she thinks that makes her funny."

Still not entirely trusting this, I say, "What would we watch?"

Maybe this is when he'll say something mean and stupid or crude and taunting.

Instead, he shrugs. "We'll find something."

It doesn't make sense in my brain, but... I think he's serious.

"I should probably put on some clothes so Parker can pay attention to the movie," he states, smirking. "Meet me in the media room. Bring popcorn."

Flames erupt beneath my skin and heat my face, but Landon just turns and heads inside the house without another word.

Hannah's eyebrows rise and she looks over at me. "Well, that was unexpected."

"It sure was."

WHEN WE ENTER the media room with popcorn and drinks, I'm half-expecting it to be dark and empty.

It isn't.

Landon isn't standing outside his bedroom on the other side of the hall smirking at us for being stupid enough to think he really wanted to hang out with us.

He is spread out on one of the couches, having apparently made himself comfortable while he waited for us. His hair is still damp from swimming, but he's wearing gray sweats and a white T-shirt.

The TV in this room is massive and takes up a whole wall—literally like a movie theater screen. This time it's Hannah's turn not to be impressed—her house has one of these rooms, too —but I can't believe I live in a house that has its own *movie theater*.

Hannah and I sit on the couch next to Landon's, but I make her sit closest to him since I know he won't mess with her. Prior to him finger-fucking me at the dinner table with our parents just on the other side of a window, I may have thought her presence in the same room was enough, but I've since reevaluated.

Landon doesn't call me out on using Hannah as a buffer. I

grab the faux fur snow leopard blanket that's big enough to cover us both and curl up under it with Hannah while Landon scrolls through the movie app looking for something to watch.

"Ooh, what about Hunger Games?" Hannah suggests when he gets to it. "I haven't watched that in a long time." She looks over at me. "Remember in middle school when we were obsessed?"

I smile. "Yes. Team Gale forever."

Hannah shakes her head. "I can see the appeal, but you know I'm a Peeta girly."

"Ugh. Enjoy your bread boy," I tease, grabbing some popcorn.

"I will. Enjoy your hard-headed hunter."

"Well, since I don't know what either of you are talking about, I guess we'll watch that," Landon states, selecting the movie and pressing play.

IT'S nice escaping into a movie for a little while.

It's even nicer having Hannah around to play chaperone so I don't have to do any mental gymnastics in anticipation of my next moves to avoid Landon.

When the first movie ends, we decide to keep going and watch Catching Fire. We stop after that, not only because it's almost time for the parents to come home, but because I only love the first two movies, not the second two.

"And that's how the story ends," I state, reaching my arms over my head and stretching.

"On a cliffhanger?" Landon asks, cocking an eyebrow.

"Technically, there are two more movies," Hannah begins to explain.

"But we don't speak of those," I finish for her. "And we certainly don't watch them."

"Parker hates them," she tells Landon.

"Why?"

"Too many reasons to name. We should probably head downstairs, anyway," I say, lighting up my phone on the armrest. "My mom and your dad will be home soon."

Hannah is still filling Landon in on the abrupt end to our trilogy experience. "I don't know if you've ever listened to Parker reading before, but she was constantly huffing and muttering over *Mockingjay*. Then we watched the movies and realized they broke the last book into two parts. We watched them."

"Once."

"But a good time was had by no one."

"Bleak bullshit. Ruining Gale," I mutter, throwing off the blanket and standing. "Let's go eat happy food. I'm getting hangry."

"Do you have dinner plans?" Hannah asks, standing and grabbing the throw so she can fold it back up.

I shake my head. "Antonia just shopped yesterday, so we should have plenty to choose from."

"I love a freshly stocked pantry," she says, almost dreamily.

"You are so weird."

Hannah grins. "What?"

I shake my head and make my way out of the theater room.

I make it to the hall first, and my gaze drifts to the side where Landon's bedroom is. I've looked at that door with dread and anticipation before, but right now, we're not alone, so I feel relaxed.

My phone buzzes and my heart flips over.

That relaxed feeling melts away and my gaze shoots to Landon.

He's watching me, but not with suspicion—until he notices my deer in the headlights expression, of course.

"I have to pee," I state abruptly, before ducking back inside the theater room so I can use the bathroom.

Once the door is closed and locked, I lean against it and look down at my phone.

Then I see it was only a text from Mom, so I didn't need to panic, after all.

My shoulders sink with relief as I shoot her a quick text back. I decide I probably should pee while I'm in here. It will only highlight my strange behavior if I return promptly, looking like I did exactly what I actually did—hid in the bathroom so I could check a text.

"Shady ass behavior," I mutter to myself as I sit down. "I need to get it together."

Apparently having invited fate to mess with me, right as I'm washing my hands, my phone goes off again. I'm casual this time when I look, expecting it to be Mom.

This time it's Javi.

I make quick work of drying my hands, then I swipe open the message.

"I'm off tonight. You should come over and impress me with your cooking skills," it says, with a winky emoji following the text.

Oh my god, *what?*

Excuses fly one after the other through my brain before I stop to think: do I *want* to go over?

I can't because Hannah's here, but Hannah could go home. She's probably only still here because she knows I can't be left alone with Landon.

I have homework to do because I've just spent over four hours lazing around watching movies with Landon and Hannah. True, but when we started Catching Fire, I already resigned myself to having to stay up late tonight to get my homework done.

Suddenly, the wood behind my back reverberates violently as Landon pounds on it. A surge of panic has me jumping away from the door, my stomach twisting and my heart exploding in a flurry of activity.

"Hannah and I are going to start dinner. Meet us out by the grill."

Heart in my throat, I try to shake off the cold fear that was triggered by him beating on the door of a room I locked myself inside and call back, "Okay."

My voice is shaky and uncertain, and I realize *that* is why I never considered going, only which excuse I could use for why I wouldn't be there.

It's probably only because we were in a dark room with a buffer between us and not interacting with each other, but Landon invited us to watch that movie and then we had a nice time.

It feels... a little like he's reaching out.

I've spent *years* waiting for that, so apparently, no matter what he's done, I can't just smack his hand away the first time it actually happens.

My Landon shit is *so* not handled.

Sighing with disappointment, I quickly type back, "I don't think I can tonight, sorry. We're about to eat dinner, and I have a lot of homework."

I feel guilty as soon as I press send.

It's all true, but it's not *the* truth.

And I like Javi. I know if I went over to his place and made dinner with him instead of Landon, we'd have a nice time. It would be easy. At no point would I feel anything comparable to locking myself in a bathroom because I'm afraid the guy I'm with might see my texts and hurt someone over it. I would experience nothing close to a trauma flashback when the criminal outside reminded me of his past sins by banging on a damn door.

That feeling in my gut gets worse when he types back, "no problem. Enjoy your dinner," with a smiley emoji that makes me feel gross.

I can't pinpoint the exact reason for my feeling of revulsion, but I don't want to examine it, either. I need to go downstairs and live with my choices.

IT TURNS OUT, my choices are delicious.

With Landon grilling and Hannah on sides, we get flavorful, delicious veggie and meat skewers served with a crisp, refreshing salad that tastes too good to be healthy.

Hannah clears our plates before I can stop her, then she brings out a tray of cute little glass dessert dishes filled with what appears to be a strawberry mousse with a dollop of whipped cream between the two fruity layers.

"That was delicious," Hayden says once he's finished the last of his dessert.

"It sure was," Mom agrees. "Maybe we should let the kids make dinner more often."

"I did nothing," I say, just to make sure I don't get any credit I don't deserve. "It was all Landon and Hannah. Clearly, we need to move Hannah in so we can all enjoy a delicious, peaceful meal much more frequently."

Landon smirks at my subtle emphasis on the word peaceful. I didn't *mean* to emphasize it, it just slipped out.

Hannah smiles faintly. "I'm afraid now that we've finished eating, I need to move *out*. Anae is probably home by now, and I haven't started my own homework, let alone..." She trails off, grabbing her glass to finish the last of her water and grabbing her own dish. "I'll put these in the sink. Would you like me to—?"

"Don't you dare," I interrupt her.

"I feel guilty just leaving so many dirty dishes."

"I will do the dishes when I get back," I assure her. "You don't work for us. Until you live here, you don't need to help with the chores."

Hannah shakes her head, smiling, and then says her good-byes while I grab my own dishes and take them to the sink.

Since I gave her a ride here, I have to take Hannah home as well. It's not a long car ride and her phone is on silent, but I can tell it's blowing up from the way it vibrates every other minute.

"Do you need to get that?" I ask, more to ask who is bothering her so much than because I think she wouldn't feel comfortable enough to take a call around me if she *did* need to take it.

Hannah shakes her head, glancing my way. "It's just Anae. She always hates when I'm not at her beck and call, but today she has been riding me even harder than usual. I think it's because of this morning," she says, looking down at her lap with a smile that lacks amusement. "If Dare *was* setting a trap, I think I may have stepped right into it by messaging him."

"It's none of her damn business who you message, frankly," I say with annoyance on her behalf, even while knowing logic has no bearing on all this.

Hannah shrugs. "It's fresh on her mind, so of course I get sniping, 'I see how it is, you'll answer Dare's messages but not mine' comments. She texted me a few times during the movie, but I didn't want to be rude," she adds, realizing I'm missing some context. "Obviously, she doesn't like to be ignored, so on top of this morning... she's just all riled up."

Unease dances down my spine. "Are you sure you want me

to take you home? We have all your school stuff. We can go straight to my room and start on homework if you want. I know you don't have clothes at my house, but you can borrow something of mine. You could totally spend the night."

Hannah shakes her head. "I'll be fine. I'm used to her moods. But thank you."

"Are you sure? Hannah, I hate leaving you here."

"It's my home," she says gently as I pull up to the gate.

As if to edit the period and put an exclamation point at the end of my fears about what awaits her inside, her phone goes off again.

Hannah sighs softly and grabs the phone so she can send a text back.

"Why don't I at least go inside with you?" I say, trying to ease my anxiety as I pull past the gate and down the driveway.

"That won't help. It will only make her angrier if she sees evidence I was out having fun."

"But then if she comes at you, I can grab a fistful of her fake hair and rip it the fuck out," I point out.

Hannah smiles faintly. "I'll be fine. I swear."

I know she says that, and I know, according to Hannah, she's always fine.

But I also know the reason she's so good at using makeup to cover bruises doesn't have a goddamn thing to do with hickeys.

I feel sick as I put the car in park. I want to say I didn't mean to get her in trouble. I didn't even consider that she would *get* in trouble. It has been so nice all summer not having Anae around to worry about, and I was distracted by needing to protect *myself* from Landon now that I live with him. I didn't even think about what it would cost Hannah to play chaperone, and of course she didn't mention it.

I'm not the only one with a psycho at home who wants to

control me, but Hannah's isn't reined in by anyone else at home who cares to protect her.

I want to beg her to stay the night again, but I know she won't.

I want to tell her I'm sorry, but there shouldn't be anything to apologize for.

I should be able to have my damn friend over to watch movies and have dinner with me. There should be no conflict about her returning home after having spent some time doing something for herself instead of serving these ungrateful assholes.

I know Jackie is technically Hannah's guardian, but only for one more month.

I want so badly to help her, but she won't let me.

Powerlessness is perhaps my least favorite feeling in the entire spectrum of human emotion.

It's all I feel as I watch Hannah climb out of my car and walk up to her door.

Restlessness moves through my veins like a livewire as I sit here watching the house. I know it's probably pointless, but I want to linger here for a minute just to make sure Hannah doesn't need any help.

It's probably my anger that makes me do it.

The powerlessness that I can't stand.

I'm *not* powerless. I've never been powerless. I'm Parker Johansson, and I can move objects out of my way with nothing more than the power of my mind.

I wish that were true.

It doesn't feel true right now.

So, I use my fingers.

I've always had a temper. It's not my finest feature. Usually, I control it pretty well, but nothing triggers me like the possibility of someone I love getting hurt.

I don't follow Aubrey because I've never met her, and if I'm being honest with myself, maybe I have developed a slight aversion to the girl based on all the trouble she has caused my best friend. I know that may not be fair, though. That horrible, uncomfortable feeling I get not being able to protect Hannah from Anae? She probably gets the same one from not being able to protect Aubrey from Dare.

I just don't care about Aubrey, so I try to ignore that.

I care about Hannah and her well-being.

Someone needs to protect her, and I'm all she's got.

That's why I use Aubrey's profile to find Dare's, and then I click the message button.

"You don't know me, but I know you," I type out. "I don't know what kind of game you're playing with Anae and, frankly, I don't care. But leave Hannah out of it. Leave her alone. Block HER if you didn't invite her into this on purpose. Whatever sick game you're playing with the girls in your life, just leave her out of it. She has enough problems without you making everything worse for her."

Normally, I would read and reread a message like this, tweaking words and moving commas to make sure it's perfect before I send it, but the rational part of me knows the longer I have to think about this, the greater chance I'll never send it.

Maybe that's the right call, but it feels too much like doing nothing, and I've had my fill of that tonight.

Deep down, I don't even expect Dare to read this message. We aren't friends, so it will go in a separate request folder that he probably doesn't even check. As unfortunate as it is, while he has a black soul and no heart to speak of, he is *tragically* nice to look at. Consequently, no matter how evil or taken he may be, I'm sure a few hopeful strays wind up in the message request section of his inbox, and since he has never met me, he has no reason to fish me out of it.

Which is why I'm surprised when, a moment later, he responds.

"Of course I know you, Parker. I saw your picture on Hannah's dresser when I visited her bedroom. Well, her former bedroom."

My face heats to about a thousand degrees at the satisfaction I feel coming off the flat line of text. I remember Hannah saying she was moved out of her room because she "displeased the king," and Dare was Anae's evil king, wasn't he?

"Hannah is the sweetest, kindest person in the whole world," I type back furiously. "The fact that you have a problem with her says more about you than her."

"How is lovely little Hannah? Sounds like she's having a bad night. What a shame."

This smug bastard. I hate him so much.

My stomach feels sick and alarm bells start going off. As angry as I am, something else is warning me to pull back. It's Anae and Hannah's words about how meticulous Dare is. How he never does anything by accident or without a purpose.

Would that include messaging me?

I wanted to yell at him and tell him to fuck off and leave my friend alone, but in doing that, perhaps I'm only feeding him more information.

And *lovely little Hannah*, what the fuck is that?

I think about Anae's rabidness this morning and lick my suddenly dry lips. She would lop off someone's head in anger if she saw Dare refer to Hannah that way—probably Hannah's, even though she hadn't done a damn thing to poke the bear.

I did.

I am.

I'm poking the stupid, evil bear.

Fuck.

I don't know how to play Dare's games and I have no

interest in learning, so as wrong as it feels not to respond, I quickly delete the message so there's no evidence of it in my phone.

That should be enough, right?

I can't remove the message from *his* phone to ensure he can't send Anae a screenshot, but both Anae and Hannah seemed to be in agreement that a screenshot is too basic for Dare. He has to leave breadcrumbs and play mind games and make people work for the information he wants them to have, and I don't think I said enough to give him another move.

Did I?

Now I kind of wish I hadn't deleted the message so I could look back at what I said.

Dammit.

I wait in the driveway for several more minutes.

I'm waiting to make sure I don't hear from Hannah, but I'm also waiting to see if he'll message me again since I cut the conversation off so abruptly.

He doesn't. I guess he was interested enough to engage when I reached out, but not interested enough to give chase.

I tell myself that's probably good, but truthfully, I have no idea how to interpret Dare's motivations. I kind of thought Hannah and Anae were drinking too much Kool-Aid before five minutes ago, but even the minimal contact I just initiated has me in my head and more anxious than I've been all night.

And that's saying something.

IT'S damn near impossible to fall asleep tonight.

I was up late doing homework, and before and after that, I was thinking about Hannah. Kidnapping her is getting more and more appealing. I know she wants to stay in her mother's house that her father built for her, but how important is autonomy, really?

I just want to keep her safe.

I also want to sleep. Desperately. My eyes burn and my body is so tired, but I can't get it to relax enough to let me drift off.

Sighing, I roll over with a huff and adjust my pillow. I resist the urge to check my phone and see what time it is, and train my gaze out my floor-to-ceiling bedroom windows instead.

My ocean view is so spectacular, I can't believe it's mine, but as I watch the moon's reflection dance upon the gentle waves, I wonder if I should close the curtains.

I never close the curtains on school nights. I know I'll be up early in the morning, and I should be asleep before it gets too bright, but tonight, I'm not so sure, and I have to get *some* sleep.

Mercifully, watching the tranquil waves makes *me* tranquil enough to finally relax.

My body, anyway.

My mind is a muddled mess, and even in my dreams, I find myself running from some shadowy threat, going through door after door trying to find the magic one that will lead to safety.

When my eyes open, I'm surprised to find the room still dark.

Why am I awake?

For a foggy moment, I'm unsure, but then I'm swept up in a wave of pleasurable stimulation I don't understand.

My body feels alive, too alive for sleeping. Pleasure ripples through me. I don't know why I'm feeling it, but I moan softly at the sensation, my hand finding the edge of the mattress and instinctively holding on.

Why...?

Another moan.

I try to focus, to heighten my awareness despite my sleepy confusion. Yes, it feels so nice I don't want to question it, but where is this coming from?

My pussy is wet. Something brushes my clit and I cry out softly, still fogged from sleep and confused at the pleasure, but god, it feels so nice. All the tension in my body is drawn to one spot, and that dreamlike caress promises to ease it.

Am I dreaming?

I wasn't dreaming of anything nice. Certainly not anything sexy, so I don't know why I'm turned on.

I don't feel asleep.

I gasp as the sensation heightens again, another stroke rubbing against my clit.

Sighing with pleasure, I let my eyes drift closed. Like that first night I got to enjoy the Atwater pool, I enjoy the intoxicating hit of pleasure and the quick, skillful strokes.

If it were only pleasure, maybe I could believe it's a dream, but I'm grounded in reality when the provider of my mysterious pleasure turns greedy. When at the height of my pleasure, he stops. He kisses my pussy like it's my mouth, then turns his head and peppers my thighs with hot, hungry kisses.

It's the kisses. His stubble scratching against my sensitive skin.

I wouldn't feel that in a dream.

Before I can grab onto it, he's spreading my pussy open and feasting on me again, and as soon as his tongue swipes my clit, all I want to do is come.

Just let go.

This isn't supposed to be happening.

My brain tries to fully wake up, but it's like wading through quicksand. The pleasure is fighting to overpower it. I can't stop moaning as lick after lick, my pussy is bathed in the promise of a release I desperately need.

Fingers. I feel a hand holding my thigh open.

Wait.

Wait, this isn't right.

The only way for me to be feeling this is for someone to be *making* me feel it, because I'm not touching myself.

I should be alone in my bedroom. Nobody should be in here with me.

Panic mixes in with the tantalizing pleasure and dulls it as reason compels me to throw off my blanket and look down.

The room is dark, but enough moonlight spills in that I can make out the clear silhouette of a man with his head planted between my spread thighs, his mouth latched onto my pussy.

"Landon!"

His grip on my thigh tightens.

I fight to free them, my heart pounding and my stomach doing somersaults as I twist away from him. He keeps my thighs pinned so I can't really move, but his mouth disconnects from my pussy when I reach down and grab a fistful of his hair.

All I can think to do is tug it, so I do. I pull hard, pushing at his shoulder and—

I cry out when he quickly regains his bearings and his grip on me now that I'm awake and fighting, and his tongue pushes into my pussy.

I wasn't awake the first time he did it. I didn't feel the invasion of his tongue, his ruthless insistence as he entered my body without permission. I feel it now, and my stomach tumbles as he assaults my clit.

He knows I was close, and he's trying to make me come. That will temporarily incapacitate me. I'll be boneless and defenseless for long enough… He'll be able to do anything he wants to me.

"No," I try to free my thighs, but he's too strong.

I reach down and dig my nails into his shoulders, dragging them across his flesh.

Landon groans against my pussy, but he doesn't stop.

I'm horrified to find the pressure building despite the struggle. There's a telltale quickening when his tongue hits that sensitive spot again and again, a tremble in my thighs, a plea from my body to just let it happen.

No, no, no, no.

This *cannot* be happening.

"Get off me," I hiss, pushing his head to force him off me. "Get out of here, Landon. Get out of my bedroom!"

How did he even get in here? The door was locked.

Wasn't it?

I couldn't have possibly forgotten to lock it.

It's part of my nightly ritual.

Although, I did run downstairs to grab a bottle of water while I was studying.

Did I lock it when I came back up?

I don't know. I was distracted thinking about too many things... I can't remember.

The moment Landon's mouth isn't locked on my body anymore, I throw my weight and sit up so I can smack him. He can't restrain both thighs and my arms at the same time.

"Get off me," I growl, shoving him and using the small victory to move my legs.

There's a Taser in my bedside drawer. If I can just get to it, then I can stop him.

He catches my thigh before I can fully turn.

His steely grip is bound to leave bruises, but he doesn't let me go. Instead, he fights to keep control of me as I fight to get away from him. The adrenaline coursing through my veins should help me get free, but he still manages to be stronger. To keep me pinned beneath him.

As soon as I stop flailing violently to catch my breath, he dives between my thighs again.

"No," I cry out, reaching down to push at his head. "Stop it, you—"

Rather than eat my pussy, this time he bites the inside of my thigh. I cry out at the shocking savagery of it, then at the twisted spike of pleasure when he runs his hot mouth over my sensitive flesh and kisses the spot as if to soothe the pain he just inflicted.

I can feel my heart pounding in my throat and heat gathering low in my belly. I *have* to get away from him before he gets that twisted mouth on me again.

There's a lot of kicking and slapping and struggling involved, but I finally get my body free enough to roll toward the other side of the bed.

I don't know what the plan is. All I can think of is getting away, but where? Out to the hall. Do I call for help?

If I do, it's all over. There's no way in hell Mom's staying here after this. Or, I guess I should say there's no way *Landon* is, because his dad would surely kick him out over this.

Shit.

If he were anyone else sneaking into my bedroom in the middle of the night to prey on me, I would *gleefully* throw him to the fucking wolves.

But he's Landon.

I remember how I felt watching him and his dad argue before he went to stay with Malek for a few days.

Can I really throw our family into another tailspin like that?

Can we even survive another one?

He takes advantage of my faltering determination to drag me down the bed and climb on top of me. I'm tummy down, so he uses his weight to pin me, then slides his hands up my arms. He stops when both of our arms are stretched over my head, his bigger hands covering mine while he uses nothing more than his thumbs to corral my wrists and keep them from breaking free.

"I can do this all night. Can you?"

The hairs on the back of my neck prickle as his hot breath hits my skin. They're the first words he's actually spoken to me since I woke up to him eating me out, and the fact that he's only speaking now to let me know how futile my efforts to stop him are...

His audacity makes me so mad, I try to slam my head back quickly and headbutt the asshole, but he's too quick and moves before I can make contact.

He chuckles, injecting a fresh burst of fury straight into my veins. "Nice try."

"Go to hell," I snap back.

"So feisty," he murmurs almost playfully, sending a shudder through my body. "Unfortunately, you're also *so* predictable."

My breath catches as he brings my hands together and locks his right hand around both of my wrists.

"Unfortunate for you, not for me," he specifies.

His hand skims my side, making my body tense up as awareness dances down my spine.

"And, to be fair, only unfortunate because you insist on fighting this thing between us. I don't mind it anymore when you fight me. It used to annoy and confuse the shit out of me. I knew you liked me, so why wouldn't you just stand still? Why did you run every goddamn time I tried to catch you?"

My chest seems to be shrinking as I fight to breathe beneath his crushing weight.

"But then I figured it out. You weren't *really* rejecting me. You didn't *mean it*. You were just making me work extra hard for you. It makes sense. I was such an asshole to you in middle school, you couldn't let it be easy. And besides, you like to be chased."

I fight to free my wrists, but he's too damn strong. "You think you stopped being an asshole to me in middle school? Maybe you need to spend some time at that hospital Anae went to last year."

Ignoring my commentary as his hand slides over my ass, he goes on. "We'll dig into why that is eventually. Maybe it's Parker-style daddy issues. Can't love a man you believe would ever leave you, even if you ran from him."

"Maybe it's because you're an asshole," I fling back.

He chuckles. "Maybe." His lips graze the back of my neck while his fingers dance across my lower back, and he murmurs, "But I think you like to be hunted. It really clicked for me tonight when you and Hannah were talking about those books you used to like. You weren't into the nice guy who was willing to sacrifice himself so she could carry on without him. You were drawn to the hunter who proved himself a capable partner and only didn't get the girl because at the exact moment she wanted to run off with him, he put something else before her. Something noble, sure, fighting to save civilization, but who cares? He committed the ultimate sin in your book. He let go of *her*. I bet you lost interest in him after that, didn't you?"

I refuse to answer him.

I can hear his satisfaction. "Yeah, you did. You don't give up on people easily, so you probably gave him a chance to win you back over, but he didn't manage it, did he? He was no longer her fearless hunting partner, focused on taking care of her and their family above all else. He took his eye off the ball and turned you off. I know you think you're more rational than anything, Parker, but you're not. You run hot. You're primal. A lioness who can't accept a weak, unfocused mate."

I gasp as he wrenches my thighs apart and wedges himself between them.

"That's why the first hint of that noble bullshit put you off. You don't want everyone's hero; you want a man who only cares if he's yours. And you don't want a man coming after you if he can be stopped." He kisses the shell of my ear and sucks the air out of my lungs. "Only one way to see if he can be stopped, isn't there?"

My heart hammers in my chest as I feel Landon lining himself up at my entrance like a battering ram outside a castle keep.

"Landon, this is not some kind of test to see if you can be stopped."

"Sure, it's not."

"It isn't," I insist, my words ending on a gasp as he nudges his cock closer. "Please... think about what you're doing here. There's no going back from this."

"I'm not interested in going back." As if to give weight to his words, he pushes himself forward just a tiny bit.

"Landon..."

"If you really want me to stop, you can try begging," he murmurs, his words a taunt as he kisses the side of my neck.

"I'm not going to beg you for anything," I say softly.

"No," he murmurs. "It was asking you to beg that got the cops called on me last time, wasn't it?"

It's sick that he sounds amused more than anything over my literally getting him arrested.

"I get it. You have a lot of pride."

It's hard to feel very proud right now as the asshole who has made it his mission to torment me for the last six years pins me to my bed with his cock forcibly prodding my entrance.

"You came to me once, and I rejected you. You were never going to come to me again. I could have waited six more years. Twelve. The rest of our lives. This is the only way it was going to happen. I had to hunt you down, *claim you*. Make my intentions clear." In a gesture that feels oddly tender despite his current position of dominance and control over my body, he gathers my hair and moves it off to one side so he can kiss my shoulder. "In case I've left any doubts, I consider you mine, Parker. And there's nothing you can do to change that."

He slides his cock deeper into my pussy and I gasp, pulling at my wrists to try to free them. "Wait."

"No," he murmurs. "I've waited long enough."

"Landon." Slightly panicked, I buck my body since I can't pull my wrists free. "I'm warning you right now."

"Yeah? What are you going to do to me, bookworm?"

My skin heats with anger at his amused tone. "I'm serious, Landon. I'm not one of your playthings. If you do this and then you fuck someone else afterward, you will kill every bit of softness I've ever felt for you. I will carve out your fucking heart—and then I'll let someone fuck me in front of your corpse."

I feel his warm chuckle against my skin. He slides a hand around my throat, his other hand still firmly gripping my wrists. "Baby, a move like that would bring me back from the dead. If you *ever* let anyone else touch you, I'll carve *their* heart out. I'll use their blood as lube when I fuck every hole you have to remind you who you belong to."

This is too depraved.

Why do I kind of like it?

That's a scarier thought than anything.

My heart thuds. "Are you still seeing Brittany?"

"Who?"

He has me pinned down pretty good, but I try to look back at him so he can see my unimpressed side eye.

He smirks at me. "She's irrelevant. Worry about yourself."

"That's not an answer."

"I'm tired of talking." I feel him draw his hips back, stopping before his cock leaves my body. "This may hurt a bit. Try to relax."

I grab the top edge of my pillow and squeeze my eyes shut. "You better be sure."

"Oh, I'm sure."

Then he drives his hips forward, slamming his cock into me and breaking the fragile barrier that kept him out.

I'VE NEVER HAD SEX, but I've read enough about it to feel prepared.

At least, I thought I had.

I wasn't surprised by the bite of pain as he rammed his cock into me, but I'm surprised by the way my skin pulls and struggles to accommodate the brutal invasion. I'm surprised by the thrill in my stomach when I feel him push all the way in, and he murmurs, "Fuck," against my skin.

He releases my wrists, needing to touch my body and needing both hands to do it.

He didn't bother to take my shirt off, but he slides his hand beneath my top to touch my flushed skin. I'm not wearing a bra, so he easily palms my breast. I'm surprised by the gasp of pleasure when my beaded nipple grazes his warm palm.

He's paying enough attention to my responses to pick up on it, so he slides his thumb down and teases the tight little bud. I gasp, arching back against him.

While he teases my nipple, he carefully slides his cock out of the tight channel, then pushes it back in, more slowly this time so I feel every inch of his exploration. He bends to kiss my neck, and that added stimulation is almost too much. Sensation dances across my brain, knocking out all the power so all I can do is feel.

It feels incredible.

I feel... possessed.

His hips rock and he drives into me again. My body puts up less resistance this time, but I can still feel him moving inside me. I'm so full of him when he shoves deep, we feel like one person.

The way he grips my throat and kisses the side of my neck leaves me breathless. The potent mix of domination and tenderness.

His body seems to say: *I own you.*

But also: *I adore you.*

I feel a thrill in my stomach, then his thumb brushes my nipple and a shudder passes through me.

"It's too much," I whisper.

"No," he murmurs against my skin.

I nod, my eyes closed. "It's too much. I can't take it."

"Stop trying to control yourself. Just let go and enjoy it."

"I can't," I whine, pressing my face into the pillow.

He teases my nipple almost idly, then he stops. I'm simultaneously relieved and saddened by him doing what I requested and lessening the intensity.

Until I realize that's not what he's doing at all.

His hand slides beneath my body, snaking down until he's touching my pussy from the front while pushing into me from behind. He thrusts into me again, this time sliding a finger into me as well. His finger curls up to find my clit, and I gasp at the sharp spike of pleasure.

He fucks me slowly, paying more attention to my pleasure than anything. He had me so close with his mouth, and now with all this other physical stimulation.

I grab the pillow, my body moving restlessly as he teases my clit.

"Landon," I cry, whining, panting against the pillow as the pressure inside me builds.

"Let it happen."

His command is all it takes.

I cry out so sharply, he covers my mouth with his hand to smother the sound. My body trembles and shakes as ecstasy shoots through me. Landon fucks me through the orgasm, his thrusts picking up in speed and intensity. I can feel my pussy convulsing around him. I'm dimly aware of him groaning and muttering, "Fuck," against my shoulder, but then my awareness drifts off down a beautiful stream of bliss.

Peace washes over me.

It's only for a second or two, then friction and the force of Landon pounding into my pussy brings me back to the moment.

I'm freer this time, though.

Able to enjoy the feel of him claiming me, the impossible fullness in my body when he's deep inside me and it's like we're one.

At some point, he releases my wrists so he can hold onto my hips better. He fucks me like he wants to break me even though I know he doesn't. I'm not complaining. I love it when he's as deep as he can go.

When he pulls out and flips me over, my heart flies into my throat. Before now, I could feel him claiming me, but I didn't have to look into his eyes.

It's a whole different experience when our gazes are locked while he pushes his cock into my body.

More intimate.

More powerful.

Definitely scarier.

I swallow, then I slide a hand around his neck and pull him down so I can reach to kiss him. Just a little one at first, at the corner of his mouth. Then I kiss his full lower lip. Before I can kiss him full on the mouth, he shoves me down against the mattress, locks his hand around my throat, and dominates my mouth while he fucks me.

It is, without question, hotter than anything I could have ever imagined.

"You're mine," he whispers against my jaw as he nips at it.

My heart is already pounding from the intensity of being fucked, but it beats extra hard when he says that.

Since he made me come already, I didn't expect to feel the pressure building inside me again, but it does.

It's different, though.

It feels like it comes from somewhere deeper.

I begin to grasp frantically as Landon's cock slams into me again and again, his movements harder and faster. I whine and grab the edge of the bed with one hand. I close my eyes and pant, then my heart nearly stops when he grabs my throat again, my eyes opening wide in surprise.

Landon looms over me, shaking his head. "You look at me when you come."

That fucking does it.

Pleasure erupts inside me. I cry out, slapping my own hand over my mouth when I realize I'm being too loud, but fuck, I can't help it. Dizzying, soul-deep pleasure pours through my body as my pussy convulses, squeezing his cock and pumping his cum into me as he explodes with a rugged groan, his beautiful body tensing above me. He growls and rams into me again, forcing every drop as deep as he can get it.

When the climax ends, he collapses on top of me, and I wrap my arms around him.

I'm still breathing heavy, my heart racing, but I just want to hold him close.

He's done fucking me, but I can still feel his cock inside my body, and I want to keep him there.

I know now that it's over, he'll probably pull out, but I don't want him to.

It feels like everything will be different when he does.

I'm not ready for that.

So, I close my eyes and allow myself to float in this enjoyable feeling of softness and bliss. I hold him like I'll never have to let go.

I let myself enjoy tonight as if tomorrow will never come.

THE UNWELCOME SOUND of my alarm clock is what wakes me.

I'm confused at first, annoyed at the sound and the too-bright light streaming in through the windows.

At first, it's just like any other morning following a long night of not sleeping enough, but while the burning of my eyes is a familiar sensation, another is not.

Between my legs, I feel wet and sticky. A bloom of horror breaks open inside me when I touch the inside of my thigh and memories of last night come rushing back to me.

Landon fucked me last night.

I swallow, looking at the empty side of my bed. There's no sign he was ever there, so he must have left after I fell asleep.

I fish my panties and shorts that he took off while I was sleeping out from beneath the comforter, then I gaze with horror at the stained bed sheets.

Oh my god. What do I do?

Antonia is coming today, but I can't let her see these.

With shaky hands, I do the only thing I can think to do.

I call Hannah.

"Hello?" she answers, sounding a little alarmed since I don't usually call her in the mornings.

"Hey, I have a question."

I can hear my voice shaking. My legs feel wobbly with panic, too.

"Okay," she says tentatively.

"It's a cleaning question. Um, it might be kind of gross."

"Okay," she says, her tone even more unsure.

"Do you know how to get blood and cum out of sheets?"

For several seconds, she doesn't say anything.

"The maid is coming today. Or the housekeeper or whatever, but I don't want her to see them because she might tell my mom or Hayden. I don't know what the housekeeper code is, but I'm guessing something like that might be reported. And then if that gets reported, I have to explain it, and I *can't* explain it. So, I don't know what to do. I have these sheets on my bed and I... should I just steal them? Should I shove them in my backpack and ditch them at school? Should I burn them? Can I just clean them? I don't know what to do, Hannah."

"Breathe," she says calmly, since it's clear from my ramble that I'm panicking. "Take a deep breath, then let it out."

I do, blowing the breath out audibly as I try to gather my wits.

"Now, are you okay?" she asks.

"I'm fine. I'm okay. I just don't know what to do with these sheets."

"Are you sure? Did he... hurt you?"

"No. He... didn't hurt me. I don't want to talk about that right now, I just need to figure out..."

"The sheets," she says softly. "We can handle the sheets. As it happens, I do know how to get both of those things out. If you want, you can bag the sheets and bring them to me. Or I can walk you through it."

I nod. "Okay. Yeah. Thank you."

"Of course."

I FLEE the house without breakfast, opting instead to stop and get myself a breakfast croissant on my way to school. I eat it in the car, gazing up at the looming school building and thinking it has never looked so intimidating before.

It's not until I'm on my way in and I realize Landon's parking spot is empty that the feeling shifts.

I'm running a little behind since I stopped to buy myself breakfast, but presumably Landon ate whatever Antonia made for breakfast.

He should be here by now.

I don't know what it means that he isn't, but it makes my stomach hurt.

The prospect of *seeing him* made my stomach hurt, too, so maybe a stomachache was inevitable today.

I feel better knowing where he is, though.

As I enter the building, I pull my phone out of my purse to make sure I don't have any texts from Mom. My thoughts go to catastrophic places. Something happened to him, or somehow Hayden found out what happened even though I know that's unlikely.

Unless he caught Landon leaving my room.

I fell asleep with Landon still inside me, and I have no memory of him leaving, so I have no idea what happened.

My heart flips over when I see a text notification, but plummets when I see who it's from.

Javi sent me another picture of the ocean, this time with a

brighter sky since it's later in the morning than when he goes for his runs.

I feel a pinch of guilt looking at it, but I don't have the time or mental energy to deal with that right now. I know I should be exhausted since I barely slept last night, but I feel wired, bordering on jittery, when I check in on the book drive to make sure everything is on track.

The nervous energy helps keep me awake, but makes it harder to focus on classes today. My focus is especially shaken when the first class I'm supposed to have with Landon starts and he still isn't here.

I check my phone again but there's still nothing, so I shoot my mom an innocuous text about my club meeting after school and wait to see what she says.

Of course, she chooses today to be busy.

I don't get to check her return text until after class, but her response is just, "got it. Have fun!"

"Ugh," I mutter, looking down at my phone on the way to lunch.

Hannah catches up to me for the first time since she walked me through cleaning my stupid sheets this morning. "Hey."

"Hey," I murmur, slipping my phone back into my purse. I try to ignore her paying extra close attention to me, but it's like walking outside and trying to ignore the sun. "I'm fine," I say shortly. "I don't want to talk about it. I don't even know what 'it' is."

"Okay," she says easily. "If you change your mind, you know where to find me." Without dwelling on it, she looks ahead down the hall. "Are we eating in the cafeteria?"

I nod. Then, despite saying I didn't want to talk about it, I add, "I don't think he's at school today. He wasn't in class."

She shakes her head. "He wasn't in the class we usually have together, either."

Sighing, I try my best not to care, and hate when the very first thought to spring to mind is... "Do you have any classes with Brittany?"

I told Landon the one sure way to blow things up like they've never been blown up before, and he loves to detonate things.

While I did it to protect us if there was ever going to be an us, to protect *him* because I know deep down, I'm the one keeping his life together, I knew the risks of handing the nuke codes over to someone as volatile as Landon.

But I meant what I said, and I hope he knows that. I wasn't running my mouth to cast a certain inflated impression of my badassery; I was delivering information that is crucial to our survival.

If he does the one thing I warned him about the very next day, the gloves are coming off. One-way alliance over. I won't protect him anymore, and he won't make it another week without me.

But maybe that's okay. Fuck him. If he's intent on living in chaos, he can live in it alone and leave us to our peace.

"Yes, she was in class."

I sag with relief, a thousand pounds falling off my shoulders.

I was talking a big game and I meant every word, but I did *not* want to have to follow through.

Why can't he just let me be nice to him?

"It is so like him to do this," I say with much less defensiveness now that the worst of my fears has been dissolved. "I fell asleep with him in my arms, and I haven't seen or heard from him since."

Hannah grimaces. "That sucks. I'm sorry."

"It sure does," I mutter.

CHAPTER 30

PARKER

AT THE END OF A LONG, stressful school day, I have even more school.

Normally, I'd be eager to head off to the Uplift club meeting, but today, it's the last thing I want to do. I'm exhausted physically and mentally, and I do not have the patience for Anae Richards.

Sighing heavily, I gather up my books. Everyone else files past me and makes their way out of the classroom. I'm the last to leave, so I make my way to the teacher's desk before I go.

Mr. Clark looks up at me from behind his spectacles, cocking an eyebrow in question.

"Can I get an extra paper packet to take home for Landon Atwater? He was absent today and we live together. I can give them to him tonight so he can catch up over the weekend."

"Oh. Yes, here you go," he says, grabbing a stapled pack of papers off his desk and passing them to me.

"Thank you," I murmur before turning to walk out.

When I step through the doorway and into the hall, I'm caught off guard by someone pushing off the wall and sauntering toward me. My eyes widen and my cheeks warm as my gaze rakes over him quickly. He's wearing a black T-shirt that hugs his athletic frame and a pair of dark wash jeans.

"Landon," I say, not bothering to hide the surprise in my voice.

I don't miss the way his gaze briefly rakes over me, either. I'm wearing an emerald green button-down top and a black skirt that felt an appropriate length all day, but now that he's looking at me, I feel like it provides minimal coverage.

Maybe it's the memory of him in my bed last night that makes me feel so exposed.

The knowledge that, while I wasn't awake to witness it, the depraved lunatic stripped off my clothes before helping himself to a snack between my thighs.

That memory really makes my face hot.

Forcing myself back to the present, I glance back at the classroom I just walked out of. Instinctively, I move away from the door.

We should start walking before the teacher comes out and sees Landon loitering in the halls after skipping class.

"What are you doing here?" I ask uncertainly as I start down the hall.

In answer, he holds out a smoothie I hadn't noticed him holding. "Thought I'd bring you a little pick me up before your meeting."

My eyebrows rise in surprise. "You skipped school and then showed up at the end of the day to bring me a smoothie?"

"And they say I'm not a nice guy," he retorts.

I crack a smile, hesitantly reaching for the icy beverage. "This isn't spiked, is it?"

He chuckles. "No. Didn't think you'd want to get caught imbibing at school."

"You figured correctly. Thank you," I say, still a bit uncertain.

He nods wordlessly, letting go of the drink and watching me eye the label. It reads "reg. strawberry cranberry smoothie."

I take a sip, and it's delicious. A slightly different flavor than I'm used to, but probably because of the cranberries. I don't typically order my smoothies with cranberry.

"So, why weren't you around today?" I ask.

"Decided to sleep in. I had a late night."

My face heats like I just strapped on a fire mask.

"Nah, that's not true," he says a second later, surprising me. "I just thought you could use a break from me today."

Frowning, I look over at him in question.

"Last time, you seemed to want a break from me afterward."

Last time was different.

I open my mouth to say the words, then decide better of it and take a sip of my smoothie. I'm not even sure how true it is.

"We will need to talk about that," I tell him. "I can't right now because I have a club meeting, but if you're not doing anything after, maybe..."

God, this feels so awkward.

If this is what talking to guys is like, maybe I'm glad Landon has banned me from dating for all these years.

It doesn't help that I have no idea where we stand. He said a lot of things last night in my bed, but in general, Landon isn't the best communicator. That's why it caught me off guard. Why I let him...

I can't think about that right now. Not at school, not with him walking next to me.

I take another sip of my smoothie to cool down. If he weren't standing right beside me, I would press the cool cup right against my face.

Seemingly unfazed by the enormous awkwardness of our

situation, Landon nods. "Sure. I'll pick you up. We can go for a ride."

The giddy sensation that rushes through me when he says that takes me *completely* off guard.

There's no way he should still be able to trigger that in me. It's just a ride—with *him*—in his car, but...

That old crushy feeling makes a startling reappearance and I have to make an effort to jam it down.

We are not going to like Landon that way again.

Are we?

I'm afraid of the answer, and *more* afraid that it's even still a possibility because I was certain he had cured me of it.

The fluttery feeling inside when he stops outside the meeting room, slides his hands into the pockets of his jeans, and gives me a little smirk seems to indicate otherwise.

Crap.

This is such a bad idea.

"See you in a bit," he says.

"Bye," I say with a stupid little wave that *horrifies me* the moment my body decides to do it.

The only way to describe the way my insides feel is shrink-wrapped.

Like my brain, apparently, because I can't focus on a single thing throughout the meeting. All my concentration is centered on him.

This is the worst.

This feels kinda... nice.

Both things can be true.

Landon Atwater is not a safe person to like. There are dozens of girls at this school who could attest to the fact.

Hell, *I* can attest to the fact myself.

But, apparently, those facts fly right out the window when he offers you the passenger seat in his car.

Ugh.

I want so badly to override all the stupidity I'm feeling right now, but maybe I need a second—kinder—opinion.

GRABBING Hannah's arm dramatically as we walk out of the club meeting, I survey our surroundings to make sure Landon isn't lurking nearby.

"What are you doing?" she asks, looking over at me since I'm behaving strangely.

"I need advice."

"All right," she says easily.

"I think I like a boy."

"You don't say," she murmurs, lightly amused.

"It's Landon."

"Why didn't you warn me to sit down first? I could break something fainting from the shock."

I slide her an unamused look. "You could at least pretend to be surprised."

Shrugging daintily, she says, "I don't like lying. I'm not wasting one on the worst kept secret of all time."

"I don't know what to do. My stomach is in knots and my brain has gone haywire. I'm going for a ride with him after school."

At that, Hannah opens her purse and draws out her wallet. I frown, watching her, then my eyes widen when she passes me a condom.

"Why do you have that?" I ask, utterly baffled.

"For emergencies. Just in case you do any *other* riding. Make sure you use one of these this time."

"Oh, my god," I say, my face flushing with humiliation. I snatch it anyway, partially because I have no idea what to expect, partially because I don't want anyone else to see her offering it to me.

I know Hannah carries *everything* in her Mary Poppins purse because she likes to be prepared, but I did not expect her to have a condom.

I also can't have Hannah financially supporting my sex life on her limited income, so as I tuck the condom she gave me into my purse, I tell her, "Don't buy a replacement. I'll buy an emergency pack myself and give you one of those."

"As long as you're prompt about it. Anae knows I keep one on me, so sometimes I'm the only reason she makes responsible choices. The last thing anyone needs is Anae procreating."

"God, can you imagine her as a mother?"

"Sure," she says breezily. "She'd buy the baby cute accessories, share photos on her socials and brag about how she really can have it all. And I'd be the one actually raising it."

"Sounds about right," I mutter, rolling my eyes.

"But it's probably better if we all wait until at least after college to start that chapter of our lives, so..." She looks pointedly at my purse.

"Trust me, you're preaching to the choir. If I had known it was going to happen, I would have had emergency condoms in my bedside drawer. On reflection, I probably should have anyway, but..." I glance over at her. "Which brings me to what I needed advice about. I know liking him is... probably not the smartest thing I could do."

"But you do."

"It's looking that way. But since I *know* going in it's a bad idea, I'm partially trying to burst my own bubble. Part of me says just enjoy it while you can, the other part is like 'you know this can't end well,' and I have trouble arguing with that flawless logic."

"And you want my input."

I nod. "Weigh in, so one of the sides has a buddy."

She cracks a smile. "I think you should let yourself enjoy it. Be smart. Be safe. Don't ignore any red flags that pop up. But considering how long you've liked him, it just seems mean to deprive yourself of the fun now that it can *be* fun. If it crashes and burns, jump out of the car, but for the time being... enjoy the ride."

"You give the best advice."

"I do what I can," she says lightly.

I feel a little better now that Hannah has given me permission to do what I wanted to do anyway. If she agrees with me, maybe it's not the most reckless thing I could do.

And realistically, what's the alternative? Things keep going the way they have been? How much longer can I keep that up? Is it even still a possibility now that Landon has dragged us both across this line?

Maybe it's an excuse to support that action I want to take, but it's also where we are right now. Landon has brought chaos and stress into all our lives since the moment we moved in. Is it unimaginable that I want a break from that?

It sounds good, but a little voice in the back of my head whispers that I may have it wrong. As controlling and chaotic as Landon was when he had *no* viable claim on me, couldn't it be worse if he feels he does?

But I tell myself I'm putting the cart way ahead of the horse.

Like Hannah said, I'll keep watch for the red flags. I'll play it smart; I'll keep things under control. I can control more from the inside when it's just the two of us, and honestly, now that he's fucked me, he doesn't have the same arsenal he had before.

I can handle Landon Atwater.

I've had to for years.

Hell, years ago, I *wanted* this.

Maybe somehow, it won't end in pain and heartbreak.

Maybe now he'll actually let me in.

LANDON IS WAITING for me in his spot in front of the school.

I'm reminded of the first day when he was supposed to give me a ride home, but he was too busy being a jerk.

I wasn't looking forward to getting in his car that day anyway, but the apprehension I feel now is unmatched.

Lower the stakes, Parker.

There's no need to psych myself out. It's just a car ride. With Landon Atwater. What could possibly go wrong?

I crack a faint smile at my own joke, but it helps bring me back down and level out the giddiness as I approach the passenger side of his car.

"Hey," he says when I open the door.

"Hey," I say back, pushing my hair back over my shoulder and sliding into the seat.

"How was your meeting?"

"Great. The book drive did okay even though we threw it together last minute, so we packed up the books and went over everything pertaining to that. Anae took black and white pictures to post online as if we're doing God's work," I say with a roll of my eyes. "It's kind of an uninspired group this year; they don't plan to really start on any side projects until the next meeting, but we are helping organize Fright Fest next month, so we'll start working on that. I don't know, the load feels light to me. I may dig around and come up with something else to put on the docket."

Landon smirks. "You always have to be doing something extra, don't you?"

I shrug. "I like to keep busy." Glancing over at him, I ask, "What about you?"

He cocks a dark eyebrow. "What *about* me?"

"You don't play football anymore. Swim team is in the off season. Ever think about joining any clubs?"

"Nah, I'm not much of a joiner."

I nod. "I get that. But colleges like to see extracurriculars on your application. Plus, clubs can help you find things you're genuinely interested in and passionate about."

"And you're passionate about helping people."

I shrug. "Yeah. What are you passionate about?"

"Not helping people," he says dryly.

I shoot him a look. "Hilarious. Maybe you should join comedy club."

"Oh yeah, I'm a riot."

"I'm serious," I say, lightly shoving his arm.

He shakes his head. "So am I. I'm not into clubs. It's bad enough I have to do 18 hours of community service this year like I'm some kind of criminal."

"You *are* kind of a criminal," I remind him. "I'm starting on my community service hours next week. I'm volunteering at a pet shelter. You should come with me."

"I suppose animals *are* better than people."

I nod my agreement. "Immensely better. And the company wouldn't be too bad, either."

He cracks a smile, glancing my way. "I might be okay with the company."

That shouldn't make my tummy flutter, but it does. Unable to hold his gaze, I shift mine to look out at the road as he drives. "Where are we going, anyway?"

"You'll see."

And soon, I do.

I didn't expect him to bring me to the beach.

It doesn't appear to be an impulsive decision, though, as he grabs an oversized beach towel and a little blue cooler out of the trunk. A gentle breeze blows my hair and I turn toward the ocean, breathing in so I can catch the salty scent.

I love the ocean.

I wasn't sure he would given his history, plus the fact that we live in a mansion that boasts beautiful ocean views and he chose a room without one.

We walk down closer to the shoreline and Landon puts down the beach towel. He drops down and gets comfortable, then he looks up at me and pats the empty spot beside him.

Cracking a smile, I tuck my hair behind my ear, then settle in on the beach towel.

Landon unzips the little soft-shell cooler he brought and takes out a container of grapes with a container full of sliced cheese stacked on top of it. He opens both and puts them between us, then he grabs a pack of crackers out of the side pocket.

"A cheese board," I say, delighted.

"Kinda. Figured you'd want a snack."

"You know me so well," I joke, reaching for the crackers.

He's in a better mood than I'm used to, so I'm still not entirely sure what to do with it. He reaches in the cooler and draws out a clear capped bottle. If I didn't know any better, I'd think it's the sunset lemonade I like from the club.

Alarm takes hold when I consider that it could be. I hope he didn't go there without me. I don't even think he should be welcome there after what he pulled before, but the prospect of him encountering Javi with no one around to keep an eye on him... it's not my favorite thing to imagine.

When he passes me the drink, I think about asking, but I don't want to invite an argument right now. "Thanks," I say instead, giving it a little swirl, then uncapping it so I can take a sip.

It *is* the sunset lemonade. Or maybe something close. It tastes a bit different, but mostly I can still taste the flavored lemonade and splash of grenadine I enjoy at the club. "This is really good," I say, taking another sip.

"It's spiked," he volunteers, halting me midway through sipping. He holds up a bottle of tea for himself. "Mine isn't since I'm driving you back to your car, but I figure it's Friday. You can afford to blow off a little steam."

I swallow the drink in my mouth, but I cap the bottle, unsure I'll take another. Thankfully, he also brought bottled water, so I grab one of those. "You have got to stop spiking my drinks and not telling me."

"I did tell you. Just now."

I shoot him a look. "*Before* I take a drink would be the appropriate time. In fact, asking beforehand if I would *like* alcohol in my drink would be the best-case scenario."

Immediately rejecting the suggestion, he shakes his head. "Nah, not my style."

"Yeah, I gathered you're more the 'ask for forgiveness, not permission type'," I mutter dryly.

Landon's eyebrows rise and he leans back on his hands, stretching his legs out in front of him. "When have I ever asked for forgiveness?"

"I... don't know. Presumably at some point in your life."

He shoots me a look that seems to convey *if you say so* but doesn't comment.

I stare at him. "Please tell me at *some point* you have expressed remorse for any number of the terrible things you've done."

He shrugs. "I don't know. Most of them were to you. You remember an apology?"

Certainly not.

"So, you just don't care who you hurt, huh? Fuck everybody? Then why should anyone care about you?"

He shrugs again, looking out at the water. "I doubt anyone does."

My heart flips over in my chest, but decidedly not in the good way. It's the flippant way he says it more than the words themselves. I know Landon has a chip on his shoulder, everyone knows that, but he doesn't say it like some bullshit meant to draw out my sympathy. He says it like it's an established fact he made peace with a long time ago.

And *that* reminds me of the Landon I tried to approach in middle school.

The one I went to that stupid party for.

The one I wanted to kiss.

Shaking my head, I pick at the label on my water bottle. "That's not true, Landon. A lot of people care about you. Your dad cares about you. I know you guys don't have the best relationship, but he does care. He wouldn't try so hard to protect you from yourself if he didn't. Malek obviously cares about you. He's always trying to keep you from getting into trouble. Clearly, I care about you. We wouldn't be here right now if I didn't."

His mouth tugs up slightly at the corners. "Yeah, but you care about everybody."

I scoff. "That is *not* true."

"Sure it is. Miss Uplift Club with all your community service." He lightly mocks me, but there's no true malice in it this time, he's just ribbing me. "I'm just one of the strays you volunteer to help out with."

I shake my head. "No. Because if one of those strays bit my face off, I'd throw its little ass in the cage and never approach it again. When I had the chance to put you in one, I didn't. I'm no overly loving angel. I'm not made of forgiveness. I'm prickly and opinionated and not one bit reluctant to stand up for myself. It was a conscious choice to let you off the hook. It is a conscious choice every single day that I wake up under your roof and commit to making this work. It's not some... natural compulsion that I just passively give in to. I always want to give you a chance, and even though you've made me regret it each time I have before, I'm still here. If that doesn't show you I care, I don't know what would."

I'm so fired up by the end of that, it takes me a minute to process the smirk on his stupid, handsome face, the amusement dancing in the depths of his green eyes.

"You're fucking with me," I realize.

"Would I do that?"

"Yes," I say, wide-eyed. "You absolutely would. You asshole." Then, letting my temper get the best of me, I uncap my bottle of water and dump it right over his head.

The smirk disappears instantly, and although my temper also dissolves instantly at the sight of him soaking wet, I'm still a little sorry I can't hold back a laugh.

Landon pushes off the beach and sits forward, pulling his wet, clingy T-shirt away from his skin. He looks over at me slowly, unable to believe I just did that, and I try shooting him my most innocent, don't-kill-me smile.

"I'm part Irish," I explain. "We have tempers."

"Oh, I'll show you a temper."

I crawl away, hastily making my way to my feet. "You deserved it! You can't get me back."

I turn to run away from him, but before my foot can even hit the beach, he grabs me from behind, yanking me back against his wet body.

I shiver when his breath hits my skin and he murmurs in my ear, "Remember what I told you would happen next time you spilled something on me?"

"Yeah, but are you really a man of your word?" I ask lightly as he drags me back toward the oversized beach towel.

"You bet I fucking am."

PARKER STRUGGLES to break free of my hold, but her weak little ass doesn't stand a chance against me. All she manages to accomplish with her thrashing is to turn me on even more than dumping her water over my head and then trying to run from me.

My temperamental little runaway, always thinking she stands a chance when she doesn't.

"Let me go, you big jerk."

I smirk at her insult, dragging her back to our picnic spot and wrestling her little ass to the ground so I can climb on top of her.

Huffing, she glares up at me. "This isn't fair. You were manipulating my emotions. I deserved a little revenge."

I unbutton the first button of her green top. "Take all the revenge you want; just know I'll always pay you back with interest."

Her nose wrinkles up and she pouts at me. "That's not fair."

"Such is life."

When I get to the third button, she tries to hold her shirt

together, her gaze darting around us. "Landon, stop it. You cannot undress me on a public beach."

"Why not?"

"Because this isn't France, and you may be fine with having a criminal record, but I'm not."

I already made sure the spot I took her to didn't have anyone else around, but I check now just to make sure no one has shown up since then. Seeing the beach is still empty, I tell her, "There's no one around to see. Relax."

"That could change at any time. If you wanted to maul me, you should have taken me to *our* actual private beach."

I push her shirt open, looking down at her pale, freckled skin and the white no-nonsense bra she's wearing underneath. I can't help but smirk. "I see you went all out for our date."

She smacks me in the stomach, glaring up at me. "Like everything else that happens with you, I didn't know this was coming."

"It's cute. Very Parker. Bet you have on no-nonsense panties to match, huh?"

Her cheeks flush, and she tries to smack my hand away as I draw up her skirt to get a look.

"Knew it."

"I hate you."

"No, you don't." I lower her skirt and look down at her, not bothering to hide my amusement. "You care about me, remember? You just said so. No takebacks."

Parker sighs heavily with annoyance, and I drop down to the ground, lifting her up and settling her on top of me. She grabs my sides to maintain her balance, then looks down at me with those big doe eyes once she's straddling me. "What are you doing?"

I pull up my wet shirt, then pull it off over my head and drop it on the towel next to us.

Parker's eyes go to my chest like magnets. She's not the first girl to openly admire my well-honed physique, but she is the only one whose approval matters.

I let her soak it in for a moment, then I reach up and grab a fistful of hair, using it to bring her down closer. "Get licking."

Her tongue darts out and she licks her lips. She looks up at me, but she can't move her head too much comfortably since I've got a tight grip on her hair.

I cock an expectant eyebrow.

She narrows her eyes at me, but then she shifts her attention to my chest. Her touch is tentative as she runs her hands over my pecs. She has no idea where to even begin.

"Kiss my chest," I tell her.

She licks her lips again, then lowers her face and softly kisses my firm chest.

"Let your tongue dart out to tease my nipple."

She does, then she looks up at me uncertainly. "Like that?"

I nod. "Now, keep going. Just listen to your body. Do what feels nice. Whatever feels good for you will feel good for me, too."

Clearly, she doesn't have much sexual confidence, but Parker has never shied away from learning something once in her life, so despite her initial reluctance, she starts to explore my body.

I knew Parker would be a super virgin and that I'd have to teach her everything every step of the way. I'd never have the patience to deal with that with any other girl, but I've long relished getting the chance to do it with her.

Malek said I should stop being such a controlling asshole and let her play with a few other dicks so she'd know what she was doing by the time she got to me, but Malek's never been into a girl before, so he doesn't get it. A while back, he tried to get with Hannah, but unlike every other fucking girl in existence, Hannah has no interest in assholes. She rejected him—politely, of course—and I'm not sure he's ever asked another girl out since. He's fucked around with plenty of them, but like me, he tends to go for the damaged ones that don't require much to keep things going.

But me, I've been marking territory I didn't even understand I wanted since middle school. From the moment Parker stood in front of me with a shirt full of muffin crumbs and tears glinting in her pretty brown eyes after I'd humiliated her, I couldn't stomach the thought of her with anyone else. The stakes felt too high. It wasn't even about the sex. I've had plenty of sex that didn't mean anything. It was the fact that if I let another guy get that close to her, maybe she'd fall for him.

I couldn't have that.

I used to think I didn't want her to have that because I fucking hated her and I didn't want her to have anything good. Then I started to realize maybe I'd put her on hold because I wanted exclusive access to her myself.

But I tried to hook up with her at that party, and she shot me down just like I shot her down in middle school. She's been running from me ever since.

Well, until my dad helpfully locked her in the same cage as me.

Thanks, Dad.

She still runs, but now she's like a hamster stuck in a wheel. There's nowhere to go. I just let her tire herself out so I can pounce on her more easily.

Smirking at my own thoughts, I use her hair to tug her face up close to mine so I can kiss her. I fucking love being able to do that.

She's the one on top, but I'm the one in control.

That is, until her spiteful little ass wiggles around on my cock, and then all I can think about is getting inside her.

"I see how it is," I murmur against her lips.

"What?" she asks innocently. "Did that make you uncomfortable?"

"I'll show you uncomfortable." I grab her so I can catch her, then I roll her off me and onto the soft beach towel beneath us. She gasps, reaching back and grabbing the wet shirt I dropped there.

"Great," she complains. "Now there's a wet spot on my back."

That's not the wet spot I'm interested in. I push her skirt up again, then tug down her white panties. I pull them all the way off so they don't get in my way, then I shove them in my pocket and settle in between her thighs.

Parker sighs, checking to make sure no one is around again. "Landon..."

I ignore her half-hearted objection and spread her thighs, taking in the sight of her pretty pussy in the light of day. I hold one of her thighs in case she gets restless and decides to fight me, then I leave a hot trail of kisses along the inside as I make my way toward her pussy.

Her sighs aren't so annoyed now.

I lock my other arm around her other thigh to really trap her, then I yank her little ass closer. I use my thumbs to spread her open, enjoying the rush of breath that leaves her lungs when I do.

Then I kiss her right on the pussy and her back arches. "You like that?" I murmur.

"Landon," she says, much more softly. "You can't do this here. I'll die if someone comes..."

I smirk. "The only person coming in the next few minutes is going to be you—all over my face as I devour your pussy."

"Oh, my god," she says, covering her face to hide her embarrassment.

"Now, be a good girl and let yourself enjoy it."

"I'm always a good girl," she mutters. "You're the one who couldn't find 'good' if it was starred and highlighted on a map."

I grin at her talking shit, then I dive between her legs and latch onto that perfect pussy.

The taste of her makes me ravenous. I love the little sounds she makes and the way she grabs desperately at the towel beneath us while I lick her pussy. My cock jerks at her little gasps and the way her thighs tremble as she gets close.

Then she whines my name, and I growl against her aroused flesh.

I go for her clit, and I'm merciless in my quest for her pleasure. She's gasping and arching off the beach, her heels digging into my shoulders as she starts to lose control.

"Landon," she cries out, her breath hitching, her eyes closed as her whole body tenses.

I shove a finger in her pussy and feel her convulse around me, crying out as pleasure erupts inside her.

Her pleasure is fucking delicious.

When her body is limp and sated, I give her pussy one more kiss before withdrawing.

Her eyes are closed, her body completely relaxed and peaceful as she recovers. It takes some effort to turn Parker's brain off, but I had a hunch an orgasm would soften her right up.

Decency forgotten, she turns on her side and curls up against me when I lie down beside her on the beach towel. Her hand comes to rest casually on my abdomen, and her long red hair spills over my bicep.

She's so beautiful when she's like this.

She's beautiful when she's fiery and pissed off, too, but I'm enjoying the glimpse of this side of her.

I let her enjoy her bliss for a few minutes despite the insistent throbbing of my cock. She doesn't help matters by curling up so close to me, absently running her hand over my stomach in a gesture I can only take as affectionate.

Affection isn't something I've gotten much of. Girls have offered it, of course. Begged for the chance to give it to me, really, but I didn't want it from them.

I want it from her.

I want everything from her.

I'M SO cozy and comfortable, I don't think I'd move if the beach caught on fire.

Landon is lying shirtless beside me. As far as I can see past him is just sandy beach and gentle ocean waves lapping at the shore, blue skies and white fluffy clouds above us.

"It's so beautiful here."

"Yes, it is," he murmurs, but something about his tone tells me it's not the beach he's focused on.

I tip my head back to look at his handsome face. I never thought we'd be here in a million years. When I used to dream about him being my first kiss, my fantasies were too innocent to ever imagine us curled up on the beach, the breeze hitting my bare ass because Landon didn't bother to put my panties back on after he ate me out.

I can tell from the bulge in his pants and the tenseness of his body that he's not nearly as relaxed as I am. I let my hand slide down his toned abdomen, then lower until my daring fingers slide over his cock. He's still wearing jeans, so I'm not sure how good it feels caressing him through the thick fabric, but the breath that rushes out of him seems to indicate at least it's not terrible.

But then he grabs my wrist and my heart seizes.

Maybe I was wrong...?

"You don't want me to...?"

Rather than answer, he shifts our positions until I'm on my back on the beach towel again.

He reaches out to touch me, almost innocently at first as his fingers graze my arm. Goosebumps erupt across my skin when his fingertips graze my exposed stomach. My eyes drift closed for a moment, enjoying the sensation of him simply touching me.

My shirt is still hanging open, exposing a swatch of my chest and bra. Landon pushes the fabric aside, leaning in and kissing my torso just below the bra. It feels so nice, I sigh, and then he does it again, softly kissing my stomach as his hand slides beneath my skirt.

"What are you doing?" I ask, startled as his hands brush the curve of my bare ass.

"I'm still hungry," he murmurs, eyeing up my pussy.

"Oh, my god. You're insatiable."

"Your fault. You shouldn't be so tasty," he says with a devilish smirk.

There's no way I should let this happen again. I've barely recovered from the first orgasm he gave me, and with the constant threat hanging over us that someone could just come walking up the beach...

I just can't bring myself to stop him when his hand possessively rests against my pussy. A soft sigh slips from my lips when he uses his strong thumb to tease me. He nudges my entrance and stimulates me with his deliberate movements without pushing inside.

"Are you sore today?"

My eyes flutter open. I must look confused, because he goes on.

"I wasn't sure how the whole virgin thing worked."

"Not your usual type, huh?" I ask lightly.

"Nah. Too clingy." He says it off-handedly, and an answering surge of annoyance flares up despite the gentle pleasure he's currently kindling inside me.

"You've got some nerve accusing virgins of being too clingy. Pardon them for attaching to some jerk they've given intimate access to their body for the first time. Sex is *supposed* to be an expression of intimacy that garners closeness. I've never given you access to anything and you've—" My words cut off on a gasp as he shoves a finger deep into my pussy.

Smirking, he says, "I didn't mean *you*. I meant other girls."

"I'm aware of what you meant. I was defending other girls, not myself. I'm not clingy. But I've seen the girls you date. If you pounce on someone with self-esteem issues because you know she'll be easy to mistreat, and then *you're* her introduction to sex, I think you have some fucking audacity complaining that she got too clingy."

Landon shakes his head. "I'm not speaking from personal experience. *I* haven't had a virgin before you. Not interested in that much responsibility when it comes to casual hookups. But I have friends that have. I've seen the clinging that comes after."

"My argument stands. *All* your friends are assholes," I state.

He smirks. "I guess that's fair criticism." Then he curls his finger, wrenching a gasp out of me. "But I'd strongly prefer you don't talk about my friends when I'm inside you."

"Oh, yeah? I'll make a mental note for when you get on my nerves."

"I wouldn't recommend it."

"But what would Arden say? Maybe we should text him and get his opinion."

Leveling me a flat look of annoyance, he shoves another finger inside me, much more roughly than the first.

"Don't threaten me with a good time," I murmur.

"You little pain in the ass."

I open my mouth to respond, but then he plants his face between my thighs and my brain switches gears.

Darting a gaze left, then right, I reach down and push at his broad shoulder. "Landon, no. It's too stressful. I won't be able to keep an eye out when you... do that," I say with some effort, already losing steam as his tongue brushes my clit. A shudder passes over me, just a glimpse of the pleasure I know he could give me.

It feels greedy to chase more pleasure, but he doesn't give me much choice. I didn't even think I could get aroused again so quickly after coming, but he's so good with his mouth.

It's a slower build this time, but when the pleasure reaches toe-curling heights and my fingers dig into the ground beneath us, I have the sense that it's going to be more intense this time. I'll be falling from a taller height, and I'm so drunk on the pleasure, it's all I want in the world.

I gasp and cry out, my thighs trembling as I near the peak.

And then he stops.

The breath rushes out of me. I look down, my eyes wide when I see him moving from between my legs.

"What... what are you doing?" I ask, a bit dazed.

He smirks, smacking me on the ass. "You thought I was going to let you come after you taunted me? Have you even met me?"

"I didn't mean it," I whine, pouting.

He nods at the ground. "On your hands and knees. If you please me, maybe I'll let you come while I'm fucking you."

God, that shouldn't be so sexy. What's wrong with me?

I mull it over as I sulkily roll over to get on my knees, but

I'm so distracted by the need to come, I almost forget to tell him to put on a condom this time.

My memory is jogged when I hear him unzip behind me.

"Wait! My purse. There's a condom in my purse."

Not sounding altogether thrilled, he asks, "Why do you have a condom in your purse?"

"Hannah gave it to me."

Now he just sounds baffled. "Why does *Hannah* have condoms?"

"I don't know, but can you just grab it? I would like to remind you we are risking indecent exposure charges if someone decides to come to the beach today."

I will need to get on birth control, though. It's harder to remember that step than I expected it to be.

When Landon reaches into my purse, my desire-muddled brain reminds me of something else I didn't think about.

My phone is in my purse.

I haven't heard from Javi today, but if he texted me while I've been with Landon and Landon sees it...

"Here, give it to me. I'll get it."

Landon frowns, looking down at me as he reaches inside the bag. I wait for him to grab it and hand it to me, but instead, he roots around.

"I know where it is. It'll be quicker."

"Is there some reason you don't want me in your purse?"

"No, I just... want to get it for you so we can get going."

"How romantic," he quips.

"Don't tease me with orgasms and then expect me to be patient."

He grabs the condom, but rather than put it on and resume fucking me, he tosses the unopen packet on the beach.

I gasp when he places a hand between my shoulder blades

and shoves me down so I'm pressed face first against the beach towel.

Landon lowers himself so his hard body is pressed against my back, and his hot breath causes the tiny hairs on the back of my neck to prickle, sending a shudder through my body. "You sure that's all it is?"

It's not an easy movement when I'm flattened against the beach with him right on top of me, but I manage a nod. The sense of being trapped causes my lungs to shrink, my breath to come in shallower draws.

"Because if it's something else, now's the time to tell me." He grabs his cock and brings it between my thighs. He shoves in, just the tip, but it feels distinctly threatening.

My voice wobbles a bit when I tell him, "If you're going to fuck me, you have to use a condom. I'm not on birth control, and I don't know how careful you've been."

"Does it feel like you're in a position to make demands?" he asks, pushing another inch of himself into me.

My heart thuds. "Landon, I'm serious."

"So am I."

He certainly sounds serious, but despite the steely tone of his voice, he draws his cock out of me and grabs the condom off the beach.

I sigh softly with relief, but it's short-lived.

As soon as he gets the condom on, he drives his hips forward, impaling me in a single thrust that makes me cry out. I claw at the beach, realizing I *am* sore, but he doesn't take it any easier on me.

Thankfully I'm wet and the condom eases the passage more than his bare skin did, but I still feel the aching fullness of him inside me. Since I've pissed him off, he draws back and slams into me again. It hurts, so on instinct, I try to crawl away from him.

"I don't fucking think so." My heart thuds as he grabs a fistful of my hair, pushing me down on the ground and caging me in with his body.

"Landon," I gasp, my heart hammering in my chest.

He forces himself inside me again. The passage isn't quite as tight this time, but it's still uncomfortable. Especially because he holds me down and does it again and again and again.

I don't even feel like a participant in what's happening.

I pant as he groans and thrusts into me. "Fuck, Parker," he cries.

I lie here, my face hot and my heart pounding as he slams his cock into me again, harder this time. Somehow it feels like he goes deeper. Making more room for himself inside me than there naturally is.

He's a greedy bastard. He wants more, more, more.

Despite the mildly claustrophobic feeling of being held down and fucked like a thing instead of a person, I can feel a telltale pressure building inside me as he slams forward, driving his cock deep. It's dizzying, and it feels dirty and depraved to feel pleasure when he's using me like this, but my gasps aren't ones of horror because it feels like he's trying to destroy me. They're pleasure because he fills me so fucking full of him. I'm not even sure I want him to, but he doesn't care. He's never cared.

When he gets closer to his own climax, he gets rougher, but my body is used to it by then. He grabs my hair and pulls it, forcing my head back against his shoulder.

"You fucking like that?"

"Do you care if I don't?" I bite out, but the way I can't help from pushing my ass back into his thrusts probably outs me for the dirty liar I am.

He chuckles lowly, kissing my neck, then biting it. "No. No, I don't."

"Asshole," I hiss, cutting off on a gasp as he slams in again and hits just the right spot.

"Damn right," he mutters, sinking his cock deep into my pussy. "Do yourself a favor and don't forget it."

He rises, taking the pressure off my back. I breathe a deep sigh of relief, but it's cut short by him repositioning me, bringing my knees in closer to my belly, then folding me over them almost like I'm kneeling to pray.

This time, when he shoves his cock into me, I lose my everloving shit. He angles my hips and keeps a hand pressed against my back so I don't try to get up, but as uncomfortable as this position is, it's worth it.

"Oh my god," I breathe, my whole body trembling as he fucks me. "Oh my god, oh my god. Landon."

"Keep your ass right here, baby." He keeps the hand on my back, but slides his other hand under me so he can stroke my clit while he fucks me.

"Oh, no." He teases my clit as he pushes inside me. The pressure inside is too much. All I can chant is, "No, no, no, no," because what's brewing inside feels unbearable. "I can't. I can't."

"Shh. Shut that pretty fucking mouth and take what I give you."

Oh my god.

I'm already so wet I don't know how the towel isn't soaked, but when he says that, I feel my body's response like he turned on a faucet. I hear it in the wet noise when he slams into me again.

It's too much.

"Stop. Stop, I can't..."

He strokes my clit even faster. "Yes, you can."

"No," I whine.

But then it's out of my hands.

I feel it in my clit first, the sharp spark of pleasure that steals my breath away, but a fraction of a second later, I feel it deep inside, an eruption of pleasure that explodes so violently, my vision goes black. My body shakes and I cry out, whimpering as Landon continues to fuck me through it. My pussy convulses around him, squeezing him as I cry out.

When it finally ends, I can't move or think or breathe properly. I feel wetness on my cheeks, under my eyes.

Am I crying?

I'm too far away to process, to think.

My body is still jostled back and forth as Landon grips my hips with both hands, driving into me, chasing his own pleasure. "Fuck. Oh, Christ, Parker."

He drives deep, groaning through his climax, thrusting a few more times, but with much less force. He's just giving me every last drop.

When he comes down on the beach beside me, I feel so raw, so vulnerable, so exposed, I crawl close and wrap my arms tightly around his neck. I need him near me. I need him to hold me.

He seems to understand.

His strong arms lock around me and he holds me like he'll never let go.

In this moment, I don't want him to.

I bury my face in his neck and kiss him. A thank you, though I'm not sure he deserves it. Whatever he just did to me was fucking magical, and I think I'm starting to understand why Brittany and all the girls before her put up with his bullshit.

The desperation I feel to kiss him is alien to me, but I can't seem to stop. I move my lips across his jawline. He turns his head, and I kiss his lips with what little energy I have left.

He holds me and pets me while I calm down. It feels so nice.

Once the frantic, needy feeling ebbs, I feel so exhausted, I can't move. And he's so warm.

I almost fall asleep there in his arms, but Landon recovers his senses before I do. Gently, he eases out from under me and slides my skirt back over my ass before pulling his own clothes back on.

I want to lie here on this beach forever.

I never, ever want to leave.

Landon packs the cooler. I'm too spent to move, let alone help.

As he zips it up, he looks down at me and our gazes meet. "You doing okay?"

I nod, but I still feel like overcooked spaghetti. "I think you may want to consider the possibility that a girl's virginity isn't why she'd cling to you."

"No? Why, then?"

"It may be because you're a sex god."

"Oh. Maybe." He nods like that makes sense.

"You should have told me."

"What fun would that have been?" He smirks, then offers me a hand. "Come on, time to get up."

"I can't. You melted my bones. I need a walker. Maybe a wheelchair. A covered litter carried by four hulking men." I throw a hand across my forehead dramatically. "Carry me."

"I would, but I have to carry all this other crap instead. Unless you want to be thrown over my shoulder and carried that way?"

"Hmm. Maybe I'll just stand."

"You sure?" He watches with amusement as I drag myself up and try to convince my legs to work.

"Almost upright."

"You're so brave."

"Made it," I say, dusting off the back of my skirt and realizing I'm missing something rather important. "Where are my panties?" I ask, looking around. I blink when he pulls them out of his pocket and holds them out for me to take. "Thanks," I murmur, feeling my face flush as I awkwardly step into them.

He nods and bends down to finish packing up the cooler.

"I feel bad," I say, stepping off the towel onto the sand since he's about to grab that next. "We hardly ate any of the food you brought us."

Smirking faintly, he says, "Hey, there were better options on the menu. Can't be mad about that."

We drift away from the cliff's edge where Landon put down the towel for maximum privacy and make our way down the beach toward the parking lot. Right when we're about to step off the sand, a lady with wavy blonde hair and her boyfriend also carrying a cooler go breezing past us.

Eyes wide, I look back at them, then I lean over to murmur to Landon, "See? We were almost criminals."

He looks back and smirks, but he doesn't seem all that concerned. "Would have been kind of funny."

Impossibly, my eyes widen more. "It would *not* have been funny."

"Kinda. My dad got interrupted when he was banging your mom on a beach because I got arrested. If we *both* got arrested *for* banging on the beach and he had to bail us out? Kind of a full circle moment. Gotta appreciate it."

"Ew," I say, smacking him on the arm. "Why would you say something like that? Also, I know you were joking, but in case it was not abundantly clear, our parents *cannot* know about this. My mom would flip the fuck out."

"I'm pretty sure my dad already knows, but yeah, I don't see your mom taking it well. That's likely why he's ignoring it."

My stomach somersaults. "You think he knows? Did he see you coming out of my bedroom or something?"

"Nah, but he's employed tactics that make it pretty clear. He's an observant guy. He doesn't miss much."

My brow furrows. "I'm surprised he would keep something like that from her if he really knows."

"He's a lawyer. It's his job to know when to keep pertinent information to himself." Glancing over and seeing me still frowning, he says, "You don't have to worry. It doesn't mean anything bad. He's crazy about your mom. If he's keeping his mouth shut, it's because he thinks he's protecting her. Same reason *you* keep *your* mouth shut."

I guess that's true. I like Hayden a lot so it would be tremendously disappointing if he turned out to be an asshole. Well, *more* of an asshole than I already know he is.

WE'RE on the way back to school so I can pick up my car when I realize we never *really* talked about the one thing we definitely needed to talk about today.

I told him during sex that if he wanted to fuck me, he needed to use a condom, but it's probably a good idea to communicate that when we both have all our clothes on.

"So, I've never had to talk to a guy about this because... well, you know. You always scare them off."

"Right."

I crack a smile. "But, um, the sex thing? We need to talk about it."

"What do you want to talk about?"

"Obviously, I haven't been active. But just as obviously, you have. Since you didn't use a condom last night, I was wondering if I should... get tested," I say, grimacing. "There's not a way to ask that doesn't sound icky. I'm sorry."

Landon smirks. "You're fine. You don't have to get tested, but if you don't want to take my word for it, knock yourself out. I've never... I've always used a condom."

This is a bit awkward, and awkwardness makes me talkative, so I nod. "Okay, good. That's good. I mean..."

He nods, partially to stop me from launching into a ramble about his sexual responsibility. "Anything else?"

"Um, you never really confirmed you broke up with Brittany."

"I was never *with* Brittany. We weren't dating. It was casual."

"Still. She deserves to know it's over."

"Fine. I'll text her."

"Thank you," I say, but then I frown, because that seems an odd thing to thank him for. Shrugging it off, I focus on what else needs to be said. "I mentioned this during sex, but I don't know... that's probably not the best time for cogent conversation."

"Seems to be for you," he says dryly.

I shoot him a look. "I am not on birth control. I'll get on some, but I have to make an appointment, and that will take time. If we're going to keep doing this, I need you to use a condom until I tell you otherwise."

"Eh, I don't really like condoms. I liked it better without."

"Um, yeah, that doesn't really matter. I am not protected," I say slowly, so he gets it. "If you fuck me without a condom, you could get me pregnant."

He shrugs indolently. "Then I get you pregnant."

My eyes bulge. "Are you *insane?* We are in *high school.* Our parents are getting *married.* You are *not* getting me pregnant."

He shrugs again, not taking this nearly as seriously as he should be. "Maybe I already did."

"That's not funny."

"Who's joking? Not only did I come inside you, I stayed for a while after you fell asleep. Why do you think I brought you a cranberry smoothie?"

At this point, it's an anatomical feat that my eyeballs are

still in my head. "I will *kill you* if you impregnated me our first time having sex."

"You can't kill me. Then who's going to rub your feet when you're tired from waddling around all day with my baby in your belly?"

"Stop," I say, covering my ears.

Clearly, his appetite for tormenting me hasn't died out because he continues. "Imagine how hot I'd look with a baby carrier strapped to me, a mini-Landon gnawing on his little fist."

"I am no longer listening to you," I inform him.

"Hey, look on the bright side. We wouldn't have to worry about how to break the news to your mom anymore. Surprise! You're gonna be a grandma."

"Stop talking. Just... no more words. This is now a silent date."

Landon smirks, looking pretty damn satisfied with himself.

Since he prefers silence, it's no trouble for his broody ass to keep quiet the rest of the way to the school. Since I'm annoyed at him, it's no trouble for me, either.

When we get to the school, Landon pulls his noisy-ass car up next to my quiet one and kills the engine.

I've never been dropped off at my car after a date before, so I'm not sure of the proper protocol. I expect Landon to walk me to my car, but when I walk around the front, he walks around the back to get something out of his trunk.

I don't know if I'm supposed to wait, or the date is over and he's just grabbing a cold bottle of water or something.

After dawdling uncertainly for a few seconds, I open my driver's side door and slide in.

Landon comes over right as I'm pulling my foot in the car and grabs the door so I can't close it. "Not even gonna wait for me, huh?"

I blush at his teasing. "I didn't know what you were doing. I thought I'd been dismissed."

He shakes his head. "I had to get something out of my trunk."

"Was it a body?" I ask solemnly, my gaze drifting to the hand he's hiding behind his back.

"Sort of. Close your eyes."

"Why?"

"Because it's a surprise."

"I don't like surprises."

"I don't care. Close your damn eyes."

Sighing, I say, "If this is something gross, I swear to God…"

"It isn't something gross. I got you a present. Now, hold out your hand, you little ingrate."

I chuckle despite myself, then I bite back a grin and hold out my palm.

He places something soft and fluffy in the palm of my hand, and my eyes pop open immediately. I gasp at the sight of an *adorable* octopus plushie. "What is this?" I say, petting his soft little head.

"It's reversible. Turn it over."

The side facing out right now is aqua with an adorable grumpy expression on its cute little face. I turn the little octopus inside out, and the other side is pink with a friendly smile.

"I figured you can use it like a signal. When you're mad at me, you can turn it that way. When it's a Landon-friendly zone, you can turn him pink."

I grin up at him, delighted, as I hug the plushie. "This is hands down the cutest 'keep out' sign in all existence."

He cracks a smile. "I'm glad you like it."

"I do, thank you." Since he's outside the car and I already got in, I step back out so I can give him a hug.

I forgot I got him all wet until I feel his shirt soak through mine.

"Shit," I say, pulling back and looking down at my shirt. Since our parents are probably waiting for us at home, it's probably a bad idea to show up together, both of us wet. "I don't have a replacement shirt in the back seat of this car yet. I used to keep one in my old car for emergencies, but this one was so nice and clean—"

Landon interrupts. "It's fine. I figured we probably shouldn't show up at home together, anyway. I'll head to Malek's and toss my shirt in the dryer for a few minutes. If anyone asks, I can just say I went for a swim at his house."

"Okay." I nod. "And if Mom asks, I was at school late working on Uplift stuff and I spilled my drink. Not that you would know that, so I don't know why I'm telling you..."

Landon smirks and leans in, kissing me on the corner of the mouth and making my heart stop. "Anyone ever tell you that you think too much about everything?"

My stomach flutters when he locks a strong arm around my waist and pulls me against him now that we have our alibis sorted. "If they did, I wouldn't listen."

He kisses me again, slower this time, a hand sliding up to find my neck. He kisses me until I'm dizzy and drunk on him, then he pulls back and lets me go.

I give him a tiny smile and slide back into my seat, but I'm still a bit high on his kisses when he's walking back to his car. I sit there for a minute to get my bearings and clear my head. Just when I'm about to leave, my phone in the cupholder buzzes.

My blood freezes for a split second when I see I have a DM —*the only person I have sent a DM recently was Dare*—but relief hits me when I recognize Landon's handle.

"You okay to drive?"

"Of course. I had like one sip of the lemonade."

"That's not what I meant," he says with a wink.

"Ugh," I type back, then I look over at him still parked beside me. I turn my octopus plushie to the grumpy side and hold it up for him to see. Landon laughs, then he finally pulls away.

***

SINCE I HAVE a new secret boy situation and I want to talk to Hannah about it without fearing I'll be overheard, I ask her out to do a little shopping with me on Saturday.

Before I leave, Landon slips into my bedroom for a little "snack," and as I'm pulling up my panties, he suggests we meet up with him and the guys afterward for lunch.

That's pretty much the last thing I want to do. Lunch with Landon and Hannah, sure, but he's hanging out with Malek and Arden, and that doesn't sound like the best time.

I suppose I'll have to compromise, though, so I tell him I'll message him when we're about done and then we can figure out where to meet up.

"So," Hannah says, as she grabs a cute blue and white checkered dress off the rack and turns it around to look at the back. "How's the Landon thing going?"

"It's going... well? As well as a secret situationship can, I guess? At the moment, it's a lot of lying and sneaking around, but obviously we have to keep it from our parents."

Hannah nods thoughtfully. "What do you think would happen if they found out?"

"I don't know. I'm trying not to think about it. I never expected this to happen, you know?"

She smiles faintly. "Yeah, since just a few days ago I was over at your house playing babysitter because you couldn't be left alone with him, I do know."

"I know," I say on a groan, walking to the next rack. "It's crazy. I know it is. He spent six years being a shithead to me, and now... I don't even know. We're a match made in hell. We have nothing in common. I'm not even sure I *like* him as a person. But the sex is so good," I finish miserably.

"Because you have so much to compare it to," she says lightly.

"Well, no. But instinctively, I'm certain he's an exceptional lover."

She doesn't hide her skepticism. "Really?"

"I know." I nod. "I'm surprised, too. I thought for sure he'd be selfish. *Nope.* We've been sneaking around for like... three days, and he has already given me..." I stop to count on my fingers. "Five orgasms? Six?"

Eyebrows rising, she says, "Seems like a pretty good ratio."

"And not just quantity, the quality is there, too. We had sex on the beach yesterday after school, and it basically changed my life."

"Guess all the practicing he did was good for something," she says lightly.

"It really was. I was never impressed by the rate at which he blew through girls, but he *knows* what he's doing. Honestly, I can see now how he could convince a girl to load up all her self-respect and throw it straight in the trash. I have a much better understanding of Brittany now. I thought she was kind of an idiot, but now I get it. She couldn't help herself. No one could. He should come with a warning label."

"He does," she says, smiling faintly. "A ton of them."

"Well, they should be more specific," I say with a sniff.

Hannah laughs. "That must have been some sex on the beach."

"It was," I say, a bit dreamily as I recall it. "It really was."

"YOU NEED to stop fucking texting her."

I put my phone down on the table, glancing over at Malek. "You need to mind your own fucking business."

"We're family. You are my business. I know how bad the Atwater men are at not fucking up their relationships with their bullshit behavior, and I'm telling you now, you're on the fast track to blowing up this relationship before it even gets off the ground if you don't knock it off."

"Malek Atwater, relationship expert," Arden says dryly.

Malek slides him a look. "Stay out of it, pretty boy. You're no good at them either."

"I've never tried to be," Arden states, his tone bored. "He's been chasing her since middle school and he's still going to fuck it up."

"All right, we're done talking about my relationship with Parker. I shouldn't have even updated you two fucks about what was going on."

"You should have broken up your parents first," Arden advises, despite the fact that I didn't fucking ask. "If *you* don't screw it up, they surely will the moment they find out about it. You can't date your stepsister. This isn't Arkansas."

A notification pops up on my phone screen. A DM from Parker that reads, "We're here! About to park."

I stand abruptly, my legs shoving back my chair. "They're here."

I don't take the time to say anything else since I need to get to the parking portico before she does so I can make sure she doesn't talk to the fucking valet.

Her Prius is just about to pull up when I get outside. Aladdin is waiting behind the stand until he sees it's her. Then he grabs a ticket and walks around to open Hannah's door since she's in the passenger seat, and she just has the vibe of a girl you're supposed to open doors for.

"Thank you," Hannah murmurs, flashing him a polite smile before climbing out of the car.

Parker's exit is much less graceful, but a smile tugs at my lips as she comes striding around the front of the car with her brisk, no-nonsense pace. The smile dies when her gaze flits to the valet, and I cross my arms when she makes her way to me.

"Hey," she says, flashing me a quick, empty smile. I know she's nervous. I keep a close watch as she tries to figure out how to handle both of us being in the same place at the same time.

Since I don't particularly want her to get a chance to interact with the guy, I call out, "Hey, Javi."

Frowning, he looks back at me.

"Make any good wishes lately?"

Parker sighs, shooting me a half-hearted glare. "If I had my octopus right now…"

I crack a faint smile, but it grows when she quickly mutters, "Sorry about him," then gives her keys to Javi without lingering and swiftly makes her way to me.

"Do you *have* to be such a jerk?"

"I do. It's the rule."

Parker rolls her eyes. "Like you care about rules."

"Hey, Landon."

"Hey, Hannah. The guys are already at the table, but we haven't ordered anything yet. Figured we'd wait for you."

"I may not be able to stay long," Hannah tells me. "I have a lot of work to do at home, and also I... don't want to," she states so honestly, I almost choke on a short burst of laughter.

"Nice hanging out with you, too," I say dryly.

"It's not you," she murmurs, but she doesn't expand on that since we're approaching the table.

I don't care much about Hannah, but I know Parker does, so I take a step back and watch to see which of my friends she doesn't want to be around. Too late to do anything about it today, but it might be useful information to have in the future.

It's hard to tell looking at the guys. Malek glances up at her without bothering to greet her, but that's just Malek. Arden regards her as if she walked up to the table naked, but that's just Arden.

Despite her prior comment indicating she wasn't thrilled to be eating with at least one of them, Hannah is the queen of politeness, so she gives both a measured smile as she sits down.

What little interest I had in investigating Hannah's possible discomfort dries up when I see Parker reach for her phone. There's enough nervous energy coming off her to power her car, and her hands tremble a bit as she quickly types out a text.

Which begs the question...

Who the fuck is she texting?

IT FEELS like the surface of my skin is approximately one thousand degrees when we sit down. We have a spot in the air-conditioned dining room, but I'm still feeling anxious from having to see Javi for the first time after not texting him for a few days—and in front of Landon, which could not be less ideal.

He texted me right before I got here, but I was driving, so I couldn't respond.

> Your stepbrother's here.

Quickly, fingers trembling as I type, I answer.

> I'm sorry about him. I hope he wasn't too much of an ass to you.

I have *no* idea how to handle this Javi situation. It feels like I should say *something* since we were texting and really seemed to be liking each other, but I can't exactly tell him why that's not appropriate anymore, either.

I don't think Javi would do anything deliberately to hurt me, but I don't really know the guy that well, either. Even if that isn't his motivation, if I confirmed this thing with Landon to him, there's a risk of him saying something to one of our parents about it. He could even mention it in passing while gossiping with a co-worker and it could get back to them that way.

I've never had a secret relationship before, but I know it won't stay a secret for long if everybody knows about it.

I'm guessing that's why our friends are here now—to act as our camouflage. We can hang out in public without drawing attention since we're here as a group.

I just hope he doesn't think this is going to be a regular thing. I can deal with Malek and Arden in small doses, but I don't want to be besties.

When I finally extract myself from the bubble of anxiety, I look across the table at Landon and find his gaze locked on me. Impossibly, my face heats more. I'm going to melt soon, like a snowman in the sun.

I'm about to look around for anything else to focus on, but, mercifully, the waitress approaches to take our drink order.

Once she's jotted them all down, she hustles off, and I dare a glance in Landon's direction. My attention is snagged, though, by a notification lighting up his phone.

That wouldn't bother me, but he immediately grabs the phone off the table and shoves it into his pocket.

"Why'd you do that?"

He looks up at me, probably not expecting to be immediately called out on it. I didn't think about it, it just struck me as odd, so why not ask?

"Because I keep getting fucking text messages I don't feel like dealing with right now. I shouldn't have listened to you about taking the time to let Brittany know I wouldn't be fucking with her anymore. She's taken it as unusually meaningful since it's not my style."

"Are you kidding me?"

"I should've made you text her since you were so worried about it," he mutters.

Well, that's annoying. "I was just trying to do the right thing. I knew she liked you, I didn't want you to fuck her over."

"Well, since I didn't, she thinks I care. So, good job."

"I'm sorry. I still don't think it was bad advice, but Jesus, I wish that girl would get a grip."

"Seems like she has a pretty firm one," Hannah murmurs lightly as she peruses the menu.

I shoot her a look. "Hilarious."

She shrugs. "I'm just saying."

"She's sending him Spotify links to songs," Arden says, not bothering to hide his amusement.

"Taylor Swift. My fucking favorite," Landon says dryly.

I bite back a wave of utterly inappropriate amusement. "Are you serious?"

"Which song?" Hannah asks.

"I don't fucking know. I didn't listen to it. Some month... April, August..."

"Gotta be August." Hannah sighs, shaking her head. "Poor girl."

"Poor lunatic. She needs a fucking restraining order," Landon mutters.

"Just block her," Malek says, rolling his eyes. "This is not as hard as you're making it."

"I should have just ignored her out of existence like I originally intended, but no. Parker had to be nice."

"I'm so sorry for not being a heartless asshole," I say dryly.

"You guys had better be careful at school," Arden advises, eyebrows rising. "In all seriousness, if she realizes you two are hooking up, she might get the bright idea to rat you out so you have to break up and Landon will be available again."

"I hope she's not that fucking stupid," Landon says, looking at his menu.

Malek says, "Pretty sure she is."

"If she does, we can sic Anae on her," Arden says, amused. "She's pretty good at revenge."

Hannah shifts uncomfortably and focuses harder on her menu, but I can tell by her face she's feeling stressed.

I feel awkward asking with all the guys here, so I take my phone out of my purse and shoot her a quick text.

"You okay?"

Her phone lights up. She grabs it, reading the message, then typing back. "Yeah. I just don't like hanging out with these guys."

Hannah has always been sensitive to the energy of people around her. I think it's one of the reasons getting sucked into Aubrey's bullshit with Dare last year was so tough on her. I never met him in person, but I saw how taxed Hannah was dealing with him, and that tells me all I really need to know about his energy.

I suppose Arden echoing the same sentiment when it seems like Dare is *actively* in the process of trying to sic Anae on *her* for revenge... doesn't make her eager to sit next to him.

I should have probably sat there and insulated her a little better. This is a table for six, so the seat between me and Landon is empty. I could have put her there and sat next to Arden myself, but I didn't think about it when we sat down.

"You want to switch seats?" I ask her via text. "We could go to the bathroom and when you come back, just sit in the one on my other side."

"No, it's ok. He'll know I'm moving because of him, and I'd rather not deal with his smugness."

Interrupting, Arden asks, "Are you ladies having a nice conversation? Want to loop the rest of us in?"

I look up. "Sure. I was just telling Hannah how funny I think it is that big, bad Arden Prince needs Anae Richards to do his dirty work for him," I say, smiling sweetly.

Arden's jaw locks, and his already glacial blue eyes cool. An answering shiver shoots down my spine.

It's pure physical instinct, though.

I'm not afraid of him.

Most people are because he has far too much money and painfully few morals. As a spoiled rich boy who has always had access to everything he could ever want, he's also prone to boredom and given to wrathful swipes at anyone he considers an enemy. The drama spices things up for at least a little while.

But he also has a very simple weakness: his beautiful face. Truly, annoyingly gorgeous, as if sculpted by the universe's finest sculptors. He's done a little modeling just for fun, and women fall at his feet everywhere he goes. While he doesn't *have* to hang his hat on his good looks given his family's money and consequent power, he's vain, and very much *enjoys* knowing he's the most handsome man in any room he steps into.

And, friends or not, Landon would not hesitate to wreck that pretty face if he turned his wrath on me. He's lost friends for me before and didn't bat an eye over it. Arden would be no different.

Arden also isn't an idiot, so he knows that.

Sure, legally, he knows Landon's not allowed to hit him, but he also knows Landon does whatever the fuck he wants. And his father is Hayden Atwater, so he always finds a way *out* of the trouble he finds his way *into*.

Most importantly, Landon just doesn't *care* about the consequences, so it would be unreasonable to expect restraint from him.

I can see how annoyed Arden is to have to exercise restraint when he'd like to verbally eviscerate me, but he doesn't run as hot as Landon. He runs much colder.

Arden is intelligent and articulate. He solves problems with his mind and his resources, not his fists. He can be measured and strategic, and as I'm going over it in my head and hearing the echoes of familiarity, I'm realizing those are probably qualities that make Hannah uncomfortable around him.

The last time she brushed with a cold-hearted strategist, it didn't go so well for her.

She didn't have me in that fight, though.

Hannah looks like an easy target because she's visibly alone in the world. Her parents are dead, her guardian takes advantage of her. Without anyone around to protect her, she's the perfect prey for a cold-hearted rich boy to play with.

Anae never would have protected her, so Hannah hid from Dare right in plain sight for a long time. She recognizes a predator when she sees one, even if it took everyone else a little longer to notice.

But then, *he* noticed *her*.

Going back over our recent interactions, I'm realizing Arden has made an unusual number of inquiries about her this year. One of them even included a comment about how vulnerable she is to those who would seek to prey on her.

"I bet they'd sell her to me if I made a good enough offer."

I took it as a distasteful joke, but now I'm overthinking it.

That creep had better not set his sights on my best friend.

Aubrey didn't protect her from Dare, but I would protect her from *anyone*.

Mercifully, before I can decide to preemptively take on the current king of Baymont High, the waitress comes over to see if we're ready to order.

Less fortunately, Arden is unaware of my stance on octopus as a food and leads with, "We'll start with the charred octopus."

Before I can say a word, Landon does.

"Nope."

I smile faintly, impressed and thinking about how I'll repay his consideration the next time we're alone together. The thought leaves me a bit thirsty, so I reach for my drink.

Arden looks over at Landon, cocking an eyebrow. "No?"

"Eat pussy, not octopus."

I choke on my lemonade, and Arden appears amused. "I didn't realize I had to choose," he says dryly.

Landon smirks, his gaze finding mine. "Yeah, well, some of us do. We're not ordering the fucking octopus."

WHEN I FINALLY RETURN HOME AFTER dropping off Hannah, I have just enough time to shower and change into something comfy before movie night 2.0.

As anxious as I was about sitting on the couch with Landon in front of Mom and Hayden last time, I'm actually more concerned this time.

I've had to bend the truth a lot lately, but I'm not particularly skilled at long-term deception. If Mom and Hayden pick up on the weird energy between us tonight, I don't know how I'll respond if we're put on the spot.

When Mom and I go to the kitchen to get the snacks while Landon and Hayden look for a movie, she takes the opportunity to check in with me.

"How was school? You stayed so late at your club meeting yesterday, we didn't get a chance to talk when you got home."

"Oh, yeah." My heart beats a little faster. "Well, it was the first meeting of the year, so you know how it is. We went over some longer-term projects like the Fright Night benefit and the Fright Fest itself, then we had to touch on some of the more immediate projects we want to tackle."

Mom nods. "Do you guys need donations for the silent

auction? I'd be happy to donate some classes like I did last year."

"Yeah, I'm sure we will. We haven't started organizing the lots yet, but I'll definitely let you know once we do."

"I can't believe Anae joined the club. How does Hannah feel about that?"

"You know Hannah. I'm sure she's not thrilled, but she hasn't complained about it. At least yesterday, Anae was pretty harmless. As long as she wants to stay out of the way and snap pictures to collect the credit, I truly don't care." I rip open the popcorn bag and distribute it between the two bowls. "I won't be home after school on Tuesday, either. I'm starting my volunteer hours, so I'll be doing a shift at the pet shelter I told you about."

"Oh, okay. That will be nice. Your credit card hasn't come in the mail yet, but if you need to buy anything for a donation to take with you, just let me know."

"I probably will. I know I'm volunteering my time, but I feel weird showing up empty-handed when I know they have a wish list." I'm not completely sure about bringing him up, but maybe it's better to do with something small like this. "I'm trying to convince Landon to come, too."

As predicted, Mom's eyebrows shoot up. "Oh yeah?"

I shrug, trying to play it off as no big deal. "He's a senior at Baymont, too. Everyone has to log their 18 hours of community service if they want to graduate, so he might as well."

"I'm just trying to visualize Landon volunteering."

I chuckle. "I know, it doesn't come easy to the imagination." I grab the bowls and head for the living room, feeling good about the limited time we've spent talking about him and not wanting to push it.

Landon is watching me when I walk back into the room. It's hard not to smile and give myself away, but what he said earlier flashes through my mind, and I glance over at Hayden.

He's watching me, too, and that makes me much more antsy.

Mom follows me in and puts the drinks on the coffee table before smoothing down her skirt and sinking into the spot beside Hayden. I smile faintly as he instinctively slides his arm around her to pull her closer.

"Did we find a movie?" she asks.

"We did. Before we start it, though," he begins, giving her a look, "I was thinking we should talk to the kids about that thing we discussed."

Mom instantly grows more anxious, but she attempts a smile and nods. "Sure."

That sounds vaguely ominous. I'm wary as I stay standing rather than take my own seat on the couch. My gaze shoots to Landon, and of course he doesn't look worried, but he doesn't care about anything, so why would he be?

"Is everything okay?" I ask.

"Yes, of course," Hayden says, clearly wanting to put me at ease. Gesturing to the couch, he says, "You can sit down. I just wanted to toss out an idea we had to see what you thought about it."

Still uneasy, I take a seat on the couch next to Landon and look over at Hayden.

"Your mother and I were talking, and while, of course, we hope you two will come home for the holidays once you're in college, there's always a chance you won't. Parker could get a boyfriend. Landon could... be busy," he says, since apparently the notion of him having to accommodate a girlfriend is too outlandish to consider. "This is the last year we *know* we will all be together. And when Gemma and I were dating—"

"For five minutes," Landon interjects mildly.

"—One of the things we talked about was the family vacations we'd been on separately. I was thinking, wouldn't it be nice if we all went on one together?"

My eyes widen. I have to resist the temptation to look over at Landon and see what he thinks.

"I was thinking we could go soon, a fall or winter trip when you'll have a little time off school."

"Where are we going?" I ask, anxious but eager. Mom and I didn't have the money to go on many trips before, but I know Hayden doesn't have to worry about a budget, and—of course—I would love to do more traveling.

"Well, it's up for discussion, but we were thinking Florida."

"Oh. Why?"

Mom chuckles and Hayden smiles faintly. "Your mother mentioned that since you were a little girl, you always wanted to go to Epcot. She also told me she finally saved up and took you a few years back, and it rained the whole time you were there. Obviously, it would be easy for us to go to Disney*land*, but we don't have Epcot here. I was thinking maybe we could take a trip to Disney World and spend some time in all the parks. And Landon hasn't been since he was a little boy, so he may not even remember it."

"I remember bits and pieces," Landon volunteers. "But my autograph book *is* pretty outdated," he adds dryly, looking at me for a reaction. "I'm guessing you're into this idea."

I can't ignore the rush of excitement the possibility gives me. I've never had a two-parent family vacation before, and getting to take my... whatever Landon is as well would be pretty cool.

Plus, when Mom and I went, I *was* disappointed when it rained the whole day we were at Epcot. We still had fun while we steamed like vegetables in our oversized ponchos in the swampy Florida heat, but I felt a lot of pressure to have the *most* fun despite the bad weather. I knew it was an expensive trip that Mom had spent years saving up for, and I was acutely aware of every dollar we were spending. There was a restaurant I really wanted to go to, but it was too expensive. We brought snacks we bought at a Publix on the way to the resort from the airport and shared cheaper quick service meals instead.

It would be nice to go on a trip and not have to worry about that stuff, to see Mom get to relax and enjoy herself with a man who would undoubtedly take care of everything.

Also, I was a bit miffed when the Frozen ride opened right *after* we went there.

"I am definitely into the idea. I don't want to shock anyone, but I will begin researching immediately."

Hayden chuckles, his eyes glinting with pleasure. "Excellent. I know they have holiday parties and things like that, so take a look. We can figure out when would be the best time to go and then we'll look at our schedules and see when we can make it happen."

Unable to contain my excitement, I look over at Landon.

He sighs.

"We are going to have the best time," I state.

"Uh-huh."

"They have mouse ear headbands."

"I'm not wearing one of those."

"And delicious snacks."

"That I can live with."

"And a pretty castle, and foods from all around the world!" I look back at Hayden. "When Mom and I went, we stayed in a Little Mermaid themed room at one of the resorts. Will we stay on property?"

"Sure, if you want to. When we went, we stayed at the Polynesian."

"Not there," Landon says. "I don't want to stay at the same hotel we went to with Mom."

"That's fine." Hayden glances at his son briefly, but continues before we hit a snag. "We can stay wherever you want. Both of you. You should check out the different resorts and let us know which one you prefer. As long as a suite that meets our needs is available, that's where we'll go."

"I don't care which hotel we stay at, just not that one," Landon mutters.

I understand he probably just wants to protect his memories of his mom since he said he does remember parts of their vacation there when he was little, and I want to keep this conversation successful, so I say, "There's another resort with a park view if we want to stay that close. Mom and I saw it when we were on one of the rides."

"The Contemporary," Mom says softly. "It looked very nice."

I nod enthusiastically, barely resisting the urge to pull out my phone and look it up right now. "I will look at all the resorts and compile a comparison chart of the ones I like most."

"Of course you will," Landon says, shaking his head with mild amusement.

"Keep picking on me and our next movie night will just be a patented Parker Johansson PowerPoint presentation on Disney resorts."

He smirks. "Don't threaten me with a good time."

I blush, remembering when I said that to him yesterday at the beach.

He winks, and I widen my eyes at him in warning.

Landon enjoys living on the edge so his eyes glint with amusement, but he has a vested interest in behaving himself now, too, so he doesn't keep pushing.

"Do you like rollercoasters?" I ask him.

"Of course I like rollercoasters."

"Hm. I don't."

"Damn. I guess we can't go then."

I shoot him a look. "There are plenty of non-coasters for me to ride. I liked the dark rides a lot. What was your favorite ride when you were a kid?"

"I liked the flying carpets."

I eye him skeptically. "Really?"

His eyebrows rise. "Sure. Why would I—?" When he belatedly makes the Aladdin connection, I know he *did* mean it. And I just accidentally reminded him of Javi, so his eyes darken with annoyance.

Hayden is as attuned to his son's moods as I am right now, so before another word can be said, he picks up the remote control. "We should probably start the movie now."

I nod my head, shifting my attention to the screen. "What'd you guys pick?"

I no more than ask, and Hayden wakes the TV up, revealing my favorite Norwegian snow sisters and an endearing reindeer.

"Your mom said it was one of your favorites," Hayden remarks. "We thought it would be fitting."

I look over at Landon, delighted. "Is this because of the reindeer are better than people song?"

He frowns, apparently uncomprehending.

"When I harangued you into volunteering with me and we said animals are better than people. I'm taking your continued confusion as a no."

"I haven't seen the movie, that's why we figured we'd watch it."

"*What?*"

Since this is an amiable enough conversation, Mom joins in, telling Landon, "Elsa is Parker's favorite princess."

"Queen, technically," I murmur. "But yes, she's my favorite. Hannah and I were Anna and Elsa for Halloween one year. I had to be Anna since she's the blonde and I have all this red hair, but I was Elsa-adjacent." Shaking my head, I say, "I'll stop talking so we can start the movie. But I am already getting very excited about outfit ideas."

Hayden finally starts the movie, and I curl up on the couch beside Landon.

It's a very different movie night compared to the last one. I still have to be hyper-vigilant, but not to fend off a possible attack this time. I just don't want our parents to get suspicious.

Landon still sits on the couch next to me and touches me whenever he can without risking detection, but this time, I want him to.

"I LOVE THESE PRETTY LITTLE TITS."

I sigh with pleasure as Landon's hot mouth roams across my nipple. He nips at my tender flesh and wrenches a gasp out of me, then he turns his attention to the other boob so it doesn't feel left out.

My eyes drift closed, another shock of pleasure shooting through me when he tongues that beaded nipple. Tension builds between my thighs as he teases it again and again. He turns his head, deliberately scratching the sensitive skin with his stubble, then he eases the sting with his soft, perfect lips.

While he teases and torments my breasts, his hand slides down between my thighs. I open them wider, letting my knees rest against the bed so he has better access to me.

This is heaven.

Landon's hand closes over my pussy possessively, and the heat from his body makes me sigh. He slides his fingers down to rub me, then he uses them to spread me open.

I'm arching against his mouth, waiting for him to push a finger into me when, suddenly, I feel as if a bucket of cold water has been dumped over my head.

There's a knock at my bedroom door.

Everything freezes, and my eyes pop open wide. Landon lifts his head, and adrenaline floods my system.

Oh my god.

"Honey, it's Mom."

Oh my god!

"Hide," I whisper furiously, pushing him off me. "Get in my closet."

Landon pushes off me and moves off the bed. My heart pounds and my stomach sinks with dread, but to his credit, he manages to get to the closet quickly and quietly.

"Just a second!" I call, trying to keep the panic from my voice as I jump off the bed and grab my nightshirt off the ground. I frantically pull it on, yanking it down and then looking around for my panties.

"Everything okay?" Mom calls back.

Yeah, fine, just dying. No big deal.

I can't find my stupid panties, so I finally give up and just hastily make my way to the door so I can unlock it.

I feel like a deer caught in the headlights even as I rip the door open. Landon only slipped into my room a few minutes ago, so I shouldn't look *too* ravished yet... but what if she can tell?

Greeting her with a smile I hope looks more casual than it feels, I ask, "What's up?"

Mom glances past me a little uncertainly. "Can I come in?"

"Of course," I squeak, dying a little and telling myself to *get it the fuck together.*

It's hard to get it together when I have to scan the floor, hoping and praying she doesn't find my panties.

My guilty gaze shoots to the closet door as I take a seat on the edge of my bed, then reconsider and climb under the covers, settling the comforter on my lap in case my shirt rides up.

"What's up?" I ask, trying to sound cool and casual.

"I just wanted to pop in for a minute before I go to bed. See how you were feeling."

"I'm good," I assure her, smiling faintly.

"Things between you and Landon seemed a bit friendlier tonight."

I nod. "I think he's starting to adjust. I told you he probably just needed time."

Mom nods, looking down at her lap. "Well, since Hayden brought up going to Disney, I wanted to steal a minute to talk just the two of us to see how you're really feeling about it."

"I'm feeling great about it. I think it sounds like a lot of fun."

"Yeah?" she says hopefully. "Good. I thought so, too. I wasn't sure Landon would be on board, but... Anyway, it won't be like when we went. We don't have to all sleep in the same room. Hayden said we'll likely get a suite with at least one separate bedroom, probably two, depending on what's available. I looked at a few of the suites and it looks like there are a few ways we can do it. You could have your own room and we could put Landon on a bed in the living room area, or we could stay girls in one room and boys in the other."

"I'm sure Hayden would love that," I say dryly.

She rolls her eyes good-naturedly. "He's survived without me in his bed for this many years, I think he can make it another week. Obviously, I feel best about that option. If we aren't able to get a suite, like if we're not planning far enough in advance, we could even get adjoining rooms. Hayden and Landon could take one, we could take the other. We'll be spending most of our time in the parks, anyway. I just wanted to make sure you know we'll figure out the best sleeping arrangements. I want you to be comfortable."

I place my hand over hers reassuringly. "I appreciate that,

but honestly, don't stress about it. I may look at rooms on my phone before bed because I'm excited and I want to get an idea of what's available, but you don't have to stress about Landon. He really seems to be making an effort, and I don't think he'll do anything to ruin our trip. I think everybody will have fun."

"I hope so."

I nod. "We will. I'm sure of it. Do you know if Hayden has a resort preference? Also, is there any kind of budget?"

Mom shakes her head. "No budget. I don't think he cares where we stay, either, but they are used to staying in the nicest places, obviously," she says, gesturing around the room. "So, don't bother looking at the budget hotels. I know you might think you'd be doing a good thing, saving him money, but I think Hayden would rather spend the money and be more comfortable."

"Remember we had to walk like 80 million miles to get to the buses from our room?" I say, smiling.

Mom rolls her eyes at herself. "I had no idea what I was doing when I booked that trip."

"Nah, you did great," I say, smiling at the memory.

She smiles, too, then pats my leg through the blankets. "All right, I should probably get to bed. Don't stay up too late researching."

"I make no promises."

Mom stands, and I watch her walk to the door. "Lock this behind me?"

I nod. "I will."

"Okay. Goodnight, honey."

"Goodnight, Mom. Love you."

"Love you, too."

With that, she closes the door, and I breathe a huge sigh of relief.

I throw back my blankets and walk over to open the closet

door. Since it's a huge walk-in closet, there's a chair over by the shoe shelf. Landon is sprawled there like a king on his throne rather than stressing like I was.

"Coast clear?"

"Yes," I say softly. Then, stepping back out of the closet, I quickly walk over and lock my door just in case Mom remembers something and tries to come back.

Landon comes up behind me, locking his arms around my waist and tugging me back against his warm body. "Now, where were we?"

"Are you crazy?" I ask, glancing back at him. "We very nearly just got caught."

"Nah. The door was locked. We were fine."

My eyes widen. "That wouldn't have helped if she would have come two minutes later and heard me in here moaning and panting."

He smirks. "Then maybe you need to learn to be quiet. I can cover your mouth for you if you get too noisy."

"I bet you could," I murmur.

"Mm-hmm." He pulls my hair away from my shoulder, then leans in and kisses my neck. "I can restrain you. Hold you face down while I fuck you. Make sure your cries are smothered in the pillow as I pound that pussy."

Fuck.

"Stop turning me on."

Rather than obey me, he brings a hand up to squeeze and caress my breast. The way he handles me, so confident as he squeezes and teases my nipple.

"Landon," I say on a sigh, half complaint, half plea.

Knowing he's got me, he walks me back toward the bed. When we get there, he releases me so he can draw my sleep shirt off and toss it on the floor behind us.

I was already completely naked when we were messing

around in my bed, but he's only half-undressed. His incredible upper body is on full display, but he's wearing black sweats slung low on his hips. I slide my fingers down the front of his waistband and reveal the snugger waistband of his boxer-briefs.

I sit down on the edge of the bed and pull him closer, then I lean in and kiss his abdomen. I kiss my way over it and down, then I experiment with letting my tongue dart out to trace the curves of his muscles.

Landon slid his fingers through my hair, mindlessly playing with it while I kissed him, but as my tongue travels lower, his grip on my hair tightens.

He uses it to tug my head back and force me back on the bed, then he climbs on with me, straddling me and grabbing my hand. He guides it to his cock, and I feel a burst of heat between my legs when I feel how hard he is.

I rub him through his pants, watching his beautiful face and body as my touch brings him pleasure. His head lolls back, but only for a few seconds. Then he reaches down and palms my tits, sucking some of the air from my lungs when he does.

"So fucking pretty," he rumbles, and my blood turns to liquid heat in my veins.

He pushes my hand off his bulge and leans down to give me a kiss. He tangles a hand in my hair and cradles my jaw with the other so he can completely control my movements. I'm hungry for his kisses, but he pulls back and leaves me wanting.

Then he lets go of my face and shoves down his pants. My heart thuds when he shoves down his underwear next.

Apprehension takes hold. My body is still warmed up for him, but I've never done what I think I'm about to do.

I swallow, looking up at his face as he strokes his cock.

"Are you a good girl?" he asks me.

I nod wordlessly, still looking up at him.

"Good," he says, his tone warm with approval. Then he

holds my chin with one hand, his cock with the other, and he guides himself to my mouth.

I feel a bit panicked with him on top of me, literally restraining me with his strong thighs. It's an instinctive physical reaction, though. I like when he pins me down.

I like the firm way he holds my chin to keep me from moving, too, though the way my stomach sinks, it's hard to tell. Instinctively, I brace my hands on the bed and tense up as his thick cock slides between my lips.

"Relax." He absently caresses my jaw with his thumb as he eases in. Once his cock is in far enough, he reaches down to squeeze and caress my breast, stimulating me and making my body respond as I take his cock deeper into my mouth. "That's so fucking good, Parker. You look so beautiful with a mouthful of my cock."

Yearning shoots through me, my mouth softening up around him because I *want* to please him. I want to taste him. I want him as deep inside me as he can get.

I cry out around his cock as he slides a little deeper, but it's because he squeezes my nipple and the pressure makes my thighs shake. He does it again a little harder and I moan around his cock, feeling the reverberations in my throat.

"Christ," Landon says sharply, releasing my jaw so he can shove his fingers into my hair and get a better grip on my skull. He shoves his cock deeper and my throat tries to reject him, but then he pinches my nipple and...

I can't breathe, but my body is on fire.

He pulls his cock out of my throat, and I gasp, catching my breath as he waits. His cock is still in my mouth, so I experiment, running my tongue over the swollen crown while it's not as deep.

Landon moans, and I lap at him again.

"That's perfect, baby. Just like that."

He lets me lick and suck him for a couple of minutes, then he eases his cock back into my throat. I still feel faintly panicky when it gets hard to breathe, but I'm more prepared for it this time.

Once he's sure I can handle it, he picks up the pace. His firm grip on my hair keeps my head where he wants it, and once more, I'm less a participant and more an orifice he's fucking to bring himself pleasure. I don't know why I find it so intensely hot to be used like this, but my body hums as he fucks my mouth.

When he's getting closer to coming, his grip on my head tightens. He stops occasionally tweaking my nipples and grabs my neck, groaning and growling as he pushes deep into my throat. It's hard to take him when he goes that deep, but I do my best to keep up. Not that I have much choice. Between his firm grip on my hair and him holding my neck like this, I couldn't object if I wanted to.

Landon's body tenses and he drives his hips forward, filling my mouth so full of his cock, my lips are practically at his pelvis. He pulls my hair and forces my face closer, and I cry out, choking on him, gagging around him.

He pulls out to let me catch my breath, but then he does it again.

He thrusts once, twice, a third time. And then, with a strangled groan and a bruising grip on my jaw, his hot cum hits the back of my throat. I swallow it down eagerly, wrapping my tongue around his jerking cock to make sure I get him nice and clean.

When he's finished using my mouth, he pulls out. I lay there with my heart pounding, feeling a strange sense of accomplishment that I was able to please him, even if it did get a little more intense than I was ready for at the end.

"Fuck, Parker." He lets go of my hair and sinks into the spot beside me on the bed. Then he immediately snakes an arm under me and pulls me against his hard body.

He takes a moment to catch his breath. I didn't get to come this time, so my body is still buzzing so much, I have to physically stop myself from rubbing against him.

"Not bad for a first time?" I ask hopefully.

"Truly excellent regardless of experience level," he assures me.

"Yay," I say lightly, curling close and tenderly kissing his chest, then I settle in with my head resting against his bicep.

He caresses the sides of my face and pulls me in closer so I'm snuggled against his chest. "You're okay?"

I nod, enjoying his warmth. "Yep, I'm good."

He nods, letting his thumb caress my jawline as he looks down at me. I think he's going to say something sweet by the look in his eye, but if the thought passed through his mind, it passed right out of it before it could happen.

Instead, he rolls me on my back and dives beneath the covers.

I gasp when he spreads my thighs, then plants his face between them.

And then his mouth is on me, and every bit of tension in my body travels to the spot he's licking between my legs.

Experimentally, since it felt so nice when he did it, I squeeze my own breasts and tease my nipples while he devours me. Maybe it's that, or my heightened arousal from what he just did to me, but it only takes maybe a minute before I'm smothering my cries in my pillow as I come.

He looks pretty damn satisfied when he emerges from beneath the blanket and drops back into the spot beside me. "Damn, I think that was a record."

I try to shove his arm for making fun of me, but I feel too good. I curl up in his arms again, pressing our bodies as close together as possible. Then I give him a little kiss on the lips before nuzzling my face against his neck.

"Don't let me fall asleep," I murmur drowsily. "I still have to look at hotels."

He snorts, absently kissing my forehead with a slight chuckle. "Okay."

ON SUNDAY, we have our first *real* family dinner.

We make dinner at home instead of going out so as not to tempt fate, and I try not to blush every time I look at Landon and recall the night before, when he pinned me to my bed and fucked my throat.

He did let me fall asleep, but he woke me up at around two in the morning. I spent close to an hour looking at resorts with him on my phone, then the insatiable man rolled me onto my stomach and fucked me again before he went to his room.

My pussy is sore and my throat's a bit sore today, too.

I still hope he sneaks into my room again tonight.

I have an appointment with my gynecologist tomorrow to get on some birth control. He used a condom last night, but he was the one to remember, not me. I'm confused by my brain's inability to remember such a crucial thing because that's so not like me, but nothing about sex with Landon is anything I was prepared for.

Besides, I kinda like when he comes inside me.

I just don't want to have a baby right now since that would ruin literally all of our lives. I don't understand how that's not a strong enough incentive to remember condoms, but... here we are.

"So, have we narrowed it down to The Contemporary, then?" Mom asks once I've spent most of dinner detailing my vacation research.

"I think so, but we'll have to have to pick our dates. I was originally hoping we could go for the Halloween party, but there's stuff going on throughout October that we won't want to miss here. There's homecoming, Hannah's birthday, the Fright Night and Fright Fest stuff. There's only one week that even works in October, and we don't have any days off school that week, so we'd have to miss five whole days."

"Some of us don't have a problem with that," Landon says as he spears his last glazed carrot.

I nod. "But others of us aren't as keen on all that catch-up work, so I'm thinking November would work. Then we can do a Christmas party. Otherwise, we should wait until after Christmas. No parties if we go then, and even the holiday festival... do we want to do that *after* Christmas?"

"So, November is the best time," Hayden surmises, nodding. "All right. Well, I'll look at the school calendar and check my work schedule to see when we can go, then we'll go ahead with booking."

"If we have to miss a couple of days, I can manage that, but I'd rather not miss a whole week," I tell him.

"And I'm not giving up Thanksgiving," Mom states.

"We could do December after the winter ball but before Christmas if we absolutely had to," I state.

"And I have no problem with any date you could possibly choose. Aren't you glad I'm an underachiever?" Landon says.

"So proud," Hayden says dryly.

I crack a smile. "I already accounted for swim team. If we

go in November, there's no conflict. If we go after Christmas, there could be."

He shrugs. "I can just blow it off if I need to. Doesn't matter."

We are *such* different people.

When the last plate has been cleared, I tell Mom I'll do the dishes so she can spend a little time with Hayden.

Landon says he'll help, much to everyone's surprise, and I eye him warily as I back into the kitchen.

He smirks. "What?"

I narrow my eyes at him. "You know what."

He grabs my hips, walking me back against the counter.

My eyes widen. "Knock it off," I whisper.

"Hey, I'm just here to be helpful."

"You can help by making sure the dishwasher is empty while I rinse off the dinner plates," I inform him primly. Then, more seriously, I ask, "Have you ever even done dishes before?"

"Nope."

I push his hands off my hips, my gaze darting to the kitchen entrance as I put some space between us. "Behave yourself," I say quietly, before turning to face the counter.

Landon walks over to check the dishwasher like I asked, then he leans against the counter right by me, folding his arms over his chest and watching me rinse off dishes.

"Can I ask you a question?" I ask him, turning on the water so I can rinse the first dish.

"What's my favorite Disney character?" he mocks.

I roll my eyes, smiling faintly. "No. A serious question."

He nods, watching me. "Sure."

"What are your plans for after high school?"

"My plans?"

I nod, looking over at him. "Are you planning to stick around here, or...?"

A guarded look slides into place, one I haven't seen in a few days—and to be honest, I hadn't missed. "Why?"

I shrug. "Just wondering." Since he seems reluctant to answer, I decide to share my plans first. "I'm planning to go to college. It doesn't seem like you're that into school, so I wasn't sure if you were, or...?"

He glances toward the living room. "My dad wants me to. Baymont basically requires it. Gotta send us off to the next stage of becoming a master of the universe, after all."

I smile at his faintly mocking tone. "Sure. But it's not what you want?"

He shrugs. "Considering our species is on the fast track to extinction, just doesn't feel like four more years of school is the best use of my time."

I snort. "Yeah, we're not doing so great, are we? You could always be a climate scientist. That would be exceptionally hot."

He smirks. "You wanna nerd me up?"

I nod. "Absolutely. Change nothing physically. Just study up and then launch a 'hot nerd' social media empire. Film yourself working out while you give relatable lectures and sell eco-friendly merch like sweat towels made from recycled plastic bottles. People will watch the videos to ogle you, then later, when they're about to throw something recyclable in the trash, they'll be like, 'wait. Didn't LandonLifts say something about this?' Before you know it, they'll be composting and installing solar panels."

He shakes his head, smiling. "Sneak attack."

"Exactly. They'll never see it coming. They'll get educated even if they didn't want to, all because they wanted to drool over some hot guy."

"Sounds like you got it all worked out."

Nodding, I say, "I can come on part-time as your brand strategist. I think it's a good plan."

He nods. "It is. Probably not gonna happen, but a good plan nonetheless."

"Oh, come on. Don't you want to save the world?"

"Not particularly." He nods at me. "What about you? What's your plan?"

"Mine is much less focused on aesthetics and branding, but obviously, I have a pretty strong drive to make a difference. I plan to go into education, so I obviously don't agree that it's a waste of time."

"After you go to school for a million years, you want to *work* at a school?"

"Probably at the college level, but yeah. I think educating people and helping open up their worldview is super important. College is when a lot of that tends to happen. Before college, most people aren't really in school to learn, and after college, the majority of people get too busy or too distracted to keep feeding their minds. If you don't use it, you lose it, so that tends to be the way it goes. I want to be there when people are at their hungriest, offering up a delicious plate of brain food for their eager consumption."

Landon smirks. "You're such a fucking nerd."

"Thank you."

"You'll be good at that, though. Professor Johansson," he teases.

I sigh, smiling. "Sounds good, doesn't it?"

"Better than LandonLifts," he says dryly.

"Hey, I came up with it on the spot. Give me a break."

He smirks. "You want kids?"

I nod, rinsing another plate. "Someday. One or two. You?"

"Maybe. Depends on who I'm having them with. I'm not that worried about securing my legacy—"

I nod solemnly, playing along. "What with the extinction and everything."

He smirks. "—But with the right person, sure."

Smiling faintly as I run a salad plate under the faucet, I joke, "Well, you can't be *too* picky about it." Then, lowering my voice, I tease, "You didn't seem overly concerned about the possibility of knocking *me* up."

I expect him to have a comeback that makes me roll my eyes, so my heart slides into my throat when instead, he says, "Like I said. With the right person, I'm open to it."

My gaze snaps to his, searching for some sign he's messing with me, but there's no hint of malice or mischief. It seems like... he means it.

Before I can respond, Mom peeks around the corner. "Hey, are you guys going upstairs after you're done in here, or do you want to stay downstairs with us? Hayden wants to be a couch potato and watch some home improvement shows."

Swallowing, trying to coax my heart out of my throat, I look back at Mom. "I'm always down for home improvement shows."

"Great." She flashes me a smile, then looks to Landon.

"Yeah, sure," he murmurs, pushing off the counter. "I guess we can keep doing the family thing."

"Yay," Mom says, clapping her hands a couple of times. "Do you want to come in and help us pick?"

I'm sure Landon suspects that part of her motivation is to lure him out of the room he's in alone with me, but rather than the annoyance I expect to see when I look at him, there's a faint smile tugging at his lips. "Sure."

"I'm almost done in here anyway," I say. "I'll meet you guys in there in just a minute."

"Sounds good," Mom says brightly.

Landon follows her out, but before he leaves the room, he glances back at me.

I shoot him a smile to let him know I appreciate his cooperation.

He rolls his eyes, but then he gives me a faint smile, too, before rounding the corner.

OVER THE NEXT couple of days, things go pretty smoothly. It's easy to pretend I'm in a normal relationship with a normal guy and there's nothing to worry about.

I even get my period, which is a relief, but a bit annoying when we get to the pet shelter. Like Landon, dogs have no interest in manners, so one shoves its face between my legs to sniff much more aggressively than it did when it greeted Landon.

"Tigger, you rude, rude boy," says Melissa, the manager of the pet shelter we're volunteering at, as she grabs the lead and tries to pull her dog away. "I'm sorry about that."

My face warming, I assure her, "It's okay. Dogs are gonna dog."

"Where do you want this?" Landon asks, nodding at the big box he's carrying. It's a vacuum cleaner that boasts its ability to handle pet hair without wearing out as quickly as an ordinary vacuum cleaner.

"Oh, you can put that right over there," she says, pointing to an alcove housing a shelf lined with toys, treats, and assorted pet supplies. "Right by the shelf. Thank you so much for bringing that, by the way. We never expect our volunteers to bring presents as well."

I watch Landon put the box down, then flash her a smile. "I saw it was on your wish list and figured it was pretty important. It's brand new, obviously. We just picked it up on our way here."

"Thank you so much. Our old one broke down and we've been in desperate need, as I'm sure you can imagine."

Now that he's restrained and not more in my business than my gynecologist was yesterday, I bend down to give Tigger some scratches behind his big, floppy ears. "Happy to help."

Landon comes back, looking decidedly *less* happy to help, but I got him here, so I'm calling it a win.

"Well, let me put this guy away and then we'll get you guys started," Melissa says, turning to take Tigger back to the row of cages lining the wall.

I lean closer to Landon. "Should I film you for your first LandonLifts episode?" I tease.

"So I can do bicep curls with a puppy in each hand and talk about pet shelter overpopulation and the importance of spaying and neutering?"

"See? You're a natural."

He shakes his head. "Too much talking for my liking. Film yourself. You're the one who likes to lecture, Miss Future Professor."

"Yeah, but I'd have a likability issue. If you do it, people will be like, 'aw I love this.' If I do it, they'll be like, 'why don't you shut your stupid whore mouth and mind your own business, you self-righteous pain in the ass.'"

His eyebrows rise. "Wow. That's a lot of contempt for someone just trying to slow down animal euthanasia."

"Yep. Welcome to life as a woman."

"Eh, fuck the haters. We don't need 'em, anyway. I'll always have more than enough money to fund whatever save the world project you've got in your head. If I need more, I have all the contacts I'll ever need to make money without even doing much. When you have a lot of money, it's easy to make more."

"Funny, when you don't have money, it's hard to make *any*.

Must be nice to come into the world knowing you'll never have to worry about such things."

He shrugs. "I guess. Didn't always love that my dad worked so much, though. After Mom... I didn't care so much, but when I was younger, I always wished he would care less about work and more about spending time with us. Like he said the other night, in twelve years, he took us to Disney once. We could afford to go on a family vacation every goddamn month if we wanted to, but... we didn't. He was always too busy." He shrugs, tucking his hands into his pockets. "If I ever do the family thing, I'm not going to be too busy. I'd rather do shit with the people I love than spend every second of every day making money I'll never need."

I drift close and lean my head on his shoulder. "I like that," I say softly. "I obviously grew up on a budget, so we have had vastly different experiences with money. When you don't have enough, it's stressful, but because of your dad, you do, and... I think it's really healthy that you're able to see when enough is enough, to be able to stop and let yourself actually enjoy it. I didn't know your mom, but I bet she would be proud to hear you say that."

His fingertips graze the side of my hand, then he grabs it, and my tummy flutters as he links our fingers together. Generally, he spends a lot of time smirking, but when his lips tug up this time, all I see is tenderness etched across his face.

Then he turns his head and drops the cutest little kiss on the tip of my nose.

My heart seems to free fall down an empty elevator shaft and a smile I can't suppress steals across my face.

But before I can say or do anything, before I can respond at all, Melissa comes walking back over to us without the outgoing pup. She clasps her hands together and looks from Landon to me. "All right, are we ready to work?"

Reluctantly, I pick my head up off my shoulder and take a step away from him. "We sure are," I say.

"You guys have any particular talents I can put to use?"

"She's good at everything," Landon says. "I'm pretty strong."

Blushing, I mutter, "I am not good at everything."

Melissa smiles. "How are you with computers?"

"I'm no coder, but I'd say I'm pretty good with them."

"We could use some help updating the website if either of you are proficient at that sort of thing. We like to post our adoption numbers for the year, and currently we still have last year's up. It's just something I never seem to have time for. Of course, we keep the adoptable pets photolisting up to date since that's the most important thing, but we do have a whole litter of puppies, a six-month-old female, and a senior male that need to be photographed and listed. They also need to be posted to socials. If you're any good at filming videos, some of our volunteers will take videos and set them to like... Sarah McLachlan music to get the hearts engaged online."

I chuckle. "I can do all that. I'm a pretty good writer, so I can write up their bios as well if you tell me a little bit about them."

"That would be wonderful." Since I have a bunch of tasks to get started on, she turns her attention to Landon. "Do you have any interest in dog walking? We have a German shepherd mix that pulls, so a lot of my girls won't walk her, but you look like you could handle her."

He shrugs. "Sure."

"When you get back, can you hold the puppies while I take their pictures for the website?" I ask him. "If we can't lure them in with Sarah McLachlan, maybe we can give them false hopes of meeting the muscled hunk snuggling the puppies in the pictures online."

"You are ruthless," Melissa says. "I love it."

Landon smirks. "Yeah, sure. Let me walk this damn dog first, then I'll let you objectify me."

I lean in to give him a kiss. "Thank you, baby."

He smirks, squeezing my side before letting go. "You can thank me later."

SINCE THURSDAY IS the day Mom spends most of at the dance studio, Hayden typically works late that day. Expecting to have the house to ourselves, I tell Landon we should take advantage of the camera his dad hasn't had fixed yet and go for a swim.

We enjoy playing in the pool for a while, but having me in a swimsuit is apparently too much temptation for Landon to resist. He won't stop trying to grab me—*and sliding his fingers beneath the fabric to touch my pussy when he catches me*—so I finally splash him in the face and tell him I'm getting out.

I'm towel-drying my hair when he comes up behind me, locking his arms around my waist and pulling me back against him.

"Don't even think about it, buddy."

"Oh, I'm thinking about it." He kisses my neck. "What good is it having the house to ourselves if I can't fuck you in places I can't when the parents are here?"

My skin warms at the imagery he inspires. "It's too stressful. The whole time, I would be thinking about your dad walking in on us. Is that what you want?"

Making a faint noise of disgust, he says, "Well, you killed it. Good job."

I look back and flash him a smile. "We should have smoothies and watch that house flipping show."

His fingertips graze the small of my lower back, knocking out some of the strength in my knees, then his hand slides down so he can grab my ass. "We could probably do that."

Once we've finished drying off, Landon tells me to go make the smoothies while he goes upstairs to grab us some clothes to change into so we don't get the living room couches wet.

I'm in the middle of grabbing straws for our smoothies when he saunters into the kitchen.

I don't usually like to wear two-piece bikinis, but since Landon has seen me completely naked and I didn't mind giving him a reason to rub sunblock all over me, I wore a two-piece today.

Consequently, when he comes up behind me and unties the string around the back of my neck, the flimsy fabric falls and my tits spill out.

I gasp as Landon palms them, pulling me back against him immediately.

Warmth ripples through me and I lean my head back against his shoulder, my eyes drifting closed as he runs his thumb over my nipple.

"What are you doing?" I murmur.

"I locked the front door. I have a clear view from here. You don't have to worry about being caught off guard. Besides, your mom isn't here. He has no reason to come home early."

"Landon," I say on a sigh. "We can't right now."

"We can do whatever we want," he murmurs, his hot breath against my neck. Then he grabs one of the smoothie glasses and presses the frosty glass against my nipple.

I gasp at the shock of cold against my flesh.

After only a few seconds, he takes the glass away and replaces it with his lips, licking and teasing the aching peak until I'm trembling in his arms.

My body hums as his hot mouth covers the flesh he just made cool, and a shiver shoots down my spine.

I don't *want* to tell him no, but I have to.

Sinking my finger into his dark hair, I lightly tug his head back. He releases my nipple and looks up at me. "I'm serious," I tell him. "No funny business. I want to watch TV."

He straightens up, in front of me now, then locks his arm around my waist and grabs my ass. "And I want to fuck you. Who do you think stands a better chance of getting what they want?"

"I can't right now," I tell him, pushing against his arm and stepping back out of his embrace. "Can I have my clothes, please?"

He frowns at me holding the bikini top against my breasts to cover them. I don't bother tying it since I'm planning to change, but if I leave myself exposed to him, he'll just keep trying.

He doesn't offer my clothes, and that annoys me, so I grab them out of his hands.

That annoys *him*. I can see it in the way his powerful jaw tightens. His eyes seem to darken as he straightens, looking down at me from his full height.

My tummy flutters, more with nerves than interest, though there is an unwanted whisper of that, too. He shouldn't look so good when he's looking so menacing, but a familiar wave of fear washes over me, reminding me how he used to be.

Things got a lot better once I let him fuck me, but I didn't think if I turned off the sex faucet even temporarily, he would start being an ass again.

Maybe that was naïve.

He's been an ass to every single girl he has ever been with. Did I really think I wouldn't get glimpses of that side of him, too?

Right now, he looks like the Landon that broke into my house, so I don't even want to look at him.

"I'm going to change," I murmur, turning and heading for the bathroom.

I hate that I walk fast, slightly worried he'll chase me.

Beyond that, worried that if he chases me, he'll catch me, and if he catches me...

It shouldn't be like that when we're basically together, should it?

As soon as I get inside the bathroom, I shut and lock the door.

Then I have a moment of clarity where I feel really icky about feeling the need to do that when the guy I'm trying to keep out is practically my boyfriend.

I haven't thought of Landon as my boyfriend because he can't *be* my boyfriend. But he's as close as he could possibly be.

What if this whole thing was a mistake?

Hannah's words about not ignoring red flags reverberate through my mind, but I tell myself to just relax. I'll change into my dress, give him a minute to cool down, and then we can enjoy our smoothies and watch TV together for a bit.

But when I emerge from the bathroom, Landon is nowhere to be seen.

I frown as I look around the living room, outside by the pool, then I make my way to the kitchen. Both of our smoothies are on the counter, but Landon is gone.

Finally, not really believing he actually left, I go to the door so I can peek outside. The sight of his car will de-escalate the situation in my mind. I'm sure he just went upstairs, or to the room he hangs out in downstairs, or...

I'm honestly expecting that, so my jaw literally drops open when I step out on the landing and see his car is gone from the driveway.

He left.

He actually fucking left.

I swallow, trying to ignore the sick, anxious feeling twisting in my stomach.

My first impulse is to grab my phone and message him to ask where he went and, frankly, if he's fucking serious. We weren't even *fighting,* I just mildly annoyed him by not wanting to have sex right now because I'm at the tail end of my fucking period and I felt too awkward explaining that. But I shouldn't *have to* explain why I don't want to have sex.

In the end, I decide, fuck it.

I don't message him.

I go to the kitchen and transfer our two smaller glasses of smoothie into a big-ass cup with a taller straw just for me.

Fuck him.

If he wants to storm out like a child, fine.

I have homework to do anyway.

I'M NEARLY FINISHED with my history homework, but it has taken twice as long as it should have to get this far.

I can't concentrate.

Two hours have passed since Landon left and he hasn't come home. Hasn't texted me.

Then, I gave in to my absolute worst impulses and looked at Brittany's social media.

Her last post was an hour ago of her sitting on a beach with her pretty, pedicured toes dipped in the water, and it's cryptically captioned, "heaven can't help me now."

Landon liked it.

I feel *ill*.

The desperate urge to text him is present, and it makes me nauseous.

Well, message him. I don't even have his goddamn phone number, so maybe I'm the crazy one for thinking he's anything remotely close to my boyfriend.

But I want to reach out, to remind him that I'm so fucking serious about what I said to him. If he touches her, he's fucking dead to me.

I don't, because I shouldn't have to remind him.

I don't want a man I have to remind to act like he's mine.

So, I leave it.

I deal with being slowed down and force myself to focus on work every time my mind tries to wander.

I also turn my octopus to green and snap a picture of it to post on my own social media account in hopes he'll see it. Because honestly, I don't want to see his stupid face. If he sneaks into my room tonight, I'm Tasing his ass.

My phone vibrates on the bed beside me and my heart lurches as I grab it, looking at the notification that just popped up on my screen.

Then my heart falls because it's not him.

It's Javi.

"Hey, haven't heard from you in a while. You doing ok?"

"I've been better," I shoot back. "How are you doing?"

"Good, just busy. I figured you have been too. Bookworms gotta bookworm," he adds with a wink.

A faint smile claims my lips. "My head is buried in a book as we speak, actually."

"Anything good?"

"Nah, just school stuff."

"Aren't you usually into school stuff?"

"Usually. Having a hard time concentrating tonight."

"Sounds like someone needs a break," he says.

"Maybe," I type back. "The good news is it's almost weekend, so a break is imminent."

"You got any free time this weekend? Maybe we can meet up."

My heart drops.

I haven't been talking to Javi since things got more physical between me and Landon, but with the way he's acting tonight and Brittany's stupid post on social media... I don't really know what's going on.

I know Landon can be wrathful and mean, but he knows where my boundaries are, and if he thinks he can fuck around anytime he gets mad...

Well, he's gonna find out.

"Maybe," I text back. "What did you have in mind?"

"Bonfire on the beach?"

"Sounds fun. Will other people be there, or just us?"

"Just us. What do we need other people for?" he jokes.

Biting down on my bottom lip, I consider what to say before I start typing. I did like Javi when we were talking before, we just didn't get to talk for very long before Landon got in the way.

But if Landon is out there doing what I'm afraid he's doing right now, then Landon and I are done. There's no reason I can't hang out with Javi.

I don't *know* if he is, though, and that makes it harder.

"Can I get back to you?" I type out. "I'm not 100% sure if I can."

"But you want to?"

My heart skitters. I feel vaguely guilty even as I type out, "Yeah, of course."

It felt like the nice thing to say, but as soon as I see the words on the screen, I feel a bit sick.

"I have to go for now though, gotta get back to that homework."

"All right," he answers. "Don't be a stranger."

"Fuck," I whisper, dropping the phone on my bed like it's on fire. My skin is suddenly so warm, I feel like if I dunked myself in a tub of water, it would steam.

Since I need a break to clear my head before I can finish my homework anyway, I make my way to my bathroom for a nice, cool shower.

I'm feeling a little better by the time I emerge, rubbing lotion into my hands before walking over to my bedside table to check my phone. I left it on charge while I showered since my bedroom door is locked.

Nothing new.

Sighing, I climb back on my bed and turn my attention back to my books.

Thankfully, I'm less distracted this time and finally manage to get it done.

I'm out of water by the time I finish my homework, so I tiptoe down to the kitchen for a fresh bottle. I hear Landon's car outside as I reach in for the water, so my heart drops and I slam the fridge door, making a mad dash up the stairs before he gets inside and catches me.

My heart pounds when I get back inside my bedroom and get the door closed behind me. I lock it, turn off my light, then walk softly back to my bed. I cleared my schoolbooks before I ran downstairs, so I fold back the comforter and climb underneath.

I'm hyperaware of the sounds outside my bedroom. His room is down the hall from mine, so I listen for the sound of his door shutting to indicate he's inside.

My body tenses when instead, I hear a quiet knock on my door.

I wait, not even breathing, for a sign it's not him. If it's Mom, she'll announce herself so I know I'm safe to open the door. Hayden doesn't typically come to my room, but he would announce himself, too.

So when the person on the other side doesn't say anything, I figure it's him.

Then he startles me, slamming his hand against the door once before dragging his fingers down the wood the same way he did the night he broke into my house and trapped me in my bedroom.

"Let me in," he says lowly.

Not a chance.

Since my light is off and it's late, he can just assume I'm sleeping.

If he wanted to talk to me, he has had all evening to reach out. Instead, he waits until it's late and expects me to just let him sneak into my room like everything is fine.

He waits outside the door for a while, but eventually, he gets the message and walks away.

A small part of me is relieved, but a larger part is disappointed. I'm not playing with him. I'm not running right now because I want him to chase me. But whether I wanted him to or not has never played a very big role in Landon's decision to come after me. He talked a big game about being unstoppable, then at the first sign of conflict, he took his ball and went home.

Maybe I should have known better than to believe him.

His years of meaningless hookups with random girls may have taught him to be great in bed, but they haven't done shit to show him how to be a good boyfriend...

Or whatever the hell he is to me.

Maybe it was naïve to think that, for me, he would learn.

SLEEP IS ELUSIVE TONIGHT, but that's no surprise.

I can't stop listening for noise in the hall, inventing excuses to leave my bedroom that I know I'll never use. My pride won't let me. Still, I waste time coming up with them.

My senses are confused when I hear what sounds like a door sliding open, but that's impossible. My bedroom door doesn't slide, and it's locked, and—

I emerge from my comforter cocoon just enough to peek and reassure myself it's only my imagination, but I nearly scream when I see a man entering my room via the sliding door that opens out to my balcony.

My heart rate ramps up and I quickly sit upright, watching as the man gently closes the door.

His back is to me, but I'd recognize the back of that head anywhere.

"Landon, what the hell are you doing in here?"

CHAPTER 41

PARKER

LANDON TURNS around to look at me. All my lights are off, but he's still illuminated by the moonlight spilling in through my windows. My gaze rakes over him, taking stock. His mussed dark hair, the way his gray sleeveless shirt—an old one with the school logo on it, from when he was on the football team—hangs off his strong frame. It's the outfit he threw on earlier after we went for a swim, and it looks damn good on him, but I don't want him to come any closer.

I don't want to risk smelling her on him.

"Stop," I say, unsure what to do. If I throw back the blanket and stand, he can grab me more easily, push me around and kiss me, even if I don't want him to.

Of course, if I stay in bed, he could just join me—again, whether I want him to or not.

I decide to stand. He watches wordlessly as I peel back the blanket and climb off the bed.

I don't move any closer since I want to keep space between us. I cross my arms in a subtle gesture of self-protection, then I stare at him. "How the hell did you get in my room?"

He gestures back at the sliding door. "Balcony. You didn't lock the door."

Eyes widening, I say, "No, I didn't lock *that* door. I'm on the top floor of the fucking house and I wasn't trying to keep out Spiderman. How did you get on my balcony?"

"Who cares?"

"I do. It couldn't have been safe."

He moves closer and, since I don't want to end up on the mattress with him, I inch toward the foot of my bed.

"Eh, I survived," he says flippantly.

"Well, don't do it again. You knocked on the door and I didn't let you in. That was your answer." Since I'm close enough, I grab my octopus plushie off the bed and hold him up like a peasant trying to ward off an approaching vampire with a holy cross. "And maybe you were too busy looking at Brittany's posts to notice mine, but the octopus is green. This was our agreed upon 'keep out' signal."

Apparently, this vampire is immune to supposedly meaningful totems because he grabs the octopus out of my hand and tosses it back on the bed as he continues toward me. "I saw your post. I said you could use that thing to signal me; I never said I'd listen."

I shoot him a look. "Cool. So it's as meaningless as your word, then. Good to know."

His expression hardens. Seemingly not appreciating my jab, he stops wasting time on pursuit and lunges for me, grabbing my wrist and then my waist and yanking me against him.

"Get off me," I say, shoving against his chest to try to put distance between us.

He keeps a firm grip on me, rendering my struggles useless. "You think my word's meaningless?"

"Yeah," I fling back, glaring up at him. "I do."

He nods, his eyes dark and angry. "Okay." He pushes me backward, but keeps hold of my shoulders.

"Let go of me," I say, not appreciating his dominant bullshit one bit in this moment.

He doesn't stop pushing me until my back's against a wall, then he leans in close, grabbing my neck and tipping my chin up so I have to look at him.

I smack his hand away—or try to, anyway.

Being *literally* pushed around after the bullshit he pulled today pisses me off so much, I want to slap him.

He must see the desire glinting in my eyes because he smirks, running his thumb along my jaw in a tender caress even as he challenges me. "Go ahead. I dare you."

I swallow, the hairs at the nape of my neck standing up in response to his low, husky voice. "No," I say shortly. "That would just give you an excuse."

His smirk widens and he leans in, kissing the corner of my mouth even as I turn my head to try to evade him. "Baby, I don't need an excuse to take what's mine."

"I'm not your baby," I say cooly. "I'm not your anything."

"Yes, you are."

"No, I'm fucking *not*," I say, shoving against him with all my strength.

He releases my neck and my face, grabbing my wrists and pinning them against the wall. "Stop fucking fighting me," he growls, nuzzling his face against my neck.

"No. Get off me," I hiss, trying to free my hands from his grip and growing more irritated when I can't. "I don't want you near me, don't you get it?"

"Oh, I get it," he murmurs lowly. "I just don't fucking care."

"Of course you don't," I snap. "You don't care about anything. Obviously."

"I care about *you*." His tone is still low and annoyed, but his words are barbed specifically to take the air out of my resistance, and I'll be damned if I make it that easy for him.

"No, you don't. Someone who cared wouldn't have abandoned me at the first opportunity and gone running back to his old ways. I don't want anything to do with someone who behaves that way. It's pathetic," I spit, hoping my words are not only barbed, but dipped in fucking venom.

He smiles, shaking his head at me. "You think you can talk to me like that?"

My wrists are still pinned so my movement is limited, but I lean forward as much as I can so I can look up at him and meet his gaze. "You've been handed enough in your life, rich boy. If you want my respect, fucking earn it."

His eyes glitter with malice as he gazes down at me, but I get the sickest sense he's enjoying this.

He releases my wrists and grabs me, dragging me back over to the bed.

"No," I say, knowing where he's going with this. "Landon—"

"Shut your pretty fucking mouth."

Before I can object, he shoves me forward. I catch myself on the mattress, but I don't want to *be* on the mattress, so I try to climb back off.

"Nope," he says, grabbing my ass with both hands and lifting me, pushing me forward on the bed. His fingers hook into the waistband of my sleep shorts, and as I try to crawl forward since he's behind me, he drags them off.

"Landon, stop," I cry out, frustrated. Not only frustrated, but embarrassed. I didn't put a new tampon in after my shower because my period is almost over, but I put a pantyliner in just to be safe and I don't want him seeing it.

I hear him unzip behind me. My heart pounds in my chest and my fingers grip the bedding as I try to pull myself away from him.

His fingers dig into my hips as he drags me back and positions me where he wants me on the edge of the bed.

"No!"

He forces my legs apart and moves between them. He presses on my back to shove me down against the mattress, then he slides his hand up to grip my throat.

I pant, my skin feeling as if it's on fire. When I swallow, I can feel the movement against his hand.

"You belong to me, Parker. Clearly, you don't understand what that means, so let me fucking show you." His forceful grip tightens around my throat. I gasp, alarmed at the constriction, then I gasp again, my whole body stiffening as he shoves his cock into my pussy.

I wasn't ready for it and it doesn't feel like he put on a fucking condom, so my skin stretches around him as he forces his way deeper.

"This pussy is mine. If you even *think* for a fucking second about letting anyone else have it, I'll fucking kill him. Do you understand me?"

"I understand that you're an asshole," I bite out through clenched teeth as he shoves himself so deep, I feel the fullness of him everywhere.

"You knew that," he states, drawing back and driving his hips forward again with little concern for my comfort. "You knew exactly what you were getting into. And I fucking told you, there was no going back. You don't get to tease me with a glimpse of what it's like to have you and then come at me with this 'I'm not yours' bullshit. The fuck you aren't. You've always been mine, Parker, and you always will be."

"You left," I cry out fiercely, my voice jagged with pain. "Did you go to her?"

"No, I didn't fucking go to her," he says, his tone annoyed and insulted like it should be common sense.

Which is a pretty fucking convenient take from the one who *wasn't* completely in the dark the whole time he was throwing his tantrum.

I'm still pissed off at him, but I feel a bit of venom drain when he says that. "You liked her picture."

"Yeah," he says. "It's not the first time I've used her to fuck with you."

My heart sinks as he says that, his voice rough as he shoves his cock deep in my still resisting pussy. "You can't do that anymore," I say, my voice strained as I grip the comforter tightly. "And you can't leave me like that."

My voice drops at the end. Landon pulls out of me, pushing me over so I'm on my back, then he climbs on the bed, between my legs, and leans down to look me in the eye. "I will never leave you. Not even if you want me to."

Those words shouldn't soothe the hurt, but they kinda do.

Licking my lips and sliding a hand through his dark hair, I tell him, "Next time I do something to piss you off, you have to talk to me. You can't run. That's *my* thing," I add lightly.

His green eyes sparkle with amusement, then it disappears and he dips his head, stealing a searing kiss that steals my breath away.

The last of my resistance melts out of me and I wind my other arm around his neck, locking my legs around him to keep him close.

This time, when he thrusts deep into my pussy, I feel a flutter of excitement. It's not punishing and aggressive, he doesn't leave me aching to get away from him. He makes me ache for more.

His mouth is ravenous, like a man feasting after a bout of starvation. His greedy hands roam my body, squeezing and stimulating while he fucks me.

When I come, he holds his cock inside me, his body taut as

my pussy pulses around him. I lie there breathless and boneless, expecting him to finish fucking me so he can come, too.

Instead, he pulls out.

I think maybe he's switching positions, but I gasp in surprise when he lifts me up. He moves under me, positioning me so I'm facing him, but I'm on his lap.

"Spread your legs," he commands. "Let me in."

I spread my legs wider, scooting closer until our pelvises are as close to touching as they can be without him being inside me. And then he *is* inside me, and I arch my back, surprised at the sensation of him sliding deep.

There's no getting away from him like this.

He has one arm locked around my waist, the other squeezing my tit under my shirt as he thrusts into me. I was wrong about him being close when I came, because he holds me and makes me take his cock like this for so long, I can feel the tension building again.

"Landon," I cry helplessly, shamelessly grinding against his cock as he fucks me.

He squeezes my nipple and I cry out, throwing my hand over my own mouth to muffle the sound. Head thrown back, I keep my eyes squeezed shut and my hand sealed over my mouth, dizzy with desire as he gives me his cock again and again. The friction is so delicious, and combined with the possessive way he handles me...

"Let go," he commands, squeezing my tit until it's almost painful.

And then I do. My cries are held back by my hand, but the whimpers sneak out of my throat as I come again, my pussy convulsing around his cock. He drives his hips up and goes deep a few more times, then warmth fills my pussy as he shoots his cum deep inside me.

Panting and weak, I fall forward and melt against him with

my head on his shoulder. His arms always feel strong, even when I feel weakest, and he locks them around me now to keep me close.

Today was rocky and scary, and I wasn't even sure I ever wanted to see him again.

But now, I'm back to never wanting him to let go.

"I NEED A FAVOR."

Hannah closes her locker and turns to regard me skeptically, a couple of books hugged close to her chest. "From me?"

I nod, checking the hall around us first to make sure no one who matters is looking. Then I grab two fifties out of my pocket and pass her the cash.

She frowns, looking down at the folded up money in her hand, then back up at me questioningly.

"You know those muffins you make that Parker likes?"

"Pumpkin, banana nut, chocolate chip...? You'll have to be more specific. I make more than one type of muffin, and Parker likes all of them."

Annoyed, I glance around again before looking back at her. "The ones she brought me in middle school."

She only brought me muffins once in middle school, so that's all the information she seems to need. "Ah. My famous banana nut muffins." Stepping away from her locker and starting down the hall, she asks, "What about them?"

"I need you to make her some."

"Why?"

"Because I don't know how to bake," I say sarcastically.

Hannah smiles faintly. "I'd offer to show you, but I'm not even sure I'm supposed to be talking to you after yesterday."

"We kissed and made up. A couple of times," I assure her.

She wrinkles her nose up at my crude implication. "Then why do you need my services?"

"I still have an octopus to win over," I say dryly.

Hannah blinks.

"Can you do it or not?" I ask her.

She nods. "I can. When do you need them?"

"Can you get them done tonight?"

"For $150 I can," she says sweetly. When I look at her with a cocked eyebrow, she raises hers. "What? It's a rush order. You have to pay rush order prices."

"I don't have any more cash on me, but I can bring the rest when I pick them up."

"Okay," she says pleasantly. "I'll stop for the groceries I need after school." She takes her phone out of her purse and holds it out for me. "I don't have your phone number. You should probably put it in here so I can text you when they're ready."

I eye the phone, then say, "Why don't you just DM me."

Sighing, she says, "Always in the DMs."

"What?"

"Nothing."

"DO YOU WANT SOME HELP?" I ask Antonia as I stride into the kitchen to grab a cold bottle of water.

She's standing at the counter prepping dinner, but she smiles when she looks at me over her shoulder. "No, I have everything under control. You go enjoy your weekend."

I head back to the couch, but I don't know what to do. I'd watch my house flipping show, but Landon isn't here, and since we've been watching it together, it wouldn't feel right to watch it without him.

I guess I could start on my homework.

My brain objects, and since what I really want to do is let myself relax, I pull out my phone to text Landon and see when he's expecting to be back.

My heart stalls when I'm greeted by a notification before I can even open my texts. A new text from Javi.

Shit. I forgot he asked me about the beach bonfire.

"How's this weekend looking?"

I stare at the message, chewing on my bottom lip. Now he'll see I've opened the message, but I don't know what to say back.

"Parker, do you have a minute?"

I look up, surprised, when Hayden emerges from his study.

He came home a bit early today, but he's been shut inside working ever since.

"Sure," I say, darkening my phone screen and slipping it into the pocket of my jeans as I stand.

He leads the way, and I follow him into his office. Once I'm inside, he closes the door so we'll have privacy, and it makes me a little nervous.

Landon's claim that he suspects his dad knows about us surfaces, making it difficult to look Hayden in the eye.

Lucky for me, there's plenty in this study to look at, so I admire my surroundings as I drift closer to Hayden's desk.

He sits down in his executive's chair on the other side, so I drop into the chair on this side.

"Everything okay?" I finally ask, since he isn't speaking and his silence is grating on my nerves.

He nods, forcing my gaze back to him when I'm trying to look anywhere else. "Ready for another movie night tomorrow?" he asks conversationally.

"Oh, yes. I'm eager to finally watch this *Goodfellas* movie you've been hyping up."

He cracks a smile. "I think you'll like it."

"More or less than Landon liked *Frozen*?" I joke.

His smile widens. "I'd say a little more."

"Setting the bar high," I joke. "I like it."

"It's actually Landon I was hoping to talk to you about," he says, apparently seeing an opening.

My heart drops. "Oh. Okay. Sure. What about him?"

He regards me from the other side of his desk, his posture strong and sure of himself while I feel like crawling beneath the chair.

Finally, he speaks. "I can't help but notice Landon has been... behaving rather well lately."

My stomach rocks and I look down at my lap.

"And I know my son, so I know how unlikely it is that his good behavior is a gift he's giving us. It's being paid for, and I know *I'm* not footing the bill."

Nausea roils in my stomach, making bile rise in my throat.

I know I should speak, but I can't seem to open my mouth. If I do, I'm worried about what will spill out.

Maybe it's my prolonged silence that makes Hayden sigh. Maybe it's the reality of our situation.

"I have to tell you, Parker, I am not a hero. Make no mistake, I love your mother immensely and I intend to spend the rest of my days making her happy and treating her fairly. But I wasn't always able to override my worst impulses. Landon is my son, after all. When I was younger, my ruthlessness was not so carefully controlled. Fortunately, I fell in love with a woman who demanded it of me. Sally couldn't love a man who couldn't be a good man for her. She knew what she deserved, what Landon deserved, and she wouldn't have stayed with me if I couldn't straighten up and become that man. So, I did."

Now I'm even more uneasy.

I know Landon said not much slipped past him, but exactly *how much* does Hayden know?

"Sally has been gone for a long time, though, and meeting your mother... it's the first time in all those years I've found a woman I'm afraid of losing. I would do just about anything to keep your mother, and Landon is the single biggest threat to our relationship. I am tempted to look the other way. I've been battling that temptation since you moved in here. I hope you don't take offense, I'm just being honest with you."

I shake my head. "I'm not offended."

Hayden nods, then tells me with no pleasure whatsoever, "My basest instinct here tells me not to look the gift horse in the mouth. If someone else wants to pick up the check for my happiness, let them. My commitment to your mother isn't the only one I've made, though. When I committed to her, I also made a commitment to you, to be as much of a father to you as possible, and I can't make the conscious decision not to protect you and convince myself I'm doing that."

I swallow. "I appreciate that, but I really have everything under control."

"You keep saying that, so why do I doubt it?"

I crack a smile. "Because you know your son?"

His mouth tugs up as well. "Yes, I suppose that's why." He pauses, his gaze drifting as he thinks. When his gaze hits mine again, I see that gleam of intelligence that has always appealed to me. "Well, if that ever changes, please don't hesitate to come to me."

"I won't."

"And don't wait until you're pushed into a corner. The sooner you speak up, the more options we have. Once you're cornered, the options tend to be much fewer and much more drastic."

I nod my understanding.

He watches me, still not appearing content. "Landon has never been with a girl he's afraid to lose, Parker. He may not know how to approach it."

That feels more like acknowledgement of this whole thing than I'm comfortable with, so I glance down at my lap, a faint smile tugging at my lips. "Believe me, I know."

"Don't let him get away with anything."

That advice surprises me so much, my gaze snaps up to his.

I might have expected Landon's father to advise me to be patient with him, to be forgiving while he figures out how to behave in a relationship he actually values. Especially considering how many times Hayden has bailed his son out of trouble.

But maybe that's why. Maybe he has learned the hard way,

and he wants to spare me the troubles he has had to deal with over the years.

He's giving fatherly advice on *my* behalf, after all.

"He may push your boundaries to see where they are, to see how far you'll let him roam past them. That's his nature. He'll have to learn to control it the same way I did. Sometimes, we can mistakenly think it's an expression of love to let someone traipse all over us and everybody else without consequence. I can tell you from regrettable experience, it is not. Let him know your boundaries early, and then stick to them."

Last night resurfaces in my mind.

Maybe Hayden picked up on trouble brewing from the way his son stormed out, or the fact that I went out looking for his car not long after.

His voice drags me back to the present.

"The moment you start letting Landon get away with things he shouldn't, you start down a path you can't turn back from. It is not what's best for him, and certainly not what's best for you. Landon needs to improve his self-control and learn how to treat people if he wants them to stick around. He needs to learn his actions have consequences, and regrettably, I let go of the reins a long time ago, so I've failed to impose that upon him. It may be too late for me, but I think *you* still have a chance."

I think so, too, but I don't say that.

"If you enable him, even if you think you're protecting him, all you'll really be doing is encouraging his bad behavior. If you don't like something, do not hesitate to tell him that. Communicate what's important to you so he knows where you're at, and then, if he deliberately ignores your boundaries, cut him off immediately. If you tell him there will be a consequence, you have to impose it. One warning is all you can give him. If you continue to warn him, your words will turn into empty threats, and he will learn not to believe you—and consequently, he will not respect you. If you let go of the reins long enough for him to slip away, you'll never get them back. Eventually, you'll have to leave him wandering and walk your own path. It will be the only way you find peace."

I'm looking down by the end of that, but when I look back up, I see the sincerity on his face.

"You're a fantastic girl, Parker, and you have a fresh start with him. If you love him in *any* capacity, hold him to a higher standard than I have. Make him behave like a man who deserves you, or leave him and find one who does."

"HEY, CAN YOU TALK FOR A MINUTE?"

I look at the text on my phone for Hannah, then I shoot her a text back. "Sure. What's up?"

A few seconds later, my phone rings. My eyes widen because we don't usually call each other, but I answer quickly in case it's urgent.

"Are you okay?" I ask immediately, ready to spring into action and grab my car keys if not.

"Yeah, I'm fine," she murmurs, but she seems to be keeping her voice low. "Is Landon back yet?"

My brow furrows. "No," I say slowly, a bit uncertainly. Why does she even know Landon isn't home?

"Good." She sighs, then lowers her voice a little more. "Listen, I don't know what's going on, but some weird stuff is happening today, and I think you need to be looped in."

My stomach drops. "Okay. What kind of stuff?"

"Landon approached me earlier at school. He wanted to ask me to do something for him. I told him I would and then he went on his way and I went on mine, but as soon as he walked away, I realized I forgot to ask him a question. So, I went looking for him. And I found him. Talking to Anae. I wasn't close enough to hear what they were saying, and I didn't want to be seen so I couldn't go closer, but the conversation looked kind of intense. It looked like they were arguing."

Scowling in confusion, I sputter a bit, trying to find words and failing. "Why would he be arguing with Anae?"

"I don't know," she says. "But since I didn't want to jump to any conclusions and I didn't hear what they were arguing about, I figured I wouldn't say anything."

Yet here she is, saying something.

"So... what else happened?"

She pauses for a few seconds, then she sighs heavily. "I don't even know how to..." She searches for words the same way I did a moment ago. "Parker, Anae brought that valet from the club back to the house tonight. They got here right after Landon left. Right now, they're on a lounger by the pool eating each other's faces."

My jaw falls open, my eyes widening. "What?"

"I sent you a picture. I feel like I need verification because I don't even trust my own eyeballs at this point."

I pull back the phone to open the message she just sent me, and sure enough, it's a photo of Javi on a lounger by the pool at Hannah's house, Anae planted on his lap with her tongue shoved halfway down his throat.

Putting the phone back to my ear, I say, "I am very confused."

"You and me both," she says. "Didn't you say he texted you asking you to hang out this weekend?"

"I did. I mean, I never answered him, so I guess maybe he got tired of waiting for me..."

My words trail off. They're feasible, but they don't really make sense. How do you go from wanting to hang out with me to making out with Anae *that* fast?

Besides, he just texted me a little bit ago.

I didn't even tell Hannah about that one.

Frowning, I pull back the phone again so I can look at the text.

An idea strikes me, so purely for science, I text back, "I think I can meet you tomorrow night if you're still free?"

Back on the phone with Hannah, I tell her, "Can you see him?"

"Unfortunately, yes."

I bite back a wholly inappropriate smile. "Keep watching. I just texted him. I want to see if he..." I cut off, my eyes widening as the three gray bubbles dance across the screen. "Is he texting?"

"What? No," she says, confused.

"Are you sure?"

"His hands are occupied," she assures me, "But not by a phone."

She swears he isn't texting me, yet a new message comes up on my screen.

"Yeah? Great. I can't wait to see you. Want me to pick you up?"

How...?

"Hannah, are you *sure* he didn't just text me?"

"Parker, I have never been more sure of anything in my life."

"Well, someone just responded," I say flatly.

"Well... it wasn't the guy you introduced me to at the club, that's for sure."

No. It sure wasn't. I saw the picture for myself, and that was definitely Javi.

Looking down at my phone, I type back to my deceitful pen pal, "No, don't come here. Things with my stepbrother are a little weird right now, but I'm tired of having to live my life around him. I'll just tell everyone I'm going to my friend's house. I hope you don't mind sneaking around," I tap the winky, kissy emoji pretty aggressively, then I press send before I can think better of it.

And a moment later, "Javi" responds, "not at all," with a wink of his own.

Well, that confirms it.

It's not Javi I've been texting.

I sit there for a moment, simmering over the implications.

My skin is so hot, I need to go jump in the fucking pool.

But I don't know how long I have until Landon gets here, so I don't waste time.

I go back to Hayden's office and knock on the door before entering.

Hayden looks up at me.

I flash him a smile, hoping I don't resemble a freckled tomato. "Can I have Landon's phone number? I just realized I need to ask him if he could pick up something on his way home, and we never actually exchanged numbers."

"Of course." He takes his phone out of his suit pocket and holds it out for me.

I hurry over to grab it, then I open a new message and type in the number.

And sure enough, I *do* have Landon's number.

Saved in my phone as Javi.

CHAPTER 45

LANDON

I INTENDED to head straight home after I left Hannah's house, but after I got those texts, I had to pull the car over.

Now, I look down at the destroyed muffins I threw against the ground and think I probably should have saved at least one to take home to her, but fuck it.

I don't care if Hannah asks her about them tomorrow and she's confused, wondering what the hell she's talking about and what happened to the muffins.

Same fucking thing that happened to them last time. I destroyed them.

Well, last time I only destroyed one of them.

I never told Parker, of course, but when I was sitting in that lonely fucking house, suddenly devoid of all the love and laughter in the world, I did eat the muffins. And they were fucking delicious.

But it wasn't about the recipe. It was the love Parker put into them for some asshole kid she didn't even know.

I was enraged when I slammed the baked goods against the road, but I just feel fucking sad now as I bend down to pick up the muffin container. It's the same one Parker delivered them in when we were in middle school. I thought she'd get a kick out of me still having it.

I'm tempted to hurl the goddamn thing off the side of the cliff now, but I settle for knocking the fallen sugar and crumbs out of it, then I toss it on the floorboard on the passenger side.

I drive around for a while.

I consider going to Malek's, but he'd want to know what happened. Considering he's been telling me I needed to stop pretending to be the fucking valet and just tell her the truth, I know how fucking smug he'd be, and I can't handle that right now.

You're looking for trouble, and I'm telling you now... you look long enough, and you're going to find it.

Of all the fucking things for him to be right about.

Malek has trust issues so I understood him not trusting Parker, but I knew better.

At least, I fucking thought I did.

For a while, I'm just fucking mad at her.

But the longer I drive, the more time I have to think, and the more time I have to think, the more I realize this is my fucking fault.

So, I drive over to Brittany's.

I still have her number saved in my phone—not for any good reason, I've just spent so many years using certain methods to fuck with Parker. I didn't realize I'd have bad habits to break.

"Come outside," I text her, sitting in her driveway.

I thought about using her for the Javi bait, but she's too volatile. I realize saying *Brittany* is volatile when *Anae* was the alternative is a little crazy, but maybe what I mean is she's more emotional. Parker's not wrong about Brittany. She's a total wreck. Her dad was a piece of shit and fucked her up real good, making her pretty easy pickings for any asshole who wants to come along and take advantage.

Parker has long reviled my being just such an asshole, so when Brittany comes bouncing excitedly down the driveway, I almost fucking feel bad.

What has this girl done to me?

"Hey," Brittany says cheerfully, bright-eyed and ready to go. She even brought her fucking purse.

I shake my head. "We're not going anywhere."

"Oh." Her smile weakens at my tone, but she maintains her smile. "Okay. You want to come in? My mom isn't home."

"No. I just need to talk to you for a minute."

Sensing I'm serious, her smile drops and she nods. "Okay. What's up?"

"I wasn't very fair to you, was I?"

She shrugs uneasily, not wanting to agree with something that insults me. "It's okay."

"It's not okay." I shake my head, looking past her. "I was an asshole, and I'm sorry. But the only reason I'm sorry is that there's a girl I'm completely fucking crazy about," I say, shifting my gaze back to hers since I know this could get out of control quick if I'm not careful. "And when I started to pull the same asshole shit with her, she didn't let me. She's spent years of her life investing in me, and the first time she thought I was out fucking around, she withdrew every penny of her emotional investment. Account closed. I managed to open it back up because I wasn't dumb enough to actually do what she thought I did, but..."

Brittany's eyes are glinting with unshed tears, but she still tries to hide it for me.

I sigh. "I thought she believed me, but I'm not sure. She may have some doubts. I need you to tell her we weren't together yesterday. You made that fucking post, and I liked it to fuck with her... I know I have no right to ask, but..."

Brittany swallows, looking wobbly is the only way I can fucking describe it. But she nods, and she swallows again, and then she clears her throat. "I can make like a video or something."

That she's near tears and still offering to help me save my relationship with some other girl...

Maybe it speaks to who I am as a person that despite seeing how emotional she is and knowing what a fucked up thing it was to ask for, I open my phone and turn my camera to video.

"Can you tell Parker that I was not with you yesterday?"

Brittany offers a watery smile. She's unsure of herself, but she wants to help. "Hey, Parker. I should have known. Anyway, Landon wasn't with me yesterday. I was just having a bad day and listening to some music at the beach by myself." She shakes her head. "He wasn't with me, though. He hasn't texted me back since he told me to stop texting him."

I press the record button to stop the video, then I slide the phone back into my pocket. "Thank you."

She nods, looking down at the driveway.

I start to turn and leave, but I think better of it and turn back. "Can I give you a last bit of advice before I go?"

"Landon Atwater, giving me advice?" she asks, a bit playfully despite how she's feeling.

"Yeah, I know." I roll my eyes at the gesture myself. "But for real. You and I hardly know each other. We never talked about shit. Stop giving so much to guys who don't give enough fucks to give anything back to you."

"After you, right?" she says dryly.

"Of course, after me," I say, smirking at her as I back away. "Thanks for the video."

"Asshole," she says, chuckling a little to herself as I walk back to my car. But then, because she can't help herself, she calls, "You're welcome."

WHEN I FINALLY PULL IN the driveway, the sun is about to go down.

I'm more or less empty-handed. I don't bother taking the empty muffin container in with me, but I have the video in my phone.

I've managed to lock my temper back up in its cage, but as soon as I walk through the front door, there's a slight resurgence. Parker's message echoes in my head.

I hope you don't mind sneaking around.

I haven't minded sneaking around, but that's because I was drunk on these first few sips of her. It all felt easy enough, I didn't think much about the hole we were digging right beneath our feet.

But I can see how our situation may have made Parker feel that, regardless of what she wants, nothing serious can ever really happen between us. Parker is fiercely protective of her mother's happiness, and there's not a shot in hell she'd put her own before it.

I am not so selfless.

They're all gathered on the couch in the living room. Gemma's next to my dad, and his arm is around her shoulders, propped against the back of the couch. Parker is facing them with one leg curled up beneath her and her hands going. Whatever she's telling them, she's animated about it. Under different circumstances, the sight would make me smile.

Her enthusiasm ebbs when I walk into the room.

The conversation goes quiet.

I'm used to it at this point. I don't really care.

"There you are," Dad says, as if they've been waiting for me.

"Here I am," I confirm, making my way over to the couch.

Parker scoots over to make room for me. "We were just about to watch—"

Her words are cut off when I get to her, grab her by the neck, and bend down to kiss her full on the mouth.

Gemma gasps as if someone just ran a fucking sword through her, and Parker gasps too, her shock caught between my lips as I taste her.

I don't linger too long.

I pull back, gently releasing her neck, and Parker stares at me, her eyes as wide as saucers and her jaw hanging open.

Then I drop onto the couch, prop my feet up on the coffee table, and slide my arm around her, the same way my dad has his around Gemma.

"Now, what are we watching?"

CHAPTER 46
PARKER

I SIT on the couch with my head in my hands, the sound of the clock ticking the loudest noise in the room.

The television has been forgotten, of course.

Hayden grabbed my mom and took her into his office as soon as she regained the ability to talk.

We were all shocked when Landon kissed me, but Mom was the most shocked. Hayden knew something, I knew everything, and poor Mom just sat there, stunned and confused, as she watched her daughter's attempted attacker *mark her* on the goddamn couch.

I feel immense guilt and no small amount of fear the longer they're in there.

I don't know what's going to happen.

In my mind, the most likely outcome seems to be Mom coming out, sad and teary, and making me go pack a suitcase so we can go back to our house.

Landon sits on the couch next to me, not nearly as stressed as I am.

"I cannot believe you did that."

He shrugs his broad shoulders with his arms crossed over his chest. "Had to be done."

"No, it most certainly did not have to be done," I state, glaring at him.

"Yeah, it did. You were only worried about your mom's relationship. I'm worried about being able to legitimize ours. It's impossible until they know. Maybe they'll struggle and be uncomfortable for a time, but they'll just have to get the fuck over it and then we can all move on with our lives."

Eyes wide, I turn to face him. "You think so, Landon? Because I think it's more likely they're going to break up, and it will be all our fault."

He shakes his head dismissively. "My dad won't let that happen. The guy's a lawyer, he makes arguments for a fucking living. He's been training his whole life for this. He'll find a way."

I shake my head. "You don't know my mom."

"And if you think a little thing like her waning interest is going to stop him from marrying her, you don't know my dad," he states.

I look back at him. "Is that supposed to be comforting?"

"It is. Did I do it wrong?"

I roll my eyes at him and sigh, sinking back into the couch cushions.

At the end of the day, I'm taking the blame for this.

I should have known better.

I knew Landon was crazy, I just never thought in one hundred million years he would respond to me agreeing to meet Fake Javi for a bonfire by blowing up all our lives in such grand fashion.

My bad.

I should have seen it coming.

In hindsight, it makes perfect sense.

He is *the worst*.

I'm irritated when he gets out his phone. "Oh, I'm sorry. Is the complete destruction of our lives not interesting enough for you? Gotta check the socials to keep your attention?"

He shakes his head, swiping the screen. "I'm not checking my fucking socials. I wanted to show you something." Then, he hands over his phone.

My eyes widen because it's a video and the still is Brittany's face. "What is this?" I ask warily.

Since I didn't do it, he reaches over and presses play.

She looks like an abandoned puppy filming a "have a nice life" video for the assholes leaving her on the curb.

"Hey, Parker. I should have known," she says with an uneasy smile. "Anyway, Landon wasn't with me yesterday. I was just having a bad day and listening to some music at the beach by myself. He wasn't with me, though. He hasn't texted me back since he told me to stop texting him."

My eyes widen in actual horror as I look over at him. "Please tell me you did not make that poor girl record this video."

"I sure did."

"Oh my god, Landon. What is wrong with you? That was so mean."

His eyebrows shoot up in disbelief. "I don't give a fuck. I won't put us all in this position again, but I did this time, and I needed to fix it. You think I'm going to let our relationship get off to an uncertain start because you're not sure you should believe me when I can easily clear it up for you instead?"

"Easy for you, not easy for her."

"I don't care about her," he states simply.

"Clearly," I murmur, sighing. "It was unnecessary, anyway, because I believed you. I know you have a temper and a history of bad behavior so when you were gone and we weren't talking, I wasn't sure, but once you told me you didn't go to her, I didn't doubt you."

His brow furrows, but before he can respond, the study door opens and steals our attention. I stand abruptly, turning to face Mom. My heart sinks immediately when I see she has been crying, and I look to Hayden with dread, expecting to see a similar expression of defeat on his face.

But Landon was right, he hasn't given up just because victory is impossible. I can see it in the firm set of his shoulders, the sharpness in his eyes. This is just another court case for him, and he's not prepared to lose.

He glances over at me, his star witness, and I know what he needs as he hands her off to me.

Mom sniffles. I want to go over and hug her, but she looks too fragile to be touched right now. "Can we go to your room and talk for a little bit?"

"Of course." I make my way over to her and follow her up the stairs. I glance back and see Landon walking toward his father, then they turn toward the study, so I guess they're having a talk, too.

Great.

I send a plea into the universe for Landon to please, please just be cooperative. This is so important, and if I fail at holding it all together now, when we're actually getting along, after suffering for the cause before that...

I can't accept that reality.

But it feels like the *only* reality.

When we reach the top of the stairs, I head toward my room, but Mom glances toward hers. "Go on in your room. I'll be right in," she says, pressing her hands to her hot, tear-stained face. "I just need a moment."

"Okay," I say, my heart heavy with dread.

I sigh heavily once I'm in my room, allowing my shoulders to slump.

It has been a *day.*

While I have a moment to myself, I remember what I wanted to check before everything blew up. I make my way over to my jewelry box and pull out the card Javi gave me that day at the country club.

I sit at my desk and put down the card, then I take out my phone and pull up the contact screen with the phone number I put in.

I'm expecting them to be different, so I'm utterly baffled when I see... they're not. The number on this card *is* the number in my phone, and I don't understand how that's possible when I watched Javi write his name on the back of this card and hand it to me himself.

It would be much easier to imagine Landon somehow got his hands on my phone after I saved his number and I just didn't notice, but then, I guess that wouldn't make sense, either. As soon as I saved the number, I sent Javi a text to make sure I had saved it correctly before I tucked the card away. If I had been talking to him that night but Landon ever since a theoretical number change...

But it can't be that. Landon's phone number is written on the back of this business card.

I can't figure it out. There's no way it makes sense. The only plausible thing I can think is that somehow, Landon forced Javi to write his number on that card and give it to me, but going over that interaction, it just doesn't make sense. Javi was relaxed and charismatic despite my awkwardness. Unless I was *utterly* wrong about him and he really is just an opportunistic creep, I can't see him so easily going along with Landon's plan to manipulate me.

Then again, he was making out with Anae Richards earlier tonight. I have a difficult time believing anyone who would go for her has an upstanding sense of morality.

Maybe Landon was right and he was just looking for a "rich girl" to mess around with.

Still doesn't explain all this, though. Not to my satisfaction, anyway.

The bedroom door opens behind me and I turn, putting down the card. Poor Mom looks so emotionally spent, so I walk over and give her a big hug.

She wraps her arms around me and hugs me back. "I feel like I've failed you," she murmurs, and that's all it takes for the dam to break.

I can't stand to see her cry.

"No," I tell her fiercely, shaking my head. "You haven't." Pulling back to look at her so she can see I'm serious, I tell her, "This isn't like before. I know he has done a lot of bad things in the past, but the kiss, this thing between us... it isn't that anymore. He really likes me, and I really like him. I know how cliché this sounds, but there truly is a side of him you haven't seen. And haven't you noticed he has been nicer lately? I know 'nicer' for Landon isn't exactly a high bar, but he has been more open to doing all the family stuff. He's stopped being such a jerk to you."

"That doesn't make me feel better. Oh, my daughter *wants* to kiss the boy who has preyed on her for a good chunk of her life? Yay."

I bite back a faint smile despite the stakes of the moment. "Well, sure, when you package it that way, it's not great. But let me package it differently. You know how since before you even met Hayden, you started feeling anxious about losing me when I go away to college and start a chapter of my life that doesn't include you as much? How you've literally lost sleep imagining me wanting to spend the holidays with my boyfriend's family instead of you? You will never have to worry about that as long as I'm with Landon because… it's the same family! And I understand that's a little weird, but honestly, who cares? If it works for us, that's all that matters, and this *does* work for us. I swear, Landon is being a good boyfriend so far, and if that changes, then I'll end it. And sure, that could be a little awkward if we were exes and we still had to spend the holidays together, but more awkward than him being the asshole who tormented me at school and I have to do holidays with him? Probably not. There was always going to be some awkwardness here. Honestly, the only way the awkwardness leaves permanently is if Landon and I *are* together. Then we really can be one big happy family, and yes, as I'm saying that, I know how twisted it sounds, but… it really isn't. And I know he doesn't have a track record of treating girls well, but it's different with me." I roll my own eyes. "And I know *that* sounds idiotic, but in this case, I swear it's true. I wouldn't be with him if it weren't. You just have to trust me. I'm not a kid anymore, Mom. It means so much to me that you want to protect me, it really does, but this isn't something I need protecting from. Landon likes me and I like him, and Hayden loves you and you love him, and those two relationships do not need to interfere with each other."

I have to take a breather after that patented Parker ramble, but I'm ready to go again the moment she brings up something I forgot to touch on.

Instead, she smiles a faint, watery smile.

"What?" I ask.

She shakes her head. "It's just funny. You and Hayden used some of the same arguments. His were more authoritative, of course."

"Of course," I say, smiling mildly.

"But he also assured me that while the optics may not be great, this is a very manageable situation."

"It really is."

"And that it's better if Landon likes you because at least then I don't have to worry about him being mean to you," she adds, trying to get on board.

"An excellent point. You don't have to stress about going out to dinner with your husband because some psycho might be trying to hurt me at home. He's just cuddling me on the couch while we watch house flips. Totally an improvement over our previous situation."

Mom cringes. "In some ways, yes. In others..." She looks at me. "I know you want to convince me this can be a totally normal situation, but under normal circumstances, I would never allow my teenage daughter to *live with* her boyfriend."

I nod, ceding her point. "That's one of the weirder aspects."

"Living together totally changes the dynamics of a romantic relationship, honey. And this one is new. I don't even know how new. How long has this been going on?"

"Not long," I murmur, mentally counting back the days. "But it isn't *totally* new. I know it's weird to think about, but Landon has had his eye on me for a while. It's why I never went on any dates before. Any guy who asked, he scared them off."

"How comforting," she says dryly.

"You were never going to get to pick out my first boyfriend," I point out gently. "I get that you would have probably preferred a nice guy who doesn't live in the same house as me..."

"I dream big, what can I tell you?" she says dryly.

I crack a smile. "But I think it was supposed to be Landon. I knew in middle school, it just took him a little longer to figure things out."

"Yes, well." She brushes a piece of invisible lint off her skirt. "Boys are stupid."

I laugh, and she looks up at me with a reluctant smile.

"If we're going to even attempt this, there will have to be rules," she states.

I nod, though I feel a bit reluctant. It has been nice living in the wild west era of our relationship, no rules, no labels, no complications aside from our personalities.

"I don't even know how to go about setting them because this is such an unusual situation," she adds.

"I'm not sure, either," I admit. "I don't think we need a ton of rules. You know me. You know I'm responsible. You know I'm not a reckless person."

"I do, but everything I know about Landon is exactly the opposite of that. I don't even understand what you could possibly have in common."

"Not much," I say honestly. "This is definitely one of those opposites attract situations, but I think it works. We balance each other out. You and Hayden are nothing alike, either," I point out.

"That's true," she allows. "But we do share values. When it comes to the important things, we pretty much see eye-to-eye. And even when we don't, we respect each other enough to compromise."

"Trust me, Landon respects me. He does compromise. I know you don't see it, but he has already."

"And you're so young, honey," she says, shaking her head. "You've never even been in a relationship before, let alone one this serious. Living together... it forces the serious aspect of the relationship to develop at a much more accelerated pace."

I can't tell if this is what she's worried about, but in the interest of honesty and sparing her that uncertainty, I decide to be completely truthful. "In the interest of transparency, I know this is awkward, but... um, we have already slept together."

Knowing dread passes across her anxious face. "That's exactly what I was worried about. You've been seeing him for days. Under no ordinary circumstances would you ever sleep with a boy you have only been seeing for days."

"And if he were anyone else, I still wouldn't have," I say gently. "You know me, Mom. I can't be pressured into doing things."

I mean, I was *literally* forced into doing this particular thing, but this is not a time for complete honesty. Looping her in that it happened is one thing, but she absolutely does not need to know the gory details of my sex life.

"I'm with him because I want to be," I tell her, since at least that's true. "Maybe things *will* develop a little faster because we live together, but honestly... who cares?" I shrug, shaking my head to appeal to her less sensible side. "As long as we're happy and healthy, how important is a timeline, really? It doesn't change anything in the long run if we get to where we're going a little faster than we would have if we lived apart."

"No, but that seriousness that develops way too fast does make it more difficult to leave even when you know you should. Believe me, honey, I know. I shouldn't have stayed with your father as long as I did, but I got stuck. Right now, things with Landon may be lovely because they're new, and even not-so-great men can change briefly when they're in a new relation-ship. But then the newness fades and the reality of who they are comes out, and if you've rushed the relationship and your lives are entwined in a way that's very difficult to separate, it is much more difficult to get out of it. Especially you. I know you, you're like me in certain ways. Look at how hard you've worked to keep things smooth with him because you didn't want to mess this up for me. Do you really think if things changed in your relationship with Landon and you wanted out, but he didn't want to let you out, that he wouldn't use that against you?"

I press my lips together, considering how honest I want to be here.

Landon would obviously do that. Without hesitation, without question. She's absolutely correct, and I won't lie, I hadn't thought about that.

But I guess it just doesn't matter. I've already dealt with him using this situation to his advantage, but he won't have the same advantages going forward. I'm not afraid of things I've already conquered.

Being with him has cured me of the fear, and it was the fear he could really use against me.

I don't see us breaking up anytime soon unless he regresses to being a big dumb idiot, but even then, when I look at the arsenal at his disposal, I don't see anything that can break me.

Sure, he might slip into my bedroom or the bathroom or any other semi-private area and force himself on me, but that only shocked me the first time. After I recovered from him coming in my panties to punish me for wearing the shorts in front of his dumb friends, I knew I could survive it, and since I've allowed him access to me since then, the threat has lost its power. If he takes what I want to give him anyway, it doesn't damage me. At worst, it pisses me off.

Conjuring the image now, I can see it. He did something stupid and I had to dump him over it. I'm heartbroken, sure, but also pissed because he was so fucking inconsiderate as to do this *before* I left for college. It could have been so much cleaner then. But he's Landon, he has to be chaotic, so I'm sucking it up to spare our parents a hostile home environment while we live out the rest of our days together. But while I'm me, he's him, so of course he doesn't want to be held accountable for his bad behavior. He didn't want the relationship to be over, he just lost his cool and made a stupid mistake I refuse to forgive him for. So, at the first opportunity, he sneaks into my bedroom. He tries to reason with me, but I'm done, so I tell him to get out. He doesn't. He insists I'm still his, even though I tell him no the fuck I am not, and then he has to show me. He's stronger than I am, so I can't fight him off. All I can do is take it as he pins me down and fucks me despite my protests, even coming inside me because he's a fucking asshole and he'd love to get me pregnant when I'm trying to leave him. What an incredible advantage that would give him in getting me to stay.

This is a very awkward moment to feel turned on, so I promptly shove the image from my mind and shake it off, shifting my attention back to Mom. "I can handle him," I assure her.

Mom looks down at her lap. "We should probably get you on birth control."

"Already done. I went earlier this week."

"You never did tell me when this all started."

"It's hard to put a date on," I admit. "About a week. Two if we're going from the first kiss."

"The night of the party?" she asks knowingly.

Feeling my face flush, I nod. I'm sure giving her a timeline is exposing some of the lies I've had to tell, but she doesn't call me out on it.

"I know I haven't been totally honest with you up to this point," I acknowledge. "I didn't feel like I could be. I *did* feel like I needed to keep things concealed to protect you, but I don't feel that way anymore. When Landon first kissed me downstairs, I thought he was ruining everything, but I'm starting to think he was right. This had to come out so we could all move forward. There's nothing to keep from you now. And I don't want there to be going forward. I've hated lying to you, and if we can just get through this and make space for that openness, there's no reason to worry about the scenarios you're worried about developing. We'll talk about things, just like we would if I were dating any other guy. I won't have to be afraid my relationship is going to wreck yours. That's what we need to get rid of. That's the stressor for me. I know that you are so well-intentioned, but honestly, I know your heart, and I know that you would give up anything to protect me, but right now, I need to know you're *not* going to do that. If it works out with me and Landon, awesome. If it doesn't, that sucks, but it's not going to impact your relationship. You're still going to marry Hayden because Hayden can't help what his son does, and none of us are going to make anyone but Landon pay for Landon's choices."

A wobbly smile tugs at Mom's lips. "When did you get so grown up?"

I roll my eyes good-naturedly. "Sometime around when I learned to read, I think."

"Sounds about right."

"Realistically, I was probably bossing around my stuffies even before then."

Mom leans in and wraps her arms around me, giving me a hug we both need. "I don't know how this will work, and I'm still very worried about things progressing too fast, but... I suppose we can give it a try."

Sighing with relief, I squeeze her. "Good. Great. Just remember, it's not about how fast things happen or what things are conventionally supposed to look like. I want us all to live together, regardless of the intricacies that may entail. I'm going to be with Landon, but I want you to marry Hayden. I want you to be happy. I want me to be happy, too. Don't make me lie to you in order for us both to be happy."

USUALLY, Landon is the one sneaking into my bedroom.

Tonight, I sneak into his.

It's a long night of long conversations with the parents. Newly aware that he's my boyfriend and not just my longtime tormentor, Mom finds reasons to keep me downstairs late. Landon reaches his limit on family time for the day and heads upstairs, and when Mom can barely keep her eyes open, I start yawning and tell her I'm tired, too.

I go to my own room for a while, but once Mom and Hayden are in bed long enough that I imagine they're asleep, I grab the business card off my desk and tiptoe down the hall toward Landon's room.

I don't bother knocking. When I turn the handle, there's no resistance, so I shove open the door.

Like mine, Landon's bedroom has windows all over the place, but at least tonight, he has the shades down so the room is dark.

Since I know it's tidy and I don't risk tripping over anything, I slip inside, close the door behind me, and carefully make my way to his bed.

My eyes adjust to the dark by the time I place my hand on

the mattress. For a few seconds, I think he might be asleep because he isn't saying anything. He's in bed, but his back is to me, so I can't tell.

Trying my best to be gentle in case he is awake, I climb up on my knees on the bed. I crawl forward, but the moment I do, he turns over.

"Well, well, well. Look who's breaking the rules now," he teases.

"You have *no* room to talk about rule breakers."

His hands find my hips and he lifts me, positioning me so I'm straddling his hips. "I wasn't complaining."

I let him situate me so I'm sitting on him because I like it, but I'm appreciative of the dark so I can't get distracted by the view. "You have some explaining to do, mister."

"*I* have some explaining to do?" he demands, his tone sharp with disbelief.

I grab his hand, then I place the business card in his open palm.

His fingers close around it to feel what it is, but he can't see what it is. He shifts beneath me, reaching for something on his nightstand. A second later, his phone screen lights up so he can use the dim light to see.

I cross my arms, watching his face for recognition, but he doesn't give anything away. "Turn it over."

His gaze slides to mine, and I register the flicker of annoyance just before the screen goes dark again.

He doesn't need the light anymore, so he puts the phone back.

"Explain," I demand.

Rather than give the contrite vibe I'm looking for, he slides his hands around to grab my ass. "Explain how you thought you were sending some other asshole your sexy tooth brushing pics so clearly you need this little ass beat?"

"No," I say, leveling him an unamused look he probably can't even see in the dark. "Explain how you did it. Javi handed me that card himself. Why would he write your number on the back?"

"I guess he didn't want to stand in the way of true love."

"Landon."

"Maybe he's not that bright and he just forgot his own phone number. Happy coincidence that he jotted down mine."

"I'm serious. Did you blackmail him? Threaten him with something? How did you get him to do your bidding?"

He's quiet for a second, then he says, "I didn't. He didn't write my number on the back of the card he gave you." Handing it back to me, he says, "This is a different card."

"But that's his handwriting."

"It's not. It's just a really good forgery."

I'm quiet for a moment, absorbing his words, and he's quiet, too.

It's his quiet that activates prior knowledge I haven't thought about in ages.

After Hannah's dad died, Anae used to torment her with forged notes and letters from him. She'd leave them places for Hannah to find when she was alone. I remember when Hannah finally told me about it, how she held the notes with trembling hands, her face white and her eyes brimming with tears. We were just kids back then, and she started to believe that somehow her dad was still alive, and he needed her help... until Anae, apparently bored by the mystery and wanting credit for her cruelty, jotted one down in front of us and then cackled like the witch she is.

You stupid idiots. Ghosts aren't real.

Anae laughed at Hannah believing the letters were really from her dad, but she fooled me, too. The handwriting looked *exactly* like his.

"Anae... she can copy handwriting." That dissolves the good humor I had about this fucked up situation. "You used *Anae Richards* to manipulate me?"

"I had her swap out the cards, that's it. I know you hate her—"

"She's the fucking worst, Landon. She's a monster. She has spent half her life *tormenting* my very best friend." I try to crawl off him because I don't feel like sitting on him anymore, but he grabs my hips to keep me from leaving. "And what did you have to do for her in exchange?" I demand. "Because Anae Richards might be a malicious bitch, but she doesn't work for free."

"It doesn't matter."

"It matters to me," I state.

"I didn't do anything for her."

"Bullshit. Don't lie to me.

"I'm not lying," he says, annoyed. "You know Anae and I aren't friends. I took advantage of her wanting to curry favor with Arden. He asked her to do it for me after he saw what went down at the club that day, so she said yes. It has nothing to do with you or us."

I shake my head, thoroughly uncomfortable with everything he just said. "I don't like that. I don't trust either of them. And how did Arden even know about it?"

"You saw him at the club that day."

"Yeah, I saw him, but he wasn't around when Javi gave me his number."

Landon cocks an eyebrow. "Are you sure he wasn't around?"

I am, but the way he asks makes me doubt myself.

"Or did you just not notice him because you were swept up in your Hannah bubble and not paying attention to your surroundings?"

Dammit.

It *may* have been the Hannah bubble, but I didn't know I needed to be on watch, either.

"Well, I certainly didn't see him. Either way, I don't particularly care for Arden, and I don't want him in my business. I certainly don't want him enlisting Anae Richards to work on your behalf."

"Obviously, I won't need to use her again. But you forced my hand. You knew the score by that point. Did you really think I was going to let you talk to some other fucking guy, Parker? I would've intervened one way or another as soon as I knew what was going on. You're lucky Arden was there and I was able to intervene before you ever *really* talked to the guy, because if he hadn't been and I found you *actually* sending that fucker pictures, I would have had to carve out his fucking eyeballs."

"You're an ass," I state.

"I think I was actually pretty fucking considerate. I knew you'd be pissed if I went after him, and I knew I'd been pretty hard on you, so I let you have a little fun."

"With you," I say sourly.

"I'm the only man of a fuckable age you're allowed to have fun with. Sorry."

"You're a deceitful jerk."

"Sure, if you look at it with that attitude. Reframe it. Think of it as roleplay, you just didn't know it was happening."

"That is literally not how roleplay works," I state as he pushes me back on the bed and rolls over so he's on top of me.

"You want me to do that 'ask for forgiveness' thing you mentioned before?"

Will he?

Out of sheer curiosity, I say, "Yes."

He scowls at me, then leans in to nip at my neck. "Wrong answer."

I push against him to get him off me, but despite my aggravation, I let my hands slide up his muscular chest. "No distractions. We are not done talking."

"Since when has fucking ever stopped you from talking?" he asks dryly, leaning in again to kiss my jaw.

"No," I say again, pushing him away harder. "I still have questions."

"There's only one question. Will I do whatever the fuck it takes to keep you to myself? You know the answer, so act accordingly and I won't have to do any more psycho shit."

Sighing dramatically as he attacks my neck, I ignore the pleasant shiver and tempting tug of arousal. "You don't deserve a reward for bad behavior," I mutter.

"Yeah, well, lucky for me, I don't sit around waiting to see what I deserve." His fingers slide into the waistband of my sleep shorts, and he pushes them down.

"Landon," I complain, trying to push him off me.

He grabs my wrists, pinning them to the mattress and coming down on top of me so his weight is crushing me. "We're done talking about this," he informs me.

My heart leaps and I feel a twinge between my legs, but also a grinding in my brain. "It's like you actively *try* to piss me off."

He smirks, sliding his hand down my panties and grabbing my pussy and feeling how slick I am. "You don't feel very pissed off to me."

I sigh with defeat as he pushes a finger into me.

Fuck.

"I swore I wasn't going to let you distract me with sex."

"Then you set yourself up for failure. Good job, bookworm," he murmurs, pushing his finger deeper into my body.

A light bulb goes off in my head belatedly. "Bookworm. You called me that when you were pretending to be Javi."

He nods, sliding a second finger into me. "I called you that in person once, too, to see if you'd catch it. I dropped you a couple of other hints, too. You missed them."

"Damn. I guess I was off my game," I murmur, my eyes drifting closed as he curls his finger and teases my clit.

"Almost like someone had you distracted," he murmurs teasingly.

My head lolls back, arousal tempting me to give up the fight and just enjoy what he's doing to me.

Amusement thick in his tone, he leans down to kiss my jaw while he finger fucks me. "Maybe I'm not such a dumb jock after all."

"I never called you that," I mutter, though I'm not even sure it's true. He makes me mad a lot. I probably did say that at some point.

"Maybe not to my face," he says wryly.

I can't help smiling as his kisses reach the corner of my mouth. "Whatever insult I flung your way, you more than earned it."

"That's all right. You run your mouth all you want. Just know I'll punish your little ass for it."

His suggestive tone makes my body hum. "Oh, no. Not a punishment," I say, my tone flat. "Anything but that."

Landon grins against my mouth when his kisses finally reach my lips. "Who knew Parker Johansson would be such a freak," he murmurs against them.

"You know what they say. It's always the quiet ones."

How are your muffins?

I'M SITTING at the counter with Landon enjoying some strawberry-topped oatmeal when my phone lights up with a text from Hannah.

Frowning as I read it, I drop my spoon and grab the phone to text her back.

What muffins?

Landon didn't give you the muffins?

I've been so busy with my life blowing up, I haven't even had time to loop Hannah in on what's been happening.

Looking over at Landon sitting next to me, looking sexy as all hell in his workout clothes, I show him the phone. "What's she talking about? What muffins?"

He glances at the screen initially, but then he stops when I ask the second question. "I smashed them."

My eyes widen. "You had Hannah muffins in your possession and you *smashed* them?"

Unapologetically, he says, "Like I'm the motherfucking Hulk. It was right after you told 'Javi' you'd meet him on the beach. I was mad."

"How dare you."

He shrugs. "At least I didn't smash 'em against your tits this time."

"I mean, that would have been more enjoyable. Then you could have licked me clean."

He smirks. "Tell her to make more. I'll pay her double."

That makes me snicker as I text her back. "She charged you?"

"Damn right she charged me."

"That's hilarious. Hannah never asks people to pay for her baked goods."

"What can I say? She must really like me."

A moment later, Hannah confirms.

Sure did. Gave him the bad boyfriend discount.
I'll make more and give them to you directly.

Thank you, my beautiful muffin making angel.

"Why do you do that?" Landon asks.

I look over, surprised to see him reading my texts. "That's shady. Do what?"

"Flirt with her."

My eyes widen slightly. "I don't *flirt* with her. We're friends. When girls are friends, they say nice things to each other. It's basically the opposite of boy friendship."

He rolls his eyes. "All I'm saying is you've never called *me* your beautiful muffin making angel."

"You've never made me muffins *or* been an angel. And I tell you how hot you are all the time." I put the phone down and pick my spoon back up. "Besides, Hannah lives with people who do their best to tear her down at every turn. As her friend, I consider it my responsibility to give her little boosts to make sure she never forgets they're pieces of shit and she's amazing."

"She should move out."

I nod my agreement. "I've been running a campaign to get her to move into the pool house, but I haven't had much success. I know it's Hannah, and she's not one to get off the ship she's emotionally attached to even if she knows it's sinking, but I really think that house is more of a noose around her neck than anything at this point."

His eyebrows rise. "I didn't mean here. Why don't you let her move into your old house instead? Not like we need to sell it. I think Dad already paid it off, so as long as she paid the utilities... frankly, I'd be willing to pay them for her if it keeps her out of my pool house."

"Hey," I say, shooting him a dirty look.

"She'll take up too much of your time if she lives here. You know I'm a greedy bastard."

"But think of all the fun movie nights we could have."

"I would rather have more time alone to fuck you," he states.

"Well, that's nice to walk in on."

I light up with a mix of horror and humiliation when I turn to see Hayden striding in, dressed for work with a briefcase in hand.

My spoon clatters as it fits the edge of the bowl. "Oh, my god," I say, covering my face because I *can't* look at him.

"Good morning, Parker," he says dryly, walking over to the coffeepot.

I remain hidden. "Parker has died, this is her ghost."

"Your mother's about to leave for work, so she'll be down any minute. If you two could keep it PG until we left, that would be much appreciated."

"What'll you give me for it?" Landon asks.

Hayden slides him a dry look. "Don't push your luck."

"I'm just saying, I think if Parker and I could share a bedroom on this vacation we're all going on, I could probably muster a little goodwill."

"We might even be able to get him in Mickey ears for a family photo," I suggest.

"Hey, now," Landon says, sliding me a look. "Whose side are you on?"

I shrug innocently. "I'm on my own side. I want the

picture."

He shakes his head. "It's a no on the ears. I might consider one of those stupid shirts, but it's gonna cost you."

"PG," Hayden reminds him.

"Yeah, yeah, yeah. Nobody in this house ever lets me have any fun."

Hayden smirks at me and I smile too, despite the intense embarrassment of what he overheard.

SUNDAY ROLLS around and for the first time since we've moved in, Mom and Hayden go out for a date night and leave Landon and me home by ourselves.

I could tell Mom was still a bit anxious, but I assured her we were just going to bum around and watch TV. Nothing exciting whatsoever.

Before their car is even out of the driveway, Landon is on the floor in front of the couch, spreading my legs and helping himself to his favorite "snack."

We really do get to have a lazy day after that, though.

My body is relaxed as I snuggle up against him, sliding my arms around his middle and resting my head on his shoulder while we watch our home improvement show.

I've become deeply invested in the personal lives of the couple that host the show.

Well, former couple. They were married when the show started, but they got divorced a couple of seasons ago and things got a little messy.

For a while, we watched them throw jabs at each other and try adjusting to their new relationship dynamic as divorced coworkers. The end of the last season was a bit rough. The ex-wife missed a few episodes, and the ones she was in, she was trying to stay out of frame to cover up what appeared to be a baby bump.

In this episode, she was introduced with a new last name, so it seems she has officially fully moved on.

Landon rolls his eyes as the former husband and wife bicker, with her laughing about his new efforts at manscaping, and him teasing her about how good he looks at the beach now.

"This guy's so fucking lame," Landon says, grabbing a handful of popcorn out of the bowl between us.

I pop a piece in my mouth, too. "He's trying to make the best of a less than ideal situation. I'm sure it's super awkward having to try to navigate a whole new relationship dynamic on TV."

"Should've made the situation better before she divorced him, then there wouldn't *be* a new dynamic to figure out. Now he has to watch her bounce around the house with some other guy's last name instead of his. It's embarrassing."

"I think he filed for the divorce, actually."

"Had to be because he knew she was going to, then. Wanted to beat her to the punch. He seems petty like that, but she's clearly the one that got sick of his shit, not the other way around. You can see he still wants her, it's just fucking embarrassing because she *was* his wife. Guy had the ball in his hands and he fucking fumbled it."

"People fumble balls sometimes. It happens. And sometimes people get along better once they separate," I point out. "At least they can still work together to provide for their family. It's how they make their living. What, you would just let your kids go hungry because you couldn't set aside your own petty bullshit to work with your ex-wife?"

His eyebrows rise. "My kids will never have to worry about going hungry, and I'll never *have* an ex-wife. You think I'd let my wife leave me, run off and marry some other fucker, have his baby, and then I'd swallow that shit and poke fun at her with a camera crew around to watch the spectacle? I don't fucking think so. My show would be a true crime documentary about how I murdered the asshole she tried to leave me for and convinced her to help me bury him."

I shake my head, grabbing some popcorn. "That's so mean."

"Mean, my ass. The vows say 'til death do we part. Don't marry me if you don't mean it."

"I'm gonna marry you and leave you for someone I don't like just to get you to do my dirty work for me. Ha, you thought I liked that jerk. Joke's on you. Thanks for the help."

Landon smirks. "Easier ways to get it done. I'm gonna be real mean to you in bed for a while to pay you back for liking some other asshole. If you want me to take out the trash for you, just ask."

"I can't believe you're so anti-divorce. I never even pictured you getting married."

He shrugs. "I don't care about the party or the paperwork. Whether we're married or just doing life together without the ring exchange... I don't care what your last name is, but what's mine is gonna stay that way." Glancing at me, he says, "You should know I take commitments very seriously. Hell, I've been holding you to one you didn't even realize you were making when you were 12 years old."

I smile, grabbing another piece of popcorn. Honestly, I'm low key delighted by his stance on all this, but for science, I have to keep poking at him.

"What if we got divorced and you met the hottest woman you've ever seen in your life, and I met the coolest guy you've ever met in your life, and we could have the coolest blended family ever? It would be like your ultimate dream group hang."

"Nope. I don't blend. You marry me, that's it. You're staying married to me."

"Period?"

"The end. No returns. No exceptions."

I smile and lean in for a kiss. "You're unreasonable," I tease.

His hand curls possessively around my waist, pulling me a little closer. "Damn right."

ONCE WE'VE TIRED of the lazy part of lazy Sunday, we get some stuff done—together. I solve the mystery of whether Landon does homework when we do some together. I have an Uplift club meeting this week, so I spend a little time preparing for that in case I'm too busy over the next few days with Landon time now added to my schedule.

Afterward, he says he's going to hit the gym. I decide to tag along. Not to work out, but I want to watch.

Watching Landon work out is *definitely* superior than getting myself sweaty. Although watching him get sweaty does get me a little hot.

When he's done working out, as he peels off his sweaty shirt on his way to the shower, he glances back at me. "You coming?"

I bite down on my bottom lip uncertainly. Landon has seen me naked when we've been in bed before, but this feels different. Not more intimate, exactly, but familiar in a way that feels new.

"I don't know," I say, playing off my uncertainty as I follow him into the bathroom. "I mean, you've seen selfies of me brushing my teeth. I don't know if I can live up to that level of sexiness."

He smirks, embodying sexiness himself as he reaches in the

shower and turns on the water to let it warm up. His body is so beautiful, even the way it moves doing such a casual thing makes me sigh.

Turning back to me, his green eyes warm and affectionate as he saunters toward me, he ebbs some of my doubts.

I let him grab my hips and pull me toward him, then I slide my arms around his neck and look up at him. "Hi."

"Hi," he returns with an intimate smile that's just for me, one that makes my stomach explode with butterflies. He pulls me in for a kiss that makes my heart kick up a speed, then he lets his fingertips move lightly down my spine before he grabs my ass. "Now, take off your clothes and get your pretty ass in the shower."

"So bossy," I tease, lightly nipping his bottom lip before pulling back.

By the time I'm finished undressing, the shower is steamed up and ready for us. Landon put a couple of towels on the counter for when we get out, but I'm just realizing we have no clean clothes.

"Should I run upstairs and—?"

He grabs my wrist, tugging me toward the walk-in shower stall.

"Okay, guess not," I murmur, following him in. "This will shock you, but I've never showered with anyone before."

"I know," he says before moving under the spray.

I stand behind him, licking my lips as the hot water soaks his hair and runs down his body, hitting every ridge of his slick muscles. My gaze naturally follows the stream down his abdomen,

My tummy jumps and I look away. "Sometimes I think it's offensive how hot you are. Like... eat some cookies."

He smirks, his muscles flexing almost just to be contrary as he runs his fingers through his hair. "I'll eat cookies if you make 'em for me."

I feel a bit awkward standing here with him just looking at me while he showers, so I cross my arms and try to shake the feeling.

His dark eyebrows rise immediately. "Don't do that."

"What?" I ask, playing dumb.

He slides me a knowing look. "Hide yourself. That pisses me off."

"The list of what *doesn't* piss you off would probably be shorter," I half-joke.

He steps out from under the spray, coming over to grab me, then he pulls me under the spray with him.

I like it better over here. His warmth provides a bit of coverage for me, too, as our fronts touch. I wrap my arms around him, and my scalp tingles pleasantly as he runs his fingers through my hair to get it all wet under the spray.

Since we're entwined the way we are, his lips are near my ear when he murmurs, "There is not one inch of this body I don't want to be intimately familiar with. I know we joked about your toothbrush selfie, but I wasn't joking. I think everything you do is sexy."

A shiver dances down my spine as he pulls me close, his grip firm, and holds my body possessively against his while he kisses my neck.

My eyes drift close as he makes his way down my neck, then I sigh with pleasure when his greedy mouth gets to my breasts. He squeezes and sucks, leaving love bites with one breath and soothing them with the next.

Lust curls through me when he grips his cock, then takes my hand and guides it there to take over.

He's kissing my shoulder, so I feel the reverberations of his low groan against my skin as I stroke him.

I want to do more than stroke him, so I sink to my knees and look up at him. "I want to taste you."

He looks down at me, running a hand through my wet hair. "Fuck, Parker." His other hand goes to my face, and I lean into his hand like an eager pet greeting its master.

That lights a fire in his eyes. His cock hardens in my hand, and feeling emboldened by his sweet words, I bring it close and kiss it before letting my tongue dart out and licking him base to tip.

His hand in my hair tightens and his head lolls back. I take that to mean I'm doing a good job.

I want to keep doing a good job, so I grip his cock and take it into my mouth the way he showed me to. Water streams down his stomach and drips on my face, but I don't care. I kneel here and pleasure him until he stops me, then I stand, my pussy throbbing and ready for him.

He turns me to face the wall, grabbing my hands and planting them where he wants them. Then he tells me to bend over, and I do.

I expect his cock to slide in a moment later, but as I stand here with my legs spread, I notice the spray change and I look over to see him grab the shower wand. Wide-eyed, I look at him. "What are you doing?"

"You know I prefer getting two orgasms out of you than one. Might as well make use of the tools available to us."

"Landon, I don't—"

But before I can object, he comes up behind me, pressing his slick body against mine. He slides a hand down between my legs to spread me open, then he uses the other to position the shower head right against my pussy.

I gasp in shock at the force of the spray against that sensitive flesh.

He lets it hit me for a few seconds, but then he moves the

wand, testing out my response to different areas. The sharpest inhale is where he stops and focuses his attention. My hand slides and I quickly fix my grip on the wall, my body shaking as the hot spray assaults my clit.

"Landon..."

He kisses the ball of my shoulder, then splays his hand across my stomach to hold me back against him.

The spray is so hard, I don't know how much more I can take. Pleasure ripples through me and I let go of the wall with one hand, reaching back to grab his hip. He rotates the spray away and makes me shudder, then he brings it back to the best spot and brings it even closer.

I cry out sharply, my fingers digging into his hips as my body tenses. And then pleasure erupts inside me, bright white light exploding behind my eyes as it pours through me.

I can't take it anymore, so I reach down to push the spray away, sagging as all the strength vacates my body.

Landon quickly turns the spray back so it's coming down on us, positions me against the wall again while I'm still woozy, then guides his cock between my thighs and pushes into me.

My pussy is so sensitive, I groan as he pushes in. He doesn't take his time to ease me in, either. He shoves deep until I'm so full of him, I feel it in my guts, then he starts fucking me when I can barely stand upright.

By the time I've come the second time, I'm ready to melt into a puddle on the shower floor.

I don't have the strength to stand, but he does, so I hang onto him, eyes closed beneath the spray as I wait for strength to come back to me.

"We should probably start getting clean," he says lightly.

"Can't," I murmur against his slick skin. "Can't move."

He chuckles, then he grabs the shampoo bottle and—to my immense surprise—starts lathering up my hair. The shower is hot and fragrant, and my scalp tingles as he works his fingers through my hair.

It's such a tender thing, him washing my hair.

I feel so loved. So cherished.

So well taken care of.

I've regained enough strength to rinse the shampoo out of my hair when the time comes, but I let him do it because it just feels nicer.

When he's done washing my hair, he starts lathering up his own, but I enjoyed when he did it to me so much, I decide to return the favor.

That leads to another round of fucking, which, on reflection, I probably should have predicted.

We've used far more than our fair share of water by the time we emerge, but I'm so satisfied that I can't bring myself to care.

Since we have no clean clothes to put on, we have to wrap ourselves in the fluffy white towels and scamper upstairs. I make Landon check around corners since he just has a towel wrapped around his waist and I feel more naked than he is. He's not shy, anyway, but the coast is clear.

We make it to his bedroom, then I ditch the towel and climb into his bed beneath his comforter. Once I'm nice and cozy, I peek out to watch him drop his towel, then climb on the bed with me.

"Am I allowed under here?"

"I suppose so."

He rips back the blanket and slides in with me, then he grabs me and squeezes my side. "So kind of you to let me into my own bed," he teases.

"I know," I say primly. "I'm basically a saint."

He smirks and lean in to kiss my sainted lips, which, of course, makes me feel like quite the sinner.

"I don't have the stamina to go another round," I warn him.

He chuckles, sliding his hands under me so he can pull me against him and wrap his arms around my waist. "That's okay."

I was nice and warm snuggled up under the covers, but I'm even cozier wrapped up in his arms.

Before long, I fall asleep. Inevitable given how nice it is to be cuddled up in his arms naked.

Unfortunately, what wakes us is a knock on the door.

"Just a sec," Landon calls, his voice rough from sleep.

"Shit," I murmur, holding the blanket tighter against my chest.

"Is Parker in there with you?" Hayden asks through the door.

I grimace. One of the rules we all agreed on was that we would exercise discretion. This probably isn't it.

"I'll be out in just a second," I say apologetically.

I hear Hayden sigh on the other side of the door, and the horror of disappointing an authority figure has me out of bed quicker than anything. "I'll be waiting right here. Make it quick, please."

"Go in my closet," Landon mutters, rubbing his eyes as he reluctantly sits up. "You can grab one of my T-shirts."

I'm flustered as I hustle over to the closet and open the door. His T-shirts are all hanging up, so it's easy enough to grab one for me and one for him. I tug the one I picked for myself on, but my legs are still far too bare.

"Do you have sweatpants I can borrow?"

He nods. "They're in the drawers. Pants, shorts. Take whatever," he says, grabbing the shirt I brought out for him.

I head back to the closet, but being in here alone while he waits on the bed feels almost as invasive as it felt the night I packed his bag for Malek's.

Suddenly remembering the time Brittany left her shirt here

hoping he would find it, I call back, "I'm not going to find a treasure trove of random girl clothes in here, am I?"

He startles me, appearing in the doorway as he pulls on his shirt. "Why would I have girl clothes?"

"From all the panties that have been dropped at your feet," I say dryly. "Ugh, I don't have panties. God, I need to stash an emergency outfit in your room or something."

Landon joins me in the closet, reaching into a basket overhead.

I'm horrified when he hands me a pair of panties.

"Ew, I'm not wearing some girl's panties, Landon."

He smirks. "They're yours."

"What?" I scowl at him.

He steals my panties all the time and puts them in his pocket, but I always end up getting them back. And these aren't even panties, they're... bikini bottoms.

Recognition hits me, and my jaw drops open when I realize why they're familiar. "These are the bikini bottoms I was wearing at that party sophomore year."

He nods, reaching into a drawer to get himself some pants.

"You kept them?"

"Obviously."

"Why?"

"Why do you think?" he asks, stepping into a pair of fitted sweats.

I stare at the bikini bottoms I lost years ago. To be honest, I was in such a rush to get away from him that night, I didn't even think about what happened to them. "It's not exactly a great memory," I point out, feeling a touch awkward to have to bring it up.

He shrugs. "Good memories, bad memories. They're all memories of us, so I'll take 'em."

I crack a smile as I step into them. "That's kind of sweet."

Before I can say anything else, there's a less patient knock at the door.

Spurred to action, I quickly pull up the sweats I stole from Landon and steal a glance in the mirror.

That was a mistake.

My hair is a frizzy mess of bedhead and my skin is flushed from sleeping in the arms of the sexy space heater standing behind me. I look bedraggled and ridiculous in his clothes, but Landon catches sight of my reflection and smiles, wrapping his arms around my waist and gazing at our reflection like I'm the prettiest girl in the world.

"I can see why you're so obsessed with me. Look at me rocking these sweats," I joke.

"Right?" he says, kissing my neck. "Eleven out of ten, easy."

He makes me blush and smile like an idiot. "You're a ridiculous liar."

His eyebrows rise. "You better watch how you talk about my girl. I'll beat your pretty little ass."

"Don't threaten me with a good time."

Landon smirks and gives me a smack on the ass, but since his father is still waiting in the hall, he also finally lets me out of the closet.

Hayden is waiting on the other side of the door, looking excessively unimpressed. The look intensifies when he looks at me in Landon's clothes, with my hair looking like I've just been ravished.

"This isn't what it looks like," I assure him. "We fell asleep, but we weren't doing anything. I mean, just now. Up here! In his bed at all. I mean..." I grimace. "I'll just stop talking."

"That would probably be for the best," Hayden says wryly. "Your mother is waiting downstairs. We brought home dessert from the restaurant."

"Ooh, yummy." I shoot him a teasing look. "How was your date?"

"We had a very nice time," he assures me.

"Think you'll see her again?"

He cracks a smile. "I have a hunch."

"Better not have gotten handsy with her," Landon says, surprising me by joining in. "We practice discretion in this house, young man."

Hayden shoots his son an unamused look, but I laugh, feeling good about an actual, playful interaction between them.

It may not seem like much between most fathers and sons, but considering their relationship up to this point, I'd say it's a very good start.

"HEY, have you seen Parker around here anywhere?"

I don't ask Hannah why she's dressed up the way she is when I catch her coming out of the bathroom. To be honest, I might not notice except for the fact that she has a dab of black makeup on her nose as well as black lipstick, and that is not her usual look.

Hannah opens her mouth to answer, but before she can, Parker comes charging out of the girl's bathroom in an identical costume and my jaw fucking drops.

Parker looks immediately guilty, and now I see why she snuck out of the fucking house without me this morning when we usually ride to school together.

Like Hannah, Parker is wearing a fuck ton of face makeup with some dabbed on her nose and black lipstick. Her long red hair is tied up in buns on each side of her head, and she's wearing a skintight black miniskirt with a cropped black and white fuzzy panda sweater that bares a swatch of her midriff.

What the fuck.

"Nope," I say immediately.

"Before you say no," Parker attempts, but I cut her off.

"Too late. I already said it."

"It's for the pandas," she states, shooting me a disgruntled look. "Official Uplift business. The kid we put in charge of the 'save the pandas' fundraiser completely dropped the ball. He had weeks to fundraise, but he didn't, and the deadline is today. We have to raise $5,000 *today* in order to reach our goal, so we're dressing like this to draw extra attention to our cause."

"There's no way in hell those skirts aren't violating the dress code."

"Look who's concerned about rules all of a sudden," Hannah murmurs.

I shoot her a look and she plays at innocence while Parker simply defends her position. "They're definitely against dress code, but I'm basically a rich kid now. I can wear whatever I want, and no one will say anything about it," she says haughtily.

"I will personally rip those clothes off your body if you don't go change right now."

She shakes her head, reaching into her bag and pulling out a clipboard. "Nope. I'm not changing until we've raised the money. If you'd like to help us collect donations, maybe we'll get there faster, but—"

I grab the clipboard out of her hand. "Give me a pen."

She reaches into her bag and hands over a pen.

I write my name in the first slot, then I jot down $5,000 under donation amount. "The pandas are saved," I state, handing back the clipboard. "Now, go change your fucking clothes."

Parker gapes at the clipboard, then her big doe eyes shoot back to me. "Is this a serious donation?"

"Sure is."

"You have to actually pay this amount."

"Is that how a donation works?"

She shoots me a look, but then she looks down at the clipboard and brightens. "Wow. Well, I guess we did it," she says, looking over at Hannah.

Hannah tugs at the bottom of her tight skirt. "Great. I figured it would take all day, so I didn't bring a change of clothes."

"At least it's Halloween weekend," I say.

"Do you want my clothes to change into?" Parker offers. "I can just steal clothes from Landon."

Hannah shakes her head. "That's okay. We went to all this trouble. I'll just wear it. Maybe I'll get more donations," she says brightly.

"Save the pandas even harder." Parker nods. "I like it."

"Bring your clipboard by my table at lunch and you can easily double it if you're wearing that," I advise her. "Not you," I tell Parker, pointing back at the bathroom. "You go put on something that won't cause me to beat people up."

"You know only *you* can cause you to beat people up, right?" Despite her words, she comes over to give me a kiss.

I glance down the hall, then back the other way. Since there's no one around, I slide an arm around her and tug her in for a better kiss.

"I don't know how good this lipstick is. I might get it all over you," she murmurs, pulling back when her lips are inches from mine.

"It's a risk I'm willing to take," I say before closing the distance.

"Mm. Do you like my sexy panda costume?" she teases, her lips still close enough to kiss.

Since my hand is resting on the soft fabric at the small of her back, I can tell it feels nice. "You can wear it for me later while the parents are at Fright Night."

Sighing, she says, "I love when they have date nights."

"I'm just glad I spent my time making panda sweaters for *your* benefit," Hannah remarks with light amusement.

Parker pulls back, smiling faintly at her friend. "Hey, they *did* get the donation we needed, just not in the way we planned. They're great sweaters, so soft and cozy. Maybe you could repurpose yours and wear it for Halloween."

"Eh, maybe," she says, but she doesn't sound interested. "I was working on a different costume, but I haven't had time to finish it. I suppose I could have spent the time I wasted making these on that, but I didn't realize we could just threaten Landon with someone seeing your legs and he'd hand over a check. My mistake. I *should* have known that."

Parker wraps a comforting arm around Hannah's shoulders. "You just don't possess the loan shark mentality required for brainstorming shakedowns."

"If I had a dollar for every time that was a problem for me," Hannah jokes.

SINCE PARKER DIDN'T WANT Hannah to be a lonely panda, she kept the sweater on, but paired it with black leggings instead of the short skirt. She also left on the panda makeup since there wasn't time to take it off before school started, so she and Hannah spend the rest of the school day canvasing for donations between classes.

Anae gets annoyed at lunch when she realizes she was left out of the panda prostitution ring, and even *more* annoyed when Arden pledges $10k after Parker strategically showed off my donation. The guy can't be outdone.

Given Arden is *her* date to his Fright Fest afterparty tomorrow night, Anae is also enraged watching him not bother to hide his enjoyment of Hannah's skimpy costume before coaxing her to come hold the clipboard for him while he jots down his donation.

Either unaware of or indifferent to Anae's intensifying anger, when he hands the pen back to Hannah, he asks, "You're coming to my party tomorrow night, right?"

Hannah flushes, focusing her attention on the pen as she slides it beneath the clip. "Um, I'm not sure."

"You better," he teases, with his usual easy charm. "I won't have fun without you."

Hannah flashes him an uneasy smile before turning and hightailing it back to the table she sits at with Parker.

Ordinarily, I would not give a fuck, but given my girlfriend is fiercely protective of the girl, I know if Hannah has a bad time, I'm gonna have a bad time, too.

"What are you doing?" I ask him.

"Good deeds," he said dryly. "I hear the pandas need saving."

"Not the donation." I shake my head. "Don't fuck with Hannah. I don't want to hear about it. And didn't you ask Anae to the party?"

"We're coordinating costumes. We're not getting married."

"She'll fucking kill you both, and I'm not exaggerating," I state.

Arden rolls his eyes, reaching for his drink. "I'm not afraid of Anae Richards."

"You're not gonna score with Hannah Dupont, either," Malek says, inserting himself into the conversation. "That girl's untouchable."

"For you, maybe," Arden says with a smirk, causing Malek to roll his eyes. "I know who's already touched her, and I happen to think I'm just her type."

"Bullshit," Malek says, not buying it for a minute. "Anyone who claims to have scored with Hannah's a fucking liar."

Arden shakes his head, and I frown at the smug look on his face, like he knows something we don't. "Didn't have to be told. I saw it for myself."

At that, Malek scowls. "Who?"

Arden smirks, enjoying having information someone else wants. Especially Malek, because they're friends, and while Arden would probably never admit it, he needs to best everyone—especially us. "Let's just say the last guy who played with Anae Richards got a two for one deal, and I'm interested in the same package."

Now it's my turn to call bullshit. "I don't know what you think you saw, but I have it on very good authority that Dare never fucked Hannah."

"You know he and Anae essentially had an open relationship? She let him fuck whoever he wanted. And you think he *didn't* take advantage of the knockout bringing him drinks at his girlfriend's house?" Arden asks, cocking an eyebrow in disbelief.

"I know people said some shit about how he used to sneak into her room when he was dating Anae, but honestly... even if he did, it was against her will, and he never went all the way with her. I know for a fact Hannah's still a virgin."

Arden shrugs. "So she's his unfinished business, then. I'm happy to finish it for him."

"You keep dreaming, asshole," Malek says, grabbing at his French fries rather aggressively.

"I don't have to dream. I have a plan, and it's already in motion."

"Keep telling yourself that."

"Since you're so sure I won't succeed, why don't we make it interesting?" Arden suggests, steepling his hands on the table.

Malek's eyebrows rise in challenge. "What'd you have in mind?"

"Before the end of the year, I'm going to complete Dare's hit list. Anae's a given, I'm already working on that, but I'll do what he couldn't. I'm going to fuck her virginal little stepsister, too."

Unease causes my shoulders to tense. "I don't fucking like this."

Malek's gaze is locked with Arden's. He leans forward, his eyes glittering with anticipation. "Name your stakes, pretty boy."

"When I succeed, you have to *give* me the Aperta. If I fail, I'll buy it from you for double its value."

Malek considers his offer. He's been taunting Arden with that fucking car since he got it. Under normal circumstances, Malek would be happy to sell it, but since Arden *can* be such an asshole, he's held off on selling it to *him*.

Malek doesn't need the money, but he hates the fucking car and he'd rather buy something else. If Arden could find one, he'd probably buy his own Aperta just to spite him, but it's a very limited-edition Ferrari, and frankly, there haven't been any on the market.

"You're going to pay me six million dollars for that fucking car?" Malek asks, eyebrows raised.

"*If* I lose."

Malek smirks. "Done."

I stand, grabbing my tray as they reach across the table to shake on it.

Malek's gaze shifts to me as he drops Arden's hand. "Where the hell are you going?"

"To sit with Parker. I can't be a party to this bullshit." Looking back at them, I warn them, "If anyone ever finds out about this stupid fucking bet, I was not here. Anyone who says otherwise can count on a fucking fight."

AFTER A LONG ASS day at school, all I want to do is relax at home with Parker.

Actually, I can't wait to peel off that fucking panda sweater and feast on her pretty little tits, but we have to wait for the parents to leave before I can do that.

Halloween is a whole thing at Baymont High. There are two full nights of events. Tonight is Fright Night, a fancy fundraising thing Baymont parents attend to raise money for the school. The venue changes annually, but tonight, they're hosting it on the Prince family's superyacht.

Tomorrow night is Fright Fest, this lame fucking thing the school puts on for the students. Parker has been helping plan it so I have to go this year, but usually I skip it and hit up Arden's party afterward.

After the bullshit he pulled today, I don't know if I even want to go this year. Parker's not much for parties, anyway. Maybe I'll entice her to stay in by suggesting she invite Hannah over to our place after Fright Fest. We can watch scary movies in the media room instead. That way, I can also make sure Hannah doesn't wind up there without really getting involved.

I don't think Hannah would go for Arden, honestly, but I know the guy, and I know once he has his sights set on something, he finds a way to get it.

"Hayden, I can't find my purse."

Gemma's tone is anxious as she glides through the living room with the grace of a dancer, her long off-white gown fanning out a bit as she turns on a dime.

I think Gemma's always a little anxious, but I haven't seen her *this* tightly wound in a few weeks.

When she first discovered I was sleeping with her daughter, she was anxious and uncomfortable every time I was near her.

I get it. I've been a problem in Parker's life for a long time, and even as a romantic interest, I'm hardly known as a guy who sticks around. I understood her skepticism, and I understood from what Parker told me that Gemma probably had a sensitivity about it, anyway, because of Parker's dad blowing up their family and making Gemma a single mom. If I had to guess, it lurks at the back of her mind that I'm exactly the kind of guy who would do the same thing to her daughter.

She's wrong, but I would have let her be wrong about me. Doesn't matter much what people think as long as Parker knows.

It was upsetting Parker, though, so one day I caught Gemma out by the pool alone when she was waiting for my dad to get off work and sat down with her.

I told her I understood why she didn't like me, and I knew I hadn't done myself any favors in that department, but she'd never have to worry about me hurting her daughter. I told her I may be an asshole, but I'm the asshole who adores her daughter, and I'd sooner cut off my own arm than break Parker's heart. I told her if Parker ever gets married, it's going to be to me. If she ever gives her grandbabies, I'll be their father. I told her I was completely serious about her daughter, that it's not a game to me, and there is virtually no chance we will ever break up. Then I told her since what we both wanted was to see Parker happy, it might be a good idea if we tried a little harder to get along.

My speech seemed to ease some of her anxiety while probably contributing to a few new sources.

But since then, I think she's gotten used to the idea that I'm not going anywhere. More than that, seeing me with Parker every day, I think she finally believes me. While she was tentative about me being her daughter's boyfriend, since I announced my intention to be her *husband*, she realized it *would* be best to embrace me.

Personally, I don't care about Gemma's motivations or if she likes me. But it's important to Parker, so I had to take care of it.

I watch Gemma being a neurotic mess, and my father's steadying grip on her arms as he pulls her in and demands to know what's wrong. I expect her to say she can't find her purse since that's what she was just bitching about, but she looks up at him and says, "Maybe this isn't right. Parker has panda makeup on."

He blinks at her. "What?"

"I know it's just us, but I do want a nice photo of us all together to remember it by. And what if...?"

He stops her before she can continue. "I'll make sure Parker is ready. You just go upstairs and find your purse. Grab a different one if you need to. We have to get going."

"I'm not even sure about these shoes," Gemma murmurs, but she turns and heads upstairs anyway.

My dad watches her until she's out of sight, then he comes over and approaches me. "Can I talk to you for a minute?"

I nod, and he takes a seat on the couch beside me.

"I need to ask a favor."

"Need a Xanax for the wife?"

He appears unamused. "No. Parker's costume, why is that happening?"

"School thing. She was fundraising to save pandas. Dressed up for the occasion."

"All right. Well, when we leave, can you get her in the shower?"

I smirk. "Now that's a favor I can grant."

He ignores my comment and soldiers on. "I need you both

dressed and ready to leave at around 9:30. The event ends at 10. Wear something nice. Have Parker wear a pretty dress, something somewhat formal."

I frown. "Why?"

"Because I need you to meet us at the marina at 10. The plan was for it to be a surprise, but while surprising Parker is fine, given our history... I wanted to talk to you ahead of time."

Meet him at the marina?

I sit up a little straighter.

"I know you haven't gone out on the boat in some time," Dad begins. "I don't want to bring up bad memories for you, and I'm not sure this will even make sense to you, but... your mother is *why* I want to do this. It's the last place she was happy, the last place she was *with us*. The sea is her final resting place, and in a sense, I feel like if we do it there, some part of her is with us. And I truly believe she would like Gemma. That she would give this her blessing if she could."

"You're going to marry her."

He nods slowly, his blue eyes glinting with emotion. "That's the plan," he says, almost gently. "I want to do it tonight, on the boat. The captain can marry us. It will be just us, an intimate thing. Gemma hasn't been married before, but she knows I prefer a very intimate wedding. I married your mother by the water. I'd like to marry Gemma there, too, but I would like your blessing."

I stare at him, my jaw locked and my arms crossed. My father isn't a man who can be intimidated, but I can tell from the tension in his body, he's uneasy about what I'm going to say.

With reason.

But, for all the resistance I put up when he first moved Gemma in, I don't have it in me to object now. Not only would I break my dad's heart, but Parker would be so pissed off, she'd bury me in a grave of angry green octopuses.

"You have it," I say simply.

The tension eases out of his shoulders immediately. "Thank you, Landon."

I crack a smile and nod. "Guess that explains why she's spiraling over a purse."

"She's nervous."

"I'd be nervous too if I were marrying you," I say dryly.

Dad rolls his eyes, preparing to stand. "I don't know what you mean. I'm a delight."

"You're something, all right."

"DO you think these shoes are okay?"

I smile faintly as Mom turns in the mirror, popping her leg through the sexy slit and examining her nude heel. "You look amazing," I assure her.

"Maybe I should have worn white. At least white heels. I should have bought new shoes for this," she murmurs.

Mom has been so much more relaxed than this lately, I can't believe she's freaking out over shoes. Shaking my head, I help her pick out a purse and convince her that her shoes are perfect, then I hurry her downstairs so they're not late leaving.

I'm looking forward to being lazy with Landon tonight. We finished our house flipping show, but there are spinoff shows for each of the hosts since they split up, and I'm dying to start hers.

Landon was supposed to make popcorn while I was upstairs helping Mom get ready, but when we finally get them out the door and I return to the living room, there is no popcorn.

"You didn't make snacks."

"I'm afraid I have bad news. Good news, too. But... there's bad news."

My enthusiasm ebbs. "What's the bad news?"

"You're going to have to wait until Sunday to start your show."

I plant my hand on my hip and look up at his trouble-making ass as he approaches. "Now, you listen here. I'm always happy to fuck you, but that does not take four hours. We can push off watching the show until later if you want, but—"

Smirking, he cuts me off, wrapping a hand around my waist and tugging me close. "That's not what I meant. Our plans have changed. Not because I want to fuck you. I do, and I probably will at some point before the night is over, but not right now. Right now, I need you to take your pretty little ass to the shower, and make it quick."

Intrigued, I ask, "Where are we going?"

"Shopping. Then you have a hair appointment, and we need to try to get there before the salon closes."

I blink. If he would have told me were going to a field and picking daisies, I could not be more surprised. "What?"

"You'll see."

I HAVE OBVIOUSLY NOTICED—AND appreciated—that Landon has a dominant streak, but in no reality did I ever imagine him taking me shopping and helping me pick out a dress.

He doesn't care about fashion, but he still picks out the dresses he wants me to try on. He helps me with zippers when I need it, lingering in the dressing room with me and admiring the way the gowns fit on my body, and especially the way they come off.

I don't know why I need a gown. We already went to homecoming, but he said I couldn't wear that one, that I needed a new dress for tonight.

We narrow it down to two.

One is feminine and flowy on the bottom, but the top is fitted and sexy with thin straps. The bottom is such a pale pink it almost looks white, and the top is a darker shade, closer to rose gold, and sparkly.

The other is a gorgeous, fiery gown with a plunging V neckline. It's tighter than the first one, and I think the mix of browns and reds suits my complexion better—especially after Anae made fun of me for wearing pastels when she came over that one day.

Annoying to have her voice in my head when Landon picks that one to buy.

"Are you sure?" I ask him.

His brow furrows. "You don't like it?"

"It's beautiful, but do you think it looked good on me?"

His expression turns stony. "What kind of question is that? Of course it looked good on you."

"Anae said I don't look good in pale colors. She said I look like a sickly Brontë heroine."

His eyes darken with anger and he rips the hanger off the hook. "Anae's a fucking idiot. Why would you listen to anything she says?"

I know he's right, but sometimes the mean things people say tend to hang around in my mind longer than the praise.

I loved the dress, and if Landon thinks I look pretty in it, it doesn't matter what anyone else thinks, anyway.

"Can we stop by the shoes before we go?" I ask.

He hasn't told me what we're doing yet, but it seems like we're having a double date with our parents. Since Mom was anxious about her shoes, and since I have a credit card I can charge on freely now, I want to pick up a pair of white ones for her.

"Yeah, but you gotta make it quick," he tells me.

***

WE GET to the salon right when they're about to close, so we have the place all to ourselves.

Landon leaves me alone to get my hair styled and my makeup done. When he comes back, I'm chatting with the stylist, but my words dry up at the sight of him.

Landon is wearing an off-white suit that perfectly complements mine. Underneath, he's wearing a white dress shirt with the top couple of buttons undone and no tie.

He looks gorgeous.

He smirks when he sees me gaping, and the stylist takes advantage of my open mouth to finish off my lips.

As soon as she's done and I blot, she spins the chair around so I can see myself.

Landon had me change into the dress before the appointment so I didn't fuck up my hair, and now I'm glad he did. I'm a little stunned at how pretty I look with my makeup done and my hair blown out and curled. The tight rose gold bodice makes my boobs look amazing, and as I stand, the flowy bottom part dances around my legs and sways with every step I take. I do a little spin, and I feel like a fairy princess in a gossamer gown.

Landon catches my wrist, turning me to face him, then tugging me close. "You look beautiful. You ready to go?"

"Are we getting married?"

For a split second, he looks stunned, then he laughs. "What? I haven't even asked you yet."

"I know, but this dress gives me wedding vibes, and we're matching, and you brought me to the salon, and let's be honest, would not having asked me yet really even be a factor if you had the idea in your mind?"

He smirks, tightening his grip on me and pulling me in for a kiss. "I guess not."

"If we are getting married, you shouldn't ruin my lipstick," I state, since our faces are dangerously close.

"We're not getting married. Not tonight, anyway," he teases, and my tummy fills with butterflies at the mischievous look in his beautiful green eyes. Then he kisses me, and the swarm grows. "Though I do appreciate knowing you'd be up for it."

I shrug. "I mean, I don't have anything better to do tonight."

Landon squeezes my side and makes me laugh, then he pays the stylist while I thank her for staying open for us.

After that, he drives me to the marina.

I know Mom and Hayden are there, so I figure we're meeting them. I know Landon's dad owns a yacht here because I had to lure Mom to it over the summer when she tried to break things off with him and he decided to slightly kidnap her so he could change her mind.

"Are you kidnapping me?" I ask Landon, holding his hand as we walk down the dock toward the boats.

"That's it. You caught me."

I nod, lightly swinging his hand. "Well, not to be a difficult captive, but I do need to be back by tomorrow evening. I helped organize Fright Fest, and I can't miss it just because of a little kidnapping."

"Hostages don't get to make demands," he informs me.

"What if they're really sweet about it?" I tease, snuggling close to him as we approach the ship our parents are on.

He smirks. "Then it's a request, not a demand, and you'll have to take what I give you."

"I do enjoy taking what you give me," I murmur suggestively.

His eyes glint with affection as he looks down at me, but movement out of the corner of my eye draws my attention away from our flirting.

Arden's family yacht is docked on our left side up ahead. It's decked out with sophisticated Halloween décor and still packed full of people, but I see Mom and Hayden disembarking. They must be in a hurry because everyone else is still lingering and talking while they make their way off the boat.

Mom looks really happy, that's the first thing I notice. They haven't noticed us yet, and as soon as they step on the dock, Hayden spins her, causing her to laugh. He catches her around the waist and pulls her back in the same way Landon does to me, then he brings her closer, his eyes warm and full of love, and he kisses her. I watch with a soft smile as Mom winds her arms around his neck and melts against him, and that's when it hits me.

I gasp softly, squeezing Landon's hand. *"They're* getting married," I whisper, just realizing it.

Landon gives my hand a squeeze back, then he tugs me forward and we start toward them.

Mom's still smiling, looking light and happy when she spins around in Hayden's arms.

It's a relief that now when she sees us together, it doesn't steal her joy. She remains smiling, and it isn't some brave face she's forcing for my benefit. Landon made the effort and had a talk with her one day. I don't know what he said, but whatever it was, it seemed to ease her mind.

She lights up when she sees me now, letting go of Hayden and rushing over to look at me. "Oh, honey. You look so pretty!"

"Landon took me shopping and got me all dolled up. He didn't tell me why, but..."

Mom looks past me at him. "Thank you," she says genuinely.

He nods, a bit uncomfortable with the warm emotion from anyone but me, and shoves his hands in his pockets.

When Mom looks back at me, I can't suppress my smile. "This is a secret wedding, isn't it?"

Mom grins and nods. "We're eloping. Surprise?"

"I love that," I say, grabbing her and giving her a hug.

"I know we talked about waiting and planning a big ceremony and reception, but..."

I shake my head, pulling back. "If this is what you want, then this is what it should be."

"I know it's fast."

Seeing how fast I've fallen deeply in love with Landon, I honestly have a lot less to say about that than I did when they first announced their whirlwind engagement. "You know he's the one. Why waste time planning a party when you can get married tonight?"

Mom grins, hugging me again, clearly grateful for my support.

She should know she has it, though. Even if I did think she was crazy, as long as it made her happy, I would support her.

But I don't think it's crazy anymore.

I'm relieved that they're getting married. I want them to. I *want* us all to be a family, and I don't care how it looks from the outside.

I've never been on Hayden's boat before, and it takes until we're boarding hand-in-hand and Landon is dragging behind a bit for me to realize this is the boat he took out with his mother that day that she didn't come back.

I slow down, letting Mom and Hayden get ahead of us so I can have a moment of privacy with him. "Are you okay?"

He nods. "Yeah."

"You sure?"

He nods again, but I can tell his jaw is locked tight.

I know he must be having some weird memories, so I drop his hand and slide an arm around his waist instead, giving him a little sideways hug as we board the boat.

Hayden takes Mom to see the captain. We follow, but not as close behind so we can keep talking.

"I'm surprised he wanted to do this on the boat," I murmur. "Was that the last time you were on it?"

Landon nods. "He asked me first. That's how I knew what we were getting ready for."

"Still."

"I get it," Landon says. "He's always loved the water. Like you," he says lightly. Then, he goes on. "I used to love the water, too, but it's hard to keep loving something that took so much from you."

My heart swells up with sympathy. As soon as we reach the level Mom and Hayden are on, I turn and give him a hug. "I'm sorry."

He caresses the back of my hair. "I know."

I lean back so I can look up at him, but I remain in his embrace. "Can I ask you a question?"

"Of course."

"Why the swim team? It seems like that's the worst possible club for you to be a part of."

He shrugs, still with his arms secured around me, then he looks out at the water almost rebelliously. "I've been swimming since I was practically a baby. I'm a strong-ass fucking swim-mer. I *should* have been able to find her, to grab her, to pull her back to the surface before it was too late."

My heart lodges itself in my throat, and I remember what he said to me when I gave him the muffins. When he asked if they were good enough to make him forget his mom was dead and it was all his fault.

"It wasn't your fault, Landon. You were just a kid."

"I know." He nods. "But I should have been strong enough to keep my family together. I never wanted to look at the fucking water again after we lost her. I switched bedrooms because I couldn't stand to look at the ocean every day. Didn't even bother making the new one my own, I just... lived there like a visitor looking forward to the day I could finally leave." His gaze drifts to me. "Until you moved in."

Surprise causes the question to slip out. "Am I in your old room?"

He nods, then looks out at the ocean. His jaw locks, his green eyes stormy and irritable, like he's regarding an enemy instead of a body of water. "But after the initial grief passed, when my dad disappeared on me, and... it was like I'd lost both of them." He looks down. "I had to know if I ever found myself in a position like that again, I'd be prepared. I had to be stronger. I needed to be the strongest fucking swimmer that had ever lived. I needed to be able to hold on to what mattered to me and not let it slip away."

It breaks my heart hearing that.

I knew Landon changed after his mom's death. He wasn't like this before, angry and pugilistic and controlling. He was mischievous, but he never had a chip on his shoulder. He was one of the popular kids at school, amusing and handsome and athletic. He was well-liked and friends with everybody. The whole world was his playground so he had no reason to hate it, but then, in the space of one afternoon, his whole world changed. Darkened.

He lost so much.

He was never the same after that.

I suppose I wouldn't be, either.

He was only twelve, but even losing my mother now, when I'm basically an adult, would emotionally cripple me. I don't know how you recover from a loss like that.

I don't think Landon ever has.

And it's impossible not to notice how he applied all the new mental processes he adopted to me.

I don't know why, whether it was fated or just because I was the only one who approached him that day wanting to offer a life raft when I saw him drowning, but it's clear I'm the thing he practiced holding on to once he lost her. I was the thing he monitored and controlled and refused to let slip through his fingers.

No amount of resistance ever would have worked. He would have torched all the lives around us and still kept chasing me because he *had* to. He couldn't stop. He would get himself arrested, blow up his own future and anyone else's who got in his way. He'd ruin his father's life, burn every bridge with every friend he ever had, and he would have just kept coming.

I guess it's fortunate I got hung up on him, too.

It does make me wonder, though...

Do I like being chased because that's who I am, or because I've spent my formative years running from him?

I guess it doesn't matter. We're together now, and if I'm honest, I know we'll be together forever. He wouldn't have it any other way, and whether my brain is wired to accept that naturally or because Landon forced it to with his years of relentless pursuit, I wouldn't, either.

Maybe he has always been mine and I've always been his, and it doesn't matter why.

And maybe it *is* a little twisted, but I've always been protective of Landon, ever since that day in middle school. Even if I was his target, the notion of things having gone differently and him *not* getting me... I don't just feel overwhelmed on my own behalf by the knowledge that I never would have known peace in my life as long as he was drawing breath. I also feel sad for him at the idea that he wouldn't have gotten the one thing he wanted more than anything.

I'm grateful it was me.

Sighing softly, I hug him again, then I place a soft kiss on the corner of his mouth. "I love you, Landon."

His perfect lips tug up and his arms tighten around me, even now, not able to get me close enough. "I love you, too."

It's not the first time we've said it, but it's the first time we've said it with all our clothes on. It usually slips out in bed after he's obliterated all my senses and I'm desperate to get as close to him as possible.

It wasn't an event the first time we said it in bed, either, though. We were both very much aware of how we felt.

I think we've always loved each other, even when we hated each other.

And I know we always will.

The Coastal Elite world continues with ***Surrender***, coming soon to kindles near you! ;)

BONUS SCENE

In *Contempt*, we discovered Hannah hasn't been sleeping well. That she's haunted by nightmares.

So, after the lipstick party, when she and Parker spent the night in her old bedroom, Hannah reached out to her own personal Freddy Krueger to see if his answer might ease her mind.

That is where and when this scene takes place.

Enjoy.

Dare to Dream
Hannah

Parker lies beside me, fast asleep.

My eyes are burning and my body is exhausted, but my brain won't stop and I can't sleep.

It's the norm for me these days. Not my brain being in overdrive, but the not sleeping.

No matter how exhausted I am when I fall into bed at the end of each day, it's so hard to fall asleep.

I've come to dread bedtime, even though nighttime used to be the time of day I most looked forward to. Jackie and Anae are asleep, the house is quiet. It's like it's mine again.

Just one more thing he's taken from me, I guess.

Now, I lie awake, anxious, knowing that when my eyes can't stay open anymore, I'll fall into his sick, dark world.

He'll be there waiting for me.

Watching, chasing, tormenting.

On the worst nights, leaving me with such an overwhelming sense of horror, I can't shake it even after I wake up.

And now, after Anae's lunacy before the party, there's one more thing weighing on my mind.

Am I tattooed on his arm?

She's crazy, but so is he.

Just because it's crazy doesn't mean it isn't true.

I can't curb my awareness of the phone charging on my old bedside table, the potential link to my Voldemort, but also... maybe the answers to some of my questions.

Technology makes it so easy. All I have to do is reach for them.

It's a bad idea. I know it is. Parker's right, I shouldn't open up that portal. I should let him be on the East Coast with me on the west, and just... forget about him for as long as he lets me.

Only, I know how completely impossible that is. Parker can say it and not know she's basically telling me to walk on water, but I know better.

How can you forget someone you see almost every night?

My gaze flickers to Parker to make sure she's sleeping soundly. She is, so I reach for my phone slowly, wrapping my fingers around the thin, smooth surface and easing it off the nightstand.

The screen lights up when I unplug the charger. It feels brazen and I'm afraid Parker will wake up, so I turn down the brightness before I open the app.

I never had Dare's number, of course, so I navigate to his social media page, the one Anae spends so much time stalking. I feel as crazy as she is creeping on his profile in the middle of the night, but I'm not here for the pictures.

I'm not here for them, but I can't help noticing them, anyway.

His latest post is a picture of Aubrey peeking out from beneath the covers, a cute playful smile on her face that brings one to mine.

Parker's right, she does look happy.

I'm just right, too. She's happy because she's living in a land of smoke and mirrors, and it could be hiding the reality of real danger.

Especially if he's communicating with Anae behind her back.

It's hard to ever be sure what Dare is thinking, but in the past, I have had a clearer view than most. It's never comfortable to connect with him, but when I do, I feel like I can see through a lot of his smoke.

I scroll away from the pictures and click the message button. The screen jumps to a blank window with alarming ease. My stomach rocks to let me know this is a bad idea. My gaze drifts to his picture in the circle above the message.

Should I really do this?

Probably not, but I tell myself it's harmless. Just a message. Just one little question. Maybe I'm wrong about the tattoo. Maybe he'll tell me I never pass through his mind at all, and I can *finally* find some peace.

Maybe the dreams will stop.

Deep down, I'd love nothing more than to sever the tether I feel between us.

Maybe this will accomplish that.

Maybe the truth could set me free.

Maybe it's all in my mind—a desperate attempt to hold on to some link to Aubrey, a valid reason not to accept being pushed out of her life.

I'm gonna do it.

I chicken out far too much in life. I'm doing this.

It's just a message. It can't hurt anything.

I type out, "Can I ask you a question?" but I look at it for a full minute before I can convince myself to press send.

It doesn't occur to me until after I've pressed it and my heart is firmly resting in my stomach that he's probably asleep.

Oh my god, what did I just do?

As soon as the thought hits, I feel guilty, but I don't know why. I had no ill intentions, but I picture Aubrey lying beside him and wonder what she would think if she saw the message pop up on his phone screen.

I wish I could delete it.

I need to unsend, but that's not an option.

What if I blocked him? Would he still be able to see I sent

him a message? I'm not sure; I've never blocked anybody before.

My hands feel shaky as I navigate away from his profile and click on Aubrey's. My heart pounds just looking at her picture. I need to think clearly, so I squeeze the button on the side of the phone to darken the screen.

Maybe I should message her. We haven't talked since prom because Dare won't let us be friends, but maybe—

The phone screen brightens with a new notification.

I hold my breath as I lift my phone to look at it.

It's a message from Dare.

Oh my god.

It's short, so I can see what it says before I even open it. "Sure."

I didn't expect him to respond at all, but certainly not so quickly.

What do I say? What do I do?

"Are you always up this early?" I type back.

"You're reaching out just to ask about my sleep schedule? How thoughtful."

I flush. "I didn't think about the time difference when I sent the message. I didn't realize it was so early where you are. Once I did, I didn't think you'd be awake."

"I wasn't," he answers simply.

"Did I wake you? I'm sorry."

I also hope I didn't wake anyone else.

"You're as well-mannered as ever, I see," he answers.

That makes me flush even more. I suppose I don't owe him any apologies, ever. I could cut his face off and not have to apologize after the mean shit he has done to me.

Thinking about that brings me back to the reason I'm texting him. "Anae's out," I type.

"I know."

I don't know why I wait for some nicety like him to ask how she's doing. I know he doesn't care, and he has no reason to pretend to right now.

"She was stalking your profile earlier tonight, looking at your pictures. She thinks you didn't block her because you wanted her to see your tattoos. She thinks you're leaving her breadcrumbs. She thinks..." I pause and backspace, my fingers not wanting to commit that thought to text, but it's why I reached out in the first place, so I force myself to type the sentence. "She thinks I'm on your arm."

I wait, my heart pounding in my throat, for him to answer.

I wait. And I wait. And I wait.

Oh my god, why isn't he answering?

My palms feel sweaty. It shows he read the message, but maybe he got pulled away? I have to know, so I send another message even though he hasn't answered the last one.

"Is that a Cinderella tattoo on your arm?"

This message also shows as instantly read, so it seems like he has the message open, he just isn't typing anything.

He's toying with me.

He probably won't answer.

He'll just sit there, amused, waiting to see how many times I'll ask before I give up.

Jerk.

My stomach roils. I place a hand on my belly, begging it to calm down. In fairness, if it had a mouth, it would probably beg me not to do dumb things to fill it with anxiety-acid in the first place.

My breath catches when he finally responds. "Maybe."

Oh my god.

That maybe feels like a yes, but of course without *being* a clear yes, because Dare is intent on slowly driving me mad.

I swallow.

"Why would you have a Cinderella tattoo on your arm?" I ask.

"What fun would it be if I told you that?" he answers.

"We're not in each other's lives anymore, why does it matter? Just tell me so I can get some sleep."

"Am I keeping you awake at night, Hannah?"

I can *hear* how much he enjoys that even through the uniform line of text on the screen. It could be from anyone, but it's from him, so it's fucked up and complicated.

Yes.

But I'm not going to admit that to him. He doesn't deserve the satisfaction he would get out of knowing just how much he torments me, even from afar.

"I have to go," he types back before I can formulate a response. "My mermaid is stirring. Get some sleep. You can think about me more tomorrow," he says, adding a wink.

Ugh. I roll my eyes, torn on whether or not I should type a message back.

It feels rude not to. I feel like I should at least tell him to have a good day since it's early morning where he is, but I also struggle to respond to a message from him that includes a winky face. Feels too much like being complicit in something shady. I don't want to play games with him, I just want to know what he's up to.

I mull it over for a second, then send back, "Tell Aubrey I say hi," so it's clear this communication doesn't need to be kept secret.

I wait another moment, but the message doesn't show as read, so he's probably not looking at his phone anymore. I still feel better having sent it.

I navigate away from the message between us and switch over to my Aubrey message chain.

I kept every message we ever exchanged, so I spend a few

minutes scrolling through and rereading them to put better thoughts in my head before I go to sleep.

My eyes are getting heavy, though.

As if my body is obeying Dare's command to get some sleep, I find myself unable to keep them open, my arm drooping and resting against the mattress as the darkness tries to suck me in.

I can't fight it anymore. Not tonight.

I check the message chain to ensure I didn't accidentally push any buttons and send her anything while I was drifting. Seeing I didn't, I close the app, put my phone back on the end table, and curl up with my back to Parker.

I feel like I still need to keep an eye on my phone, even though I know it's unlikely I'll get another message.

He said he had to go.

Aubrey was stirring.

I bet he has his arms wrapped around her even now, her soft skin flushing beneath his fingertips. I bet he's touching and kissing her, marking her like he always used to and making sure she knows who she belongs to.

Ugh.

I adjust my pillow, trying to shove the miserable thoughts away.

It's easy because my brain is exhausted and just wants to rest.

I don't expect real rest from sleep anymore, though. Hard to feel recharged after a night of excruciating torment.

When my body finally gives out on me and my eyes drift closed, I anticipate tumbling into the now-familiar darkness.

But, for the first time in a long time, it isn't darkness I fall into.

For the first time in a long time, I finally get some rest.

AUTHOR'S NOTE

I hope you enjoyed Parker and Landon's story (and the rest of Hayden and Gemma's) (and then finally, a peek into Hannah's mind. Wow, I packed a lot in here, didn't I? lmao)!

It occurred to me that I usually address questions in my Facebook reader groups (Sam Mariano's General Reader Group, and then there is a Coastal Elite spoiler room where readers theorize and I occasionally answer questions for anyone who wants to go more in depth with this world and its characters) but not everyone *has* Facebook.

Now that you've read *Contempt*, you probably have a better feel for how the stories in this series will overlap. Obviously, Parker and Landon's story began in *Undertow* and concluded in this one. You'll see them again in *Deception*, but they'll be side characters. The struggle part of their journey is over. Beyond this, it's just fluff.

The question I get most is "Will Hannah get a book?"/" When will Hannah get a book?" I love this question because I also adore Hannah and I am *obsessed with her love story*, but it's not a simple question to answer. Hannah's story is obviously sprinkled throughout this series (she was introduced in *Even if it Hurts*), and her love story will span more than one book, but it most certainly will get told. Wild horses couldn't stop me. ;)

And honestly, I cannot wait.

I've been daydreaming about Hannah's story for a really long time. It spills over into my life even when I don't want it to. It distracts me from other projects. I dream about it. I think about it when I'm driving or showering or cooking. Scenes have been coming to me from all over the timeline of her love story for so long, I can't believe it's finally time to write it.

Well, almost.

The next book in this series is *Surrender*. Hannah isn't in Silvan and Sophie's story (which was originally titled *Sophie's Surrender* and released as a standalone for three months late last year/into early 2023), but she *is* in the Coastal Elite bonus content I added to the end of that book. It basically picks up where *Contempt* left off, but in Boston with Dare and Aubrey so we can see how their Halloween is going.

Deception is technically Hannah's book, but her story won't fit in one book. My intention is to hold off on releasing Deception for a while after I've finished it so I can write ahead. I want to release the rest of the series pretty close together so you guys don't have to wait long for the conclusion.

I am loving the hell out of this series, so I hope you are, too!

Silvan and Sophie's story is the last book that will work in any capacity as a standalone. Beyond that, you're either all in or you're out.

I know Hannah's book is the one a lot of people are looking forward to, but it is the one that cannot be pieced out *at all*.

While I have crafted this series for people who are reading the entire thing, someone could read just *Even if it Hurts* and be satisfied, they could read just *Undertow* and *Contempt* and probably be satisfied (if annoyed at all the development of side characters they didn't care about since they didn't read the first book). They could very easily read *Surrender* as a standalone as long as they stopped reading when they got to the bonus content at the end of their book.

But that's where the ability to pick and choose (even if ill-advised) ends. I am crafting a complex series with a lot of very interconnected storylines, and it is intended to be read in order. I wouldn't tell you they're not standalones if it weren't true. I'm not trying to trick you; I'm simply trying to help you enjoy the story I poured my heart and soul into as much as possible.

If you want Hannah's story, you've gotta buckle up and read the whole series. That's the only way to get it. By the end of *Surrender*, I will have provided everyone with more than enough information to determine: do I want to read Hannah's story? Am I intrigued, even if I'm not sure where it's going?

If you are, fantastic. I'm extremely excited for it. In a lot of ways, Hannah is practically a prototype for my very favorite type of heroine. In others, she's quite different. Her preferences were an issue when I first met her. What do you *mean*, you don't like assholes? Do you know whose book world you showed up in?

But Hannah's story is a dark romance treasure trove, and I can't wait to explore it. Her story will challenge me to write things I never have before, while also blending in tropes and dynamics I'm well versed at writing that I really love.

There will also be a Coastal Elite spinoff novel releasing after *Surrender*, but I'll tell you more about that in Silvan's book since it will make more sense there. :)

Until next time!

-Sam Mariano

ABOUT THE AUTHOR

Sam Mariano has a soft spot for the bad guys (in fiction, anyway). She loves to write edgy, twisty reads with complicated characters you're left thinking about long after you turn the last page. Her favorite thing about indie publishing is the ability to play by your own rules! If she isn't writing her next book, playing with her mischievous pup, or hanging out with her delightful daughter... actually, that's about all she has time for these days.

Feel free to find Sam on Facebook (Sam Mariano's General Reader Group), Goodreads, Instagram, or her blog—she loves hearing from readers! She's also available on TikTok now @sammarianobooks, and you can sign up for her totally-not-spammy newsletter HERE

If you have the time and inclination to leave a review, however short or long, she would greatly appreciate it! :)